HAUNTED

Also by Kat Martin

The Silent Rose

The Dream

The Secret

Hot Rain

Deep Blue

Desert Heat

Midnight Sun

Against the Wild

Against the Sky

Against the Tide

Into the Fury

Into the Whirlwind

Into the Firestorm

Beyond Reason

Beyond Danger

Beyond Control

Pivot

The Last Goodnight

The Last Mile

One Last Chance

The Ghost Illusion

KAT MARTIN

HAUNTED

KENSINGTON PUBLISHING CORP.

www.kensingtonbooks.com

KENSINGTON BOOKS are published by

Kensington Publishing Corp.
900 Third Avenue
New York, NY 10022

Library of Congress Card Catalogue Number: 2024936513

The K with book logo Reg. U.S. Pat. & TM Off.

ISBN: 978-1-4967-4405-0
First Kensington Hardcover Edition: October 2024

ISBN: 978-1-4967-4407-4 (ebook)

10 9 8 7 6 5 4 3 2 1

Printed in the United States of America

HAUNTED

CHAPTER ONE

A LOT OF BAD THINGS HAPPENED IN THE WICKEDEST TOWN IN THE West. Men died. Women were murdered. Some of their deaths left a haunting imprint in the very walls of the buildings. The Copper Star Saloon was one of them.

It was the year 1898. The plinkity-plink of an old piano rose up from downstairs. Rough men's voices and women's high-pitched laughter seeped through the wooden floors of the rooms above the saloon. A woman sprawled naked on the bed, the big hairy body of Boris Koblinsky, one of the local miners, pressing her down in the mattress.

"You're hurting me, Boris."

"Ya know the way I like it," Boris said. "Tell me ya want it."

What Sadie wanted was to push the big bastard off her, tell him to find someone else, but Boris paid three times what the other miners did. He'd taken a fancy to her nearly a year ago, and it was worth a few bruises for the extra pay.

Boris panted and made the iron headboard slam against the wall. Lacey, the owner, would want a few coins for the damages, but it would all be over soon, and Sadie could tuck the extra money into her savings. In a year or two, she'd have enough to leave this hellhole, move to Tombstone or Bisbee, maybe even find herself a husband.

The bed kept hammering against the wall. Boris squeezed her breasts, pinching so hard pain shot through her body.

"Stop it, Boris!" She sucked in a breath and tried to roll away from his big, calloused hand. He should have been done by now, but Boris was drunker than usual, numb enough to last longer. Sadie couldn't take much more. She cried out, but the music and laugher muffled the sound.

Her anger surfaced, replacing the lure of money. She began to fight, trying desperately to dislodge him.

"That's enough, Boris. Get off me." Boris just kept grunting, ramming painfully inside her. "Stop it, Boris—you pig!"

"Pig, am I?" Fury distorted his features. Boris reared back and slapped her so hard her ears rang. "Well, I might be a pig, Sadie Murphy, but yer nothin' but a two-bit whore."

Sadie felt Boris's big hands settle around her throat, and her fury slowly faded, turning instead to fear. "Let . . . go . . . of . . . me!"

She thrashed beneath him and clawed at the thick, blunt fingers squeezing off her air supply.

"You're mine, Sadie! Ya belong to me!" Boris rammed into her again, his big hands gripping her tighter and tighter as he rode her toward release. His lust was building, his excitement reaching its peak.

Sadie's vision began to blur. Her nails dug into Boris's calloused hands, but she couldn't pry his fingers loose. Darkness hovered behind her eyes.

Boris . . . The silent word remained locked in her throat. Her vision narrowed and finally went black. Beneath Boris's heavy weight, her body went slack. Boris finally finished and pulled out of her.

Dragging on his denim pants, he jammed his big feet into his heavy leather work boots, and pulled his undershirt back on. Sliding his suspenders over his thick shoulders, Boris glanced over at the bed. Sadie lay on her back, pale legs splayed, eyes open and staring lifelessly up at the ceiling.

Got what she deserved, he thought.

Still, the sheriff might not see it that way. Boris grabbed his floppy brown felt hat, tugged it low on his forehead, strode along the hall and down the back stairs. Plenty of jobs around. Time he found himself a new one.

Plenty of whores around, too.

Boris smiled to think of the pleasure in store for him when he found himself a new woman.

CHAPTER TWO

Jerome, Arizona
October, Modern Day

THE COPPER STAR SALOON AND HOTEL ON MAIN STREET BUZZED with activity. Tourists came from all over the country to visit the remnants of the old mining boomtown the *New York Sun* had once described as the Wickedest Town in the West.

The town, a city of fifteen thousand at its peak, was now an infamous ghost town with a population of less than five hundred. It had been falling in ruins until the sixties, when artists and shopkeepers began moving in, keeping the town alive.

Built in the 1890s, the Copper Star had been ravaged by fire four times, but had always managed to survive. The molded tin ceilings, batwing doors, long wooden bar, and ornately carved back bar looked the same as they had more than a hundred years ago.

The owner, Jenny Spencer, worked behind the bar, comfortable in a business that had been family-owned for as long as she could recall. After her father had died, her uncle Charlie had run the business, then six months ago, Uncle Charlie had also passed away. Though Charlie had a son, the sad truth was, Eddie Spencer wasn't capable of running the place. He'd been into booze and drugs since his teens.

Instead, Jenny had inherited the saloon and hotel she had been running ever since her divorce.

Behind the bar, Jenny drew beers and made drinks for the tourists, smiled, and made conversation. The place was usually peaceful in the daytime, but when the town was full of summer visitors, the bars and saloons could get rowdy. Fortunately, she was well known in the small town, where everyone seemed to watch out for each other. So far, she had managed to take care of herself.

Setting two beers on the counter and retrieving the patron's money, Jenny looked up to see her tall, lanky brother shoving through the batwing doors. Breathing a sigh of relief, she rounded the bar and hurried toward him.

"I didn't know you were coming, but I'm really glad you're here."

"You look a little harried. Everything okay?"

"Unfortunately, no. The hotel's full. It's time to clean the rooms. I'm down to one girl, and the bartender didn't show up." She glanced at the customers seated at the wooden tables scattered around the saloon. "Could you possibly take over till I get things worked out?"

Dylan just shrugged. "Sure, no problem."

"Thanks. You're a lifesaver." Jenny went up on her toes and kissed his cheek, knocking aside his dark blue baseball cap where the words PRESCOTT FIRE gleamed in white letters on the front. She was far shorter than her brother's six-foot-one-inch frame, her long, curly hair a lighter shade of brown.

"Sorry." She tugged the cap back down over his forehead. "I promise I won't be long."

Jenny headed for a door on the other side of the saloon that led to the hotel lobby. Halfway there, she spotted the regular bartender coming in.

"Sorry I'm late." Troy Layton was sandy-haired and good-looking, a real ladies' man, good for business in the saloon. "Had car trouble this morning. Carburetor problem. I figured you could handle things till I got here."

"A phone call would have been a good idea," Jenny said. "At least you finally made it. I've got work to do upstairs."

"Like I said, I had car trouble. I'll call next time."

Jenny didn't bother to reply. Troy was a pain in the neck, but he was a good bartender. In a town as small as Jerome, not an easy guy to replace.

As Jenny walked through a door to the original hotel lobby, one of the guests was on her way down the stairs.

"I want my money back!" the woman demanded. Short and round-faced, pretty much round all over, she was Mrs. Friedman, Jenny recalled.

"What's the problem?"

Angry spots of color pinkened the woman's cheeks. "The problem is I paid good money for a room and didn't get a wink of sleep. People arguing in the room next door, footsteps in the hallway at ungodly hours. I'll never spend another night in this hotel! Either you give me my money back, or I go on the internet and give you a one-star review, warn people what they're in for if they book a room at this hotel!"

"I'm sorry, Mrs. Friedman, there shouldn't have been a problem. All the rooms in that section were recently remodeled. We had them soundproofed. It shouldn't have been noisy in there."

Mrs. Friedman ignored her, just dug through her purse, pulled out her wallet, and slid out her American Express card. "I paid for the room online. Please refund the amount on my card."

Dylan walked through the door just then, and Jenny cast him a beseeching glance.

"Refund the lady's money," he said. "You don't need a bad review."

"Fine." But Jenny wasn't happy about it. As soon as the woman grabbed the handle of her carry-on and marched out through the etched, half-glass front door, ringing the bell above, she turned to her brother.

"There is nothing wrong with the rooms in the new section. That woman just wanted a free place to stay."

"You just opened that section, right?"

Jenny nodded. "It's only been available for a couple of weeks.

Tourism is growing in town. Jerome has plenty of business. The hotel needed the income, and you and I both thought the increased earnings would pay off the loan fairly quickly."

"And it will," Dylan said. "Just because some old bat of a woman . . ." He paused at the look on her face. "What? What aren't you telling me?"

Jenny sighed. "This isn't the first time. I didn't want to tell you. This is my business, and you have a job and a life of your own to worry about."

"You're my sister. You know I'll help any way I can."

"I know."

Their dad had raised them after their mother had died of cancer; then he was killed a few years later in a car accident. She and Dylan were both used to being on their own.

"So tell me what's going on with the new section," Dylan said.

"That's just it. I have no idea what's going on. Guests complain about hearing things."

"What kind of things?"

"Footsteps when no one is there. Chains rattling. People whispering in the hallway."

"Chains rattling? Seriously?"

Jenny glanced away. "That's what they say."

"Come on, sis. You should be used to this stuff by now. Jerome is a ghost town, one of the most famous in Arizona, maybe the whole country. During its heyday, hundreds of people died working the copper mines. People come here specifically hoping to see a ghost. Hell, you can buy a ticket online for a ghost tour."

"I know, but this is different."

"Different how? The hotel is on the damned tour. There are stories of at least four dead people supposedly seen walking the halls upstairs."

"Those are friendly ghosts."

"Friendly ghosts?"

"I mean, if they're actually real."

He cocked a dark eyebrow, which Jenny could barely see beneath the bill of his ball cap.

"Uncle Charlie always kept those rooms blocked off," Jenny

said. "Back when he remodeled the hotel, he left that section untouched. When we opened it, the rooms still had the original furniture. I had some of it refinished and put back when we were done."

"Yes, and the rooms look damned good up there."

"Yes, they do. They're as pretty as they were back when the hotel was first built, but . . ."

"But what?"

"Charlie never talked about it, but he told me once that odd things happened in the rooms in that section. Dangerous things. That's what he said."

The skeptical look on her brother's face reminded her that he didn't believe in ghosts, except the ones the kids dressed up as on Halloween.

"I always figured Charlie just didn't want to expand the place," Dylan said. "Be more work he didn't need. Until the manager quit and you took over, he seemed to be enjoying his retirement."

Jenny bit her lip. "Maybe you're right. It's probably just a result of the new construction. That part of the building is settling or something."

"That would be my guess. And don't forget how susceptible people are to suggestion. They come to Jerome looking for spirits. They find what they expect to find."

"You're right. I'm sorry. I shouldn't have brought it up."

Dylan grinned. "You didn't bring it up. Mrs. Friedman did."

Jenny smiled. As the bell above the door rang again, her gaze shifted away from her brother to her best friend, Summer Hayes. Her family owned the Butterfly Boutique, where Summer worked. She was taller than Jenny, pretty, with a willowy figure, long straight platinum-blond hair, and a shy disposition.

"Hi, Jenny." Her face lit up. "Dylan, nice to see you." The blush in Summer's cheeks betrayed the crush she had on Jenny's brother. So far, he hadn't seemed to notice.

"I thought you might have time for lunch," Summer said to Jenny.

"I'm starving, but I'm swamped." Jenny checked the ship's clock on the wall behind the old-fashioned, slotted key holder on the wall. "I've got some paperwork I have to finish. Give me thirty minutes, and we can get something here."

Summer nodded. "Okay, that sounds good. I'll be back then." She flashed a timid smile at Dylan. "Take care, Dylan."

"Will do. You, too."

The bell rang as Summer walked out. Dylan's gaze followed, lingered a moment, before he glanced away. Jenny wondered if he had any interest in her friend, or if Summer's attraction was completely one-sided.

Jenny turned to her brother. "So, what are you doing in town?"

"My shift starts tomorrow. Eight days on before I'm off again. I thought I'd check on you before I went to work." Dylan was a firefighter in Prescott, a larger town less than an hour's drive away. Jenny worried about him. Fighting fires was a dangerous occupation. She took comfort in knowing he was very good at his job.

"You didn't have to do that, but I'm always glad to see you."

They talked for a while, but Jenny had work to do, and Dylan had begun to glance at his watch. "I better get going."

"Yeah, me, too."

Her brother walked out the door, ringing the bell once more. He was such a stand-up guy, so different from Richard, her abusive, cheating, rat bastard ex-husband.

Looking forward to a short lunch with Summer, Jenny headed to her small office in the rear of the lobby.

CHAPTER THREE

JENNY SAT WITH SUMMER AT A TABLE IN THE SALOON, EATING A Miner's Burger and Fire-in-the-Hole Fries, the specialty of the house, along with a cup of Smelter Soup.

The bar menu was limited—just burgers, sandwiches, salads, and pizza, which came frozen, but, with a few extras, actually tasted very good. There were miscellaneous appetizers, like fried mozzarella, onion rings, and chicken wings. Just enough to keep the customers happy.

It was the bar that made most of the money.

"So how's everything going?" Summer asked. She'd been living in Jerome since her mother bought the Butterfly Boutique ten years ago, and the two had moved into an apartment upstairs.

"This business is never easy," Jenny said. "But I'm dealing. It's harder now that Uncle Charlie's gone and I'm on my own."

Summer picked up a fry, dabbed it in a blob of ketchup, and popped it into her mouth. "At least you have your brother." She ate another fry. "He looks great, by the way. What's he doing these days?"

Jenny smiled. "Dylan always looks good, and if that's a subtle way of asking if he's seeing anyone, the answer is no one serious. Not that I know of, at any rate."

"Think there's any chance he would ever ask me out?"

"I don't know. I think he'd like you if he got to know you, but he's stubborn. He'd be pissed if I tried to interfere in his love life."

Summer sighed, and both of them dug into their burgers. Jenny was sipping a Diet Coke when she spotted someone pushing through the old batwing doors at the entrance.

"Speaking of good-looking," Summer said, "check out the guy who just walked in."

Jenny's attention fixed on the door. The man was at least six-three, with a pair of biceps bulging from the sleeves of a black T-shirt snug enough to reveal a set of shoulders any linebacker would envy and a heavily muscled chest.

"That's Cain Barrett," Jenny said. "He's the new owner of the Grandview Hotel."

"I've heard about him, but I've never seen him. Wow." She sighed. "Just wow."

Jenny smiled. "Can't argue with that."

"I heard he's doing a major remodel over there."

Jenny nodded and sipped her Coke. "Dylan said he went to Mingus High School, same as I did, but he was older. He dropped out for a couple of years, came back and graduated, then left town. I guess he was just too far ahead for me to remember him."

Dylan had also told her the men in the Barrett family had been miners since the early nineteen hundreds. Rumor was, they were ruffians, outlaws, and criminals. Dylan said Cain had been extremely poor as a kid, but apparently that had changed. Cain Barrett was now the owner of Barrett Enterprises, a company worth millions.

The Grandview remodel was well underway when Cain had begun showing up in the bar. Occasionally, he would come in with the job foreman or one of the guys on the construction crew. Once in a while, he came alone and sat at the bar. One of the locals told her he had dated an army of glamorous women, but he had never married.

"Oh, my God," Summer hissed. "He's coming over here."

Jenny sat up a little straighter, wishing she weren't wearing the red bandana that tied up her hair in a ponytail. Not that she was interested. After her cheating husband and her ugly divorce, men were off-limits.

"Ms. Spencer," Cain said in a deep, masculine voice as he stopped next to their table. "It's good to see you."

"You as well, Mr. Barrett."

"It's just Cain. I thought we'd settled that the last time I was in here."

Her cheeks warmed. She didn't really know him that well, but he was a good customer, and if that was the way he wanted it . . .

"All right . . . Cain. This is my friend, Summer Hayes. She and her mother own the Butterfly Boutique just down the street."

Cain smiled. "Nice to meet you, Summer." He had a solid jaw, dark brown hair, and gold-rimmed dark eyes.

"I'd like to speak to you for a moment when you're finished," he said. "I have a business proposition for you."

Summer surged to her feet. "I was just getting ready to leave." Though half her burger and fries remained on her plate, she nearly knocked her chair over trying to escape.

"I'll buy next time," Summer added. "Nice to meet you—"

"Cain," he reminded her, and Summer's face flamed.

"Cain," she repeated.

"You as well, Summer."

With a last glance at Jenny, Summer turned and hurried out of the bar. Jenny forced herself to relax as Cain pulled out a chair and sat down at the table.

"Would you like something to eat or drink?" she asked.

"I'm fine, thanks."

"So what can I do for you . . . Cain?"

"I need to hire a consultant to help me finish the hotel. I'm interested in hearing suggestions that could make the place run better. I figure you've been managing this place for a while—"

"Actually, I own the Copper Star. I've been working here off and on since I was a kid. Now I own the property."

He looked chagrined. "My mistake. I should have done a little more research. I thought Charles Spencer was the owner."

"Uncle Charlie recently passed. He left the Star to me."

"I'm sorry for your loss."

"Thank you. I miss him every day."

Cain just nodded. "Being the owner/operator, you clearly know how to run the business, which gives me an even better reason to hire you."

Jenny frowned. "Surely you can find someone a lot more qualified than I am to give you advice on how to run your hotel."

"Maybe. But I'd have to bring them in from Phoenix, find a place to put them up until we open, and take the risk they know what they're doing. Add to that, Jerome is a specialized clientele, a mix of locals and tourists. A tiny community that's extremely self-sufficient. You're accepted here, and you understand the mix."

Jenny considered the offer. She knew how to run the Star, but this was different. The old Grandview Hotel had dozens of rooms, plus a bar and a restaurant. She wasn't sure she could handle the job.

On the other hand, she could certainly use the money. Uncle Charlie had run up a debt on the business she was still paying off, and there was a second loan to cover the construction on the newly opened wing.

"I'd have to hire someone to fill in for me while I'm over at the Grandview," she said. "How long would you need me?"

"Until the hotel is finished—at least a few weeks, maybe longer. But it would only be part-time, which should allow you to handle things here as well."

At least the place was close by. She would still be driving the eight miles to and from her small house in Cottonwood, but she was used to that. "What sort of money are we talking about?"

Cain named a sum that made her head swim. Maybe she had misunderstood. "Are you . . . are you sure?"

"If it isn't enough—"

"No! That . . . that isn't what I meant. I meant are you certain you want to take that kind of risk on an unknown commodity like me?"

He smiled, and a soft flutter rose in her stomach. "I like the way this place operates," he said. "I like that the locals come here as well as the tourists. That means you're doing a good job. It also means you're an accepted part of the community. That's what I want for the Grandview."

"You were raised in Jerome. You'll be accepted as a local."

Cain shook his head. "I've never been accepted. But that's a story for another time. Do you want the job or not?"

She had offended him. She hadn't meant to do that. "Would it be all right if I took a look at the hotel before I give you an answer? It's been closed for three years. I'd like to see what I'm getting into."

Cain relaxed. "Good idea. I should have thought of it myself. I'm liking this idea better and better. Do you have time to go now, or should I come back for you later?"

"I'm afraid I can't go today. Tomorrow would work."

"All right. What time shall I pick you up?"

"We've got a shift change at five. I usually take a break about then."

Cain nodded. "Fine. I'll be here tomorrow at five."

"It's only up the hill," Jenny said. "I'll just walk."

Something that might have been irritation—or maybe it was amusement—touched his lips. Clearly Cain Barrett wasn't used to someone else calling the shots. Jenny wondered if taking the job would be a mistake.

Cain shoved his big frame up from the chair, and Jenny stood up, too. She hadn't realized how much he would tower over her. She thought of Richard, but his abuse was mental, not physical.

"I look forward to seeing you tomorrow at five." Cain turned and strode across the room. Liking the view, Jenny watched until he disappeared out the door.

The afternoon was coming to an end. Cain pulled his silver Dodge Ram 2500 diesel out of the parking lot of the Grandview Hotel, his most recent acquisition.

His grandmother was ailing. Nell Barrett had been in an assisted-living facility in Prescott for the last five years. Cain had always taken care of her needs, but her fondest wish was to return to Jerome, the place she had been born, the place she had lived with her late husband for forty-five years.

But Nell needed twenty-four-hour care. Which was the reason Cain had purchased the Grandview. For the last eight months, he'd had a construction crew remodeling the old hotel, turning it into what he hoped would be a profitable business and, more important, a place for his grandmother to spend the last years of her life.

As far as Cain was concerned, he owed Nell Barrett everything. He'd been four years old when his father had abandoned the family. A year later, his mother had dumped him with his grandmother and disappeared, too. It was Nell who had raised him, fed and clothed him, done her best to turn him into a decent human being.

He owed her for making him the man he had become and for everything he had accomplished. She wanted to spend her last years in Jerome.

By God, Cain would see that she got her wish.

He slowed the pickup to take the steep curve in front of him. There were thousand-foot drops off the edge of the narrow road. The drive wasn't for the faint of heart.

Jerome sat at a 5,600-feet elevation. There were two ways in and out: one off Highway 17 or the shorter route back to his ranch, along a formidable switchback through the national forest.

The remnants of Jerome perched on the steep side of a mountain, its precarious location alone making the place a tourist attraction.

Added to that was its violent, yet interesting history as a Wild West town—the murders, the shoot-outs, the gruesome fires that had burned the place down again and again and taken countless lives. Shifting soils, a result of the eighty-eight miles of mine tunnels, had killed thousands of miners and collapsed whole portions of the city.

His grandmother loved Jerome, with its colorful residents and western history, but the place held few good memories for Cain. Too much bad had happened. Too many gruesome deaths. Too many ghosts.

He smiled at that. He'd been around the town since he was a kid, but he'd never seen a spirit. Maybe you had to be a believer.

Whatever the truth, the Grandview was famously known as one of the town's most haunted places. The Copper Star was another.

The thought reminded him of the woman who ran the saloon, Jenny Spencer. Cain remembered Jenny from high school. Petite and always smiling, she was popular with the kids in school. He'd noticed her one day when one of the football jocks had been picking on a boy named Felipe, a Latino kid about half the guy's size.

Jenny had gotten right in the jock's face and warned him he'd better back off or else. The jock and his buddies had laughed their asses off, but they'd left Jenny and the kid alone.

She'd only been a freshman, way too young for him. He'd been a real bad boy in those days, hung out with an ugly crowd, but he never would have hurt an innocent young girl.

Jenny was no longer a kid. With her curly brown hair and big green eyes, she was even prettier than she had been in school. Her figure had matured from girl to woman, which made him think about her in a way he hadn't back then. She still had that girl-next-door appearance, and she still intrigued him.

Cain was now a respectable citizen, and after her divorce, Jenny was available. He wanted to find out more about her than the gossip he had heard, to satisfy his curiosity if nothing else.

He was meeting her at five o'clock tomorrow. Meeting her, not picking her up. The feisty young woman she had been before was still there.

Cain smiled.

It was an hour later that he arrived at his destination, the Cross Bar Ranch, the sixteen-hundred-acre property he had purchased two years ago. He owned a house in Scottsdale, not far from Barrett Enterprises, and a condo in Vegas, but the ranch felt like home, the first real one he'd ever had.

White fences surrounded the main house, as well as the barns, alfalfa fields, and pastures where a herd of purebred Black Angus cattle grazed. Turning into the fence-lined lane that led to the sprawling single-story, Spanish-style home, Cain spotted a white sheriff's SUV with gold lettering on the side parked out front.

Deputy Sheriff Hank Landry stood on the front porch talking to his housekeeper, Maria Delgado, a short woman, twenty pounds overweight, with straight black hair worn in a single long braid. She did the housework and cooked for him, but returned to her husband at night. Cain was fortunate to have her.

Maria pointed the deputy in Cain's direction and closed the front door, leaving the situation to him.

"Deputy Landry," Cain said as he climbed down from the truck. "I hope you've brought good news." Landry was lean, in his early fifties, with salt-and-pepper hair. He was relatively new to the area, having worked in the Sheriff's Department for less than six months.

"Just wanted you to know we did as you asked," Landry said. "Took a couple of deputies and went out to have another look at the pasture where you said the horse went missing."

"And?"

"It's rained since you first reported the incident. Any vehicle tracks were washed away. The department has put out a bulletin on the theft, but so far nothing useful's been reported."

"That's too bad. Looks like you wasted a trip."

"Didn't want you to think we weren't doing our job."

"Of course not," Cain said, with a hint of sarcasm the deputy missed. He wasn't happy with the effort the Sheriff's Department had put out so far. Or maybe it was just Landry, who was in charge of the district.

"I'll let you know if anything breaks on the case," the deputy said.

"I'd appreciate it." Cain watched as Landry turned and headed for his SUV.

So far he wasn't a fan. Their conversation had left him exactly where he'd been before. Minus a half-million-dollar championship cutting-horse stallion that had disappeared without a trace.

The horse belonged to him, and Cain kept what was his. It was time he did a little investigating of his own.

CHAPTER FOUR

IT WAS A STEEP WALK UP HILL STREET, A THIRD OF A MILE TO THE Grandview Hotel. Jenny crossed the parking lot, climbed the tall concrete front steps, and pushed open the door.

Cain Barrett stood in the middle of the room in conversation with one of the men in the construction crew. With his height and muscular, broad-shouldered build, the man was impossible to miss. Jenny had to admit he looked good in a pair of black jeans and a white dress shirt rolled up to the elbows.

On one sinewy forearm, a tattoo disappeared beneath the crisp white fabric. There were ugly scars on the backs of his hands that she had noticed when Cain had been sitting across from her at the bar. A pair of low-topped leather work boots covered his big feet.

Jenny had googled Cain Barrett that afternoon, found article after article written about him, the rags-to-riches story of a man who had come from nothing and become a multimillionaire. Cain had been abandoned as a child and was raised by his grandmother, whom he credited with making him the success he was today.

The article told how Cain had been a high school dropout until Nell Barrett had persuaded him to return to school. He had finally graduated, taken a small grubstake, all Nell could afford to give him, and set out to make his fortune. Which he had done in spectacular fashion.

After years of backbreaking labor in a series of Arizona mines, Cain had partnered with Barton Harwell, a fellow miner a few years older and more experienced. Together, they started prospecting on their days off. During their hunt for gold—the ore most miners hoped to find—they purchased half a dozen abandoned mining leases.

They worked the leases for three years before Harwell got discouraged and sold his half interest to Cain, who kept on working the claims.

It was brutal, grueling labor, but a year later, Cain's efforts paid off. Instead of gold, he discovered a huge deposit of molybdenum, enough to make him rich. Barrett Enterprises was a Fortune 500 company, and the impoverished high school dropout from the nowhere town of Jerome was now a wealthy, respected businessman.

Jenny thought of the painful-looking scars on Cain's hands. Mining was a dangerous game. After reading the articles, she felt a growing respect for the man she had come to the Grandview to meet.

He turned and saw her, then smiled, and Jenny's stomach did a little dip. She smiled back, but quelled the attraction she was determined not to feel.

Cain checked the stainless watch on his thick wrist. "Right on time. I figured you would be."

"You did?"

"Your place runs smoothly. You can't make that happen unless you're organized and efficient. Ready for a tour?"

"I am." She glanced around the entry. It had clearly been rebuilt, but the look of the old place shined through—the dark wood paneling, the beautiful tin ceilings, the polished hardwood floors.

The steady rhythm of hammering sounded in the distance as Jenny followed Cain into the bar. Canvas tarps covered the floors, and men on ladders were working to clean the beamed ceilings. The view across the desert to the distant mountains was spectacular.

Cain showed her the nearly completed bar and the equipment installed to run the place: ice-makers, dishwashers, sinks, glass racks.

"It looks like you've spent a lot of time thinking this through," Jenny said.

"The bones of the place were good when I bought it. We've redesigned the building and replaced all the old equipment. I could use some input on the supplies we'll need, whatever it might take to increase efficiency."

Jenny just nodded, taking mental inventory as they walked along.

The restaurant was near completion, but not quite finished yet. A wall of windows created a view as spectacular as the one in the bar.

"I need the same kind of input here," Cain said. "How much of everything we need, right down to the salt and pepper shakers."

It was a big job full of unknowns. She didn't really have that kind of expertise, and yet the excitement of a fresh challenge was rushing through her veins.

"I can give you my best estimate."

He cast her a sideways glance. "I'll need a little more than that."

He was pressing her, upping the challenge. "If I take the job, I can handle it," she said.

Amusement touched his lips, exactly where she shouldn't have been looking. *You're only human,* she told herself, and it had been years since she'd felt the slightest attraction to a man. Her mind strayed to Richard, but she blocked the thought. She refused to let bad memories control her future.

"I'll show you the meeting rooms. They're just down the hall." Past the restaurant, a set of double doors led into a big empty chamber. GRAND VISTA SALON, the sign read.

"All the walls are movable," Cain said. "One big room or a bunch of smaller ones. Whatever we need."

There were windows that looked over the valley below and the mountains in the distance. The walls were dark wood that continued the theme of the bar and restaurant.

"Be nice to have meeting rooms available. It's always been a problem for groups in the area."

"Problem solved," Cain said. "Ready to go upstairs?"

"Looking forward to it. What you've done up here is nothing short of incredible. It's all new, and yet it looks as if it were built in the 1920s, which, originally, it was." Everyone who lived and worked in Jerome knew about the old hotel that had once been a hospital.

She didn't want to think about the people who had died there or the chilling ghost stories that came from guests who had stayed in the older version of the hotel.

They went up the grand staircase instead of taking the elevator, and Cain gave her a tour of the second floor. The rooms had all been redone, the process nearly completed, and there was a gym at one end. One look at Cain, and it was clear he used the facility.

They walked past the rooms along the hall.

"We want to preserve the feeling of the times," Cain said. "We're furnishing each room with antiques or antique reproductions."

"It's going to be beautiful."

Pleased, his features softened. "Thanks. We're all working hard to make that happen."

He led her to one of the new elevators that had been installed. "All the rooms and suites on the third floor are the same as the second, so we'll skip that." Cain pushed the button for the fourth floor.

"This is where things get interesting." The elevator door slid open. "We've turned a number of rooms on this level into a spacious apartment for my grandmother."

"Nell, right?"

One of his dark eyebrows went up. "You did some digging, I see?"

"That's right. If I'm going to work for someone, I want to know as much as I can about them."

"I can usually say the same, but in your case, I've resisted. I wanted the pleasure of getting to know you myself."

Jenny paused in the hallway in front of a set of double doors. "Why?"

"I'm not sure yet," Cain said honestly. "I'll let you know when I figure it out." He opened the door into a living room with a fireplace. French doors led out to a balcony with views of the mountains. The bathroom was spectacular, but fully handicap-equipped.

"My grandmother is ailing," he said. "She wants to spend her last years here in Jerome. I want that for her. The adjoining room is for her caregiver, who's also her good friend. Another room is for any equipment necessary to see she's taken care of properly if something were to happen."

"I assume you have someone else handling the medical aspect of the setup."

He nodded. "You don't have to worry about any of that."

"And the rest of the floor?"

"More rooms, some with balconies, and my suite. I won't be here all that much, but when I am, I'll want to spend time with my grandmother, and I'll want to be comfortable."

Men were at work in the suite, so they skipped it, finished the tour, and returned downstairs.

"You said you won't be here that often. Your company offices are in Scottsdale. Is that where you live?"

"I have a house there. The place I call home is my ranch out in Kirkland. It's about an hour away. The Cross Bar raises championship cutting horses." He smiled. "If you take the job and you want to see it, I'll show it to you sometime."

She was going to take the job. She'd had no doubt from the moment she had opened the front door. She loved the Copper Star, loved running the hotel and saloon. But aside from the money problems her uncle had left her when she'd inherited the property—and the ghosts that had been troubling guests in the new wing—the challenge had been gone for some time.

Jenny looked up at him. "As I said, I like what you've done. But the finishing touches could make the difference between success and failure. I'd like to help with that."

He smiled, definitely pleased he was getting his way. Jenny wasn't sure how she felt about that.

"So you're accepting my offer," he said just to be clear.

"That's right."

"When can you start?"

"I need a day or two to make arrangements. I want to operate on my own schedule—that isn't negotiable."

He nodded.

"We're busiest on the weekends. It's Friday night. I could start . . . say, next Tuesday? That should give me time to hire an extra part-time employee and set up the scheduling."

"Tuesday works fine. I'll walk you out to your car."

Jenny glanced at him over her shoulder as he reached down to open the door leading outside. She could feel the size of him, the heat of him, and her heart beat a little faster.

"I didn't drive," she said. "It's less than a ten-minute walk up the hill from the Star."

Cain frowned. "Coming up isn't the problem. It's pitch-black out there now. The town is full of tourists, and you never really know who you might encounter." The wind blew a big gust of cold fall air through the open door. "The temperature has dropped. I'll drive you back."

She could tell it would be useless to argue, and as Uncle Charlie once said, "If you want to win, you have to learn to pick your battles."

Jenny had a feeling that working for Cain Barrett, she would face plenty of battles ahead.

Cain walked Jenny out to his big Dodge truck and opened the passenger door. As small as she was, he was glad the truck had automatic power running boards and, being the top-of-the-line model, pretty much everything else. Jenny swung into the passenger seat without his help, and he rounded the front, climbed in, and started the engine.

As she'd said, it was only a matter of minutes down the steep hill to Main Street. He could have dropped her off in front of the saloon, but he didn't like the idea, and a parking space had just opened up a little way down the block.

Nell had taught him a man walked a woman to her door. Luckily, she had also taught him etiquette and how to speak proper English. She had been a schoolteacher in her younger years. More he owed her for.

"Thanks for the ride." Jenny stepped down from the seat before he had time to get out and open her door. She waved as she disappeared into the saloon.

Unease slipped through him at the sight of the string of motorcycles parked along the edge of the asphalt. He debated for a moment, then decided he could use a beer before heading back to his half-finished suite at the hotel.

There wasn't much in the way of decoration there yet, but there was a sofa and chair in the living room, along with a big-screen TV. He had a king-size bed in the master, plus a guest room. Both bathrooms and the powder room were finished, and he kept several changes of clothes in the closet. The best part was the private elevator he'd added at the back of the hotel that went from the rear parking lot all the way up to his fourth-floor suite.

He got out of the truck and walked the half block back to the saloon. A beer sounded good, and the road down the hill to the ranch was too dangerous a drive for anyone who had been drinking. He'd stay at the hotel and head back to the ranch in the morning.

As Cain pushed through the swinging doors, country music filled the air. A man's voice, accompanied by the strum of a guitar, came from a one-man band in the corner. The room was packed, tourists mostly, a couple of guys in cowboy hats. There were a few locals in the mix and some old hippies from the days of Jerome's comeback as a tourist attraction.

A new generation of artists, misfits, and outliers ran the remodeled boutiques, restaurants, and bars—and, of course, there were the ghosts Jerome was famous for.

Cain's glance went to a group of men in biker leathers who had pulled several tables together and were laughing and drinking. Two of them had their chairs tilted back, their heavy motorcycle boots propped on the tables. STEEL COBRAS was the name on the back of their black-leather jackets.

His gaze immediately went in search of Jenny. She was talking to the bartender—Troy something—and she didn't look pleased. Cain remained next to the door, watching as she headed for the bikers, half of him uneasy, the other half fascinated.

"Gentlemen," Jenny said, her hands propped on her very appealing hips. She looked good in the stretch jeans she seemed to favor, and the bikers definitely noticed.

"Hey, babe, you come over here to get a little?" The guy was big and bald, with earrings in both ears. "Good ol' Ryder will be happy to give you some." He grabbed his crotch and squeezed it suggestively. "Let me know if you like what you see."

Jenny focused her attention in good ol' Ryder's direction, grabbed his booted feet, and dragged them off the table. They hit the wooden floor with a heavy thud, jerking the biker's neck as his chair dropped back down on four legs.

The other bikers howled with laughter, but Ryder didn't seem amused.

"The bartender says you're way over your limit," Jenny said. "I think it's time for all of you to leave."

Cain could feel his eyes widening in disbelief. Little Jenny Spencer couldn't be taking on half a dozen rowdy bikers. But clearly she was.

Ryder's chair scraped back as he rose to his feet. The music kept playing, but the conversation in the bar had stopped.

"You know what I think?" Ryder said. "I think you and me are goin' for a little stroll outside." He gripped Jenny's arm, but she jerked it free.

"I'm not going anywhere with you." Jenny pointed to the door. "Now get out."

Cain rested lightly on his feet, ready to step in if things went south, and he figured they would. He knew guys like these. They'd been among his lowlife friends back when he was a kid.

"You wouldn't want us to drive drunk, would you, sweetheart?" The second biker was tall and skinny, with stringy brown hair and a sleeve of tats down each arm, more tats on the side of his neck.

"I definitely don't want you driving drunk," she said. "I can easily arrange for the police to come and get you, give you a free room for the night."

Another round of laughter broke out, but one look at Ryder and it faded away.

"The choice is yours," Jenny said. "I'd suggest you throw your bedrolls down at the edge of town and get some sleep, be on your way in the morning."

It was reasonable. Far more reasonable than Cain would have been. He had to admit he was impressed. And the way the men were grumbling and stirring to their feet, it looked like Jenny's approach actually might work.

As the group started for the door, some of the tension in his shoulders began to ease.

Then Ryder paused and turned back. In two long strides, he reached Jenny, bent, and hauled her over a beefy shoulder. As he strode for the door, Cain's whole body tightened.

He hadn't been in a barroom brawl in years, but he hadn't forgotten how to fight. He stepped in front of the big ugly biker and flattened a hand on the man's massive chest.

"Put her down."

Jenny was struggling, calling the guy a few choice names. From the corner of his eye, Cain could see the bartender speaking on the phone, talking madly with his hands, but aside from the phone call, he made no move to help. Cain disliked him immediately.

"I said put her down."

"Stay out of this, mister." Ryder's arm tightened around Jenny's knees. She was pounding on his back, but Ryder was too big and dumb to feel it.

Cain's hand balled into a fist. "A smart man would let the lady go."

"She your woman?"

Cain looked at Jenny, whose fury under different circumstances might have amused him.

"I'm thinking about it. Put her down."

Ryder set Jenny on her feet. Cain caught her fist before she could throw a punch. "It's all right. Good ol' Ryder was just about to leave."

"I oughta kick your ass," the biker said to him. But his friends had already left, and his kind didn't like to fight one-on-one.

"You're welcome to try," Cain said mildly.

"Next time," Ryder said. "I got a long memory."

"So do I," Cain said, never breaking eye contact.

The biker's jaw clenched. Turning, he pushed through the swinging doors hard enough to rock them and walked out of the bar. The minute he was gone, the music and conversation started up again.

"I didn't need your help," Jenny said, but he noticed she was trembling. "This is my place. I handle things here."

"My mistake," Cain said.

Slightly embarrassed, Jenny blew out a slow breath and raked her fingers through her thick brown curls, pushing them back from her face. "Okay, so maybe this time I did need a little help. Thank you."

He managed to hold back a smile. "My pleasure."

"Still, I prefer to handle things myself as much as I can."

"I understand. I feel the same way."

"You do?"

"Yes. You did a nice job, by the way. It damn near worked."

She gave him a tentative smile. "It usually does." She cocked her head to the side, her gaze running over his big frame. "Next time I need a bouncer, I know who to call."

He did smile then. "Wouldn't be the first time I've done the job."

She looked intrigued, but didn't press for more. They weren't on that kind of footing. *Yet.*

"Buy you a beer?" she asked. "It's the least I can do."

"Sounds good."

Jenny tipped her head toward the bar, where Troy was calling off the law, and Cain followed, then settled himself on an empty stool. "You've got Sam Adams on tap. I'll have one of those."

She rounded the bar and drew him a beer, set it down in front of him, and drew a glass for herself.

"Would you really have fought that guy?"

He shrugged. "Not unless I had to."

"No one's ever fought for me. It was always just Dad, my brother, and me. Dylan's three years older. He left as soon as he got out of high school. Then Dad died."

She took a long swallow of beer. "At least I had Uncle Charlie. Now he's gone, too."

Cain fought an urge to tell her she could always count on him. He barely knew her, and yet he felt strangely protective. Maybe she reminded him of the sweet girl she had been in high school.

Jenny looked at him and smiled. "I think I'm going to like working for you."

Cain lifted his glass in approval and took a drink. He had wondered if hiring Jenny Spencer was a good idea. After tonight, he had no doubt.

Tuesday couldn't come too soon.

CHAPTER FIVE

IT WAS LATE. A HEAVY RAIN HAD BEGUN TO FALL OUTSIDE THE WINdows. A noise in the hallway intruded into Jenny's sleep, footsteps and whispering voices. Her eyes cracked open. It took a moment for her to remember she wasn't at home. She was spending the night in the Copper Star.

She did that occasionally when the weather was bad or the saloon had enough customers to stay open till two a.m., as it had tonight. The rowdy crowd had been enjoying the entertainment and spending plenty of money, always good.

Jenny had closed the bar and headed up to a room she'd kept unrented in the old section, knowing tonight would be a long one.

The footsteps continued down the hall, moving almost silently past her room. Her heart rate kicked up as she glanced at the clock on the nightstand. *Three-forty-five a.m.* Who would be out this late in Jerome when the entire town was closed up?

She remembered Mrs. Friedman talking about the footsteps she had heard in the hall *at an ungodly hour.* It was certainly an ungodly hour now.

Her heart tripped faster. She strained to hear more. She had heard stories from guests about ghosts making all sorts of noises, footsteps when no one was there, whispered voices of invisible people. She didn't like the idea there could actually be spirits in the building, though half the town believed the stories.

Tossing aside the covers, Jenny grabbed her jeans and yanked them on under her sleep-tee, then crept across the room to the door. She took a deep breath, pulled it open, and peered out into the hall. She didn't really believe in ghosts.

Did she?

The sound of voices reached her. Quietly slipping into the hall, she listened, trying to figure out where the sound was coming from. All the rooms were rented tonight except the one she was staying in.

The whispering drifted toward her, raising goose bumps on her skin. A man's voice, then the raw, sexy laughter of a woman, coming from farther down the hall. Jenny summoned her courage and tiptoed toward the sound.

The whispers became clearer when she reached room 7. A man had rented the room, she recalled, dark-haired, medium build, a little silver at his temples. He was only paying for a single, and he had sneaked the woman into his room.

Relief trickled through her, along with a shot of embarrassment. Not a ghost. Nothing to be afraid of. Just a guy trying to get lucky.

Not her, she thought glumly, as she turned and headed back to her own room down the hall. She'd been divorced for two years, separated from Richard for a year before that, and they hadn't really been together well before then. All in all, her marriage had been a complete and utter failure.

Jenny reminded herself she had a new life now. She was a business owner. Whatever it took, she was going to make that business a success.

Slipping quietly back into her room, Jenny closed the door, shucked her jeans, and returned to bed. As she drifted toward sleep, she thought of the man she had spent the evening with, Cain Barrett.

Barrett was as tall as the biker, and at least a hundred-eighty-five, maybe two-hundred pounds. He'd been a match for the big biker, but if trouble had started, it would have been five to one. She liked the way he'd handled himself, not hotheaded, not provocative, but confident. She had a pretty good feeling his subtle threat was real. Cain Barrett didn't look like the type to back down from anything.

She smiled. *Not even a ghost.*

Her smile slowly faded. Since Mrs. Friedman had checked out, two more guests had complained about hearing voices in the middle of the night. The voices purportedly were actually in their room. One guest said she'd seen an object lift off the dresser and tumble onto the carpet.

Jenny had no idea if any of the stories were true, but both rooms were located in the new wing of the hotel.

You're just being paranoid, she thought. *This town is full of stories about ghosts, always has been.*

Jenny closed her eyes, but half an hour passed before she finally fell asleep. She forgot about ghosts, big handsome men coming to her aid, and pretty much everything else.

When she opened her eyes, it was morning.

It was Saturday. Cain had left Jerome early enough to reach the ranch before sunrise. Working with Billy and Quinn, two of the full-time hands, Cain checked on Sultan, a big sorrel gelding with an injured tendon, then headed back to the house for one of Maria's hearty breakfasts.

Billy, Quinn, Sanchez, and Denver sat down with Cain at a long wooden table in a corner of the big open kitchen and dug into platters of bacon, eggs, and toast.

"Pass the bacon," Quinn said. He was late fifties, had worked on the ranch since he was a kid. He had darkly tanned, weathered skin and brown hair turning gray. Quinn knew more about ranching than Cain could learn in the next ten years.

Billy, who'd just turned twenty-two, had worked on the ranch summers and weekends until he'd graduated from high school, then gone to work full-time to help support his mom and little brother. Blond and lanky, Billy was a hard worker and never complained. Sanchez, nearing sixty, was one of the hardest-working men Cain had ever known. Denver Garrison was the latest addition, forty years old, a lean, fit, good-looking man, an expert rider who had trained a number of cutting-horse champions.

The ranch could probably make do with fewer people, but, except for Denver, whom Cain had personally hired, the men were part of the Cross Bar family. Along with Maria, they made a good team.

Cain thought of Jenny and wished he could show her the ranch. But Jenny was skittish. He had a feeling he would need to take things slowly.

He still wasn't sure what there was about her that had snagged his interest so strongly, but since the first time he had seen her in the Copper Star, he'd been intrigued. He hadn't remembered her at first—it had been nearly fifteen years since he'd seen her.

That first day in the saloon, she'd been patching up a kid who'd taken a bad fall out front on his bicycle. The kid was afraid to go home, afraid of what his dad would do when he found out about the ruined bike.

Jenny cleaned the scrapes on the boy's knees and the cut on his hand; then she and one of the guys in the bar had managed to put the bike back together.

Maybe some things never changed—Jenny was still more like the fresh-faced girl she had been in high school than any of the women he usually dated, females who spent most of their time in beauty salons, expensive spas, or shopping for designer clothes. For a while, he'd enjoyed having a beautiful, high-maintenance female on his arm. But at some point over the last few years, the whole scene had begun to bore him.

He'd decided it was time to make some changes. First, he'd bought the ranch, a place where he could escape the pressures of his business; then he'd bought the hotel, a place to give his grandmother her dream. It wasn't long after that he'd begun to feel better, more the person he wanted to be.

Still, something was missing. Cain was determined to find out what it was.

* * *

It was Saturday night. Last night's storm had returned midday and worsened into the evening. Still, the hotels were full, the bars and saloons as busy as they'd been the night before.

The Copper Star would be open late, so Jenny would be spending the night in town again, going home to Cottonwood Sunday morning for a day of badly needed rest.

It was early, not quite nine p.m., the bar crowded with customers. Sometime during the last two hours, she had developed a headache. It didn't happen often, but if she didn't lie down, it was going to get a whole lot worse.

Jenny said good night to Troy, who would be closing up, as he often did, spoke to the servers, Cassie and Molly, and headed upstairs.

Tonight, she'd be staying in a room in the newly remodeled wing of the hotel.

She couldn't put it off any longer. She needed to know if something suspicious was actually happening there.

The hallway was empty, room 8 a little chilly when she opened the door and walked inside. Jenny glanced around as she turned up the heat, proud of the décor in the hotel rooms, especially in the new section. An old-fashioned, queen-size four-poster formed the centerpiece of the room, while a blue-flowered porcelain washbasin and pitcher sat on an oak dresser with ornate brass handles.

With the exception of the four-poster beds, all the rooms were unique, this one done in cream and pale blue—the curtains, the quilt, and the upholstery on the oak rocker next to the round, piecrust table by the window.

Stripping off her plaid western shirt, stretch jeans, and sneakers, typical of the clothes she wore in the bar, she opened her overnight bag and pulled on a pink cotton sleep-tee with I LOVE JEROME and a heart on the front.

Just being away from the loud music, raucous laughter and conversation downstairs helped her headache, which was still pounding in her temples, but wasn't nearly as brutal as it could sometimes get.

There were no TVs in the hotel. People came to Jerome to get away from the pressures of their everyday lives. The tiny town provided the quiet visitors wanted.

Jenny turned back the covers on the bed and slid beneath the cool cotton sheets. She'd been up late last night and, after her encounter with the imaginary ghosts in the hall, hadn't gotten much sleep.

Tonight, she was sleeping in the new section. Jenny prayed none of the ghostly incidents people reported were real.

CHAPTER SIX

With a full moon to help him navigate, Cain took the curves up Highway 89A a little faster than he should have. He was driving his newly purchased, forest-green Jaguar F-type, a sleek two-door that really hugged the road.

Quinn and Denver were off to the Skeleton Bar and Grill or the Burro Saloon, not far from the ranch. Billy had met a girl from Prescott, so there was a good chance he'd be hooking up with her there tonight. It was Sanchez's weekend to stay at the ranch.

Cain had finally succumbed to an itch that urged him to return to Jerome. He had always listened to his intuition, and all day it had nagged him, telling him the trouble Jenny had faced with the bikers wasn't over.

He probably should have just called her, made sure she was okay, but the idea didn't sit well. He was worried.

Or maybe he just wanted to see her.

Either way, he reached the top of the mountain, made the sharp turn onto Clark Street, and headed downhill to Main Street. It took him a couple of minutes to find a parking place, and in the end, he had to walk a block back to the saloon.

Even a block away, he could hear the country music, same singer, same guitar as last night. He stopped in the shadows outside the bar. The same row of motorcycles he'd seen last night were parked in the same space as before. He recognized a couple of them, one black-and-chrome with silver conchos on the seat, another with red-and-orange flames streaking over the gas tank.

His strides lengthened. His intuition rarely let him down, and apparently, it hadn't tonight. He pushed through the swinging doors, his gaze going in search of Jenny, but he didn't see her.

A row of tables had been pushed together, same as before, the bikers sitting around it, though none of them had their motorcycle boots propped on top.

The Steel Cobras were there—all but one. Ryder was not among them.

Ryder was missing, and so was Jenny. Worry slid through him. He strode across the room to where Troy stood behind the bar, pouring a customer a whiskey and Coke.

"Where's Jenny?" Cain asked.

"She had a headache and quit early."

"She went home?" He knew she lived in Cottonwood. She was going to be working for him. After tonight, he was going to know a lot more about her.

"Jenny's in a room upstairs. She went up to lie down." Troy collected the cash for the drink and rang it up in the old-fashioned brass cash register next to the credit-card machine.

Cain glanced back at the bikers' table. Still no sign of Ryder. "Jenny may be in trouble. Which room is she in?"

"I'm not allowed to give out that information."

"I just want to check on her. Which room?"

"Sorry," Troy said, mopping the top of the bar.

Tired of being polite, Cain reached over, grabbed the front of Troy's black Copper Star T-shirt, and hauled him halfway across the bar. "Which room!"

"I'm . . . I'm not sure. We've got a full house tonight. She said it was in the new section, number eight, I think."

Cain let him go, turned, and strode across the room to the lobby. Praying for once his instincts were wrong, he headed up the stairs.

* * *

Something shifted in the air. Jenny felt the bed dip, and her eyes flashed open to see a man's face in the shadowy darkness above her. A scream rose in her throat, but a meaty hand cut off the sound.

"Take it easy, and you won't get hurt."

She started shaking. The man was using his weight to press her down in the mattress, trapping her arms, and he weighed a ton—Ryder, she remembered, big, bald, and ugly. She'd been worried about ghosts, not the biker she had pissed off in the bar last night.

"Now . . . here's what's going to happen," the biker said. "You and I are going to have us a little fun."

She started squirming and twisting on the bed, trying to break free, trying to push off his heavy weight, but he only laughed.

"You're gonna spread your pretty legs for me, sweet thing. You might as well get used to the idea."

She thrashed and tried to scream, but the sound was muffled by his big, thick-fingered hand. She had locked the door. How had he gotten in?

Reaching between them, he yanked up her sleep-tee, and she started fighting harder. The hand over her mouth moved a little, and she sank her teeth in and bit down as hard as she could.

"Fuck! You little bitch, you're gonna pay for that!" Ryder let go of her long enough to pull back and slap her across the face. Jenny screamed, but his fingers crushed down over her mouth again, and it sounded more like a whimper.

The buzz of his zipper sliding down was the last thing she heard before the door crashed open, splinters flew, and Cain Barrett burst into the room. He took one look at the big bald biker, yanked him off her, and smashed a fist into his ugly face.

The fight was on as the two big men swung a series of blows, but there was no stopping Cain. The fury in his eyes said he would kill Ryder if he had to.

She glanced from Cain to Ryder as she rolled out of the bed, saw that the biker's nose and mouth were bleeding, one of his eyes beginning to swell. Grabbing the brass lamp on the nightstand with shaking hands, she took a steadying breath, braced her feet apart, and swung the lamp with all her strength, crashing it against the side of Ryder's head.

The biker swayed on his feet. Cain's last punch sent him hurling into the wall, his big body sliding down to the floor, his head lolling forward, unmoving. Cain stood over him, breathing hard, his dark eyes still burning with fury. His fists were clenched, his powerful biceps bulging.

Jenny sagged down on the edge of the bed. She couldn't stop shaking. In all the years she had been around the bar, nothing like this had ever happened.

Cain bent down and checked Ryder's pulse, pulled out his cell, and called 911. A few quick words, and he ended the call. "The cops are on the way."

Since the police station was right across the street, it wouldn't take long for them to get there. She should have been relieved, but instead, the fear she'd been feeling rushed back with the force of a blow, and a sob caught in her throat.

Cain turned at the sound. He walked over to where she sat on the side of the bed. She flinched as he reached toward her, and his hand fell away. "You're all right, honey. He's not going to be hurting anyone anytime soon."

Jenny couldn't control the shaking. She wrapped her arms around herself, but it didn't do any good.

"Let me hold you," Cain said. "You're safe with me, I promise you."

She shouldn't. She was a grown woman. She didn't need someone to take care of her, and yet . . . Trembling all over, she rose from the bed, and Cain eased her into his arms.

"I won't let anyone hurt you," he said. "Everything's going to be all right."

Jenny rested her head on his shoulder, and her fear slid slowly away. She was safe. The police were on the way, and Cain was there.

She lifted her head to look at him. "Thank you. If . . . if you hadn't come along when you did . . ."

She felt the tremor that went through Cain's big body.

"How did . . . how did you know?" she asked.

"I've got good instincts. I had a hunch those guys would be back."

"I checked the door. I don't know how . . . how he got in."

"It was bolted when I got here, but I could hear you inside. Probably opened the door with a lock pick. Guy like him would know how to use one." Cain glanced at the splintered door, destroyed by a kick from his heavy leather boot. "You need to put chains on these doors."

She realized her trembling had stopped and forced herself to move away. "They're on order. I'll put them up as soon . . . as soon as they get here." At least the sound of the chain breaking would have given her some warning.

She turned to see two of Jerome's finest rushing into the room, realized her sleep-tee was ripped halfway to her waist on one side, and straightened it as best she could. Cain pulled the blanket off the bed and draped it around her shoulders. She gave him a whispered "Thanks."

"What's going on here?" one of the officers asked. Gerry Simmons, tall, bean-pole thin, and a really nice guy. Jenny knew all the guys in the local police department, which consisted of a chief, a lieutenant, two full-time, and two part-time officers.

"Ms. Spencer was attacked by the man over there on the floor," Cain said. "Fortunately, I got here in time to stop him."

"Nice work," Gerry said. "You're Cain Barrett, right? You're the new owner of the Grandview?"

"That's right."

The other officer, Neal Gibbons, a nice-looking, gray-haired man, knelt to check on Ryder's condition, then locked a pair of handcuffs around the biker's thick wrists. "EMTs are on the way. Won't take 'em long to get here."

Jerome had a well-trained volunteer fire department, with a station house also on Main Street, not far away.

Ryder groaned and roused himself enough to realize his hands were cuffed behind him.

"Take it easy," Neal said. "Paramedics are on the way. They'll take you to the hospital in Verde Valley."

"Fuck you. I don't need no fuckin' hospital."

Cain stepped in front of him, one of his scarred hands unconsciously fisting. "Keep talking and you will."

Gerry put a hand on Cain's shoulder. "We got this. But we're going to need a statement from you and Jenny."

"Tomorrow," Cain said. "Jenny's had enough for tonight."

"It's all right, Gerry," Jenny said. "I'm okay. Just tell me what you need."

Gerry cast a long, disgusted look at Ryder. "We can do it tomorrow. Like Mr. Barrett said, you've had enough for tonight."

Cain relaxed. "It's just Cain. We'll see you at the station in the morning. I'll call, let you know what time we'll be there."

The EMTs strode through the door just then, spotted Ryder, and hurried toward him. He was swearing, calling them filthy names. He loudly declined any help. The EMTs verified he was okay as far as they could tell without taking him in, and the officers hoisted him to his feet.

"We'll see you two in the morning," Gerry said, as the police hauled the biker out through the ruined door. After the shuffle of feet and Ryder's cursing disappeared down the hall, silence fell.

"I can't thank you enough for what you did," Jenny finally said.

"You work for me now. I take care of my people."

The words were like a wake-up call, putting things back in perspective. She was just an employee, nothing more. She had to remember that. "Nothing like this has ever happened here before. Whatever the reason, I'm glad you came."

Cain nodded. "Get dressed, grab your overnight bag, and let's get out of here."

"What?"

He glanced at the shattered door. "You can't stay here. Troy says the rooms are all full. You can stay over at the Grandview."

She started shaking her head. "I'll just drive down the mountain to my house."

"The storm outside is blowing like a bitch, and after what happened, you're in no shape to drive."

That much was true. Every time she thought of the attack,

about how bad it could have been if Cain hadn't arrived when he did, she started shaking again.

"I'll sleep on the sofa in my suite," Cain added. "You can have the bedroom."

The thought of sleeping in Cain Barrett's bed was enough to make hot color wash into her cheeks.

He must have noticed. Amusement touched his lips. "You don't have to worry. Ryder's in jail, and I'm nothing like him."

She managed to keep her eyes on his face. Nope, Cain Barrett couldn't be more different. "It isn't that. I just . . . I don't want you to have to give up your bed."

"I can handle a night on the sofa. You're going to be working for me, and as I said before, I take care of my people. Get dressed and let's go."

CHAPTER SEVEN

IT HAD TAKEN CAIN YEARS TO PERFECT THE KIND OF SELF-CONTROL IT had taken not to wrap his hands around the biker's thick neck and squeeze the life out of him. The thought of what Ryder planned to do to Jenny had sent him into a blinding rage.

Even in his bad-boy days, he'd been protective of women. Maybe it was something his grandmother had instilled in him, or maybe it was just part of his DNA. Whatever the reason, he felt even more protective when it came to Jenny Spencer. She was a foot shorter than Cain, a foot shorter and nearly a hundred pounds lighter than the bastard who had tried to rape her.

His stomach burned to think of it.

"Stay here," he said to her, as they reached the bottom of the stairs in the Copper Star lobby. Cain went to the door leading into the saloon to check on Ryder's buddies, see if they were still in there. The bar was about half full, but there was no sign of the men.

He looked out the front door to see if their bikes were still parked along the street, but the arrival of the police must have been enough to send them on the run. Cain was no fool. Even with Ryder gone, four to one wasn't good odds.

He kept a close eye on the shadows and the doorways of closed-up businesses as he led Jenny down the sidewalk to the Jag. Spotting no sign of trouble, he took the overnight bag she had been carrying so he could keep his hands free, clicked the locks, and opened the passenger door.

Jenny settled into the tan leather seat, and he closed the door. Cain rounded the hood of the car, tossed her bag into the seat behind him, and slid in behind the wheel.

When Jenny didn't reach for her seat belt, he pulled it across her chest and latched it, felt her flinch when his arm brushed her breast. Cain silently cursed.

She was still a little shocky. He admired the way she had managed to hold it together so far, but he figured she was close to her limit, and he was glad he had insisted on taking her back to the Grandview.

"Where's your pickup?" she asked as he started the engine.

"I left it at the ranch. The Jag drives better on curves." *And I was worried about you. I wanted to get here as fast as I could.* But he didn't say that. After what had happened, knowing he was attracted to her would probably scare her to death.

The short drive up the hill took no time at all. The outside hotel lights and the tall LED lights in the parking lot were burning. A few lights glowed through the windows of the hotel.

He drove around back and parked the Jag in his private space behind the building, close to the back door. Grabbing Jenny's overnight bag, he went around and helped her out of the car. She hadn't said a word since they'd driven away from the saloon.

Inside the hotel, Cain reset the alarm system and punched the elevator button. When the door opened, he urged Jenny inside, and the carriage lifted away. She didn't speak until the doors opened and she realized she was in the entry of his suite instead of in the hallway.

"You have a personal elevator. That's nice."

He smiled. "Yes, it is. I like my privacy."

She looked up at him with those big green eyes. "Then what am I doing here?"

He wanted to touch her, hold her the way he had in her hotel room, reassure her she was safe. It was probably the last thing she wanted. "I invited you here. That's different."

He hadn't shown her the suite when he had given her the hotel tour, and as she looked around, he could read her curiosity. She assessed the newly arrived caramel leather sofa and chairs, and the wet bar along one wall, though there still were no barstools. An end table rescued from a second-hand store sat next to the sofa, along with an old brass lamp.

"Besides the living room and master bedroom, there's a guest room and a study down the hall that still needs furniture. Obviously, the place isn't finished," Cain said unnecessarily.

Jenny seemed not to notice. Instead, her gaze took in the wall of windows that looked out at the mountains, though it was too dark to see them.

"This could be really nice with the right accents."

He was glad she was thinking about something besides the attack. "Yes, it could." A thought shifted toward the front of his mind. "I have an interior designer working on the project—several, in fact—but I'd really like your input on my suite."

Surprise showed in her face. "You would?"

"Yes. I think you might be able to give it a little homier feel . . . so it wouldn't be like my office or the house in Scottsdale."

He thought he read something in her face, interest in the solitary life he led, or maybe it was pity.

"All right, I'll give it some thought."

"The bedroom's that way." He pointed toward a door on the right side of the room, trying not to imagine her naked in his bed, the sweet curves he'd seen outlined by her stretch jeans, the full breasts he'd felt when he'd fastened her seat belt.

"The maid was here this morning, so the sheets are clean. Fresh towels in the bathroom. If you need anything, I'll be right out here."

She turned to face him. "What about you? You'll need sheets and a blanket."

"There's some extra bedding in the linen closet in the hall. I'll take care of it. There's a powder room and a guest bathroom, so I won't have to bother you. You just get some sleep."

Jenny didn't move, simply stood there looking up at him.

"What is it?"

Her eyes welled. "I'll never be able to thank you enough."

He didn't want to give her the same excuse, that he'd helped her because she was one of his employees. He didn't want to lie to her again.

"Get some sleep. I'll see you in the morning."

Jenny nodded, picked up her overnight bag, went into the bedroom, and closed the door.

Two seconds later, her head popped out. "Any chance you'd have an extra T-shirt? Mine . . . went in the trash after . . ."

"No problem."

He walked into his room, pulled a white cotton V-neck out of the secondhand dresser, and tossed it in her direction.

"Thanks." Jenny snagged it out of the air and closed the door as he walked back into the living room.

Cain sank down on the sofa. *What a helluva night.* He thought of Jenny in his big king-size bed and wondered if he'd actually be able to sleep.

Something shifted in the air. Jenny felt it the same way she had before, and her eyes popped open. It wasn't Ryder who stood at the foot of the bed; it was something different, something in the shape of a man that wasn't a man. Something dark and sinister that could float on the slight currents of air in the bedroom.

Her breathing hitched. *It's only a dream,* she told herself, but when she sat up in bed, she realized her eyes were wide open and she could see his bloody, battered face. A pair of eyes that glowed like red neon gleamed from swollen black sockets in sunken, hollow cheeks.

Jenny screamed, a shriek of terror that sliced through the walls with the squeal of a buzz saw. Cain burst through the door, which, in a show of trust, she hadn't locked.

Cain strode toward her. "What is it?" He glanced around. "Where is he?" His gaze went in search of Ryder, but Jenny shook her head. "What's going on?"

She was trembling from head to foot. She couldn't believe this was happening—not again. "There was . . . was a man at the foot . . . foot of the bed. A man but . . . but not a man."

Cain frowned. "A man but not a man," he repeated darkly.

"Yes, no . . . I don't know. I think . . . I think it was a ghost."

Cain sighed, his exasperation clear. "It was just a dream, honey. You were attacked, damn near raped. It's bound to cause some kind of trauma."

She could feel her eyes welling. She wasn't a crier, yet tonight all she wanted to do was weep.

Cain pulled her up from the bed into his arms. Stupid as it was, Jenny didn't resist. There was something about Cain Barrett that made her feel safe. She took a steadying breath, and her trembling eased, then faded altogether. Jenny clung to him a moment more, then let him go.

She raked back her sleep-tangled hair. "I'm sorry. I'm not usually like this. I'm not usually so much trouble."

Cain's lips twitched. "You're no trouble, Jenny Spencer. I'm glad I was around to help."

She relaxed and managed to smile.

"Think you'll be able to sleep?" Cain asked, and this time, it wasn't amusement she saw in his gold-rimmed brown eyes; it was heat.

Or maybe it was just her imagination, which seemed to be on a roll tonight. "I think so. I'm sorry I woke you." But seeing what appeared to be a ghost wasn't something she was going to forget anytime soon.

"No more *sorry*'s," Cain said. "Things happen. When they do, we deal with them."

"Right." She hoped that sounded strong and capable, but she doubted it. For the first time, she remembered the T-shirt he had loaned her. It modestly came to her knees, but the soft white cotton also outlined her body, and the V was deep enough to reveal the tops of her breasts. "Good night, Cain," she said softly.

"Good night, Jenny."

Cain closed the door.

CHAPTER EIGHT

Sunday morning arrived at the Grandview Hotel and, with it, the construction crew, electricians, plumbers, a pair of interior designers up from Scottsdale, and miscellaneous other members of the team. All the workers were being paid extra to get the job done as quickly as possible.

Unwilling to wake Jenny, Cain showered in the guest bathroom and put on the clothes he had worn the night before. He ignored the dark stains that were Ryder Vance's dried blood. He doubted anyone would know what it was. Cain headed downstairs.

"Mornin', Cain." Jake Fellows, a fit, well-built man in his fifties, was the general contractor heading up the remodel.

"Morning, Jake. How's it going?"

Jake lifted his ball cap to scratch his thinning brown hair, then settled the cap back on his head. "Believe it or not, we're right on schedule, maybe a little ahead."

"News I like to hear," Cain said.

A woman walked in his direction—*sashayed* might be a better word. "Good morning, Cain." It was one of the interior designers, Millicent Beauchamp. She was a statuesque redhead who'd been a little too friendly from the start. Cain made a point of keeping her at a distance.

"Millie."

She gave him a fake smile. She preferred to be called Millicent, which everyone refused to do. She had the pouty lips that were in fashion, but Cain preferred a more natural look.

"I was hoping I'd see you," she said. "The carpet's arriving day after tomorrow. We'll be installing it this week. The tile installation will be finished in a day or two, along with the hardwood floors." Millicent was an extremely good designer, the reason Cain had hired her.

"That's good news," he said. "I talked to Jake. Looks like the construction crew is almost finished with their part of the remodel."

"That's great, because all the furniture that was ordered a few weeks back should be arriving soon. We'll have it installed before the end of the month."

"I look forward to seeing it."

Millie's smiled widened. "We'll have to celebrate when we're finished. Of course, dinner will be on me."

She'd been trying to get him to go out with her since their initial meeting. "First things first," Cain said. "Let's get the hotel open and running before we start celebrating."

Millie's smile slipped a little. "Of course." She glanced over his shoulder at someone walking up behind him. Cain's sixth sense—or the disapproval on Millie's face—told him Jenny had arrived.

Cain turned toward her. She looked a little tired, but as pretty as ever. Cain's body stirred. He managed to ignore it.

"Millicent Beauchamp, this is Jenny Spencer. She's the owner of the Copper Star. You'll be working with her on my personal suite. Whatever you two come up with, Jenny will have the final say."

Millie's eyes widened. "You're letting a saloon owner decorate your suite?"

Irritation trickled through him. "I like what Jenny did with the rooms she recently remodeled at her hotel. They're a little old-fashioned, a little more traditional, more relaxed. I won't be here that often. When I am, I want to feel comfortable."

Millie kept the fake smile plastered on her face. "That won't be a problem. If you'd told me, I could have handled it myself."

"I'm sure you'll work it out. In the meantime, we're headed to town for breakfast. We'll be back in an hour or so."

Jenny opened her mouth to argue, glanced at Millie, and let the hand Cain had set at her waist guide her toward the back door.

"We'll have breakfast, and you can check on things at the Star. Then we'll come back and you can talk to Opal, get her to show you the kitchen. Maybe make a few suggestions, whatever you think might make the place run more smoothly."

"Opal's your cook?"

"That's right." The hotel kitchen, like the bathrooms, had already been completed. Opal Dorn, the cook, was stocking shelves and freezers, getting ready for the opening. "Eventually, we should have enough business to bring in a chef for the evening meals, but Opal will continue to run the kitchen during the day."

"I told you I couldn't start until Tuesday. After quitting early last night, I have even more to do."

Cain grumbled a curse beneath his breath. He was still worried about Ryder's motorcycle gang, the Steel Cobras. They might want vengeance, and Jenny could be a target.

A noise at the front door caught his attention, and Cain turned back toward the sound. He paused at the sight of his grandmother in a wheelchair, a blue knit shawl draped around her thin shoulders, being pushed by her caregiver, Emma Watters.

"All right, I'll drive you back down the hill so you can go to work," Cain said. "But I want you to meet my grandmother first."

Jenny smiled. "I would love that."

It warmed him to see that she meant it. Together, they walked to where his grandmother waited. Cain leaned down and brushed a kiss on her wrinkled cheek. He knew better than to hug her, as he always used to. Nell's bones had gotten too brittle to handle much physical contact, especially with a guy his size.

"Jenny Spencer, I'd like you to meet my grandmother, Nell Barrett, and her friend, Emma Watters. Jenny's the owner of—"

"I know who she is," Nell said, cutting him off. She looked at Jenny. "Your Uncle Charlie and I were friends for years. Good man, your Uncle Charlie. A big loss for the town—for all of us—his passing."

"Thank you for saying that," Jenny said. "It's a pleasure to meet a friend of my uncle's." She smiled. "Cain has told me a lot about you. It's clear he adores you."

Nell's gaze slid in his direction. "He's a devil, that one. You best watch yourself, girl."

Jenny looked at him as if his being a philanderer was no surprise at all. "I'm sure half the women in Jerome have set their caps for him."

Nell grunted a laugh. "They'll have one devil of a time catching him." She looked at Jenny. "'Less he wants to get caught."

Cain figured it was time to change the subject. "So why didn't you call? You drove all the way from Scottsdale, and I could have missed you."

"I knew you were here. I still got lots of friends in town. I pretty much know everything that goes on in Jerome." She cocked a snowy eyebrow in his direction. "I heard about that little tussle you had at the Star last night. Bastard deserved the beatin' you gave him." She turned to Jenny. "So Cain brought you here after the fight?"

Jenny's cheeks flushed. "The hotel was sold out, and the room I was staying in was no longer . . . well, there wasn't a door anymore."

Nell nodded her approval.

"Well, I'm glad you're here," Cain said to Nell. "I'm driving Jenny down the hill to work. Soon as I get back, I'll show you around. You can look at your suite and let me know if there's anything you want to add or change."

"You got any coffee in the kitchen?" Nell asked.

"There's always coffee in the kitchen," Cain said.

"Good. I think Jenny and I could both use a cup. You can drive her down the hill when we're finished."

Cain didn't dare smile, but he felt like it. Didn't matter how big you were or how grown up, you didn't argue with Nell Barrett.

"Yes, ma'am," he said.

Jenny took a chair at a Formica-topped table in the kitchen. Cain wheeled his grandmother into position across from her.

"I've got a couple of things to do," he said. "I'll catch up with you ladies in a bit."

Cain left the kitchen. Emma, a woman in her forties with black hair cut in a bob, quietly slipped away. Emma was Nell's caregiver and best friend. One look told Jenny that Emma was solid as a rock and loyal to a fault, a woman Cain could count on to take the best possible care of his grandmother.

Opal poured two china mugs of coffee and set them on the table, along with a bowl of sugar, a pitcher of cream, and a couple of spoons.

"Thank you," Jenny said, as Opal returned to her kitchen duties. She was a big woman, heavyset, with a short cap of salt-and-pepper hair. Just the opposite of Nell, who was thin to the bone, her hair silver-white. Faint evidence of an earlier stroke, an unnatural tilt to her lips and the veined-hand curled in her lap explained the wheelchair.

"So . . . you and my grandson . . . ?" Nell asked.

"What? Oh, no. We're just friends. Cain's very protective. He helped me deal with some motorcycle riders on Friday night, then last night he showed up just in time to keep the big one, their leader, I think, from . . . from . . ."

Nell rested a long-fingered hand over Jenny's where it rested on the table. "He's a good boy. One of the best. If he cares for you—"

"It isn't that. Not really. He just hired me to do some work for him, and he's protective of the people in his employ."

"Is that so?"

"That's what he said."

"Did he now?"

"You don't think it's true?"

"Oh, yes, I'm sure it is." Nell made no further comment, just smiled and took a sip of her coffee. "What do you think of this place?" she asked.

Nell glanced around the big, modern, stainless kitchen, making a circular motion with her finger that included the entire hotel. "Grand, isn't it? Just like its name. Who would think the old hospital could turn into such a fancy place."

Jenny thought of the dream she'd had last night, the nightmare she didn't believe was a dream at all. "Mrs. Barrett, do you—"

"It's just Nell. You call me Nell, just like everyone else."

Jenny smiled, liking the idea. "All right, Nell. You lived in town for most of your life. People believe this place is haunted. Do you think that's possible?"

"I know 'tis. The whole blasted town is full of spirits. Everyone 'round here knows that. Even the darn tourists."

"I've heard the rumors, of course, but until last night . . ."

Nell's interest sharpened. "You saw a ghost in the Grandview last night?"

Jenny shifted a little under Nell's shrewd blue gaze. "I don't believe in ghosts, at least I didn't until I saw one. I know it sounds crazy, but last night I saw a man, or maybe only the head of a man, floating at the foot of my bed."

"What'd he look like?"

Bile rose in her throat as her mind went back to the memory. "His face was hideous, bludgeoned and bleeding, his eyes deep black sockets with red, glowing orbs in the center. I thought I was dreaming until I realized my own eyes were open."

"This whole building is haunted. Four hospitals were built in Jerome over the years. The United Verde—this place—was built on top of another. History books say nine thousand people died here from 1927, when it opened, to 1953, when it closed."

"That's incredible." Just thinking about it made a knot form in Jenny's stomach.

"Some real nasty deaths, too. In the old copper-mining days, the miners died like flies. Cave-ins, explosions, deadly fights between the men. Fire in the tunnels was a big threat. Mine owners only paid the bills for the injured miners who could get well enough to work again."

"I guess there were no unions or safety standards in those days."

"It was every man for himself. Heard a story about a miner who caught fire and got his legs burnt off. Hospital kept him for a while, but when the mine owners stopped paying, they cut him loose. Gave him a big dose of morphine to take with him for the pain. No job, no money, no legs. The miner took an overdose and killed himself." She cocked a snowy eyebrow. "You don't think a fella like that would come back to haunt the sonsabitches who treated him that way?"

Jenny inwardly smiled at the outrage in Nell Barrett's voice, although the story was too awful to imagine. "So you think I could have seen the ghost of a miner who died in the old hospital?"

"Could be. Way you described him, could be the head of the ghost of Claude Harvey."

"Claude died in one of the hospitals?"

"Claude was an employee right here, worked in the hospital in the thirties. They found him dead one morning in the basement, his head crushed beneath the elevator."

Faint nausea swirled in her stomach.

"Some folks believe he was murdered. In the old days, murder was a common occurrence in this town."

"Does Cain know the stories?"

"Anybody raised here knows the stories. But you lived in Cottonwood, not Jerome, right?"

"That's right. After my mother died, I lived with my dad. In the summers when I was a teenager, I worked for Uncle Charlie in the hotel. After I turned twenty-one, whenever I was home from college, I worked in the bar." She had heard a few ghost stories back then, but she hadn't paid much attention. She'd been a lot more interested in boys than spirits.

"Charlie used to talk about you all the time," Nell said. "He was really proud of you. Said you were the first person in the family to get your college degree. He didn't care much for your husband, though."

"Ex-husband," Jenny corrected.

"Smart girl," Nell said. "Charlie said he mistreated you. No woman should put up with that."

After a couple of years, she hadn't. Richard was gone from her life, though he made an occasional appearance when he wanted something.

Jenny thought of her uncle and felt a pang of loneliness. "I really miss Uncle Charlie."

"He left you the Copper Star. That means he's right there with you all the time."

Jenny found herself smiling. "Yes, I guess he is." She liked Nell Barrett. She could understand Cain's love for the woman who had raised him.

He walked into the kitchen just then, filling up the room with his height and powerful presence. "You two have enough time to exchange the latest gossip?"

"For the time being," Nell said.

Jenny rose from the table. "It was really nice meeting you, Nell." The older woman just smiled and nodded. Jenny turned to Cain. "I can walk down the hill. There's no need for you to drive me."

"We've got an appointment at the police department. Chief Nolan is waiting for us."

Jenny sighed. "Right. I can't believe I forgot."

Cain turned to his grandmother. "I won't be long."

Nell smiled as if she knew a secret Cain didn't. "Take your time. I'll be right here."

Jenny led the way out of the kitchen. In minutes, they were settled in the Jag, driving back down the hill to Main Street. "You haven't mentioned last night," she said.

Cain slid her a sideways glance. "Which part? The monster in your hotel room, or the monster in your dreams?"

Jenny glanced out the window, looking at the buildings perched precariously along the street. She turned back to Cain. "Maybe you were right. Maybe it was one and the same." Though after listening to Nell, she didn't believe it. "I'm sorry—"

"Don't say it. It's over and done. Best to just move on."

"Maybe so, but I still appreciate what you did."

Cain turned the Jag onto Main Street. "That reminds me, I haven't thanked you for your help last night."

"My help?"

"The brass lamp next to the bed. Quick thinking and pretty damn brave. Most women would have run away screaming. Instead, you pitched in to help."

"It never occurred to me to leave you there to fight Ryder by yourself."

Cain cast her a sideways glance. "As I said, I appreciate the help, but anything like that ever happens again, you get the hell out of there and leave the fighting to me."

Jenny made no reply. There was no way she would ever abandon someone who was risking himself to save her.

From the dark look in his eyes, Cain knew what she was thinking.

Cain parked near the police department. They made their way along the street and went inside.

Chief Nolan was waiting, a robust, heavyset man with a leonine mane of thick gray hair. He took his job seriously, and he didn't like ripples like the ones created in the Copper Star last night.

Chief Nolan gave Jenny and Cain each a yellow pad. "I need your statements in writing. But first, just tell me what happened upstairs last night."

"Where's Ryder?" Cain asked.

"Transferred him to the Yavapai County Jail down in Camp Verde. Unfortunately, some fancy lawyer showed up at the jail this morning to represent him. Looks like he'll be out on bail sometime tomorrow."

Cain swore. Thinking about what had happened, Jenny felt a chill.

"If he knows what's good for him, he won't come back to Jerome," Cain said.

The chief sat down in his chair. "Take it easy, Cain. We'll be watching for him. He turns up around here, he'll be back in jail before you can count to ten, and next time he won't be getting out so easy."

Jenny hoped Chief Nolan was right. She also wondered where Ryder had gotten the kind of money to hire an expensive attorney.

They finished the paperwork and left the building, and Cain walked her the short distance back to the saloon.

"You don't need to worry," Jenny said, reading the concern in his face. "I'll be fine."

"Any of the Cobras show up, you call me."

"I've been running this place for years. I'll be fine."

"Promise me."

Jenny released a slow breath. "All right, fine. If any of the bikers show up, I'll call. See you Tuesday."

"Tuesday," he repeated, and headed back to his car.

CHAPTER NINE

CAIN RETURNED TO THE HOTEL, CHANGED INTO CLEAN JEANS AND A fresh blue-denim shirt, then gave Nell and Emma a tour, winding up in Nell's nearly completed suite and Emma's adjoining quarters, not as large, but extremely nice.

Afterward, he loaded Nell's wheelchair into the back of the Acura RDX he had bought for her, one of the easiest vehicles for the handicapped to get in and out of. Taller than Nell and thirty pounds heavier, Emma helped Nell into the passenger seat. His grandmother could walk with the use of a cane, just not well and not for long.

They stopped for lunch at the Clinkscale, once a brothel owned by a madam named Belgian Jennie Bauters—at one time, the richest woman in Arizona. In a strange twist, Jennie was murdered by her opium-addicted boyfriend, who was hanged a few months later for the crime.

More ghosts? Cain thought with amusement, then remembered an old saying, *Whoever dies in Jerome, stays in Jerome.* Though Belgian Jennie had been murdered in another town, the brothel in Jerome had belonged to her, so if you believed in spirits . . .

He smiled as Emma held the door and Cain wheeled Nell inside. Today, the building was a lovely boutique hotel with a restaurant downstairs that served the best food in town.

They ate a leisurely lunch, and then Cain helped Nell back into the car and loaded the wheelchair, and Emma settled herself in the driver's seat.

"I'll let you know when your rooms are ready," Cain said.

"It better be soon," Nell warned. "'Cause we're about to be movin' in."

Cain grinned. "One way or another, they'll be ready for you by the end of the week."

Nell grinned back. "That's my boy."

Cain watched Emma drive the SUV down the hill toward Cottonwood, heading for Interstate 17, the road back to Scottsdale, then turned and made the steep walk up the hill from the Clinkscale to the Grandview, enjoying the brisk fall weather and the exercise.

Back in his suite, he thought of what had happened last night, thought of Jenny and tried not to imagine her sleeping in his bed.

By herself, unfortunately.

He would be glad to be back at the ranch, where he could concentrate on other problems and push images of Jenny to the back of his mind.

Before leaving the hotel, Cain double-checked with Jake, then spoke to Millicent about Nell's suite. Satisfied he'd done what he could, he headed out to his Jag for the drive back down the mountain. On Monday, he had a meeting with the private detective he had hired to help him find his champion cutting horse and the men responsible for stealing him. On Tuesday, he would be back in Jerome to get Jenny situated in her new job.

Jenny. Arousal slipped though him, tightening his groin. Damn.

When he'd returned to Jerome, he'd had no idea he would run into Jenny Spencer—hell, he barely remembered her—or that if he did, he would feel an attraction he hadn't felt for a woman in years.

He wondered what Jenny thought of him and hoped the attraction was mutual. He had a feeling his money and success wouldn't make a bit of difference to her. Sort of good news/bad news, depending on how you looked at it.

Money usually bought him just about anything. Not this time. Cain wanted Jenny. He just had to figure out how to make her want him.

The weekend slipped past with only the usual problems of running a ranch. Monday morning, he drove his pickup the thirty miles to Prescott, arriving on time for his ten o'clock appointment with Nick Faraday.

Nick was former military. He'd gone into law enforcement for a couple of years after leaving the service, found out he had a knack for digging up information, and eventually gone private.

Cain crossed the lot to the office of Faraday Investigations on Gurley Street, a small, unassuming beige structure with parking spaces out front. He rapped a few times and opened the door. Nick was kicked back in the chair behind his desk, his cowboy boots crossed at the ankle on top, his cell phone pressed against his ear. He was about six feet, lean-muscled, black-haired, and good-looking.

He waved Cain forward as he swung his feet to the floor and sat up in his chair.

"I'll be in touch," Nick said into the phone and ended the call. He looked at Cain. They'd been friends for years, even before Nick had gone into the army. They had reconnected when Cain bought the Cross Bar Ranch and wanted background information on the men who worked there.

"You're early," Nick said. "Lucky for you, I've already got some intel for you." He pointed to a wooden captain's chair on the opposite side of the desk. "Have a seat."

The office had the bare essentials, a desk with a computer on top, a couple of metal file cabinets, a pair of wooden chairs in front of the desk, and a small, barely functional kitchen in a tiny room next to the bathroom. The space was painted a dull off-white, and there were a couple of posters, photos of the Arizona desert, on the walls.

Nick believed that, aside from the time he spent on the computer, being in the office meant he wasn't getting his work done.

"You want some coffee?" Nick asked.

Cain flicked a glance toward the tiny kitchen. "You call that day-old sludge you drink coffee?"

"Just brewed a fresh pot."

"That's a relief. Thanks, I could use some."

Nick brought him a pottery mug with a cactus on the side and returned to his seat behind the desk, carrying a mug for himself.

Cain took a sip. It was hot and black, just the way he liked it. He hadn't slept well last night, worrying about the Steel Cobras and Jenny. Maybe the coffee would help him focus. "So what have you got for me?"

"Let's just say you aren't the only one who's been losing livestock. The Branch Creek Ranch out in Dewey had a couple of prize quarter horses stolen, rodeo stock that earned them a pretty penny in competition earnings. They were taken two days after your cutting horse went missing."

"Dewey isn't that far from the Cross Bar."

"No, and two top-ranked Morgan show horses were stolen from the Four Winds Ranch near Cordes Lakes the week before the incident at your place. The ranch is a horse-boarding facility. Losing expensive livestock is not good for business."

"So we've got a horse-thieving ring."

"Looks like."

"Interesting that all three thefts happened in Yavapai County. What's the sheriff doing about it?"

"Deputy Landry says he's working on it."

"That's what he told me. I prefer action over words. You got any ideas who might be responsible?"

"Good chance somebody local is feeding the thieves information. No way the thefts are random. There are a lot of horses out there, but somehow they managed to pick the most valuable."

"Who would have that kind of information?" Cain asked.

"Could be as simple as digging around on the internet. It might take some time, but the info is probably out there."

Cain pondered the notion, though it didn't sit quite right in his head. "I guess you could find info on my stud. Sun King is an all-American cutting-horse champion. His offspring have won total earnings of over a million dollars. Plenty of articles written about him."

"Same goes for the show horses. There's info out there on them."

"So somebody steals them. How are they getting rid of them?"

"Good question."

"I've got some people who are good with computers," Cain said. "They can find out just about anything."

"Like who might have been searching ranch websites looking for valuable animals?"

"Exactly." Cain rose from his chair. "Keep digging. I'm not convinced the internet is the answer."

Nick stood up behind his desk. "Neither am I."

"One more thing. I need a little info on a woman named Jenny Spencer. She's working part-time for me at the Grandview. Born in Cottonwood. Owns the Copper Star Saloon and Hotel. See what else you can find out."

"Will do."

The men shook hands, and Cain left the office. On his way back to the ranch, he drove through an Arby's on Iron Springs Road and grabbed a roast-beef sandwich, then at the last minute, made a turn onto Gail Gardner Way, which led to Highway 89, the road up to Jerome.

It was Monday. Odds of the bikers showing up again were minimal. Except that he'd called the jail in Camp Verde that morning, and, as expected, Ryder Vance had made bail. The police believed he'd left the area. Cain wasn't so sure.

Jenny Spencer, with her sweet curves, pretty face, and golden-brown curls, was a temptation to any man—Cain included. But the guy who might want to punish her was the son of a bitch she had helped send to jail.

Jenny spent Sunday afternoon and Monday in the small house in Cottonwood that she and Dylan had been raised in: three tiny bedrooms and one small bath, an older track house with a single-car garage, one of a dozen that all looked the same.

Dylan had no interest in the house or living in Cottonwood, so after her divorce, Jenny had moved back in. She had managed to furnish the place, but done little in the way of decorating and felt no attachment to it.

Lately, she had been thinking of the money she could save if she rented the house furnished and moved into one of the suites in the hotel. She would lose the nightly rental fee, but the bigger rooms were harder to fill, and the mortgage payment on the Cottonwood house, plus the utilities and upkeep, weren't cheap. The money she could earn from the house would give her some wiggle room, and she spent most of her time in Jerome anyway.

She would lose the privacy the little house afforded, but once she got the construction loan on the new wing paid off and the business started earning enough profit, she could move back in.

Plus, she reminded herself, she now had a second job, which meant extra money, but also more time in Jerome.

Before leaving on Sunday, she had made a decision. Jenny told Troy and Heather Donahue, the girl behind the desk in the lobby, not to rent room 11, a small suite that overlooked Main Street.

Then she put an ad in the digital version of the *Verde Independent*, left the saloon in the hands of Barb McCauley, the other bartender, and headed down to Cottonwood. By that afternoon, she had a tenant.

Now that the decision had been made and the ball had started rolling, Jenny began packing the personal items in the house that she was taking with her, her clothes and toiletries, a set of china that had been special to her mother. By Monday, everything was boxed up and ready to go. She was committed to making the Copper Star a success. She would do whatever it took to make that happen.

Jenny refused to think of pigs like Ryder Vance and what had almost occurred.

And she firmly refused to think about ghosts.

CHAPTER TEN

CAIN SEARCHED FOR JENNY IN THE BAR AND THE HOTEL, BUT THERE was no sign of her. He finally managed to track her down through her friend, Summer Hayes, who was working behind the counter at the Butterfly Boutique.

Summer had been a little too trusting in giving out Jenny's address, but in this case he was grateful.

Cain made the eight-mile journey to Cottonwood in his pickup. Bags of grain he'd picked up in Prescott to take back to the ranch were still stacked in the truck bed. Cain pulled up in front of Jenny's small house. An older white Subaru Outback sat in the driveway, the cargo-bay door open, several boxes stacked inside.

Jenny's front door stood open, which wasn't good with Ryder Vance on the loose; it looked as if she were loading stuff from the house into the back of her vehicle. Cain was halfway up the sidewalk when Jenny walked out the front door, a big cardboard box in her arms.

"Let me have that." Cain took it before she could argue and headed for the Subaru.

"What are you doing here?" Jenny asked, propping her hands on her hips as he loaded the box in with the others.

"I had an appointment this morning in Prescott. Would you believe, on the way back to the ranch, I took a wrong turn and wound up here?"

"No, I wouldn't believe it." But her mouth tipped up, and it made Cain smile.

"It's partly true. I did have an appointment in Prescott. When I finished, I started back to the ranch, but halfway there, I began thinking about Ryder and turned on the road up to Jerome instead."

"I told you I'd call if any of the Cobras showed up."

"I know. No idea why I made the turn, but then when I got to the Copper Star, you weren't there, and Troy said you only worked half a day on Sundays and had taken Monday off. I knew you lived in Cottonwood, and that's only about ten miles from the county jail, so here I am."

"How did you get my address?"

"I have my sources." He smiled to distract her. If Summer wanted to tell her, that was Summer's business. "Looks like you're packing up? What's going on?"

"I'm renting the house and moving into the hotel. I can save money, and things always go smoother when I'm there. Plus I'll be working for you at the Grandview, so I'll be in town even more."

Desire slipped through him. Jenny would be working at the Grandview. They could get to know each other. If the attraction was mutual, sooner rather than later, he planned to have her in his bed.

Then he considered the extra hours she would be putting in. "You sure you want to work that hard?"

Jenny just shrugged. "It won't be forever, only until I get the construction loan paid off and generate a little more business. Besides, I like the idea of contributing to the success of a new hotel. What's good for Jerome is good for me."

True enough. An idea slipped into his head. "I plan to book some business conferences at the Grandview as soon as it's open and we get any operating glitches resolved. I'll be happy to promote the Copper Star. People want a glimpse of the past when they come to Jerome. What better place than a saloon that's been there for over a hundred years?"

A wide smile broke over her face. "That would be great."

Cain smiled back. Looked like the way to Jenny's heart was to help make her business successful. *You aren't after Jenny's heart,* he reminded himself, *just her sweet little body.*

He frowned. Or maybe it was more than that. He still wasn't sure of his intentions.

"I'll help you with the rest of the stuff you're moving," he said.

Half an hour later, the boxes were loaded into the Subaru, the rest in the back of his truck. One load instead of two, and they were on their way back up the hill to Jerome.

A teenager named Tim, a busboy at the Star, helped with unloading and carrying stuff upstairs to a small suite in the new wing. No kitchen, but a cozy living room, bedroom, and remodeled bath.

"You're probably starving," Jenny said when they headed back downstairs. "Lunch is on me."

He'd worked off the sandwich hours ago. A beer and a burger sounded good. "You're on," he said.

Jenny led the way into the saloon, which, during the day, was mostly filled with people eating. Cain paused just inside the doorway when he spotted a tall, svelte blonde with voluptuous breasts walking toward him.

Anna Hobbs Somerset. He had gone out with Anna years ago, after he'd returned to high school. She had been a senior, same as he, but after dropping out, then going back, he was older. She'd been a real beauty, popular with the football players, mainly because she liked sex.

She especially liked sex with him—or so she had said—as long as he didn't tell anyone. Anna couldn't afford to be seen with a poor, bad-boy, low-class guy like him.

Cain had left town after graduation, and that was the last he had seen of her—until a few months ago.

He'd run into Anna at the Hassayampa Inn when she'd been in Prescott to visit a friend. Anna had invited him to join her for supper. During the conversation, she'd told him she had married Arthur Somerset, an extremely wealthy older man, but Arnold had died, leaving Anna a widow.

"It was so very sad." Anna dabbed a napkin beneath her eyes.

"We'd only been married a few months when Arnold had a heart attack."

Unfortunate for Arnold, fortunate, indeed, for Anna, who was now a rich woman.

They had spent the night together in Anna's hotel room; then a week later, he had taken her out to dinner. He'd slept with her a couple of times in Scottsdale, where she lived.

But for Cain, the attraction just wasn't there. He hadn't called her since, and he didn't intend to.

Now Anna was in Jerome. He flicked a glance at Jenny, who watched them from where she stood next to the bar.

Damn.

Anna walked up and air-kissed his cheek, leaning in for a hug that pressed her full breasts into his chest. "Cain, darling. It's so good to see you."

"Nice to see you, Anna." That was a lie. Anna had been a vicious little strumpet in high school. From the few times he'd been with her in Scottsdale, that hadn't changed.

"I came up to visit Susan Tisdale," she said. "You might remember Suzy from high school?"

"I'm not sure. It's been a while." He hadn't the slightest memory of the girl, who probably wouldn't have given a ruffian like him a second glance.

"I was hoping you'd be here," Anna said. "While I was in town, I thought I'd drop by the hotel, see the progress you've made." She flashed him a smile from beneath her thick lashes. "I'm hoping you'll give me a tour."

Of the bedrooms, he thought. Sex was all she'd ever wanted from him. The only difference was, now that he was as wealthy as her late husband, she wasn't ashamed to be seen with him.

"I'm afraid I'm busy this afternoon," he said. "Maybe another time." He smiled. "The hotel should be open in another few weeks. I'll show you around the next time you're in town."

Anna's lips flattened out, and her blue eyes narrowed. She was pissed and letting him know it. When he looked at Jenny, he read a similar expression on her face.

He didn't give a flying F about Anna, but Jenny was another matter entirely. Clearly, this wasn't going to be one of his better days.

Jenny watched Cain talking to the beautiful blonde. She remembered Anna Hobbs from high school, one of the most popular girls in school. Even then, she was beautiful, tall and elegantly curved, with high, full breasts and slender hips. She'd always made Jenny feel short and frumpy. Her hair was the color of the sun, her lips as red as cherries.

Jenny remembered seeing her in the saloon a couple of times a few months back, not long after Cain had shown up in town. He had started dropping into the Star for a beer as construction on the Grandview grew closer to completion, but she couldn't recall seeing them together.

Anna and Jenny hadn't spoken. Anna had no reason to remember a lowly freshman while she was the queen of the senior class. Watching the two of them now, it was obvious Anna knew Cain, and not in a high school alumni sort of way. The looks the woman was giving him would melt a branding iron.

Jenny turned away and went into the kitchen to see how Myrna, the cook, was doing—anything to block the sight of Anna and Cain together. She couldn't believe she was jealous, but she wouldn't lie to herself, either.

Unfortunately, Mondays were often slow, and that was the case today. Jenny braced herself. She couldn't hide out much longer, but the thought of standing next to Anna, dressed in a sweatshirt and dirty work jeans, was simply too much.

Maybe if she waited a few more minutes . . .

Cain appeared in the doorway, tall and impressive, taking up far too much space to be ignored. "Where's that lunch you promised me?"

She'd been hoping he would just leave. Clearly, he was involved with Anna. Even if Jenny had been wearing a cocktail dress and high heels, she couldn't compete with a sophisticated woman like Anna Hobbs.

"Something's come up," Jenny said. "Go ahead and find a

table, and I'll have it brought out. Burger and fries okay, or would you rather have something else?"

Cain gave her a long, searching glance. "If you aren't going to join me, I'll take a rain check. I can get something back at the hotel."

Jenny managed to smile. "A rain check, then. Sorry."

He looked at her as if he had something he wanted to say, but in the end, he just nodded.

"I'll see you tomorrow. What time will you be there?"

"Around ten, if that works for you. I'd like to check on things here before I leave."

"That's fine. See you tomorrow at ten." Cain walked out the door, and Jenny breathed a sigh of relief. She tried not to wonder if Anna Hobbs would be spending the night in Cain's bed, but her vivid imagination was already picturing it.

She'd been stupid to pretend he might have an interest in her. She was hardly on the level of a woman like Anna Hobbs.

Which didn't change the fact she had already accepted a job at the Grandview, and it didn't change the fact Jenny intended to do that job as well as she possibly could.

It was late, the bar empty except for Troy. Jenny said good night as he walked out the side door to his car. She checked to be sure everything was locked up, then went out through the lobby and up the stairs to her suite.

She was mostly unpacked, the stuff she didn't need stored in the old stone basement, along with her mother's pretty flowered china.

She undressed and climbed into the queen-size bed, her muscles aching after a day of packing and moving, determined to catch up on her sleep. At least her head wasn't pounding. Mostly she was just bone-tired.

With a deep sigh, Jenny plumped her pillow and settled back in bed, pleased the mattresses she'd purchased for the new section were so comfortable. Her eyelids were just beginning to close when she caught a flash of light from the corner. Startled, her eyes shot open, and she peered around the room, trying to see what it was.

She spotted the object near the window, perfectly round, a bright, gleaming white spot of light, and it wasn't stationary. It was drifting around the room.

Her heart began to pound. She slowly sat up in bed, her eyes never leaving the brilliant white object. People who visited Jerome often came to see ghosts. Customers had mentioned things called orbs, supposedly connected to spirits, but she had never seen one. More than one person had claimed to have seen an orb in the saloon. One person even showed her a photo he had taken showing a bright white circle up by the old balcony above the bar.

At the time, she'd figured it was probably a problem with the camera, but now, as the brilliant circle of white hovered near the ceiling, she watched it, more intrigued than frightened. What was it? Where had it come from? Why was it in her bedroom?

The light darted boldly one way and then another, then streaked across the room and blinked out of sight. Jenny's pulse was still racing, her thoughts spinning.

So orbs were real. Tomorrow she would go on Google and find out more about them. Or at least what other people said about them.

Jenny took several deep breaths and tried to relax. An orb was just a light. Even it if it were some sort of spirit, it wasn't going to hurt her. She closed her eyes, determined to get a good night's sleep. She needed to be at her best when she went to work at the Grandview.

Went to work for Cain.

Jenny sighed into the silent darkness. She hoped Anna wouldn't be there tomorrow. No matter what she told herself, seeing the woman with Cain would make her uncomfortable.

Jenny tried to relax. If she didn't fall asleep soon, she'd take a couple of Tylenol PM.

Unfortunately, half an hour later, her restlessness continued, and her eyes kept cracking open, looking for another orb. Almost an hour passed before she got up and dug into the medicine cabinet, popped two pills, and finally went to sleep.

It was three in the morning when the plinkity-plink of an old upright piano reached her through a deep haze of slumber. Her eyes slowly opened. It took a moment to rouse herself enough to recognize what she was hearing—piano music, laughter, and the sound of glasses clinking in the bar downstairs.

She jolted wide awake, and her heart started knocking. What was going on? The bar was closed, and there was no old piano anywhere in the building.

Jenny sat up in bed. A few feet away, the closet door swung open, then very slowly closed. Her pulse kicked up. Jumping out of bed, she ran to the closet and jerked open the door. Nothing but her clothes and shoes, and the rolling suitcase she had brought from home.

Her mouth felt dry. Her heart was hammering. The music and laughter downstairs continued. Grabbing a pair of jeans, she jerked them on, pulled on a sweatshirt, and jammed her feet into a pair of sneakers. Snatching her flashlight off the floor beside the bed, she headed for the door.

Dim light from the sconces in the hall provided just enough illumination to see there was no one there. No sounds, just the creak and groan of the old building, sounds she had heard a hundred times since she was a kid.

When she reached the bottom of the staircase in the lobby, she turned and went into the saloon. Panning the flashlight around the room, she saw that the bar was empty. No piano music was playing, no people talking, no laughter or the clink of glasses.

Her pulse eased a little, but her mind still raced.

It was a dream, she told herself. It had to be. Right? Either that or she was going slightly crazy. Ghosts in Cain's bedroom. Now ghost sounds in her room upstairs.

With a heavy sigh, Jenny returned to her suite. She'd been working in the Copper Star since she was a teen. She had never seen a ghost. True, she'd heard a few eerie noises, a few gruesome tales from customers and employees, but nothing like this.

Then again, until now, she hadn't spent any time in the newly opened, recently renovated rooms in the hotel.

Did that make a difference?

As she climbed into bed, Jenny remembered Uncle Charlie's words. *Odd things happen in the rooms in that section. Dangerous things.*

Uncle Charlie had left that part of the hotel closed up. She wished she could talk to him, ask him why he had never remodeled the rooms and instead left them outdated and unrented.

Jenny closed her eyes, but she didn't fall asleep.

CHAPTER ELEVEN

CAIN WAS WAITING WHEN JENNY ARRIVED AT THE GRANDVIEW THE following morning. She was wearing dark blue jeans and a red plaid flannel shirt, her sun-touched curls freshly washed and gleaming around her shoulders.

How a woman in jeans and flannel could make him think of the night she had spent in his room—in his bed—and make him hard, he had no idea. Cain forced his mind in a safer direction, for the first time noticing the dark circles under her eyes and the pallor of her usually robust complexion.

He thought of Ryder and frowned. "You all right?"

"Bad night," she said.

"Tell me it had nothing to do with Ryder Vance."

She gave him a faint smile. "Would you believe me if I told you it was ghosts?"

"Let's get some coffee, and you can tell me what happened." He took her arm and started guiding her toward the dining room instead of the kitchen.

"Shouldn't I be getting to work? That's what you're paying me for."

"Let's talk first." As they walked along, he noticed her discreetly glancing around the lobby. Pure male instinct told him she was searching for Anna. Cain swore a silent oath.

"In case you're wondering, Anna Hobbs isn't here. I have no interest in Anna."

She paused to look up at him, one of her brown eyebrows arching. "Are you sure? The two of you looked awfully friendly yesterday."

"Anna's old news. I ran into her in Prescott a few months back. Dated her in Scottsdale a couple of times. That was it."

"By dated, you mean slept with."

He shrugged. "I'm a man, Jenny. Whatever else she is, Anna is an attractive woman."

Jenny glanced away. "Yes, she is."

Cain reached out and caught her chin, turning her to face him. "Don't underestimate yourself. I find you far more attractive than Anna Hobbs."

Her pretty green eyes widened. "You do?"

Cain bent his head and very lightly brushed his mouth over hers, settled in for a quick taste of her. When Jenny's lips softened and trembled under his, Cain lingered. Jenny relaxed against him, and Cain felt a rush of desire he hadn't been prepared for.

He forced himself to move away. Arousal throbbed in his groin, and he could still taste her on his lips. "That's just so you know I'm telling you the truth."

The color had returned to Jenny's pale cheeks, so the kiss had accomplished something. Now he also knew the attraction he felt for her wasn't one-sided.

He took a steadying breath. "Now . . . let's get down to business."

Jenny's composure returned, both of them focused again.

Unfortunately.

"Where would you like me to start?" she asked.

"First, let's have that coffee." He led her into the dining room instead of the kitchen. A few of the new wooden tables were set up, along with half a dozen high-backed chairs, more on the way. Opal brought them a tray with two china mugs of freshly brewed coffee, cream and sugar, a basket of warm biscuits and house-made jam.

"That looks delicious," Jenny said. "Thank you, Opal."

The cook smiled and returned to the kitchen.

Cain took a drink of his coffee. "So tell me about last night."

Between sips of coffee and consuming a fluffy, golden-brown biscuit, Jenny told him about seeing an orb in her bedroom, then hearing music and laugher coming from downstairs. "I have no idea if any of it was real, but that's what happened."

Nell would have believed her. Cain was a lot more skeptical.

"Maybe you were dreaming," he said.

"It's possible. I thought of that on my way down to the saloon, but after seeing the orb, I was wide awake. When I went down to check it out, the bar was empty. No piano, no people. Nothing. I went back up to my room, but I didn't hear the music or see the light again."

"Whatever it was, it doesn't seem to have been a threat. Real or not, maybe eventually you'll be able to figure it out."

Jenny smiled. "Thanks for not laughing." She looked him straight in the eye. "As for the kiss . . . it probably wasn't a good idea."

His arousal returned just thinking about it. "Maybe so, but that's what makes life interesting."

"You're my employer. Aren't you afraid of being sued for some kind of harassment?"

He almost smiled. There wasn't a whole lot Cain was afraid of, not after the life he had led.

"You're too independent to play the victim card." He smiled. "Besides, the kiss was worth the risk."

And if things went his way, the kiss would only be the beginning.

The color heightened a little more in Jenny's cheeks. She finished her coffee, said good-bye, and headed into the kitchen, as good a place as any to start. Cain could think of a lot of other things he would rather have her doing, but this was business. For both of them.

Jenny headed into the kitchen to talk to Opal and discuss making the kitchen run as smoothly as possible. She refused to think of Cain. She didn't have time for a man in her life. Even if she did, after Richard, she was too wary of men to get involved in a relationship.

Not that Cain would be interested. According to the tabloids, the man had dated a legion of women, though his brief affairs hadn't lasted long. Jenny didn't want to be included among them.

She found Opal at the big stainless sink in the huge, modern kitchen.

"Are you ready to get started?" Jenny asked.

"I am," Opal said, wiping her plump hands on a clean, white dishtowel. She was a tidy woman, her short, salt-and-pepper hair neatly trimmed and held back with clips on each side of her round, pink-cheeked face. Jenny liked her.

"How do you want to do this?" Opal asked.

"Let's just take a walk around. You can give me a rundown of how things are progressing."

"All right."

The tour started with the large pieces of equipment. Jenny liked the handy way the spices were laid out for ready access, the cookware and utensils, pots and pans in easy reach above the counter. But when she saw the flatware and dishes to be used in the dining room, she frowned.

"Those pottery plates are gorgeous," she said, picking one up and judging the weight. "But good Lord, they're heavy. The servers won't be able to carry them, or at least they'll have to carry them one or two at a time. That means multiple trips to the same table, and that costs time and money, plus it slows down the service."

Opal was nodding. "That's what I told Ms. Beauchamp, but she said the bold design statement was worth it."

"Ms. Beauchamp? You mean Millicent?"

"The decorator, yes."

A noise sounded in the doorway. Cain stood in the opening, his gaze fixed on Opal. "Millie's here to decorate the place, not tell you how to run your kitchen."

Opal said nothing. Cain's presence was definitely intimidating.

"The heavy plates are going to be difficult for the staff to handle," Jenny explained.

"So I gathered," Cain said. He walked over, picked up one of the gorgeous black pottery dishes, and frowned. "Jenny's right.

Beautiful but not practical. Get rid of them, and get something more functional."

"Ms. Millicent is gonna be real unhappy if we change the stuff she picked," Opal warned.

"Then she'll just have to be unhappy. From now on, you and Jenny have the final word in the kitchen. That goes for the service in the dining room, as well."

Opal glanced at Jenny, then back to Cain. Her smile was almost a grin. "Whatever you say, Mr. Barrett."

"It's just Cain, Opal. We're all working together here."

Opal's smile widened even more. She was younger than she first appeared, probably mid-forties. If the biscuits and jam were any indication, the lady knew how to cook.

Jenny worked through the day, sticking with the kitchen and dining area, making some inventory lists, checking equipment and ease of access.

A little before five, she left to return to the Copper Star. The after-work crowd, along with a day's worth of tired shoppers, started drifting in around five p.m. She walked into the saloon, saw that it was just beginning to fill, ducked in to check on preparations in the kitchen, then went back to spell Barb, who was overdue for a break.

Twenty minutes later, Dylan pushed through the swinging doors. He spotted Jenny in an instant and walked straight toward her, pulled her in for a hug.

"What are you doing here?" Jenny asked as the warm hug ended. "You're supposed to be at work."

"I just heard what happened Saturday night. Why the hell didn't you call me?"

Jenny sighed. There were few secrets in Jerome. The attempted rape, ensuing fistfight, and arrest would be the top gossip for days, maybe weeks. "Cain showed up in time to take care of the problem. I didn't want you to worry."

"*Cain.* So you two are on a first-name basis now?"

Jenny stiffened. "Cain fought the guy who attacked me. He could have been seriously injured. If he hadn't shown up when he did . . ." She thought of the attack, and a lump formed in her throat.

Dylan pulled her back in for another quick hug. "I'm sorry I wasn't here. If something bad had happened to you, I would never forgive myself."

Jenny reached up and touched his lean cheek. "I love you, Dylan. You're the best brother anyone could ever have. But I'm a grown woman. I own my own business, and I learned how to take care of myself a long time ago." *When I dumped my cheating, abusive husband.*

But Jenny didn't say that. Very few people knew how awful her marriage had actually been, what a vicious, lying snake in the grass Richard was.

Not even her brother.

"It was sweet of you to take time off from work and drive all this way, Dylan, but I really am okay." Jenny glanced around. "The bar is filling up, Barb worked all day, and tonight's Troy's night off. I don't have much time. I'm bartending and closing up."

One of his dark eyebrows went up. "By yourself?"

She laughed. "I've been closing up since I took over running the place. Don't worry, I won't be driving home late. I'm not even living in Cottonwood anymore. I moved out a few days ago. I'm staying in a room upstairs."

"What about the house?"

"I rented it. Once I get the Star back on track, after the lease is up, I can move back in. Or we can sell it and split the money."

Dylan ran a hand over his jaw. "All right, I get it. Sometimes I still think of you as my kid sister, and I worry."

She smiled. "I'm still your kid sister. Now go sit down at the bar, and I'll feed you. Burger, okay?"

He nodded. "Yeah."

"We may have an empty room upstairs. You wanna stay over?"

Jenny glanced up as Summer walked into the saloon. Her gaze found Jenny, lit on Dylan, and her cheeks flushed. Summer faltered, but kept walking.

"Hi, Jenny," she said. She looked pretty tonight, in a soft peach sweater, flowing, ankle-length skirt, and low heels, her silvery hair loose around her shoulders. She liked to dress nicely when she worked in the boutique. "Hi, Dylan."

Dylan smiled. "Hi, Summer." He was looking at her as if he had never seen her before.

Jenny wondered if maybe he really hadn't.

"You here for supper?" he asked.

"I just dropped by to hear how Jenny's new job is going," Summer said.

Dylan's head swiveled in Jenny's direction. "What new job?"

Summer kept talking. "She didn't tell you? She's working for Cain Barrett over at the Grandview. She's helping him get the place in order."

Jenny's eyebrows went up. "How did you know that?"

"You're working for Barrett?" Dylan asked, the frown back on his face.

"Only part-time," Jenny said. "I get to set my own hours, so it shouldn't be too hard."

Summer smiled. "Cain told me about the job when he came looking for you on Monday. That's why I gave him your home address."

Life in Jerome. No privacy whatsoever. Jenny just sighed, but Dylan was still frowning.

"Do either of you have any idea of Cain Barrett's reputation?" he said. "The man's screwed women from coast to coast. I've seen pictures of him with cover models and movie stars." He turned to Jenny. "You're in way over your head, sis. You need to watch yourself."

Irritation bubbled through her. Cain's love life was hardly a secret. No matter how much money he had, he was still just a man. She could handle Cain Barrett. The kiss they'd shared meant nothing, and she intended to keep it that way.

"I've seen the stories about him, Dylan. The job is interesting, and I need a fresh challenge. You should be able to understand that since your job is different and interesting every day. The job at the Grandview pays well, and I think I'm going to be good at it. Other than that, I'm not involved with the man in any way."

She gave him a hard stare. "Even if I were, it wouldn't be any of your business."

Dylan glanced away. He was wrong to interfere, and he knew it. "Fine."

Jenny smiled. "Now, how about that dinner? Summer, why don't you and Dylan sit down at one of the empty tables, and I'll get you some menus."

CHAPTER TWELVE

Cain was working in the study in his suite the following morning when his cell phone rang. He recognized Nick Faraday's number.

"Faraday. You got something?"

"Not a lot. Just a little info on Jeanette Eileen Spencer Thorndyke. Thorndyke's her ex. It's Jenny Spencer now that she's gone back to her maiden name."

"Thorndyke. Tell me about him."

"Richard Thorndyke. Jenny met him at Yavapai College. Her uncle, Charles Spencer, helped her pay for school, but Jenny also worked nearly full-time. Richard was a year older, married her as soon as she graduated. According to what I could find out, Jenny worked to put him through Arizona State, which took him an extra year because he was so busy screwing around."

Cain's jaw hardened. "Jenny know about it?"

"It took her a while to figure it out, I guess. Divorced him after she did. When it comes to women, Thorndyke's as smooth as they come."

"What's he do for a living?"

"Worked as a stock broker after he got out of school. After the divorce, he sold real estate for a while. When that didn't pan out, he married a woman named Margaret Eastman. She's ten years his senior, inherited the family fortune, so these days Richard doesn't do a helluva lot of anything, except play golf, squire his wife around, spend her money, and screw other women."

Cain had watched Jenny in the bar. She was always friendly to her customers, but she made it clear to the men she wasn't interested. Now Cain knew why.

He thought of the kiss. He figured he had caught her off guard. She'd probably be more wary the next time.

Cain silently cursed.

"That it?" he asked.

"I can dig a little deeper, but so far, I haven't turned up anything that would make you hesitate to employ her."

"I didn't think you would, but I appreciate your taking a look." He shifted the phone to his other ear. "Anything new on my stallion?"

"Still looking. Some good news for the Branch Creek Ranch. One of their quarter horses showed up at an auction in Tucson. The mare was running loose along the road, and the guy who found her needed money. Lucky thing was, the son of the owner was at the auction, looking to buy some stock. He recognized the animal, and the whole thing went sideways. Horse is back at the ranch."

"Interesting. You'd think if they went to the trouble of stealing it, they'd take better care of it."

"You'd think."

"I've got my computer whizzes digging around on the internet," Cain said. "So far, they haven't found squat."

"I'll keep you posted from this end."

Cain ended the call and tossed his cell phone up on the desk. He should probably go back to Scottsdale, check in at the office in person. But he had competent people he trusted, and if they needed him, they knew where to find him. Anything really important, he was only a couple of hours away.

He checked his heavy stainless wristwatch. Jenny wasn't coming in today. She was working at the Copper Star. It was nearly lunchtime, and he was hungry. Grabbing the brown sheepskin jacket on the back of his chair, he slung it over his shoulder and headed for the elevator in his suite.

* * *

It was eleven-thirty. With the October weather still pleasant and business brisk, the rooms were mostly full. Jenny had two part-time girls upstairs cleaning.

Deciding to check on their progress, she walked through the door from the bar into the small hotel lobby. At the same time, Heather rounded the desk and came toward her. She was a nice girl, a little overweight but working on it, a few pink streaks in her shoulder-length dark hair. She was quiet and efficient, an asset to the crew at the Star.

"The couple in room ten haven't checked out," Heather said. "We have another reservation for the room today, so I'm not quite sure what to do. Should I go up and knock on their door, let them know it's time to go? Or just wait and charge them extra when they leave?"

Jenny remembered the tall, slim man and the attractive woman with him. "I'll take care of it. Hand me the passkey, just in case." In case there was a problem. Most likely the couple had simply overslept.

Jenny headed upstairs. Room 10 was in the new section. There was no PRIVACY sign hanging on the door, so Jenny walked over and knocked. She knocked again, but still got no answer.

"Hello?" Knock, knock, knock. "Is anyone in there?" Pressing her ear against the door, she was sure she heard a sound, but she couldn't be sure. The room was prepaid. Maybe they'd just left and forgot to turn in their key.

Pulling the passkey out of the pocket of her stretch jeans, she shoved it into the lock, praying the couple wasn't in the middle of a quiet round of sex.

She banged again as she opened the door, giving them enough time to call out, then pushed the door farther open. A scream erupted, impossible to contain, the gruesome sight in front of her making her stomach twist.

The tall, thin man lay naked on the floor, covered in blood. His eyes were open and staring at the ceiling. The pretty flowered porcelain basin and pitcher that sat on the dresser was shattered, the man lying among the vicious glass shards.

Trembling all over, Jenny started backing up, hit the door, knocking it closed, turned, jerked it open, and raced out into the hall. *911.* She had to call 911 and get help. Dear God, where was her cell phone?

When she reached the stairs, Heather was racing toward her from the bottom, pink-streaked dark hair flying around her shoulders. "What is it! What's going on?"

Jenny realized one of her hands was balled into a shaking fist. She pressed it over her mouth, then forced herself to take a calming breath. "Call 911. Tell them it's . . . it's an emergency."

Jenny swallowed. She had to collect herself. She was the one in charge. She was the boss. It was up to her to handle the situation. She took another breath and tried to calm her racing heart.

"What's going on?" Heather repeated.

"Just do it. Tell them we need help. Tell them someone's . . . someone's been murdered."

Heather's eyes widened. As the girl jerked out her cell to call the police, Jenny thought of the woman who had been with the man when they'd checked in. She'd found the man on the floor, naked and covered in blood the color of old meat, dark and thick, his empty eyes open and staring. There was no doubt he was dead.

But what about the woman? Dear God, what if she were also injured, maybe even dead?

Gripping the banister, she started back up the stairs, her legs shaking so badly she could barely place one foot in front of the other. She could hear the sound of a siren, but all she could think of was getting to the woman, praying she was still alive.

Her knees felt weak as she shoved open the door and walked back into the room. The coppery smell of blood hit her, and her stomach rolled. She fisted her hands to keep from touching anything, trying not to look at the naked man on the floor. She was halfway across the room when she noticed a pair of fuzzy pink slippers on the other side of the bed.

Nausea rolled in her stomach as she moved closer, saw the woman lying on the floor, the trim ankles, the bare calves, the pink shorty nightgown that matched the slippers.

Jenny bit back a scream, locked it down tightly in her throat. *Be alive,* she thought. *Be alive.*

She forced herself to move closer, saw the blood on the nightgown, more of it matted in the long blond hair. Then she saw the rise and fall of the young woman's chest. *Alive, alive, alive.*

Her throat closed up. She barely felt the tears washing down her cheeks. *Thank you, God. Thank you, thank you, thank you.*

Jenny knelt beside the woman, who was unconscious but breathing, which meant her heart was beating. She had no first-aid training, but the fire department was only down the street. She dialed 911 and told them she needed an ambulance as well as the police, hung up, and knelt beside the woman.

The woman was still breathing, and the EMTs would be there any minute. She didn't want to move her, perhaps make her injuries worse.

She vaguely heard voices calling her name, followed by the sound of heavy boot steps. Rising from beside the bed, she turned, expecting to see the EMTs, but instead saw Cain striding toward her.

She must have made a sound in her throat, because he was pulling her up from the floor, easing her into his arms.

"Everything's going to be okay. Help just arrived. We just need to keep out of their way."

"The man is . . . is dead."

"Yes, I see that." He led her out into the hall, passing the emergency techs. A man and a woman in black uniforms rushed past them into the room.

"The ambulance is on its way up from Cottonwood," Cain said.

"The woman . . ." Her fingers dug into his arm. "She's . . . she's still alive."

He nodded. Drew her a little farther down the hall. She felt the tip of his finger, wiping tears from her cheeks.

"You have any idea what happened in there?" he asked.

Jenny thought of the broken porcelain pitcher and the glass shards on the floor. Some of them were big enough to cut through flesh and bone.

"They must have had a fight. Both of them were injured. The

door was locked, so I don't . . . don't think anyone came in from outside." She looked up at him as an awful thought struck. "Oh, my God. Their room . . . room ten is in the new wing. Uncle Charlie said bad things happen there. What if it was—"

"Don't even say it. Whoever killed that man was very real. You and your hotel had nothing to do with it. Come on. We're going downstairs. You have an office somewhere, right?" She nodded. "The police can talk to you there."

She didn't resist when he guided her through the maze of police and emergency services people, down the stairs to the lobby.

"Which way?"

"The door in . . . in the back on the left."

Her laptop sat on an old oak desk. There were two wooden chairs in front of the desk and an office chair behind it. Several oak file cabinets had seen plenty of use. A green-velvet settee sat against the wall. A small refrigerator hummed next to an open door that led to a tiny bathroom with a sink and toilet.

Cain eased her over to the velvet settee, went to the fridge, and found a bottle of water. He cranked off the cap and wrapped her fingers around the bottle.

"Drink," he said. Then he disappeared into the bathroom and came out with a wet paper towel, which he folded and draped over the back of her neck.

Jenny took a long swallow of water as Cain sat down on the settee beside her.

"You going to be all right?"

She took another drink of water. The cool towel helped calm her nerves. "I'm okay. It was just such a shock." For an instant, her throat tightened. She glanced up at the ceiling as if she could see into the rooms upstairs. "I've got to get back up there. I'm the person in charge. I need . . . need to handle this."

"Let me go up and—"

"No. It's my responsibility." Taking the bottle with her, she rose and headed for the door, with Cain right behind her.

Jenny turned. "What are you doing here, anyway?"

"I wanted some lunch. I got here just as the EMTs arrived. I figured whatever was going on, you'd be in the middle of it."

A faint smile curved her lips. "You always seem to show up at just the right time."

Cain smiled back. "I have a knack."

They returned upstairs together, found Chief Nolan had arrived on the scene.

"The woman's stable but unconscious," the chief said. "We found a wallet and purse in the room. Driver's license says the man's name is Brian Santana, forty years old, unmarried. The woman is Leslie Owens, thirty-three, also unmarried. Two separate addresses, both of them in Phoenix."

Aside from the information on the hotel registration form, which was the same as the information on Brian's driver's license, Jenny knew nothing about the couple that could help Chief Nolan and the police with the investigation.

She gave a brief statement to Gerry Simons, one of the officers who had arrested Ryder Vance after he had attacked her, then stood next to Cain as police cordoned off the newly opened section of the hotel, treating it as a crime scene, stringing yellow tape across the corridor and the door to room 10.

It occurred to her that she would need to find accommodations for the guests arriving later that afternoon, a thought that reminded her of the dead man and injured woman, and her eyes burned.

Suck it up, and get back to work.

She pressed her lips together as she looked at the yellow tape. Secretly, part of her was glad no one else would be staying in the new section, not until they knew exactly what had happened to Brian Santana and Leslie Owens. No until Jenny was sure something unexplainable hadn't occurred.

Cain's voice drew her from her thoughts. "You've done all you can," he said. "You ready to leave?"

"I need to talk to my staff, explain what's happened. Then I'm driving over to the hospital. Leslie Owens needs someone there when she wakes up. Until her family or a friend can get to the hospital, I want to make sure she's okay."

Cain gave her a long, assessing glance. "All right, staff meeting and trip to the hospital. We better get started."

Her head came up. "What? You don't have to do that. You've already done more than most people would have. I've been working at the Grandview. I know how much stuff you have to do."

"Lots of people work at the Grandview. Mostly, I'm just in their way."

That wasn't true. The man was as efficient as a machine, a master of making things move rapidly and smoothly.

"You go have your staff meeting," he said. "Then I'll drive you to the hospital. Once we've made sure Leslie is in good hands, I'll bring you back."

Jenny shook her head. "It's too much to ask."

"You aren't asking. I'm offering."

She wanted him to go with her. She couldn't deny it. He was the most solid, comforting presence she'd had in her life in years.

"All right, if you're sure."

Cain just took her arm, and they headed down the stairs.

CHAPTER THIRTEEN

EXPLAINING THE MURDER SITUATION TO THE EMPLOYEES DIDN'T take long. Word traveled fast in Jerome, especially at a locals hang-out like the Copper Star.

In a waiting room at the Verde Valley Medical Center, Jenny sat next to Cain for almost four hours before Leslie Owens's mother, Aida, and her aunt, Betsy, arrived from Phoenix.

Neither of the women had ever met Brian Santana. Leslie had told her mother she was dating someone new, but aside from Brian being a "good-looking, very nice man," Aida knew nothing more about him.

By the time the two women arrived to take over Leslie's care, Jenny and Cain knew the woman had suffered a concussion, but not how severe it was. Leslie was still unconscious, but the doctors were optimistic. Leslie had also sustained scratches, abrasions, and bruising, some of it around her throat.

As they were leaving the hospital, Chief Nolan arrived. He spoke to them briefly, then went in to talk to Aida and Betsy.

At least for a while, Jenny's duties were over.

"The doctors are hopeful Leslie will fully recover," she said, as Cain drove back up the hill to Jerome.

"That's good news, and they should know more by tomorrow."

Jenny watched the familiar desert landscape pass by outside the pickup's window, the wide open vistas, Palo Verde trees, prickly pear, and miscellaneous cacti. The sky was clear, the sun out and shining, but a storm was on its way, predicted for the weekend.

"I keep thinking about the murder," she said. "I think Brian and Leslie got into an argument that got out of control. Brian assaulted her, and Leslie killed him trying to defend herself."

"The door was locked when you got there, so it doesn't look like anyone else was involved. If the broken basin and pitcher turn out to be the murder weapon, you could be right, killing Brian was self-defense." He turned to look at her. "Unless Leslie murdered Brian on purpose, which would change things entirely."

Jenny felt a shiver. She thought of Leslie Owens, but couldn't see her as the type to murder someone. Then again, how would she know?

"I wonder what they were fighting about that could have caused things to turn so violent," she said.

Cain's big, scarred hands remained steady on the wheel. "With any luck, Leslie will be able to tell the police when she wakes up."

Jenny glanced at Cain, at his square-jawed, handsome profile, surprised she would notice after the trauma of the last few hours.

"Do you think Chief Nolan will tell us what he finds out?"

Cain flicked her a sideways glance. "Nolan was appointed by the mayor. If he has any gratitude for my sizable contribution to the mayor's reelection campaign, he'll be more than happy to keep us informed."

Jenny fell silent. *Money talks and bullshit walks,* Uncle Charlie used to say. She had supported the mayor as well, mostly by putting campaign posters in the windows of the Star and passing out brochures to locals.

At least Cain's money had gone to a good man.

By the time they got back to the Copper Star, Heather had found alternate lodgings for the guests who'd been planning to check in that afternoon, and the bar had returned to normal. There was a constant buzz among the customers, but people were eating and drinking as if it were any other normal day.

"Looks like the place is back to business as usual," Cain said.

"Looks that way."

"Amazing how well our employees can get along without us."

For the first time that day, Jenny smiled. "Kind of humiliating, really."

Cain laughed. "True."

They were standing in the opening between the lobby and bar. She needed to get back to work, but somehow couldn't summon the energy.

"I have an idea," Cain said. "It's been a tough day, so I hope you'll at least consider it."

Jenny looked up at him. "Of course. How could I not after all you've done to help."

"As you just said, the Star is chugging along just fine without you. You can't do anything about the room upstairs until the police release the crime scene."

"I hadn't thought about that, but you're right."

"I think you should take the rest of the day off and all day tomorrow. You deserve it, and it'll give me a chance to show you the ranch. We'll drive up, spend the night, and I'll show you around tomorrow. I'll bring you back the next morning. What do you say?"

For a moment, Jenny just stared. "Just because I let you kiss me doesn't mean I'm going to sleep with you."

Amusement lifted a corner of his mouth. "I'm not asking you to sleep with me. I'm asking you to visit my ranch as a guest. We won't be alone. I have half a dozen ranch hands milling about, plus my housekeeper, Maria Delgado. You've already spent the night in my suite, in my bed. You were perfectly safe that night, and you'll be perfectly safe this time."

She couldn't deny Cain had been a perfect gentleman. Still . . . Jenny felt torn between wariness and interest. "What about my work at the Grandview?"

"A couple of days won't make any difference."

She wanted to go. She was attracted to Cain Barrett as she hadn't been to a man in years. It was dangerous, but also exciting to have piqued the interest of a man like Cain.

Say yes, a little voice prodded.

"You need to get away from this place for a while, and I think you know it," Cain pressed. "A few days off will give you time to put things in perspective. If your people need you, you'll only be an hour's drive away."

"What if Chief Nolan wants to talk to me about the murder?"

"As I said, you'll only be an hour away."

The last of her defenses faded. She smiled. "All right. Taking off for a couple of days sounds wonderful, and I would love to see your ranch."

Being away from town, breathing fresh air out in the open desert—the appeal was overwhelming.

Jenny thought of what had happened in the room upstairs. At least for the rest of today and tomorrow, she could leave ghosts and murder behind.

Now that things were under control, Cain finally relaxed. The moment he had seen the EMTs and police arriving at the Copper Star, fear had gripped him. He'd been sure Ryder Vance had returned and attacked Jenny.

At six-foot-three and nearly two hundred pounds, not much scared Cain. Throw in dealing with the rough crowd he'd run with as a kid and the tough men who worked the mines, and fear was an odd sensation. He'd learned to overcome it years ago.

He'd been equally surprised at the relief he'd felt when he'd discovered Jenny wasn't the victim. It made him realize how important she had become to him. It didn't mean he had fallen madly in love with her. Hell, he wasn't even sure he believed in love. It was just a bit of knowledge he would stash away to examine later.

In the meantime, he intended to enjoy her company for a couple of days while he showed her the ranch.

Cain waited at the bottom of the hotel stairs, while Jenny went up to pack a few things for the trip. A police officer escorted her past the yellow tape to her room, then stood in the hall until she was finished.

Once they were loaded into his big Dodge truck, Cain headed straight for Highway 89A. No need to stop at the Grandview. He kept plenty of clothes at the ranch.

"Might as well sit back and enjoy the ride," he said as the truck rolled down the curvy mountain road. At that altitude, they were driving through timbered forest, down to the desert floor below.

Jenny said little on the way. Emotion could be a bitch. Though she was drained and exhausted, she looked pretty, with her shiny, golden-brown curls and the tiny row of freckles across her nose.

Arousal stirred through him. He wasn't taking her to the ranch with seduction in mind, but that didn't mean he didn't still want her. Denying the strong physical attraction he felt had him a little on edge.

With the sun pouring in through the window, the cab of the truck grew warm. He glanced over to see that Jenny had fallen asleep, her head curled into her hand, propped against the warm glass. A surge of protectiveness burned through him, which seemed to be a common occurrence when Jenny was around.

Cain wasn't sure he liked it.

As he turned onto Iron Springs Road, heading toward the ranch, Jenny sat up in the passenger seat. She looked out the window to see where they were. Recognizing the road northwest out of Prescott, she turned toward him.

"I can't believe I fell asleep. Not much company, was I?"

"You needed the rest. It's been a hard day."

She raked back her curly hair and sat up a little straighter. Dusk had fallen, but as he neared the ranch, it was still light enough to see the white-fenced pastures along the road and lining both sides of the lane leading to the ranch house.

Cain pulled to a stop in front of the single-story, red-tile-roofed structure and turned off the engine. Jenny was out of the truck before he could get down from the driver's seat.

"What a beautiful place," she said, glancing around, taking in the barns, the fenced paddocks, and desert vistas surrounding the property. She looked more rested, more relaxed, and he was glad he had brought her here.

"I fell in love with the Cross Bar the first time I saw it," Cain said, grabbing her overnight bag from behind the seat. He slammed the pickup door, and they headed for the house.

Maria Delgado opened the front door. "Señor Cain. Welcome home."

"It's only been a few days," he said, smiling. "Maria, this is Jenny Spencer. She's a friend from Jerome. She'll be staying with us for a couple of days."

Maria's black eyes swept over Jenny, who was about her same diminutive height, though Maria was older and much more robust.

Jenny smiled warmly. "It's a pleasure to meet you, Maria."

"*Buenos días,*" Maria said, but there wasn't much friendliness in the greeting. His housekeeper was extremely protective. Cain rarely brought a woman to the ranch, no one for over a year. Maria's motherly instincts had been aroused. She thought every women was after his money.

Mostly she was right.

"This way," Cain said, grabbing Jenny's bag and carrying it in through the foyer. Continuing down the long hallway in the bedroom wing, he walked past the master bedroom and put her things in the guest room next door.

Jenny walked in behind him.

"All the guest rooms have their own baths," he said. "If there's anything you need, just let me or Maria know."

"I'm sure I'll be fine." She surveyed the Southwest décor, the colorful striped fabric draped over a heavy wooden chair, the Native American blanket at the end of a queen-size bed with an ornate wooden headboard.

"Your house is lovely."

"Thank you. It's the only place I own that really feels like home."

They walked out of the guest room, back down the hall to the living room. It was also done with a Southwest flair, lots of bright-colored woven pillows and rugs, and heavy wooden furniture.

"You must be hungry," he said. "You haven't eaten anything all day but a candy bar and too much coffee at the hospital."

She looked up at him in surprise. "I hadn't really thought about it. Everything's been so chaotic, I guess I forgot."

He smiled. "Maria's a great cook. She feeds the hands at five. I called and told her we were coming but we'd be late. She'll have food for us waiting in the oven."

"Now that you mentioned it, I'm starving."

"So am I."

Maria was gone when Cain led Jenny into the dining room. But the Spanish-style table, a heavy slab of wood surrounded by ten ornate, high-backed wooden chairs, beckoned with dark red, yellow, and turquoise pottery dishes. Dark red napkins fanned out from inside thick ruby glasses.

"Grab a plate, and we'll see what's in the oven." Cain led her into the big, modern stainless kitchen, and they loaded their plates with enchiladas, rice, beans, and freshly made tortillas.

A bottle of Rioja Gran Reserve sat open on the table as they sat down, and Cain poured each of them a glass. There was no talk of murder or possible motivation, just pleasant, easy conversation about the Grandview remodel and the ranch.

When supper was over, Cain collected their plates, Jenny collected the rest of the dishes, and they carried them into the kitchen.

"What happened to Maria?" Jenny asked, glancing around.

"She has a husband at home. She'll be back first thing in the morning."

Jenny's features tightened. "You said there would be people around. You even mentioned Maria. What's going on, Cain?"

Irritation trickled through him. "As much as I would love to strip you out of those clothes and have my wicked way with you, that isn't why I brought you here. The hands sleep in the bunkhouse. You have your own room with a lock on the door. It's getting late. Why don't we just say good night now, and I'll see you in the morning."

He turned to walk away. He didn't need this. He had never disrespected Jenny Spencer. He wasn't planning to start.

Jenny stepped in front of him, her palm on his chest, blocking his way. "I'm sorry. You didn't deserve that."

Cain made no reply.

"I'm not afraid of you," Jenny said. "You've never given me any reason to be. It isn't you I'm afraid of . . . it's me."

He said nothing, but he was listening, curious about what she would say. "Go on."

"The truth is, when you're around, I feel things I shouldn't feel, and I don't completely trust myself."

Resting a hand on his cheek, she went up on her toes and pressed her mouth over his. It was a soft kiss, just the brush of her lips over his, but Cain's whole body tightened.

"Just so you know I'm telling you the truth," she said, repeating his own words back to him.

Cain reached out and pulled her against him. When her arms went around his neck, he kissed her the way he'd been wanting to, urging her lips apart, feeling a heady rush of desire that made him rock hard.

Jenny moaned, and Cain just kept kissing her, taking what he wanted, the rush growing stronger, his arousal strengthening. Her fingers dug into the muscles across his shoulders. He could feel the roundness of her breasts pressing into his chest, the brush of her curls against his cheek. Hungry need burned through him. If he didn't stop soon, he was afraid he wouldn't be able to.

He felt her small hands on his chest, pushing him away, and forced himself to let her go.

Her eyes were big as she looked up at him. "I shouldn't have done that." She pressed her fingers over her trembling lips. "You're my boss."

Cain laughed, grateful for a break in the tension. "Maybe I should sue *you* for sexual harassment."

Jenny's soft mouth, still moist from his kisses, curved into a smile.

Cain returned her smile and eased her loosely back into his arms. "So we're attracted to each other. What's wrong with that?"

Jenny shook her head. "I don't do things like this, Cain. I'm just getting my life back together after my divorce."

"From what I understand, it's been a while."

She sighed. "You're right, it has. I just can't seem to get back into the swing of things. I probably shouldn't have come out here with you. I don't want to lead you on."

Cain laughed. He couldn't help it. "That's usually my line."

She looked up at him with those big green eyes. "So I've been told."

Cain's smile faded. "I want you, Jenny Spencer. I'm not going to deny it. But there isn't any rush. When I want something bad enough, I can be a very patient man." Leaning down, he lightly kissed her. When she didn't push him away, he let the kiss play out, then reined himself in.

"It's a beautiful night," he said. "But the weather is going to change. Why don't we sit outside on the patio? There's a fireplace out there. I'll start a fire, and we'll finish that bottle of wine we left on the table. Tomorrow I'll show you the ranch."

Jenny looked up at him. "That sounds like a good idea." Her lips twitched. "Just don't expect me to attack you again."

Cain laughed out loud.

CHAPTER FOURTEEN

A WHITE SHERIFF'S SUV SAT IN FRONT OF THE HOUSE THE FOLLOWING morning when Jenny walked out of the guest room into the living room. Cain was nowhere to be seen.

Had something else happened at the hotel? Cold dread washed through her. She shouldn't have left. She had a duty to her employees; she had responsibilities.

She went in search of Cain and ended up in the kitchen, found Maria Delgado cleaning up the breakfast dishes.

"I'm sorry, I must have overslept," she said. "I didn't mean to miss breakfast."

"You are a guest. You can sleep as late as you like. I will fix you something to eat."

"There's a police vehicle outside. I need to find Cain."

"Deputy Landry is here. They are out in the stable. What about your breakfast?"

"Thanks, but I don't have time." A sheriff's deputy, not the police. The news didn't lessen her worry. Jenny rushed out the back door and ran toward the barn. Cain and a man in a beige uniform were just walking out from inside. Jenny hurried toward them.

"Is there a problem at the hotel?" she blurted out, interrupting the men's conversation.

"Not that I know of," Cain said. "Deputy Landry, this is Jenny Spencer. She owns the Copper Star in Jerome."

"Ms. Spencer." He touched the brim of his flat-brimmed, beige hat.

"It's nice to meet you." She glanced anxiously at Cain, hoping for more information.

"Deputy Landry is here to give me an update on the theft of my stallion. Sun King was stolen several weeks ago. Apparently, there's still no sign of him."

Jenny frowned, wondering why Cain had never mentioned it. "I'm sorry. I didn't mean to interrupt."

"It's not a problem," Cain said. "We were just finishing up."

"As you know, several valuable horses in Yavapai County were also stolen," the deputy said to Cain. "None worth the half-million dollars your stallion would bring. But the good news is, one of them has been found."

"I heard that. The mare showed up at an auction in Tucson. Owner's son happened to be there. Just blind luck, it would seem." There was a touch of disdain in Cain's voice that made the deputy's jaw tighten.

"We're still working on finding the others."

"I'm sure you are," Cain drawled, and Jenny figured she must be getting to know him because she could hear the sarcasm in his voice.

The men talked a moment more, then Deputy Landry headed for his white patrol SUV and drove off down the lane toward the highway.

"You never told me someone stole your horse." *His half-million-dollar horse.* Thinking about it, Jenny felt oddly hurt. She'd thought they were friends. It was stupid. A man like Cain Barrett had more than enough friends already. He certainly didn't need any more.

"It happened a couple of weeks ago," Cain said. "Sun King's a champion cutting horse. We train them here. Take a walk with me, and I'll show you some of the others."

She went with him, but somehow the excitement of seeing the ranch had dimmed a little. He hadn't tried to seduce her, but he had made his intentions clear. She was nothing special, just another of his women.

Stupid. Stupid. Stupid.

"Do you ride?" Cain asked.

"I used to, but not in a long time. I had friends in Cottonwood who owned horses."

"Best way to see the ranch." He glanced down at her feet to see what she was wearing.

Smiling, she pulled up the leg of her jeans to show him the pair of worn brown cowboy boots she had put on that morning. "I figured if I was going to visit a ranch . . ."

As she glanced around at the high desert mountains and the blue sky overhead, suddenly his intentions didn't matter. It was a beautiful day. She might as well make the most of it.

Cain smiled his approval. "I can probably find you a hat in the barn. Let's go."

While he saddled a big red, thick-necked roan for himself, one of the hands, a blond young man named Billy, saddled a pretty palomino mare for her. Cain grabbed a dusty straw cowboy hat off a row of hooks on the barn wall and tugged it low on his forehead. He plucked a smaller, slightly battered hat off another hook and tossed it in her direction.

Jenny snatched it out of the air and put it on, glad she had pulled her long, curly hair into a low ponytail at the nape of her neck. The hat was a little too big, but it would do.

Cain swung into the saddle, sitting the big roan the way he did everything else, with ease and confidence.

Billy led the palomino over to the mounting block. "You're all set," he said.

When she was younger, she could swing up onto the saddle without using the stirrup, but that was a long time ago, and she didn't want to make a fool of herself. Jenny mounted and rode out of the barn behind Cain.

"You raise cattle?" Jenny asked, spotting a herd of black cows in the distance as they traveled a road behind the house toward the hills.

"Black Angus. A hundred cow/calf units, just to keep things interesting. The horses are our main focus. We have twenty-four registered quarter horses—twenty-five before we lost King. Some of them appear to have great potential as cutting horses. Denver Garrison is our trainer. He's working a quarter horse gelding right over there."

Cain pointed toward a tall, lanky cowboy riding a bay horse working a group of black cows. The horse's dancing front feet dodged right and left, skillfully keeping the cattle clustered together, man and horse working in perfect unison.

"Do you ride cutting horses, too?" Jenny asked.

Cain laughed. "I've made a few attempts, usually ended up landing on my ass in the dirt. I leave that job to the professionals."

It clearly took a skilled rider to stay aboard. Jenny figured Cain had probably made a good decision.

"We were just getting ready to breed Sun King to Kitty Cat," he said as she rode beside him. "She's a four-year-old mare out of a champion cutter named Smart Cat. King's offspring have won over a million-two in competition, and Smart Cat is in the same league."

"Do you think you'll get King back?"

"I'm not used to losing something that belongs to me." He flashed her a look she couldn't read. "I've got good people working to find him, so there's a chance they'll come up with something."

Cain raised his hat, raked back his thick brown hair, resettled the hat, and tugged the brim back down on his forehead. "I just hope wherever he is, King's being well taken care of."

Jenny felt a little pinch in her chest. No matter what he thought of her, Cain was a good man. She knew he worried about his people. Apparently, that concern extended to his animals, as well.

"Before we go, is there any chance you could get hold of Chief Nolan, find out what's happening with Leslie Owens and the investigation?"

"I'll give it a try." He pulled out his cell and punched a number in his contacts. The big roan shifted and snorted beneath him, but Cain kept the horse under control.

Nolan must have picked up.

"Cain Barrett, Chief. Any news on the murder at the Copper Star?"

Jenny couldn't hear the other side of the conversation, but Cain was nodding. "When will the crime scene be released?" He flicked her a glance. "I'm sure Jenny will be glad to hear it. Thanks, Chief, I appreciate the update."

He turned in the saddle as the call came to an end. "Leslie Owens is stable but still in a coma. The doctors say that's good, gives her head time to heal. The murder victim, Brian Santana, has a criminal record. Nothing major, just a couple of unpaid parking tickets, possession of a controlled substance when he was eighteen, and a DUI about ten years ago." His gaze found hers. "At least we know he was no boy scout."

"Fairly minor crimes. Doesn't sound like a man who would assault someone."

"Hard to tell what's going on in a person's head."

"True."

"The crime scene won't be released until tomorrow."

Surrounded by the blue skies over the ranch, Jenny breathed in the fresh desert air and felt the sun on her shoulders. "At least I don't have to feel guilty for being here and not there."

"There's nothing you can do at the moment. You might as well enjoy yourself." He nudged his horse forward, and Jenny fell in beside him. Maria had packed a lunch, which was in Cain's saddlebags.

They ate at the bottom of a canyon, where a narrow stream sustained a few tall cottonwood trees. A light breeze blew some of the leaves into the stream to drift away with the current. It was a spectacular way to spend the day.

They were almost back to the stables when Cain pulled the roan to a stop, turned in his saddle, and pointed to a horse in one of the lush green pastures. "That's Kitty Cat." A beautiful sorrel with a gleaming copper mane and tail galloped across the pasture.

"She's gorgeous."

"So is King. They would have been a helluva match."

It was late afternoon by the time they rode back into the barn, the temperature cooling enough that she needed to wear her jacket. Her legs were shaking when she tried to dismount. She felt Cain's big hands wrap around her waist. Turning, he set her easily on the ground.

"Thanks," she said. "I'm out of practice."

"It takes a little time for your muscles to get used to it."

Billy unsaddled the horses, and Cain led Jenny through the back door into the kitchen. One of the hands, an older man with dark, weathered skin, was busily chopping vegetables on a wooden block on the massive center island.

"That's Sanchez. He's not as good a cook as Maria, but he isn't bad."

Sanchez grinned.

"So Sanchez is cooking for us tonight?"

"For the hands. Maria had to drive her mother to Prescott for a doctor's appointment. I've seen you eat, so I know you aren't a vegetarian. I took out a couple of steaks. It's still warm enough to barbeque. I thought we'd eat later."

So she would be alone with Cain again tonight. She should ask him to drive her back to Jerome. She needed to make sure everything was okay at the Copper Star. She needed to check on her employees, make sure they were dealing all right with the tragedy that had happened upstairs.

She shouldn't let herself get more deeply involved with Cain. But instead she lingered, watching the sunset while he grilled, then joining him for a delicious steak dinner.

Afterward, he led her out of the kitchen, watching her with those perceptive dark eyes. "If you want to go back, all you have to do is ask."

Did she really want to leave? She thought of his kiss. She wanted to feel the heat again. She wanted more than that. It had been years since she'd been attracted to a man. The few men she had been with, including her ex-husband, had all been disappointments.

Today had been one of the best days of her life. Jenny didn't want it to end. She wanted to stay, wanted to spend the night with Cain. She wanted to know if he could make her feel the fire she had always dreamed of and never really known.

"I don't want to go back," she said softly.

His dark eyes heated, turning the rings around his pupils gold. Cain walked over to the wet bar against the living room wall and poured some whiskey into the bottom of a heavy crystal rocks glass, filled another for himself, and carried them back.

He handed her one of the glasses, and Jenny took a sip, hoping Cain wouldn't notice the tremor in her hand.

"If you stay," he said, "I won't stop this time."

She looked up at him. "I'm staying. And I don't want you to stop."

CHAPTER FIFTEEN

"THERE'S A COMFORTABLE SITTING ROOM IN THE MASTER SUITE," Cain said. "There's even a fireplace. We can relax there."

Jenny just nodded. Her heart was hammering, and he hadn't even touched her. Cain led her down the hall to his bedroom. Relief hit her when he opened the door into a sitting room that matched the Southwest décor of the rest of the house. Jenny crossed the red tile floor toward a small, Spanish-style stucco fireplace and sat down on a sofa covered in bright-striped, woolen fabric.

Wood had already been laid in the hearth. "Cold enough in the evenings now for a fire." Cain set his drink on the ornately carved coffee table, walked over and picked up a long wooden match, struck it on the box, and set the kindling ablaze. As the fire leaped to life, he joined her on the sofa.

Jenny took a long swallow of her drink. There were liquor bottles on a dresser against the wall, plenty of whiskey if she needed more fortification.

"How long has it been?" Cain asked, taking her hand and bringing it to his lips. Her stomach instantly contracted.

"I've been divorced for a while, but we weren't really together at least a year before that. I stayed when I should have left."

"You have a new life now," Cain said, gently stroking her hand, kissing each of her fingers.

Jenny studied his handsome face, the solid jaw, the faint cleft in his chin. "I'm afraid you'll be disappointed. I'm not very good at sex."

Cain's dark gaze never wavered. "I am," he said.

Then he kissed her, not the ravaging kiss she expected, but a slow sensual tasting that had her stomach free-falling and heat sliding out through her limbs.

Cain broke the kiss and handed her the rocks glass. Jenny took another hefty swallow. Cain took the glass from her hand and set it on the coffee table. "I don't want you drunk, just relaxed."

"I . . . I need a shower," she babbled. "I smell like a horse."

"You smell like sagebrush and fresh air. It's a heady aphrodisiac." He reached up and pulled off the elastic band around her ponytail, then ran his fingers through her curls.

"I love your hair," he said, spreading the heavy mass around her shoulders. "It feels like it's alive." Cain kissed her again, then moved lower, his mouth burning a trail along her throat. He reached for the top button on her flannel shirt, unbuttoned it, and kissed her bare shoulders. He unbuttoned two more buttons, pressed his mouth against the tops of her breasts.

"I'm sure you're used to silk, not flannel," she said nervously.

He glanced up at her. "In your case, you have no idea how much flannel appeals to me." When he opened her shirt and unhooked her white bra, she was glad of the lacy cups and the clasp at the front.

Cain leaned over and kissed her, softly coaxing her lips apart as his hands roamed over the fullness, cupping first one and then the other, caressing and teasing, making her breath catch and her pulse pound so hard she could hear it.

"Tell me what you like," he whispered between gentle kisses.

"I-I don't . . . I don't know."

He nibbled the side of her neck. "Then tell me what you don't like." He gently bit an earlobe. "Did you like making love with your husband?"

She just looked at him. "No." Another soft kiss had her insides quaking.

"Why not?"

"Richard wanted me to . . . to service him. That was all he cared about. He liked to just lie there while I . . . while I did things to him."

Cain kissed her again, more deeply this time. "What did you want him to do?" He softly kissed the side of her neck.

"I wanted him to be a man instead of a . . . a . . ."

"Weakling?" Cain supplied, his scarred hands kneading her breasts.

Her head fell back, giving him better access. "Not exactly, but . . ."

His teeth lightly abraded her nipple, and desire burned through her, hotter than she had ever felt before. "I wanted . . . wanted him to take control."

Cain ran his finger over her bottom lip. "That's good, because I'm a man who likes to take control." And then his mouth closed over hers in a deep, hungry kiss that fueled the heat sparking between them.

Pleasure, pure and raw, burned through her. She had never felt anything like it, never felt such blazing need. She wanted Cain, wanted him to touch her. She wanted to touch him.

Cain broke the kiss, rose from the sofa, and reached for her hand.

Jenny thought of the time it would take to strip off their clothes and climb into bed, how it would slow things down and they would have to start all over again. She didn't want the fire to die, but she was afraid it would.

"I want you," she said. "I'm afraid if we have to start over . . ." She shook her head. "I want to feel the way I do right now." She reached for his denim shirt, pulled it out of his jeans, and popped open the row of snaps down the front, exposing his wide chest. She reached out and touched him. He was so powerfully male.

"Please," she said, and it sounded like the plea it was.

Jenny ran her hands over the heavy pecs and washboard abs and felt a rush of desire that made her dizzy.

"You want a real man, Jenny. I'll give you one." This time his kiss was rough and hungry. A hard, taking kiss that stirred her up until she could barely breathe. Her body was embarrassingly ready for him, desperate to join with him.

In minutes, he had stripped off her boots, jeans, and the rest of her clothes. Cain's chest was bare, but he was still wearing his Wranglers and boots. Lifting her, he wrapped her legs around his waist, kissed her fiercely, unzipped his fly, and slid himself deep inside.

A sound escaped her at the staggering rush of pleasure. Cain began to move, and the heat went hotter, wilder, fiercer. Her lips clung to his as he took the kiss deeper. She could feel him moving, big and hard, and everything inside her burned.

Her climax struck out of nowhere and seemed to have no end. She clung to Cain's powerful neck, repeating his name over and over, but he didn't stop.

Instead, he crossed the room, propped her back against the wall, and continued pounding into her, sending her into a second frenzied climax. It wasn't until her third release that he finally let himself go, joining her in his own shuddering climax.

Jenny rested her head on his shoulder as time drifted past. Cain let her go, and she slid down his body. It took a moment to realize there were tears on her cheeks.

Catching her chin between his fingers, Cain forced her to look up at him. "Did I hurt you?"

Jenny shook her head. "No . . ." A slow smile spread over her face. "You were perfect."

Cain smiled back. "My sweet Jenny." With a last brief kiss, he turned and left to dispense of the condom she hadn't seen him put on. "I'll be right back," he called over one wide shoulder.

"Your turn," he said, tipping his head toward the bathroom as he walked out. Jenny grabbed her clothes off the floor and hurried to put them on.

"There's a robe in there you can use," he said through the door. "You won't be needing your clothes tonight."

Jenny felt a rush of anticipation mixed with a hint of uncertainty. Aside from having the kind of incredible sex she'd only imagined, she couldn't afford to get involved with Cain. She was just another of his women. Whatever happened between them would be brief, perhaps only tonight. As long as she accepted that, she'd be okay.

As she lifted the man-sized robe off the hook, she took a deep breath. She didn't know how long it would last, but she was spending the night in Cain's bed.

Tonight, she refused to think of ghosts or death, or what might be waiting for her at the Copper Star.

CHAPTER SIXTEEN

THOUGH A FEW DRIFTING CLOUDS SIGNALED AN UPCOMING STORM, the sun was bright late the next morning as Cain carried Jenny's overnight bag down the hall to the living room.

After an amazingly satisfying night, they had slept late, then indulged in a round of easy morning sex before showering together and having breakfast in his sitting room.

Cain felt like a million bucks.

He wasn't sure what Jenny felt. The sex had been amazing between them. There was no way to disguise the way she had responded to him. She was nervous this morning, a little shy in the bright light of day. Cain found it charming.

He watched as she pulled out her cell phone and scrolled through her messages. "I have a text from Chief Nolan. The crime scene has been released."

"Back to business as usual," Cain said. But one look at Jenny's face and he wasn't so sure. A man had been murdered—either in self-defense or on purpose—in her hotel. Cain had dealt with death, seen friends die right in front of him when he had been working in the mines. Jenny was already worried about ghosts. Now a flesh-and-blood man had died violently in one of the rooms upstairs at her hotel.

"Someone's coming," she said, as they walked out the front door.

He looked up to see a silver Mercedes coupe turn down the

narrow lane and drive toward the house. It took him a moment to recognize the blonde behind the steering wheel—Anna Hobbs Somerset. Damn, he didn't need this today.

"Looks like you have a visitor," Jenny said, her voice a little tight.

Cain flashed her a look. "I didn't invite her. Why don't you wait for me in the truck while I handle this."

"No problem," she said in a way that sent a thread of irritation through him.

Cain opened the door and helped Jenny into the passenger seat of the pickup, then stashed her bag behind the seat. Closing the door a little more firmly than he'd meant to, he walked over to where Anna was pulling the Mercedes to a halt.

She cracked open her door and swung long, shapely legs in a pair of spike heels to the ground as she prepared to get out of the car.

"I wasn't expecting you," Cain said, holding the door in place so she had to stay where she was. "I'm afraid I was just getting ready to leave." He urged her back into her seat and closed the car door, then heard the buzz of the window sliding down.

Anna smiled. "I probably should have called first, but I was out this way visiting a friend. I figured it couldn't hurt to stop by and say hello."

"I appreciate the thought, but as you can see, I already have plans."

Anna's glance flashed toward the pickup.

"When I stopped calling," Cain said, "I figured you'd realize I wasn't interested. I don't want to hurt your feelings, Anna, but that hasn't changed."

Blue fire flashed in the eyes that fixed on his face. "Don't be a fool, Cain. We were always good together, even back in high school. Now that I've inherited the controlling share of the Somerset Bergen Group, a relationship could be extremely beneficial to both of us."

"I'm not interested in your money, Anna." He glanced over to the truck and saw Jenny watching them. Inwardly, he cursed. "Best to let the past stay in the past and get on with our lives."

Anna's gaze returned to the truck. "It's her, isn't it? That little bit of fluff who owns the saloon. I saw you watching her when I was in town a few months back. I know you've been seeing her. I suppose in a town this size, you don't have a whole lot of choice."

Cain bristled.

Anna's smile could have sliced through steel. "I remember her from high school. Shy little thing. She was nothing then, and she's nothing now."

"I think it's time for you to leave."

"She isn't worth it, Cain. Think what the two of us could accomplish together. Surely, you can see I'm right." Anna buzzed her window closed.

Putting the Mercedes in drive, she pulled a little farther down the lane and turned around. The car blew past, throwing up a cloud of dust as Cain walked back to the truck.

He cursed as he slid behind the wheel and closed the door. "With any luck, she won't give us any more trouble."

Jenny adjusted her seat belt. "It's your business," she said.

"Dammit, Anna Hobbs means nothing to me. She never has."

Jenny's eyes met his. "I guess Anna doesn't understand that."

His hands tightened on the steering wheel. "After the conversation the two of us just had, she damn well better." Cain fired up the engine.

By the time he pulled up in front of the Copper Star an hour later, things seemed to have returned to normal.

"I need to get going," Jenny said a little too brightly, popping open the door as he stepped on the brake and put the truck in park. She reached behind the seat and grabbed her overnight bag, looked up at him, and smiled. "Thanks for everything. I really enjoyed myself."

At her fake smile and abrupt departure, irritation filtered through him. "Did you?" He let his gaze roam over her suggestively. "I did my best to make sure of that."

Jenny's cheeks turned pink, but her smile remained in place.

"The ranch is beautiful. You were right—I needed to get away. Thanks again."

He'd been brushed off by women before, but it had never bothered him. It bothered him now. "So that's it? We're done?"

"Of course not. I'll see you over at the Grandview. I still have plenty of work to do." Jenny turned to leave as Cain stepped down from the driver's seat. He slammed the door and caught up with her just as she reached the entrance.

Catching her shoulder, he turned her to face him. "We aren't done yet," he said. "Not even close. I thought you'd figured that out after your fourth or fifth orgasm."

Her cheeks flushed pink. She glanced wildly around to see if anyone was listening, then pulled him out of the way around the corner as a man and a woman walked past them into the saloon.

"It was fun," she said, her lips still curved. "But I'm sure you have more important things to do than squire me around the country."

His eyes narrowed. He studied the smile plastered on her face, and suddenly he understood.

"You're afraid. That's what this is. I didn't think you were afraid of anything. Not bikers, not ghosts, not even murder on your doorstep."

When she tried to glance away, Cain caught her chin, tilted her face up, and brushed a kiss over her lips. "I'll pick you up after work, and we'll have dinner in my suite at the Grandview."

"I don't . . . I don't think that's a good idea."

"Well, I think it's a great idea. You wanted a man, Jenny. Well, now you have one. We're going to see how this works out." For several long seconds, he just stood there waiting.

Slowly, a warm, sincere smile curved her lips. "Okay, then. I guess I'll see you tonight."

Cain relaxed. He hadn't realized how important her answer was. "Will you be finished by six?"

"Seven would be better."

"Seven, then. I'll be here to get you." Turning, he walked back to his truck.

Women, he thought. But this one continued to intrigue him. No way was he ready to let her go.

The hotel was running smoothly. The police had released the crime scene, and while Jenny was away, Heather had taken it upon herself to clean up the bloody mess in room 10. The girl had spunk, that was for sure.

"Thank you for doing that," Jenny said to her. "I didn't expect it. I wouldn't ask you to do something I would have trouble doing myself."

Heather just shrugged. "Everyone sort of pitched in. The room seems pretty normal, but if you look hard enough, there are still some dark spots we couldn't get out of the carpet."

Jenny swallowed the bile that rose in her throat. "I'll have to have it replaced before we rent the room out again." She didn't want to spend the money, but she didn't feel comfortable having guests stay in a room where a murder had been committed, not until it had been completely redone. "Thanks for going the extra mile."

"No problem." Smoothing back her pink-streaked, dark hair, Heather returned to her desk in the lobby, and Jenny went to work. First, she checked on the kitchen, taking time to talk to Myrna to see if there was anything she needed. Then she spoke to the servers, Cassie and Molly.

Troy was in the bar, getting ready for the weekend onslaught. Friday nights were always busy, with people off work and ready to relax.

Troy was using a clean, white dishtowel to dry a stack of freshly washed glasses as she approached.

"Looks like you have things under control," Jenny said.

Troy smiled. "You know me. Nothing but work, work, work."

Not quite, but he did his share. "With any luck, the weekend will go smoother than the last few days."

"With any luck," he repeated, stacking the glasses on a shelf.

Satisfied that things were running as they should, Jenny headed for the office, passing the part-time bookkeeper on her way out.

"Everything's almost up to date," Betty said. "I'll be back in for a couple of hours on Monday to finish up."

"Great, thanks." Jenny shut the office door and sat down at her desk. The computer was humming. She brought up Google Chrome on the screen, finally getting a chance to research the round sphere of blinding white that people called an orb.

A list of articles popped right up. *Ghost Orbs Caught On Camera.* Another link read *Video Shared on Internet Ignites Paranormal Debate.*

Jenny clicked on that one and viewed the footage, which showed a strange white circle of light, but it looked different from the orb she had seen.

She tried another link. *Ring Camera Reveals Paranormal Orb.* That one was outside, just below the roof of a porch. It was white, but it could have been some kind of reflection.

Another piece of video taken by a camera inside the living room of a retired police officer's home didn't look quite right, but clearly orb sightings of different kinds weren't uncommon.

She clicked on an article entitled *What Is an Orb?* and started reading.

Orbs are thought to be energy that can be seen by the naked eye. A true orb doesn't have the spokes of light caused by a reflection, like a camera lens, the glass in a window, or just dust in the air. White orbs are usually thought to be positive energy, but they can also be an indication of a spirit that is trapped on an earthly plane where it doesn't belong.

A chill slipped through her. *A spirit trapped on an earthly plane.* Was that possible?

Typically, orbs are seen at night in places where paranormal phenomena have been reported; the site of a sudden violent death; or places where many deaths have occurred.

The chill was back. One thing she knew about Jerome—in the town's unruly past, sudden, violent death had been common, and a large number of people had died. There were deaths in the mining tunnels, in the fires that had rampaged through the city, in arguments that got out of hand. And murder.

Though the Copper Star was built of stone and had managed

to survive four separate blazes, undoubtedly a number of deaths had occurred in the hotel.

She glanced up at the molded tin ceiling, thinking of the couple in the room in the new section, an idea forming in the back of her mind.

For years, the hotel had kept journals that guests could fill out, brief notes or paragraphs about their stay. It was an old tradition, until Uncle Charlie had stopped it a few years back. The journals made him uneasy. He didn't like the idea of the Copper Star being described as haunted.

But he hadn't tossed out the journals.

Sitting at her desk, she tried to recall where her uncle had stashed them, rose from her chair, and walked over to the old wooden cupboard against the wall. Drawers formed the lower half. Two wide doors closed the top half of the cabinet. Jenny opened the double doors to see stacks of old papers, faded hotel notepads, and bookkeeping ledgers from fifty years back, stuff she still needed to sort through.

She found the leather-covered journals stacked on a shelf beneath a pile of yellowed newspapers.

Jenny opened the journal on top, saw the date finely scrolled in blue ink, quickly opened each of the journals in the stack, and began putting them in order by year. From the dates, it was apparent the guest-book tradition had started after the Copper Star had been remodeled in the late 1990s.

In the years before that, what had been a luxury hotel back in Jerome's heyday wasn't much more than a flophouse where rooms could be rented by the hour, day, week, or month.

Since the town's rebirth in the 1960s, legends of ghostly hauntings had been growing, attracting visitors, a way to get the struggling community back on its feet.

The journals helped grow the legends. People enjoyed writing down their experiences. Whether they were true or not didn't seem to matter. For years, the journals had been kept in the hotel lobby, to be added onto or read by visitors.

Jenny thought of the man who had been killed in the room upstairs. When guests recorded their eerie experiences, they often mentioned the room number in which they had spent the night. She started skimming the pages, looking for descriptions of paranormal phenomena, particularly happenings in what was now the new section, the rooms Uncle Charlie had closed off.

Specifically room 10.

CHAPTER SEVENTEEN

CAIN ARRIVED AT THE COPPER STAR A LITTLE EARLY. HE COULD use a beer, and after spending the day indoors, working with Jake Fellows and his construction crew, then going over last-minute changes with Millicent Beauchamp, he was way past ready to escape.

He settled himself on a barstool, and Troy Layton, the bartender, approached.

"What'll it be?" Troy asked.

"Sam Adams. Draft."

"Coming right up."

Troy's wheat-blond hair gleamed in the light of the neon beer signs behind the bar. He was tall and lanky, good-looking and clearly in good physical condition. He acted as if he was God's gift to the women who hung around the bar. As long as he did a good job for Jenny, Cain didn't care.

As Troy drew him a beer, Cain glanced around but didn't see Jenny. He took a long swallow of the ice-cold beer.

Troy stood a few feet away, mopping a spill on top of the bar. "If you're looking for Jenny, she's in the kitchen."

Cain made no reply, just quietly sipped his drink, enjoying a moment of end-of-the-day relaxation. When a blood-curdling scream came from the kitchen, he was on his feet and striding in that direction.

Troy was just ahead of him. "What's going on?" Troy demanded of the cook, who was hurrying toward a set of stairs in the back of the room.

"Where's Jenny?" Cain asked, as the cook rushed past.

"She went down to the basement."

Worry tightened the muscles across his shoulders. Cain started toward the stairs just as he spotted Jenny's head coming up. He breathed a sigh of relief. Until he saw the bleached color of her face.

"What the hell happened?"

She looked up at him. "Snakes."

"Holy shit," Troy said.

As she reached him, Cain gripped her arm. "Are you hurt? Did you get bitten?" He could feel her trembling, but Jenny shook her head.

"I'm okay, but there's a nest of rattlesnakes under the stairs. I can't imagine how they got there."

Unease trickled through him. Neither could he. Cain took her hand and led her a few feet away. "You sure you're not hurt?"

Jenny took a steadying breath. "Scared the crap out of me, but I'm okay." She raked back her curly hair. "I need to find someone who can deal with the problem. The fire department, do you think?"

Cain glanced over at Troy. "Let's take a look."

Troy shook his head. "Not me. I hate snakes."

"I'll go with you." It was a black-haired guy in his thirties who'd followed them in from the bar. Cain had met him in there once.

"Marco, right?"

"That's right. Marco Bandini. My wife and I own the sandwich shop down the street."

"Cain Barrett." Cain shook Marco's hand and turned to Jenny. "You got a couple of flashlights?"

"The overhead fluorescents are on down there, but it's dark in the corners. I'll get you some lights."

Armed with flashlights and a couple of long wooden sticks the busboy had rounded up from the alley, they headed down the basement stairs. Cain paused before he reached the bottom and shined the flashlight around, searching the shadows in the darkness.

Just out of the sight in a corner next to the staircase, a mass of writhing, hissing rattlesnakes spit their forked tongues in Cain's direction. The deadly buzz of their rattles made the hair stand up on the back of his neck.

"Jesus," Marco said. "Looks like there's at least four of them. Hard to tell the way they keep curling over and under themselves."

In Cain's opinion, four rattlesnakes were more than enough.

Marco prodded them a couple of times with his stick. "These guys are big. I used to wrangle them when I was a kid, but we need the right equipment." He led the way back up the stairs to the kitchen.

"We need the right gear," Marco said to Jenny. "I might have something in my garage, but it could take me a while to find it."

"I called the fire department," she said. "They have what they call snake-catching equipment. A couple of the guys will be right over."

"Sounds good to me," Marco said.

"Me, too," Cain agreed.

Half an hour later, the firemen used long poles with a hook-like device on the end to lift the snakes out of the pile, one at a time, and place them in burlap bags. Then they loaded them into the back of a pickup for a trip into the desert.

As soon as the firemen had left and the noise had quieted, the bar began to return to normal. People here were used to seeing rattlesnakes, just not that many in one place and not inside a building.

Standing next to him, Jenny surveyed the after-work crowd filling the tables. The country singer, a guy named Cody Reynolds, was setting up to play on the small stage in the corner.

"First murder, now snakes," Jenny said. "Around here, the fun just never stops."

Cain didn't see any humor in the situation. Not when he thought about the deadly serpents in the basement and what might have happened. "You ready to go?"

She nodded. "I'm ready."

"Where's your bag?"

Her gaze fixed on his. "I wasn't sure I needed one."

"I want you to spend the night, if that's what you're asking." Especially after what had just occurred. Too much was happening, too many dangerous things. He wanted to keep Jenny as close as possible.

"Okay, I'll get my overnight bag." She smiled warmly and something expanded in his chest. He walked her to the foot of the stairs in the lobby, then waited for her return.

He thought about the snakes. Perhaps it was just coincidence. They say bad things come in threes.

Cain wasn't a big believer.

Jenny had supper in Cain's suite. Opal had been cooking for the construction guys, who were working late to get the job done on time. She'd made beef stew, served it with a loaf of crusty bread, and baked an apple pie.

Cain found their supper foil-wrapped on a tray in the oven and carried it upstairs, along with flatware and napkins.

The hotel was getting closer to completion. A lot had been done to the suite in the past several days. Jenny could see her influence in the décor, small touches she had suggested to Millicent, who had actually liked the ideas and placed the orders. The caramel-leather sofa had been brightened with earth-toned Southwest colors. There were Indian rugs and pillows that picked up the same warm tones, items she had found in one of the shops on Main Street. Another shop had provided lamps of polished wood inlaid with turquois, covered with leather shades the color of the sofa.

"I think this suits you," Jenny said, as she glanced around. "What do you think?"

"I like it. It would have been just a place to stay before. Now it feels like an extension of the ranch, part of my home."

Jenny smiled, glad he approved. "It does, and yet it has a slightly more modern feel that makes it unique. I think Millicent is doing a good job."

"Better because of your input. I'm really glad I hired you."

Her smile fell away. "I shouldn't be sleeping with you. It's not professional."

Cain walked over and pulled her into his arms. He kissed her, long and deep, then lifted her chin with his fingers. "Things happen. The way we handle them is what makes life interesting."

His gaze roamed over her, and she didn't miss the hunger. "You're right," he added, knowing she had read his thoughts. "That's exactly what I'm thinking, but it's been a long day, and I'm sure you're starving."

She was, but not for food. Cain was uncovering an unknown part of her. She was becoming addicted to the things he could make her feel, the kind of pleasure she hadn't believed was real.

Cain went to the bar, opened a bottle of Cabernet, and poured them each a glass. They sat down to eat in front of a live-edge coffee table made from a thick slab of polished wood that complemented the lamps and leather sofa.

"Millie's putting the same kind of table by the window," Cain said. "With four leather chairs. Should make a nice eating area."

"Sounds perfect." Even if Millicent had her sights set on Cain, it didn't make her any less proficient at her job.

"So, aside from wrangling snakes, what did you do today?" he asked, digging into his stew.

Jenny swallowed the bite she had taken, which was delicious. "All the usual stuff, but I managed to carve out a little time to start going through the old hotel journals."

He took a sip of wine. "What kind of journals?"

"We don't use them anymore, but in the past, guests could

write their experiences in a leather-bound volume we kept on the front desk in the lobby. You wouldn't believe some of the stories I read."

"Ghost stories?"

"Some were complaints about things guests didn't like about their stay in the hotel. The toilet in room three ran all night. The shower dripped. The music in the bar was too loud—stuff like that."

"Sounds like the usual complaints every hotel deals with."

"Some of it was. But the idea of the journals was to write down any interesting experiences the guests might have had during their stay. Paranormal stuff, you know? Some of the stories were really creepy, and a lot of them were repeated over the years."

He tore off a crusty piece of bread. "Such as?"

"Accounts of a ghost cat. Apparently, the hotel has a resident ghost who's a cat. People felt the cat rubbing against their legs. They found paw prints on the furniture when there was no cat in the room."

"That's definitely creative."

"There were also children's handprints on the windows. This was reported several times. It seemed to happen every year."

Clearly interested, Cain listened as he ate his stew. "What else?"

"A lot of people reported hearing heavy breathing and someone groaning. A couple staying in a room in the old section reported hearing old-fashioned piano music and people laughing in the bar well after the bar had closed. When it happened to me, I thought I must be dreaming, but now I believe it was real. A couple of people also reported seeing round white lights near the ceiling in the saloon."

"Orbs, right?"

"That's what they're called. I saw one in my room one night. They're supposed to be the spirits of souls trapped on the earthly plane."

"I suppose anything's possible."

"The more I read, the more I don't really know what to believe."

They ate in silence for a while. Jenny wasn't a great cook herself, so she was enjoying Opal's delicious meal.

"How far back do the journals go?" Cain asked as he pushed his empty bowl away.

"The man who remodeled the hotel in the late 1990s started the tradition. Uncle Charlie stopped doing it a few years back. He didn't like the idea of people saying the Copper Star was haunted."

"Can't say I blame him, though there are dozens of ghost stories about the Grandview. I've pretty much just accepted the possibility and let it go at that."

Jenny thought of the bloody face of the ghostly being who'd been standing at the foot of Cain's bed. The memory stirred a shiver. "Nell told me some of them."

He set their pie plates in front of them. "So you're going through the journals year by year."

"That's right. I haven't gotten very far, but I'm writing down anything interesting, the date of the report, and what room it occurred in. I'm looking for the same events happening over and over."

"Sounds like a good approach."

She smiled. "I'll start again in the morning when I get back to the hotel. I've got meetings over here later tomorrow to discuss some options with your bartending staff. I should be around all afternoon."

Cain gave her a look that said he was thinking of a little afternoon delight.

"I'll be here to work," she reminded him.

Cain just smiled.

They finished dessert, cleaned up the mess, and snuggled together on the sofa. Snuggling led to kissing, kissing led to touching, and things heated up from there. Cain carried her into the bedroom and set her on her feet. He took his time undressing her, then stripped off his own clothes, and they settled in the big king-size bed.

Starting off slow and easy, Cain seemed determined to take his time, but in seconds, slow and easy turned hot and erotic. She loved the feel of his big body pressing her down in the mattress, sliding inside her, moving deep. Release came swift and hard. Cain's release followed.

Afterward, she curled against his side, and both of them slept.

It was the middle of the night when something awakened her. For a moment, she was afraid it was the bloody ghost she had seen before. Then she felt Cain's hand skimming over her body, caressing her breasts, moving lower, and wondered vaguely how such tough, scarred hands could be so gentle.

Desire burned through her. She was more than ready when he lifted her and set her astride him. She'd wanted a man who took control, but even when she was the one in charge, she could feel the power of him, his driving need, and it set her on fire.

She was limp and sated when she awakened before Cain the next morning. She needed to get up, get dressed, and get to work. She had a lot to do at the Copper Star, and she wanted time to read more journal entries.

Instead, she reached for him and felt his heavy arousal. The morning slipped away in slow-burning need and tender satisfaction. She was curled against him, both of them awake, but still drowsy, when she heard a firm knock on the living-room door.

"Stay here. I'll take care of it." Cain leaned down and kissed her. "I should have been up hours ago. You're a bad influence." But he was smiling. Stark naked and unembarrassed, he walked away.

Watching him, even after a night of amazing sex, Jenny felt a rush of heat.

Cain grabbed his robe off a chair next to the door and headed out of the bedroom. She should have been up earlier. She had a dozen things to do.

Forcing herself to leave the warm bed that smelled liked sex and Cain, she headed for the bathroom. After a quick shower, she dragged her hair up in a ponytail and secured it with a scrunchy. Makeup could wait. She pulled on jeans and a sweatshirt, grabbed her overnight bag, slung her purse strap over her shoulder, and headed for the bedroom door.

Thank God, Cain had a private elevator. She could sneak out the back way and walk down the hill to the hotel.

Except that when she opened the door, Nell Barrett sat on the sofa.

CHAPTER EIGHTEEN

CAIN WATCHED THE BEDROOM DOOR OPEN AND INWARDLY GROANED as Jenny stumbled into the living room.

"Well, hello there." Nell's smile held the welcome of a mama tiger protecting her cub.

"Umm . . . hello." Jenny was fresh out of the shower, her hair still damp, her face free of makeup. She looked delectable. After last night, the sight shouldn't have made him want her again, but it did.

"My grandmother wasn't supposed to get here until this afternoon," Cain grumbled, tossing a dark look at Nell. "I could hardly toss her out."

"Of course not," Jenny said.

"Besides, I knew it wouldn't be long before she figured out something was going on between us." Not that he knew exactly what that something was—aside from incredible sex and this over-protective feeling he had toward Jenny.

"I think I see a coffeepot over on the bar," Nell said from her perch on the sofa. "Why don't you go get dressed? I imagine I can persuade Jenny to make us a cup."

Cain didn't argue. He had learned not to argue with Nell Barrett when he was six years old. He hated throwing Jenny to the wolves in the guise of a sweet old lady, but he had a feeling Jenny could handle it.

Cain smiled as he closed the bedroom door.

Figuring she had no choice, Jenny brewed a pot of coffee and found two cups in a cabinet over the wet bar. "Black, if I recall."

"That's right."

Same way Jenny drank it. Neither of them had led a pampered life. Maybe black, no-frills coffee was a symbol.

"So you and my grandson . . ." Nell blew over the surface of the steaming brew to cool it, then took a healthy swallow.

Jenny just sipped her coffee. There was no way she could deny Nell's insinuation.

"All right," Nell said. "I'll tell you the truth. As soon as I realized my grandson had a woman in his bedroom, I wanted to find out who she was. He might be a grown man, but he's still my boy. I was just hoping it wasn't that Millicent woman or that schemer Anna Hobbs."

Jenny's chin came up. "I don't think he's seeing either one of them." Or he'd better not be. Jenny had no idea what was happening between her and Cain, but for the brief time they were together, she wasn't about to share.

"I can see by the look in your eyes that would be a deal-breaker for you."

"For the time we're together, yes."

"Good for you." Nell sipped her coffee. "Actually, I'm a little surprised to see you here. Perhaps my warning was too subtle."

"If you think I'm expecting wedding bells and picket fences, you're wrong. Along with your warning, my brother made me well aware of Cain's track record. What you don't know is I was married before, and it was a disaster. Marriage no longer holds any appeal for me."

Jenny set her mug down on a coaster on the coffee table. "You told me the truth, so I'll do the same. My husband and I were not . . . that is, we were not . . . sexually compatible. I thought it was my fault, that I just didn't like sex. Then I met Cain."

"Well, now, this is finally getting interesting."

Jenny steeled herself. Nell wanted to know what was going on, and though it was really none of the older woman's business, Jenny knew how much Nell meant to Cain, so she would tell her.

"I was attracted to Cain from the start. That was several months ago, when he began coming into the saloon. I stayed away from him on purpose. People talked about him. I knew his reputation with women. But he never came on to me, never used the same old, worn-out lines my male customers tossed out."

"Certainly not. My boy has higher standards than that."

"Cain offered me a job. I needed the money, so I took it. And the job presented a challenge. I hadn't realized I was missing that in my life."

"So you went to work for him." Nell sipped her coffee. "And something changed."

"That's right. Things started happening, crazy things, stuff spinning out of control at the hotel. Cain always seemed to be there when I needed him. Not once, but over and over. There's a chance he saved my life."

Nell nodded. "The night you were attacked."

"Yes. The way things were going, anything could have happened."

"So you're here out of gratitude."

Anger surged. She could feel the heat in her cheeks. Jenny took a steadying breath. This was Cain's grandmother, the person he loved most in the world.

"Cain fought for me. I'll always be grateful for that, but that isn't the reason I'm here." *In his suite, in his bed.* "When I realized Cain was also attracted to me, I decided to take a chance, find out something about myself."

One of Nell's silver eyebrows went up. "What was that?"

"I found out I'm a normal, red-blooded female, with normal female desires. I'm not the cold woman my husband made me believe I was. Whatever happens, I'll always be thankful to Cain for helping me figure that out."

Nell leaned back on the sofa, a wide smile breaking over her wrinkled face. "Bravo, Jenny Spencer. You have more gumption than I first thought." Her smile widened. "Now all we have to do is hope my grandson is smart enough to appreciate what he's got."

Jenny said nothing, just rose from the sofa, carried her mug over to the wet bar, and set it in the stainless sink.

"I'm afraid I have to go. I'm late already, and I have a ton of things to do. I'm sure Cain will get you settled in."

Nell tried to push herself up from the sofa.

"No, please don't do that," Jenny said. "I know the way out." She smiled. "Cain has a private elevator, so I can escape out the back. I won't have to embarrass myself any more than I have already."

Nell laughed. "I hope I'll be seeing more of you, Jenny Spencer."

Jenny thought about their conversation and smiled, discovering, as she had before, that she liked the older woman. "I hope so, too." So what if Nell was protective of Cain? She had raised him. She was the only mother he had ever known; she had every right to be.

Jenny tried to imagine what she would be like as a mother. There was a time before Richard when she had wanted children. She could only hope she would have done as good a job raising a child as Nell had done with Cain.

Towing her overnight bag, Jenny rode the elevator down to the parking lot and started walking across the asphalt, down the hill to the Copper Star.

Cain sat across from his grandmother and her caretaker in the dining room, having lunch. Nell and Emma were both settled in their new rooms. Emma had helped Nell unpack. There would be more boxes coming, but the basics were here.

Things were beginning to move along more swiftly in the hotel. The dining room was finished; the distant hammering and orders shouted by the men were coming from another area.

Opal was cooking, trying out different recipes, some of which Jenny had suggested, meals people consistently liked to order or happy-hour snacks that were cheap and easy to make. Done right, she said, there could be a great profit margin there.

"I like your Jenny," Nell said as she delicately picked at the chicken Caesar salad Opal had prepared for her, while Cain and Emma lunched on Swiss-and-mushroom burgers.

"She isn't my Jenny," Cain said. "Not exactly. We're dating, just like two ordinary people."

"*Dating* isn't exactly your style, Cain. I hope you realize your Jenny is a one-man woman. She expects you to be a one-woman man. At least, as she put it, for as long as it lasts."

Cain set his fork down next to his plate, not the heavy, black pottery dinnerware Millicent had insisted they use, but a lighter, more easily handled version, thanks to Jenny.

"I'm not interested in anyone else," he said. "If I start to feel an attraction for another woman, I'll end things with Jenny. I don't intend to do anything that would hurt her."

"I assume that goes both ways. If Jenny gets interested in another man, she'll just tell you, and you'll acquiesce to her wishes and let her go on her merry way."

An image surfaced of Jenny naked in his bed this morning, her long, golden brown curls spread over his pillow. The notion of another man touching her, kissing her, making love to her, sparked a red haze behind his eyes.

"What other choice would I have?" he said, deliberately keeping his voice even.

"I don't know. I guess you could fight for her. Oh, that's right. You already have."

Cain shoved back his chair. "I don't know what kind of bee you have in your bonnet, but my love life is none of your concern. It never has been, and it never will be. I love you dearly, but I have a life of my own."

He rose from his chair and spoke to Emma. "If you need anything, you both have my cell. More staff will be arriving today. You'll be able to get meals served in your rooms or come down here, whichever you prefer."

He rounded the table, leaned down, and kissed his grandmother's powdered cheek. "I'll see you both at supper. With luck, Jenny will be joining us. I hope you'll keep your opinions on our relationship to yourself."

Nell just smiled. "Of course, dear."

Cain shot her a look and headed for his suite. He had work to do in his office that would occupy him for the rest of the day. Jenny would be working in the hotel this afternoon. He squashed any thoughts of an hour with her upstairs in his suite. He couldn't afford to let her distract him.

It bothered him to think a woman could cloud his mind and interfere with his work. It had never happened before.

Cain didn't like it.

Jenny worked through the lunch rush, then headed for her small office in the hotel lobby.

She went over to the stack of journals on top of a file cabinet, picked up a couple, and sat down at her desk. The first ledger was full of the same type of entries as all the others, problems with the room or the bathroom, accounts of hearing noises in the hall or in the room—ghost experiences, the guest believed.

One reported seeing a hazy figure at the foot of the bed that disappeared. Eerie laughter, cold spots, objects moving, and doors opening and closing. She had been hearing those sorts of tales since she was a kid and never given them much thought. But after the unexplained experiences she'd had upstairs herself, she was paying closer attention.

She picked up another journal, this one dated fifteen years ago, and began thumbing through the pages. Her fingers stilled at a lengthy account scrolled delicately in what appeared to be a woman's handwriting.

Mr. and Mrs. Don Dennison October 1st, guests in room 10.

Jenny's interest sharpened.

We had a terrifying night. Don and I have been married for twenty years, and I have never seen him behave as he did last night. It was after two in the morning when I awakened to the sound of heavy breathing in the room. Someone is in here, I thought, feeling uneasy, but there was enough moonlight coming in through the window that I could see no one was there.

A ghost, I thought, amused. We had both read stories about Jerome. We thought it would be fun to actually see a ghost. I wasn't afraid. I wasn't even sure I believed in spirits.

The heavy breathing faded, and I started to go back to sleep. That's when I realized Don was awake. He was sitting up in bed right beside me, staring straight ahead.

"Don, are you all right?" I asked.

Don didn't answer. When he turned toward me, his eyes looked black and empty. The way his mouth had flattened out, the way his nostrils flared, he looked like a completely different person.

For the first time, I began to feel afraid. I started to get out of bed, but Don pulled me back down and climbed on top of me. Though he had never acted this way before, I didn't try to stop him. Not until I felt his hands slide up around my throat and he began to choke off my air. I tried to scream, but no sound came out. He was always a gentle lover, but that night he pried my legs apart and forced himself on me.

This wasn't my Don. This man was rough and cruel. It was as if another man had invaded my husband's body. I started crying, tears streaming down my face as I tried to pry his hands away from my throat so I could breathe.

I started whispering his name over and over. Don, please. Don, you're hurting me. Don, I love you.

For the first time, the words seemed to reach him. He started shaking. He looked down at me, at his hands wrapped around my throat, and his eyes widened. A look of horror came over his face, and he jerked away.

"Mary, dear God! Mary! Did I hurt you? Mary, are you all right?" Don knelt on the floor at my side. "Oh, God what have I done?"

I don't know how, but I knew it wasn't his fault. In twenty years, he had never acted this way. I told him we needed to leave. We had to get out of the hotel right this minute. We packed and headed downstairs.

There was no one in the lobby. A green glass lamp on the desk cast dim light into the room, and the journal sat open next to the lamp. I had read pages when we had checked in. While Don went to get the car, I started writing. I want someone to know what happened.

What you are reading is a true and accurate account of what occurred last night in room 10.

* * *

Jenny just sat there. Her muscles felt frozen. She had to force herself to breathe. *Dear sweet God.*

One thought after another tumbled through her brain. Uncle Charlie had closed that section of the hotel not long after the entry in the journal. Had he read what Mary Dennison had written? Or had something even worse occurred?

She sat another minute, her mind darting from the past to the present, to the murder that had just taken place in the same room. With a steadying breath, she bookmarked the page and closed the journal.

She glanced at her watch. She was past due at the Grandview. Nell Barrett would be there. Nell knew things about Jerome, things that had happened over the years.

Jenny grabbed her purse and the journal and headed for the door.

CHAPTER NINETEEN

Cain worked all afternoon. He'd left word he wasn't to be disturbed. His staff knew better than to disobey his orders unless it was an emergency.

At six o'clock, he went downstairs. Jenny would likely still be working. Handling two jobs required long hours. He admired her for it and only felt a little guilty. The experience and advice she brought to the Grandview were well worth the money he was paying her.

And she seemed to bring a spark of enthusiasm to the employees. They were excited to get the hotel finished and get it open.

He found her downstairs, sitting at a table in the dining room with Millicent, their heads bent over a yellow pad as Millie made notes. The two of them were smiling at each other—a surprise in itself—but when they saw him walk into the dining room, their smiles turned a little too bright.

Warning signs flashed in his head. When two smart women got together, there was a good chance they could find a way to cause trouble.

Cain walked up to the table. "Okay, what are you two up to? I can see by the looks on your faces, it doesn't bode well for me."

Millie laughed. "We've been discussing the grand-opening party. We figured we had better start planning now. That way, we'll be ready when the hotel is completed—which, according to your schedule, is less than two weeks away."

"A grand-opening party," Cain said darkly, since the notion had never occurred to him.

"That's right," Millie continued. "We need to send a message. The Grandview is open for business. It's a first-class hotel, a place to get away from your troubles, a hideaway in a little-known area that's easily accessible from Flagstaff, Sedona, Scottsdale, and Phoenix."

He fixed his gaze on Jenny, who so far hadn't added her two cents.

"I thought you could have a soft opening after that," Jenny said. "Open the restaurant and bar just to the locals and whatever tourists happen to be in town. Once you get the kinks worked out, you can start your marketing campaign."

"Marketing campaign," he repeated grimly.

Jenny and Millicent exchanged glances. "We just assumed you would want enough guests to make the hotel a success," Millie said. "Advertising is the only way anyone's going to know it's here."

She had a point. He'd thought of it more as a residence for his grandmother, but she was right. The place needed to sustain itself. "Just how much is this grand-opening party going to cost me?"

Jenny looked at Millicent.

"It won't be cheap," Millie said. "But if you can get the right people to show up, it'll be worth it. In the end, the party will pay for itself."

His gaze returned to Jenny. "Is that what you think?"

"I never had enough money to advertise the Copper Star. Fortunately, it's a well-established business in Jerome, part of the local history. And it sits in a prime location. Even so, if I could afford the cost of promotion, I would do it."

He sighed, clearly defeated. "All right, then. I'd like to see a cost breakdown for the event. If it looks workable, we'll have a grand-opening party."

Millicent and Jenny both grinned.

Cain shook his head. "I need a drink." Heading across the

room, he walked behind the bar and poured himself a Johnny Walker Black. When he turned, Millicent was gone, and Jenny was walking toward him.

She looked tired, but pleased at the work she and Millie had accomplished.

"You want a drink?" he asked.

Jenny shook her head. The smile was gone from her face. "I found something in the journals today. I brought it with me so I could show you."

Cain started to say something, but his cell phone rang. He pulled it out of his pocket, looked down, and recognized the caller ID.

"It's Chief Nolan." He pressed the phone against his ear. "Chief."

"I just wanted to let you know Leslie Owens is awake and doing very well. She's cooperating fully with the police investigation. The doctors are releasing her tomorrow."

"Thanks for letting me know. What about Brian Santana? Does the coroner's office have a cause of death?"

"From what we could tell, it looks like the two of them were fighting. The porcelain pitcher in the room got broken during the fight. Santana fell backward and landed on a big shard that went right through his ribs into his heart."

Cain grunted. "Rough way to go."

"Can you think of any good way?"

"I guess not. Thanks for the update, Chief." The call ended, and Cain turned to tell Jenny what the chief had said, but her phone rang before he got the chance.

Jenny looked down at the screen. "It's Nolan." She greeted him and listened, probably getting the same information as Cain.

"I'm so glad to hear Leslie's going to be okay," Jenny said into the phone. "Is she able to have visitors?" She nodded. "That's good. Thank you so much for letting me know."

"Good news," Cain said as the call ended. Clearly, the chief had spared her the details of Santana's death, for which Cain was grateful.

"The chief says Leslie Owens is awake. I need to talk to her, Cain. I need to know what happened in that room."

He frowned. "The police won't like you interfering in their investigation."

Ignoring him, Jenny brought up Google on her cell phone. "It's still visiting hours at the hospital. I'm driving down to Cottonwood to see Leslie. I'm hoping she'll tell me what happened."

He felt a pang, knowing Jenny had taken the murder personally, believing it was somehow her fault. "You know what happened, love. Leslie killed the man who attacked her."

"I want to know why he attacked her, how it happened. I read something in one of the journals today. Something that might be important."

He frowned. "You read something that happened in room ten?"

"Yes. It was years ago, before Uncle Charlie closed that section of the hotel. I'll tell you about it when I get back from the hospital. I don't want to miss the chance to see Leslie."

"I'll drive you. You can tell me about it on the way."

"What about your grandmother? I thought you'd be having dinner with her since it's her first night here."

"I was hoping you and I could both have dinner with her, but she's used to my unpredictable schedule. We'll do it tomorrow night instead."

"Okay, if you're sure."

"I'm sure this is going to be an interesting evening. Grab your purse, and let's go."

Jenny sat in the passenger seat of Cain's silver Dodge truck as he drove down the mountain toward the Verde Valley Medical Center in Cottonwood.

She had given Cain a brief description of what was written in the journal. He appeared unimpressed.

"So this passage you read . . . some woman wrote about the night she had spent in the hotel."

"That's right." The journal was in her purse, but she wasn't ready to share the actual words. She wasn't quite sure why.

"You said her husband got violent and tried to choke her."

"Mary Dennison. Her husband's name was Don."

"All right. Then Don woke up and begged her to forgive him. Mary said it was totally out of character for him to behave that way."

"That was the general drift. She said her husband had never acted that way before. She said it was as if another man had invaded her husband's body. Those were her words. She said his eyes looked black and empty. That he didn't even look like the same man."

Cain kept his gaze on the road, his hands on the wheel as the truck took the long grade down the mountain to the flat desert lands below. The sleeves of his shirt were rolled up to the elbows, exposing the tattoo on his left arm.

It was a crossed pick and shovel beneath a skull wearing a hard hat. A miner's tattoo, for sure. She wanted to know the story behind it, but it never seemed the right time to ask.

"So what are you thinking?" he said. "That there was some sort of entity in the room that was responsible for the attack on Don Dennison's wife?"

She could hear the disbelief in his voice. Maybe that was the reason she hadn't read the passage aloud.

"I don't know. Maybe. I want to hear what Leslie Owens has to say."

"Fine. For the moment, we'll leave it at that."

Jenny flicked him a glance. "Thank you."

Cain just grunted.

They didn't say more as he drove the last few miles and arrived at their destination. The predicted weekend storm loomed on the horizon, thick gray clouds rolling in, beginning to pile up overhead.

They made their way toward the entrance, walking beneath the portico of a beige-and-white stucco structure into the lobby. The main part of the hospital stood four stories high, an impressive white building that dominated the desert around it.

Behind the front desk, a short, blond nurse in scrubs sat at a computer. She looked up as they approached.

"May I help you?"

"We're looking for a patient named Leslie Owens," Cain said.

The nurse gave him a once-over, a hint of color rising in her cheeks. Clearly, she liked what she saw. Jenny couldn't blame her.

"Let me take a look," the nurse said, typing in the information. "Yes, here it is. Second floor, room two-eighteen."

Cain smiled. "Thanks . . ." His gaze went to the tag on her very impressive chest. "Caroline."

Her face flushed even brighter. "If there's anything else you need, please just let me know."

"Will do. Thanks again."

They headed for the elevators. "You're a handy man to have around," Jenny said, with only a hint of sarcasm.

Cain flashed one of his rare grins as he led her to the elevator and pushed the button. It quickly whisked them upward, and they walked out onto the second floor. The door to room 218 stood open.

With a glance inside, Jenny recognized Leslie's mother, Aida, sitting at her daughter's bedside. Aida was a woman in her fifties, with blond hair going gray and a warm smile. She rose and crossed the room to greet them.

"Hello, Jenny," Aida said. "It's nice to see you again."

"We heard the good news." Glancing toward the bed, Jenny took in Leslie's pale, battered face, the puffy black-and-blue eyes, the bandage around her forehead.

"How's she doing?" Cain asked.

Aida smiled. "Why don't you ask her yourself? I'll go join my sister in the cafeteria for a cup of coffee. If I don't see you later, thanks for helping my daughter."

Jenny just nodded. "I'm so glad she's going to be okay." Aida left, and Jenny walked over and sat down in the chair next to the bed. Cain waited beside the open door.

Jenny reached out and took hold of Leslie's hand. It felt cool but not icy, a good sign, Jenny thought.

Leslie's eyes opened and swung in Jenny's direction. "I remember you . . . from the hotel."

"That's right. I'm the owner, Jenny Spencer. The man by the door is Cain Barrett. He's a friend."

Her gaze swung toward Cain, but she didn't greet him.

"Chief Nolan called to tell us you are going to be okay," Jenny said. "He told us the doctors would be releasing you tomorrow or the next day."

"The sooner the better," Leslie said. "I just want to go home."

"I'm so sorry about what happened. The hotel belongs to me, but it's also where I live. If you're feeling up to it, maybe you'd be willing to tell me about that night. I'd really like to understand."

Leslie shifted on the mattress, trying to get comfortable. "I can tell you, but I don't know if you'll believe me. I don't think Chief Nolan believed all of it."

"Try me," Jenny said.

"Could you press the button, so that I can sit up a little more in the bed?"

"Of course." Jenny adjusted the bed, as well as the pillow behind Leslie's back, then waited quietly for her to begin.

"Brian and I didn't really know each other all that well," Leslie said. "We'd been corresponding through email for several weeks before we met and went out on a date. I liked Brian, and it seemed as if he really liked me. We were strongly attracted to each other, so we decided to spend some time together. Brian booked a two-night stay at the Copper Star, which was just far enough away from Phoenix to make it feel special, kind of a two-day getaway."

"I remember seeing you when you and Brian checked in."

Leslie's eyes filled. She wiped away tears with the back of her hand.

"We both liked the hotel right away. You could tell it had been remodeled, but it still had a cozy historical feel. We went out for supper, but came back early. We wanted to be together, you know? So, after dinner, we went up to the room. Brian had drunk a little more than he usually did. He was nervous, I think. We were still in the first stages of a relationship." More tears fell.

Jenny reached over, pulled a tissue out of the box, and handed it to Leslie, who dabbed it beneath her eyes.

"We fell asleep after we . . . made love. Everything was perfect until . . ." She shook her head. "I'm not exactly sure what happened. I remember something woke me in the middle of the night. I don't know what it was, but at first I thought there was someone in the room."

She dabbed at her tears. "The moon was out that night. The door to the bathroom stood open. I could see there was no one in there or anywhere else in the room."

When Leslie didn't continue, Jenny squeezed her hand. "What happened then?"

"I realized Brian was . . . was also awake. He was sitting up in bed, staring straight ahead. The next thing I knew, he was on top of me, gripping my wrists next to my head, pressing me down in the mattress. I-I told him to let me go, that he was hurting me, but all he did was laugh. Then he slapped me, and I knew I was in trouble. I tried to scream, but he covered my mouth with his hand."

"You must have fought him," Jenny said.

"I-I struggled. Somehow I managed to shove him off me. I ran for the door, but Brian . . . Brian was right behind me. I grabbed the pitcher on the dresser and smashed it over his head, but it . . . it didn't stop him. He just whirled me around and shoved me back down on the bed."

Leslie swallowed and dabbed at fresh tears. "Brian started hitting me over and over. Then he climbed on top of me and he . . . and he . . ." She glanced away.

"He forced you to have sex," Jenny said, remembering the journal.

Leslie's hazel eyes found hers. "Yes. I could feel his fingers wrapping around my throat, and I thought he was going to kill me."

"How did you get away?" Cain asked. Jenny hadn't heard him approach.

Leslie blew her nose. "I'm not exactly sure. When he started hitting me with his fists, I remember thinking I had to do something or I was going to die. I shoved him as hard as I could and jumped out of bed, but then I tripped and fell, and I guess I hit my head. That's the last thing I remember."

Jenny felt a burn behind her eyes. "I'm so sorry, Leslie."

"I remember thinking this man . . . this man couldn't be Brian. He was vicious and cruel. His eyes were like two black holes, and his features were twisted. He was trying to kill me, and I had no idea why." Leslie started crying.

Jenny leaned over and kissed her forehead. "Whatever happened, it wasn't your fault." She thought about the journal. "Maybe it wasn't even Brian's."

Their eyes met and held. "You . . . you believe me?"

"Yes," Jenny said, and her own eyes welled with tears. "Take care of yourself."

Leslie just nodded.

Cain was waiting when Jenny reached the door. He didn't say anything, just took hold of her hand and led her back to the elevator.

Neither of them spoke on the way to the truck.

CHAPTER TWENTY

CAIN DROVE THE STEEP ROAD BACK UP THE HILL TO JEROME. IT WAS starting to rain, a rhythmic patter against the windshield that continued to build, forcing him to turn on the wipers. He was glad Leslie Owens seemed to be on the mend, but Jenny's talk with the woman hadn't gone the way he'd hoped.

He flicked a sideways glance to where Jenny sat rigidly in the passenger seat. "Tell me what you're thinking."

Jenny shifted to look at him. "You heard what Leslie Owens said. Brian's attack was completely out of character. She said it was like he was a totally different man."

"Leslie said she and Brian had only known each other a short time. Takes a while to know what a person is capable of, and Chief Nolan told us he had a criminal record."

"No assault, nothing like that. He didn't say attempted murder or any other violent offense."

"True, but Leslie admitted Brian had been drinking."

"A little more than normal. They had just started dating, and Brian was nervous. That doesn't account for his totally erratic behavior. The thing is, Leslie's story is very close to what Mary Denison wrote in the journal."

"And?" Cain pressed, knowing there was more going on in that pretty head than Jenny had told him so far.

"And both couples were staying in room ten."

Irritation trickled through him. "Tell me you don't think your uncle closed that section of the hotel because there was a demon in room ten."

"I don't know why he did it. I don't even remember exactly when it happened. I was a teenager back then. I'm betting it wasn't long after the incident Mary wrote about in the journal."

"So you're going to . . . ? What? Close part of the hotel down again because some nut tried to strangle his girlfriend and instead wound up dead?"

"What if being in that room is the reason Brian Santana died?"

Cain's hands tightened on the steering wheel. "Surely, you aren't blaming yourself."

"I opened that section of the hotel. I wanted to make more money. Maybe by doing that, I put people in danger." *And Brian ended up dead* were the unspoken words.

"Keep talking that way, and you're going to wind up in a humdinger of a lawsuit."

"Maybe I deserve it."

"Bullshit." Cain forced himself under control. "Be reasonable, honey. Whatever happened between Leslie Owens and Brian Santana was not your fault. Even if there is something evil in the room that affected Brian's behavior, you weren't aware of it."

Jenny fell silent. As the car rolled along, a bolt of lightning flashed in the distance, zigzagging toward the horizon. "I'm going to close down room ten. I probably should close the whole section the way Uncle Charlie did, but—"

"But if you want to stay in business, the hotel has to support itself. That's just the way it is." Cain pulled into town, but didn't stop in front of the Copper Star, just continued up Main Street, turned on Hill, and drove toward the Grandview.

"It's getting late," Jenny said.

"You have to eat. Even if Opal's gone home, there's plenty of food in the kitchen." He flashed her a look. "I've been a bachelor for a long time. I'm not a half-bad cook."

Cain pulled the truck to a stop in the parking lot behind the hotel and turned off the engine.

"I don't have any clean clothes."

"You can change when you get back to the Copper Star in the morning."

"I'm not in the best mood," Jenny said. "Are you sure you want me to stay?"

Cain's gaze touched on her sweet curves, and his groin tightened. He wanted her. He couldn't seem to get enough. He also wanted her safe. "We'll eat first, then go to bed. I guarantee I can put you in a better mood."

For the first time that evening, Jenny laughed.

Warmed by the sunlight spilling in through the curtains, Jenny awoke early the next morning. The storm had passed during the night, but bad weather was expected to return this week. She glanced around Cain's bedroom. Though it was barely seven o'clock, Cain was already gone.

Jenny yawned as she climbed out of bed. A quick shower, and she would head back to the Copper Star. She needed to make sure everything was running smoothly before she returned to the Grandview that afternoon.

She smiled to think that Cain had kept his word. She hadn't gotten as much sleep as she needed, but after his skillful lovemaking, she was definitely in better spirits than she had been when she had left Leslie Owens's hospital room last night. *Better spirits.* Smiling at the pun, she headed for the bathroom.

Her smile faded as her thoughts returned to the murder in room 10. She hadn't had a chance to talk to Nell, but she planned to, and she would rather do it when she came back that afternoon. She didn't want Cain's grandmother speculating any further about Jenny's involvement with her grandson.

Her hair still a little damp from the shower, she grabbed her purse, slung the strap over her shoulder, and headed for Cain's private elevator. She needed to get back home and change into clean clothes. She wasn't secure enough to leave any of her personal belongings in Cain's suite. Neither of them had any idea how long they would be together.

The thought tugged at something inside her.

The elevator opened on the bottom floor, and Jenny pushed through the door leading out to the rear parking lot, hoping to leave unseen.

Instead, when she walked out, she spotted Cain talking to a lean, black-haired man standing next to a black SUV. She thought about ducking back into the hotel, but it was too late.

Cain waved and strode toward her. He smiled. "Trying to escape?"

As always, the man was far too perceptive. "I need to get to work. I'll be back this afternoon."

Cain nodded, but a trace of amusement touched his lips. "A friend of mine just showed up. I'd like you to meet him." Urging her forward, he led her over to the man standing next to the SUV.

"Jenny Spencer, meet Nick Faraday. Nick's a private investigator. He's been trying to help me find Sun King—and the people who stole him."

She didn't miss the edge in Cain's voice. He wasn't used to being thwarted, even by a band of thieves.

"Nice to meet you, Nick," she said.

"You too, Jenny. I understand you own the Copper Star."

She didn't ask how he knew. He worked for Cain as a private investigator. "It's been in my family for a number of years."

Nick didn't mention the murder, though it had been all over the local and not-so-local news. Jenny wondered if Cain had asked him to look into it. She wasn't sure how she felt about that.

"Nick stopped by on his way to Flagstaff." Cain turned to his friend. "Sure you don't have time to come in for a cup of coffee?"

Nick shook his head. "Thanks, but I'm going to be late as it is." He was a good-looking man, the muscles filling out the sleeves of his olive-drab T-shirt making it clear he stayed in shape.

"You were bringing me up to speed on the stolen horses," Cain reminded him, putting the conversation back on track.

Nick nodded. "The two Morgan geldings stolen from the Four Winds Ranch turned up at a rural property in Winslow. The owner called the authorities. County sheriff got involved, saw the horses on a stolen property report, and had them returned to the ranch."

"So they're back at the Four Winds."

"That's right."

"Which leaves one of the Branch Creek quarter horses and Sun King still missing."

Nick just nodded. "Did you have any luck with your computer people?"

"I spoke to Matt Reasoner in my Scottsdale office on Friday. He's still digging around, but so far he hasn't found any online searches that connect the three ranches."

"So nobody searching for info on valuable horses in Yavapai County," Nick said.

"Doesn't look that way."

Nick's gaze locked with Cain's. "You realize none of this is making any sense. Thieves steal a bunch of valuable horses, then let them go? How does that work?"

Cain's jaw looked tight. "Maybe after the thieves took them, they found out how hard it is to sell high-value, registered livestock. Without their papers, the animals aren't worth much more than any other horses. Maybe they figured it was better to get rid of them than end up going to jail."

"Could be," Nick said. "Or could be stealing the others was simply a distraction. Your stallion is the most valuable horse by far. While the police are spreading themselves thin searching for a bunch of far-less-expensive livestock, Sun King could be on his way to Mexico."

"Or Saudi Arabia," Jenny added, and both men turned to look at her. "A couple of weeks ago, I read an article online that said horses are a major part of the Arab culture. They're willing to pay just about anything to own the very best."

"Sun King isn't for sale," Cain said.

"Exactly," Jenny said.

"She's got a point," Nick agreed. "Once the horse is out of the country, selling him wouldn't be nearly as much of a problem. Or the thieves might already have had a buyer lined up."

Cain ran a hand over his jaw. "Well, something's sure as hell going on."

"I'll keep after it," Nick said. He climbed into the SUV. "Again, nice to meet you, Jenny."

"You as well, Nick."

Nick fired the engine, put the vehicle in gear, and the SUV began to roll down the hill.

"I have to get back in time to change for work." Jenny adjusted the purse strap on her shoulder.

Cain frowned. "Why don't you leave a few things here? You don't have to carry stuff back and forth every day."

It wasn't a good idea, and both of them knew it.

"You work here," Cain continued. "It's not a problem."

He was just being practical, Jenny thought. And it really would be more convenient. "All right."

Cain bent his head and lightly kissed her. "I'll see you later." There was something warm in his eyes . . . something besides the desire that made the gold in them glitter.

Jenny nodded and set off down the hill.

CHAPTER TWENTY-ONE

THE GRANDVIEW WAS BUZZING WITH ITS USUAL CONTROLLED CHAOS when Jenny returned. Carpenters working, deliveries arriving, FedEx and UPS fighting to make their way up the narrow road that led to the hotel at the top of the hill.

Jenny glanced around, but saw no sign of Cain, who undoubtedly was working. You didn't make the kind of money Cain was worth by being a slacker.

Jenny spent the first couple of hours finishing the lists of kitchen and bar supplies that still needed to be ordered. Then Millicent showed up, and they continued making plans for the grand-opening party. Which was turning into more work than either of them had anticipated, but was also exciting and something they were both looking forward to.

She and Millicent were getting along much better than she had expected. Cain's proprietary attitude toward Jenny made it clear where his affections lay—at least for the time being. Millicent seemed resigned. Or maybe she was just planning to wait until Cain began looking for a replacement.

Jenny felt a soft pang at the notion. She sighed. Whatever happened, happened. In the meantime, she was going to enjoy the time she spent with Cain.

By late afternoon, Millicent had left for the Airbnb she was renting at the edge of town while the hotel was being completed, an old, remodeled wood-frame house built in the early 1900s.

Jenny wondered if there were any ghosts in the house, but didn't think it was a good idea to ask.

Her thoughts went to the murder in room 10. She needed to speak to Nell, hear what the older woman had to say. Cain had asked Jenny to join him and Nell for supper, but Jenny didn't want to bring up the subject in front of Cain.

At five o'clock, she went back to the Copper Star to check on the Sunday-evening crowd, but the weather was turning bad, and as the fall days shortened, the customers began to thin. The weekend was over, the hotel only half full. The crime scene had been released, but so far no one had been booked into the new wing of the hotel.

Unfortunately, that would soon change. The end of October was the annual Jerome Halloween Party, the biggest day of the year for the tiny town. The hotel was completely booked—except for room 10. Everyone from miles around would be showing up dressed as ghosts and goblins.

This year, Jenny wasn't looking forward to it.

Satisfied everything was running smoothly, she went upstairs to her suite. The door had been replaced after Ryder's attack, and the room was clean, everything back in order. Still, she felt uneasy whenever she was in there. Maybe she should move to a different room.

Or maybe not. No way was she letting a creep like Ryder Vance intrude into her life, her world. She'd stay right where she was, she decided, as she packed enough clean clothes to last a few days, extra makeup and toiletries that she could leave at the Grandview, then went in to shower and dress for her dinner with Cain and his grandmother.

Instead of her usual jeans and flannel shirt, she chose a black knit sheath dress accented with simple gold jewelry. A text message arrived just as she was ready to leave.

Cain's note said he would be picking her up. Good, she wouldn't have to haul her carry-on up the hill, hoping no one would see her heading for Cain's private elevator. Hurriedly putting on her heels, she descended the stairs to the lobby, then wheeled her bag through the door out to the sidewalk.

Cain was already there, his gorgeous Jag parked at the curb. He got out and came around to take her bag and open the door, looking magnificent in a navy sport coat and tan slacks.

"What happened to your pickup?" Jenny asked, ignoring the little leap her heart took as he settled her in the passenger seat.

"I have to go to my office in Scottsdale for a meeting in the morning. I had one of the ranch hands drive the Jag up and exchange it for the truck."

Jenny grinned. "Nothing like going first class."

Cain grinned back as he closed her door, walked around, and slid in behind the wheel. "A lesson I learned long ago."

He fired the engine, which purred like the jaguar the car was named for. In minutes, they were back at the hotel, up in Cain's suite. Jenny took a moment to put her clothes away in the guest room and bath.

"You look gorgeous," Cain said. Walking up behind her, he slid his arms around her waist, pushed her curls aside, and pressed his mouth against the nape of her neck. Heat slid low in her belly.

"I've been thinking about you all day." Another sexy kiss moistened the exposed skin on her shoulder. "Wanting you."

Jenny swallowed. "I've been too busy to want you."

His hand slid into the modest scooped neckline of the dress, into her lacy black bra to cup her breast. "How about now?" His fingers rubbed back and forth over her nipple, making it peak, making her stomach melt.

"Now . . . ? Now that's all I can think about."

He kept kissing her neck, nipping her earlobe. When she tried to turn around, he held her in place.

"Not yet," he said. "I've got something else in mind for you."

She could feel his hands roaming over her hips, sliding her black knit dress up around her waist. Jenny trembled.

Cain spotted her black-lace thong and groaned. "Oh, yeah," he said, pulling her back against him. One of his hands slid over her abdomen, into the top of her thong, and moved lower.

A little sound came from her throat as he stroked her with one hand, while his other hand caressed her breasts. She was hot all over, melting inside, damp and aching for him. His hard length pressed against her, and the heat fanned out, making her tremble.

"Tell me what you want."

This time she knew the answer. "I want you, Cain. I need you." It was insane. They were meeting his grandmother in minutes, and all she could think of was having him inside her.

"Let's see what we can do about that." He gently bit the nape of her neck. Then he was bending her over the arm of the leather sofa, sliding down her black-thong panties, urging her to step out of them. His zipper buzzed down, and he was nudging her legs apart, touching her, sliding deep inside. Her hunger was so intense a whimper came from her throat.

Cain gripped her hips and started to move, and little ripples of pleasure tore through her. He moved deeper, began to set up a rhythm, and an instant later, her body exploded in climax. Cain didn't stop, just held her in place and drove into her until she came again, before following her to release.

She was weak and shaky as he pulled her back against him, his arm locked around her waist to hold her up.

"Cain . . ." she whispered.

He eased her dress back into place, turned her into his arms, and kissed her the way she had wanted him to before.

He set her back far enough to look at her, must have read the satisfaction in her face.

"There's more where that came from," he said, smiling. "Just let me know."

Jenny laughed. "We're getting ready to meet your grandmother. I can't believe you did that."

"Believe it," Cain said, his smile widening. He kissed her one last time. "We'd better put ourselves back together. We're having supper up here tonight. My grandmother will be here any minute."

"Oh, my God." Jenny turned and raced for the bathroom. By

the time she returned, Cain was waiting in the living room, his back to her, long legs splayed as he gazed out the windows.

He turned at her approach.

"I just realized . . . we . . . we didn't use a condom." She had meant to say it a little more tactfully, but the words just tumbled out.

"That's right," Cain said. "Those days are over. I got my test results back, and I'm fine, and I know you haven't been with a man since your husband. You're on the pill, right?"

Jenny's head spun. She frowned. "How did you know all that?" She remembered Nick Faraday, the detective who worked for Cain, and her features tightened. "Never mind. I think I know."

Cain walked over and drew her into his arms. "We're in this together, right? I hope you feel the same way."

Anger had her stepping back from him. "I understand why you had Faraday run a check on me, but don't you think digging into my sex life is going a little too far?"

"I needed to know."

"How would you like it if I did that to you? Dug into all your past affairs?"

"I'll tell you anything you want to know."

"Fine. From now on, if you want to know something about me, all you have to do is ask."

"I already knew everything I needed to know about you before Faraday looked into your past."

"You did?"

"I knew you were honest and kindhearted. I knew you were smart. I knew I wanted you badly. I still do."

And then he kissed her, and Jenny was lost.

Cain left for Scottsdale early the following morning. He'd left Jenny sleeping, her curls spread over his pillow. Their supper the night before had been interesting, as he watched his grandmother and Jenny interact. Nell liked her. And Jenny liked Nell. They were easy together, as if they had known each other for years.

That was a good thing, Cain told himself. But he didn't want it to change the dynamics between him and Jenny. He wasn't sure where their relationship was headed. Hell, it had taken him a while just to admit they had one.

The truth was, they weren't just dating. There were expectations between them. Fidelity, first and foremost. Jenny expected it from Cain, and Cain expected it from Jenny.

That was a first for him. He usually spent time with women who preferred to remain unattached. Who accepted that either of them could see other people. Commitments were something he had shied away from. Somehow, with Jenny, it had just happened.

The weird part was he liked it.

Cain spent the morning in meetings in the Scottsdale office. He met with his CEO, as well as the president of the company and several company VPs. Barrett Enterprises was planning to acquire Titan Transport, which built heavy equipment geared to the mining industry. Titan would be a valuable asset to the company.

After a hard day, they broke for a catered supper in the conference room, then worked for two more hours. It was eight p.m. when the last meeting ended.

Cain drove the Jag toward his house on North Pima off Hualapai Road. The three-acre property, part of Pima Acres, was surrounded by desert, the house a flat-roofed, ultra-modern structure with walls of glass and very high ceilings. With an interior done in white and black with light and dark gray accents, it was a beautiful home. Unfortunately, it felt as if it belonged to another man.

Cain still wasn't sure why he'd bought it. Mostly because the woman he was seeing at the time had loved it. It came fully furnished, and he didn't want to spend more time shopping for something else.

As he pulled into the driveway, his headlights illuminated the tall glass windows in the living room, giving him a glimpse into the stark interior.

Cain pressed the button that opened one of the three-car garages and just sat there with the car idling, trying to work up the will to go in. He had meetings scheduled for tomorrow and the next day. There was no way around it.

With a sigh of resignation, he pulled the Jag into the garage and turned off the engine. The refrigerator would be fully stocked. The housekeeper would have a casserole ready to put in the oven. The place would be immaculately clean. No one would bother him.

No one would be waiting for him.

He liked it that way, he told himself. It would be a nice change from the problems at the ranch or the chaos at the Grandview.

But when he finally went inside, the house felt empty in a way he hadn't noticed before. When he went into his spacious bedroom, showered, and climbed into bed, he couldn't fall asleep. He kept thinking of Jenny. Worrying about her. A lot had been happening at the Copper Star. Bikers, ghosts, rattlesnakes. And murder. Was it all just coincidence?

If he could have convinced himself, Cain might have been able to sleep.

CHAPTER TWENTY-TWO

JENNY NEEDED TO TALK TO NELL. THOUGH SHE'D ENJOYED HER DINNER with Nell and Cain the night before, they hadn't discussed the murder. It wasn't an appropriate topic for a special, welcome-home supper for Cain's grandmother.

With Cain already gone, Jenny had showered in his fancy marble bathroom, dressed, and headed for the Copper Star. She wouldn't be sleeping in his bedroom tonight. Their relationship was too new for those kinds of assumptions.

She'd planned to talk to Nell when she went back to the Grandview later that day, but Nell was out, spending the afternoon with friends. Needing to stay busy, Jenny put in extra hours, telling herself not to think of Cain and what he might be doing in Scottsdale. Telling herself it didn't matter that Anna Hobbs lived there. Or any number of other beautiful women.

Back at the Star, she relieved Troy and bartended the late shift. By eleven o'clock, when the saloon closed up, she was so exhausted it didn't take her long to fall asleep. It wasn't until well after midnight that a sound in the room nudged her awake and her eyes cracked open.

Her pulse beat faster. She glanced around but didn't see anything. No orb, no ghostly faces floating at the foot of the bed. She relaxed and began to drift back to sleep.

Then she heard it. A gasping sound, followed by heavy, labored breathing. It seemed to be coming from inside the very walls of the room. Jenny clutched the blanket tighter around her. She wanted to close her eyes and pretend none of this was happening.

Maybe it wasn't.

She heard the notes of a music box playing and what sounded like children's laughter. Then abruptly, everything stopped.

The bedroom went eerily silent. All she could hear was the rapid beat of her heart pounding in her ears. For an hour, she lay awake, listening, waiting for something to happen.

Eventually, her tired body overruled her fears, her eyelids drooped, and she fell asleep.

Nothing disturbed her until sunshine streamed through the curtains at the windows. Jenny had never been happier to see the dawn.

She was meeting Nell Barrett for lunch at the Grandview, then she and Millicent planned to work on the grand-opening party. Cain wouldn't be back until tomorrow. Jenny tried to pretend she didn't miss him, but like it or not, Cain Barrett was rapidly becoming an important part of her life.

It wasn't what she wanted. The thought of falling in love with him was nearly as terrifying as what had happened in her room last night.

She glanced at her watch. Though the dining room wasn't officially open, Opal was cooking, trying out different daily specials, which she'd been serving to the construction crew. Schnitzel, sauerkraut, and mashed potatoes topped today's menu.

"I appreciate your joining me," Jenny said to Nell, digging into the mashed potatoes, which were delicious. "I'm desperate to talk to someone who might be able to help me."

Nell swallowed the bite of schnitzel she had taken and delicately wiped her mouth with a white linen napkin. Her fine white hair was neatly pulled back in a bun, and there were tiny pearl earrings in her ears. She always dressed well, perhaps a holdover from an earlier time, but Jenny thought the look worked exactly right for the older woman.

"Is this about the murder that happened in your hotel?" Nell asked.

"Yes, it is. I mentioned some of this to Cain, but he wasn't exactly receptive to my thinking."

"Which is . . . ?"

"That something evil exists in room ten."

Nell's snowy eyebrows went up. "Well . . . I certainly didn't see that coming."

"I'm hoping you won't think I'm crazy, but I believe the man who was killed was under the influence of some kind of evil spirit or demon or whatever it is that lives in that room."

"Based on what evidence?"

"Brian Santana attacked Leslie Owens, the girl he was dating, and tried to strangle her. It was totally out of character. He had no record of any former violence, nothing that would indicate he was capable of something like that. Leslie said it seemed as if he had turned into another man."

"If you believe that, I'm guessing you're no longer renting out room ten."

"No. The thing is, Nell, this isn't the first time something like that happened in that room."

Nell took a sip of water from the short-stemmed goblet Millicent had chosen, a good choice, Jenny thought—elegant, yet it fit into the big stainless dishwasher.

"I know I'm getting older," Nell said, "but I don't recall another murder happening in the hotel. At least not while I was living in Jerome."

"The other incident didn't end up with anyone dead, but the attack came very close." Jenny told Nell about the journals and what Mrs. Dennison had written fifteen years ago about her night in room 10.

"Mary Dennison described her husband's behavior exactly the way Leslie Owens described Brian Santana's. Both men committed vicious attacks on the women they were sleeping with in that room. I brought the journal so you could read Mary's account."

Jenny pulled the small, leather-bound volume out of her purse and set it on the table. Nell drew out a pair of silver half-glasses, slid them on, and settled them on her nose.

She took her time reading the entry, removed the glasses, and folded them up. "I can see why you're concerned."

"Leslie Owens's story was almost exactly the same. Except that she fought back and Brian ended up dead."

Nell shook her head. "Such a terrible thing."

"Uncle Charlie closed that section of the hotel, but he never told me why. He did it not long after Mary Dennison wrote that entry in the journal. I-I'm really starting to believe the entire hotel is haunted."

Nell arched a silver eyebrow. "There's not much doubt of that, dear girl. Half the town is haunted. The spirits, however, are mostly harmless, even playful. This sounds like something more."

Jenny didn't mention the strange noises she had heard in her room last night. She didn't want Nell to think she was imagining all of this.

"I have a friend," Nell said, as the meal came to a close. "Her name is Cleopatra Swift. She was named after the mountain this town is built on."

"Cleopatra Hill."

Nell nodded. "Cleo has a gift. She doesn't talk about it to most people, but Cleo can sense the presence of spirits. She's sensitive to their thoughts and emotions. Sometimes she can help them pass into the world beyond, where they're supposed to be."

Seconds passed as Jenny absorbed the information. "So you don't think what I'm telling you is crazy."

"Not in the least. I was raised in Jerome. I've heard ghost stories all my life. Some of them could make the hair stand up on the back of your neck. I learned to be less skeptical than most."

"This friend of yours . . . Cleopatra. Will she help me?"

Nell set her napkin next to her empty plate. "Cleo might agree to help. If she does, she'll come to the Copper Star, see if she can make some sort of contact. In the meantime, I suggest you do some research. Try to find out what might have happened in the hotel in the past. Perhaps you'll even find mention of something in room ten."

Jenny smiled for the first time since she and Nell had been seated in the dining room. "I've been meaning to do that."

"The museum on Main Street would be a good place to start. They have lots of books on early Jerome. Maybe someone who works there will have information that could be useful."

"Yes. And the library. I'll start tomorrow."

Both of them rose from the table. Emma appeared out of nowhere to help Nell into her wheelchair for the trip up to her suite. Whenever she wasn't with Nell, Emma entertained herself with a bag of knitting that was always close at hand.

"I think I'll take a nap," Nell said. "I'll call Cleo a little later and let you know what she says."

"Thank you so much."

"Don't thank me yet." Nell gave her a stern look down the length of her nose. "And until we figure out what's going on, stay out of room ten."

As Emma rolled Nell's wheelchair toward the elevator, Jenny thought of the evil that could have possessed Brian Santana, and goose bumps crept over her skin.

James Randall, the president of Barrett Enterprises, had a family emergency. His mother had been in a car accident and was rushed to the local hospital. Cain had canceled the rest of today's meetings. Fortunately, the doctors believed the woman would be okay.

Though it was only six o'clock, Cain was tired to the bone. Heading straight home, he pulled into the driveway and opened the garage door. He needed to get a decent night's sleep.

The Jag idled quietly. Though the outside lights softly illuminated the carefully constructed desert-landscaped yard, the house looked as empty and lonely as it had the night before.

His breath came out on a sigh. He needed to finalize the work they'd been doing and close the Titan deal. But they had all worked hard today and managed to accomplish most of what they needed to do.

Cain studied the uninviting interior of the house. The meetings had gone well, better than expected. Tomorrow, if necessary, a Zoom call could handle the rest.

He checked his heavy gold wristwatch. He could be back at the ranch before nine. Or he could be back in Jerome.

Cain put the Jag in reverse and backed out of the driveway. There was a convenience store on the way to the freeway. A quick stop at the Circle K, a hot cup of coffee, and he was on his way.

Traffic was moderate. The Jag rolled north on Interstate 101, merged onto I-17, and continued north, the strong coffee and the demands of mountain driving keeping Cain alert.

An hour and a half later, he spotted the sign for Prescott and turned off the interstate onto AZ 69. Another convenience-store stop, and he was passing through town, heading up Iron Springs Road toward the ranch. He slowed the Jag as he approached the Y in the road, left to the ranch, right to Jerome. It was almost the same distance, but the drive to Kirkland took less time. Still . . .

Left to the ranch, right to Jerome—and Jenny.

Cain turned right.

There was a chance Jenny was staying at the Grandview. He should call her, let her know he was on his way, but something held him back. He drove the curves to the top of the mountain and pulled into Jerome, turned up the hill to the Grandview.

A quick trip inside told him Jenny wasn't there.

He should have figured she would still be working. When he drove up in front of the Copper Star and got out of the Jag, he could hear country music playing. He pushed through the bat-wing doors.

Jenny stood behind the bar. She was smiling, leaning over the counter, resting on her elbows, talking to a good-looking, dark-haired man with a two-hundred-dollar haircut, designer jeans, a cashmere sweater, and expensive Italian loafers. His buddy was romancing a redhead, while Romeo had set his sights on Jenny.

The guy laughed at something Jenny said, and she grinned. Cain felt his blood pressure rise.

As he crossed the room, Jenny spotted him, rounded the bar, and ran toward him. She threw her arms around his neck.

"You're back early," she said, smiling up at him. "Why didn't you call and let me know?"

Cain didn't hug her back. "Looks like you had plenty of company while I was gone."

"What?" Jenny followed his gaze to the guy at the bar. She frowned and took a step back. "I'm bartending tonight. Bartenders talk to people. As long as they're being entertained, they're buying drinks. You've been around long enough to know that."

When Cain made no reply, her features tightened. "You have some nerve coming in here and looking at me like I'm doing something wrong. What about you? Did you spend last night with Anna? Or was there someone new?"

Irritation trickled through him. "I was working, just like I said. I wasn't with Anna or anyone else. We made a deal. I don't break my word."

Jenny set her hands on her hips. "Well, I don't either." She was wearing a denim skirt and cowboy boots. His mind returned to the night she'd been wearing the black knit dress, the way she had looked bent over his sofa.

His body went hard. That was the trouble. He was thinking with his dick and not his brain.

He blew out a breath. "Can we talk for a minute somewhere private?"

"I'm busy. I'll talk to you tomorrow."

"Please," he said, catching her wrist as she started to turn away. "Okay, I'm sorry. I was jealous. It's a new experience for me. Can you break away for a minute?"

She gave him a long, assessing glance, then turned and asked one of the waitresses to fill in while she stepped outside.

Cain led her through the batwing doors onto the sidewalk. It was too cold to stay out there long. He was still wearing his navy blue suit. He took off his jacket and draped it around her shoulders.

"You were right in there. You weren't doing a damn thing wrong."

"No, I wasn't."

He sighed. "I learned something about myself tonight. I learned that Scottsdale isn't my home anymore. I decided to drive back up the mountain to the ranch. Then I realized what I really wanted to do was to see you."

Jenny's big green eyes stared up at him. "So you stormed into the bar, making accusations."

"I was still getting used to the idea."

Her lips twitched. Then her amusement faded. "So . . . I guess this is the moment when we decide whether or not we're going to trust each other."

He nodded. "I guess it is."

"Do you trust me, Cain?"

Did he? He knew her history, knew all about her. He had trusted her even before he had hired her. "More than any woman I've ever known."

"Except for Nell."

His lips edged up. "Except for Nell." He reached out and caught her chin, tilted her head up and lightly kissed her. "What about me, Jenny? Do you trust me?"

"When you give your word, I believe you keep it."

"Yes or no?"

"I trust you, Cain."

He frowned. "Why does that sound like you still have doubts?"

She rested her palms on his chest, her eyes still on his face. "I don't trust you not to break my heart."

Cain pulled her into his arms and just held her. He wondered if, in the end, it wouldn't be the other way around.

CHAPTER TWENTY-THREE

After their confrontation last night, Cain had been especially solicitous in his lovemaking. Such a big, virile male. She hadn't known he could be so tender. Her emotions were in even more turmoil than when he'd showed up at the bar last night, jealous and accusing.

Perhaps she had forgiven him too easily. But Cain seemed to be suffering from the same anxiety she was. She had never felt so conflicted about a man before. She wasn't ready to get seriously involved. And yet she couldn't handle the thought of losing Cain.

Maybe Cain felt the same way.

Or maybe not.

Time would give her the answers. In the meantime, she had a business to run, and she needed answers of a different sort.

That afternoon, Jenny went to the library. First, she browsed books that told the early history of Jerome. The town had come into being when some of the richest copper deposits ever found were discovered in the area. As many as twenty-three different nationalities worked in the United Verde Mines.

The town was just as wild as she had heard. The first wooden structure was Butter's Bar, a two-story brothel and saloon owned by Nora "Butter" Brown. An article dated November 27, 1879, insisted that Wyatt Earp had an encounter with Billy the Kid in Butter's Bar. An altercation in the street had sidetracked the men and saved Wyatt from having to kill the Kid.

Butter had written in her journal that she had spent the night with Wyatt, a true gentleman, one of the best nights she had ever enjoyed. No one seemed to know if the story was true, but Butter, who was murdered by her opium-addicted husband in 1905, never backed down on her claim.

Jenny smiled. For Butter's sake, she hoped it had actually happened.

Jenny finally found an article that zeroed in on the Copper Star. An earlier hotel in the same location, owned by the same man who had built the Star, had burned down twice before the turn of the century. The last conflagration had destroyed half the town, leaving ten people dead and forty missing.

The Star had been rebuilt and reopened in 1899, but in the Wickedest Town in the West, the deaths just kept mounting.

By now, Jenny knew that thousands of people had died in Jerome over the years. She hadn't known most of them were cremated in the blast furnaces, their ashes dumped on the slag piles and later used for concrete aggregate in the sidewalks.

When people visited Jerome, they were literally walking on the remains of dead people.

Jenny shivered.

The hours slipped past. A stop in the Mine Museum and Gift Shop netted a stack of books about ghostly happenings, which she carried into her office and sat down to read. A story caught her eye about a ghost in the Liberty Theatre, the redbrick building around the corner from the Star.

A woman in the theatre was supposedly murdered by her lover while the piano was playing loud enough to cover up the sounds of her struggle.

Jenny's gaze sharpened on an article about ghosts in the Star. A woman known as the Lady in Red had been seen wandering the upstairs hallways. She mostly appeared in room 1, where she'd been visited by a past owner of the hotel. True or false—who knew? Jenny had never seen her.

She sighed. There were tons of ghost stories, but none of them explained the murder that had happened in room 10.

Jenny wasn't sure if that was good news or bad.

She worked a while in the saloon, helping Barb serve cocktails and delivering food, then went back to the Grandview, arriving in time to join Cain for drinks.

The bar was nearly completed. The mahogany tables and chairs had arrived and been carefully positioned around the room. Softly lit, gilt-framed desert landscapes hung on the wood-paneled walls.

The bartender, a woman named Hannah McKenzie, an attractive redhead in her forties, was working behind the long, polished counter, sliding wineglasses onto the rack upside down by their stems.

Behind the bar, dozens of bottles of alcohol rested on clear-glass shelves: Maker's Mark, Wild Turkey, Stolichnaya, Beluga Gold, Grey Goose, Sapphire, Bombay, Cuervo, Patron, and dozens of others, all beautifully illuminated by lighting below each shelf.

Cain rose as Jenny approached. In crisp blue jeans, white shirt, and a brown tweed sport coat perfectly tailored to his broad-shouldered, V-shaped body, he looked yummy.

He turned to her, a faint smile on his lips, reminding her of what had happened in his room last night. Desire clenched low in her belly. Faraday also stood up, distracting her, thank God.

Cain reached for Jenny's hand and pulled her toward him, leaned in, and brushed a light kiss on her cheek.

"You remember Nick?" The detective was black-haired and good-looking, with a keen intelligence in his intense blue eyes.

"Of course. Nice to see you, Nick."

"You, too, Jenny."

Cain seated her in the chair next to his, and the bartender appeared at the table. Cain and Nick already had rocks glasses in front of them. Cain drank Johnny Walker Black.

"I'll have what Cain's drinking," Jenny said. Whiskey not wine. Cain's mouth edged up. By now, he knew she was different from the other women he'd dated. He would get used to it. Or not.

He turned back to Nick. "Where were we?"

"We were talking about the last stolen horse being found."

"Where?" Jenny asked.

"The gelding was running loose in a rancher's field east of

Phoenix," Nick said. "Which only leaves Sun King and makes it clear the theft of the other horses was just a distraction. Stealing Cain's stallion wasn't only about money. I believe it was personal."

Jenny's spine straightened, but Cain remained calm.

Nick continued, "Clearly, you have an enemy willing to go to great lengths to hurt you."

"I've made millions of dollars in the years since I found that molybdenum deposit. Success breeds enemies. That's just the way it is."

"I need a list of anyone and everyone who would go this far to steal something from you."

Cain laughed. "Let's see, should I start with my housekeeper in Scottsdale? She steals the toilet paper every time she cleans my house."

Nick did not see the humor. "I hardly think that's the same. Sun King's worth half a million dollars. He's a horse you want to breed. Whoever stole him wants you to feel it."

Cain took a drink of his whiskey. "All right, I'll get you that list."

"Soon," Nick said, rising from his chair. He downed the last of his drink and set the glass on the table. "We have no idea how far this guy is willing to go." He flicked a glance at Jenny. "There might be other things he'd be willing to do in order to get to you."

Cain's jaw went ironhard. He nodded. "I'll have it for you by the end of the day."

Back in his suite, Cain sat down in front of the computer in his study, and Jenny walked up behind him. Resting her hands on his shoulders, she dug her fingers into the taut muscles, kneading the tension away. Unfortunately, the feel of her small hands working him over had the opposite effect, and arousal slipped through him, making him hard.

He forced himself to concentrate on the list he was trying to make.

"Do you even know where to start?" Jenny asked.

Cain eyed her over his shoulder. "What? You think I stepped on so many people trying to make money, I can't even remember their names?"

She leaned over and kissed his cheek. "Just the opposite. You're a man of integrity, Cain. I saw that right away. I wouldn't be interested in a guy who hurt other people to get what he wanted."

Some of his tension eased. Jenny had faith in him. It shouldn't feel so important, but it did.

"I'm not saying I was a saint. I worked hard. I had to claw my way to the top. I refused to let anyone or anything stand in my way. But I stayed within boundaries. I didn't destroy other people's lives to get where I am today. I didn't lie or steal from them."

"Maybe whoever it is doesn't believe that. They think you're guilty—whether you actually did anything to them or not."

Cain sat back in his chair and breathed a sigh. It made a sad kind of sense. "So where do I start?"

"Start with the present and work backward. Nothing like this has ever happened before, so whatever you did—inadvertently or otherwise—must have happened recently."

He nodded. "Good logic." Though it might not be correct.

"You just went to Scottsdale. You said your company is buying a business."

"Titan Transport," Cain said.

"How long have you been working on it?"

"A little over six months."

"So before King was stolen?"

"That's right."

"Was there someone on either side of the deal who didn't want the sale to go through?"

Cain looked at the blank computer screen. "Okay, I get it." He smiled. "You should have been a lawyer—or a detective."

Jenny grinned. "Thanks."

Cain spun the desk chair around and pulled her onto his lap. "I can think of something a lot more fun than making a list of people who hate me." He kissed her, gently, then more thoroughly.

Cain cursed himself as he thought of what Nick had subtly warned, that whoever had stolen his stallion might go as far as hurting Jenny. Reluctantly, he set her on her feet.

"I need to do this," he grumbled.

"Yes, you do. I brought some reading with me. I'll leave you to it."

"Opal's still here. I'll call down, have her fix a tray and leave it in the oven. When I'm finished, I'll have someone bring it up, and we can eat."

"And afterward?" Jenny teased.

Desire tightened his groin. His gaze ran over her, taking in her sexy curves. "Afterward, I'm sure we can think of something to do."

Jenny laughed.

Sitting in Cain's living room the following morning, Jenny read through the rest of the books she had purchased at the museum. There were dozens of ghost stories, some a repeat of what she had read last night or heard before.

In the saloon at the Copper Star, a number of patrons had reportedly seen a short Mexican man with a big mustache standing near the bar. A customer had even taken a photo of the hazy figure.

Apparently, he was an actual man named Kito, who had frequented the barroom, cardrooms, and billiard tables in the saloon.

Her heart ached at the story of a young Mexican girl who was impregnated by one of the wealthy town bigwigs. The girl was taken out to Hulk Canyon and shoved over a cliff. People said her spirit walked the town in search of justice.

Lots of stories. No way to know if any of them were true, or which ones might have resulted in a spirit being locked between this world and the next—if there even was such a thing.

She thought of the call she had received from Nell. Cleopatra Swift would meet her this afternoon in the lobby of the Copper Star.

It was going to be interesting to hear what the woman had to say.

CHAPTER TWENTY-FOUR

"I'VE GOT TO GET GOING." JENNY HEADED FOR THE ELEVATOR IN the entry of Cain's suite.

"I'll see you this afternoon," Cain said from his seat on the sofa, his laptop on the coffee table in front of him so he could continue working on his list.

"I've got an appointment this afternoon. I won't be over till later."

Cain's head came up. "What kind of appointment?"

Jenny smiled. "I'll tell you about it when I get back." She walked over and kissed his cheek, turned and started back toward the door. She could feel his eyes on her, feel the heat, remembered last night, and knew what he was thinking.

Exactly what she was thinking. She forced herself to keep walking.

Jenny picked up her pace as she made her way down the hill to Main Street. The sun was out, but it was chilly. Cleopatra was already there when Jenny arrived, a big woman, late sixties, close to three hundred pounds, with breasts the size of melons beneath a white sweater with flowers on the front.

No more than five feet tall, she wore a pair of baggy jeans that ended above her ankles. White sneakers covered her feet.

Cleo hoisted herself up off the burgundy horsehair settee in the lobby. Thankfully, it was a sturdy piece that had lasted for over a hundred years.

Jenny smiled and walked toward her. "Mrs. Swift. It's a pleasure to meet you."

"It's Cleo, and you're late. I don't like to be kept waiting."

Jenny's face colored as she glanced down at her watch. Two minutes after the appointed hour. "Sorry. I appreciate your time."

"In that case, let's get going." Cleo hoisted her huge bulk off the settee and headed for the stairs. There was an old service elevator in the kitchen that had been there since the last remodel back in the 1990s. It was used to bring up sheets and towels, mops and buckets, vacuum cleaners and the like.

Jenny thought about asking Cleo if she wanted to use it, but one look at the stubborn way the woman attacked the stairs and she kept her mouth shut.

At the top of the stairs, Cleo stopped to study the recently opened hallway. "This is the new section," the woman said, though Jenny hadn't told her.

"That's right."

"Charlie kept it closed off."

"Yes, he did."

"Charlie Spencer wasn't a fool. You should have paid attention."

If only she had. "Uncle Charlie never told me why he closed it. It didn't seem important at the time. I guess I should have asked." Jenny felt a sweep of guilt. "Now it's too late."

Cleo grunted. "Well, maybe we can figure it out." Turning, the heavyset woman headed down the hallway, pausing every now and then, cocking her head as if she were listening for something or trying to sense something she couldn't quite grasp.

Jenny felt nothing. Maybe she was completely wrong. Maybe none of it was real.

Cleo paused outside the door to room 10. Everyone in Jerome knew about the murder, but the news hadn't reported the room in which it had happened. Perhaps Nell had told her.

Cleo reached for the doorknob, turned it, and walked into the empty room. It was completely clean, the bedding replaced, carpet pulled up, hardwood floors polished to a sheen, no trace of the gruesome murder that had taken place in there.

Cleo stood in silence at the foot of the bed. She turned. "There's . . . something."

Jenny's pulsed kicked up. "What is it? Is it in here now?"

"Not now. What's here now is like a whiff of smoke in the air. It's what's left after, only a sign something's been here." Cleo's gaze pinned her. "Is this the room where the murder happened?"

"Yes."

Cleo nodded, moving her triple chins. "I need to come back tonight, try to make contact."

"You can't do it now?"

"There are different kinds of spirits, same as there are different kinds of people. Some of them exist only in darkness."

Jenny felt a chill. "Are those . . . evil spirits?"

"Yes." Cleo turned and stomped back out the door. Jenny followed her down the hall, down the stairs to the lobby.

At the bottom of the stairs, Cleo turned back to her. "This place be closed by midnight?"

It was a weeknight. The weather was bad, business slow. "Earlier, if that's what you want."

"Midnight. Meet me here." Cleo's big body swayed back and forth as she turned and walked to the door. She opened it, ringing the bell above, and disappeared out onto the sidewalk.

Jenny's shoulders sagged as a rush of tension left her. Had Cleo really sensed something upstairs? It certainly appeared that way.

Jenny glanced over at the lobby desk. On Monday morning, she had put the most recently used leather journal, half full, back out on the desk, where it now sat open. Things were happening. She needed to know what was going on. She needed to know the truth.

Maybe she would find out tonight.

Cain wasn't happy. Jenny had called and told him she'd be working late, spending the night in her suite at the Copper Star.

When he'd told her he'd pick her up after she closed up, she had stumbled through a string of excuses.

Cain wanted to know why.

He thought of the guy with the Italian loafers and two-hundred-dollar haircut, but he didn't believe Jenny had any interest in the man. He trusted her, he realized, just as he'd said.

Something else was going on, and Cain intended to find out what it was.

He left the Grandview around the time he figured the saloon would be closing, drove the Jag down the hill, and parked on the street out front. It was eleven-thirty. Some of the lights were still on inside. Even after the customers were gone, it took a while to close the place down.

He walked up to the front door and knocked, heard movement inside the bar. Jenny's voice came back to him from the other side of the door.

"Sorry, we're closed."

"It's Cain. Let me in."

"Cain . . ." He heard the hesitation in her voice, then the rattle of locks, and the door swung open. "What are you doing here? I told you I had to work late and I was going to spend the night upstairs."

"That's what you said."

She clamped her hands on her hips. "You don't believe me? You think I'm going off with some stud muffin I met in the bar?"

Cain grinned. "No, I don't think that." He forced her back a couple of steps as he walked into the saloon. "I told you I trusted you, and I do." He glanced around the empty bar. "The question is what else is going on tonight? Because I'm beginning to know you well enough to realize you were only telling me part of the truth."

Jenny sighed. "I'm not sure I like that."

"Comes with familiarity, sweetheart. Now tell me the rest."

"Okay, the truth is I knew you wouldn't like what I'm doing tonight so I didn't tell you. Plus I figured if you were here, your disbelief might affect the outcome."

He surprised her by pulling her into his arms and kissing her. She resisted for an instant, then slid her arms up around his neck and kissed him back.

Cain reluctantly broke the kiss. "You can tell me anything, honey. If I don't like it, I'll say so."

She smiled up at him. "All right. But the same goes for me. If I don't like it, I'll tell you."

Cain smiled back. "I figured. Now what's going on?"

"I met Nell's friend, Cleopatra Swift, today. Cleo is able to communicate with spirits. She took a look at room ten. Cleo thinks there could be something evil in the room. She's coming back tonight to see if she can reach out to whatever it is."

Cain just shook his head. "Ms. Spencer, you never cease to amaze me."

She crossed her arms over her chest. "I knew you wouldn't believe it."

"I've never seen a ghost, but half the population of Jerome is convinced the town is full of them. I'm willing to keep an open mind."

"You are?"

"Yes."

Jenny relaxed and smiled. "Cleo will be here at midnight. I need to finish up so I'll be ready when she gets here."

"What can I do to help?" Cain asked.

"Seriously?"

"Sure, why not? It's not like I've never washed a dish before." Cain followed Jenny toward the kitchen.

By the time Cleopatra Swift arrived twenty minutes later, they were finished and waiting for her in the hotel lobby. Cain had known Nell's friend since he was a kid. She was even bigger and rounder than she'd been back then.

Cleo eyed him up and down. "Well, look who's here. Mr. Success himself, Cain Barrett."

Cain just smiled. "Hello, Cleo. It's nice to see you."

Her gaze flicked toward the staircase, then returned to Cain.

"So . . . are you gonna be a pain in my ass tonight, or are you going to be quiet and let me do my work?"

Cain bit back a laugh. "I won't give you any trouble. I'm just here for Jenny. And there's nothing I'd like better than to actually see a ghost."

Cleo harrumphed. "We'll see about that." Turning, she adjusted the strap of the big quilted, blue-flowered bag slung over her shoulder and headed up the stairs. Cain and Jenny followed.

"The hotel's only about half full," Jenny said when they reached the top. "I think everyone who's staying here is in their rooms by now."

"Good." Cleo marched down the hallway of the new section and stopped in front of room 10. Jenny reached out and turned the knob, and the door swung silently into the darkness beyond.

Cleo walked into the room. Resting her big, quilted bag on the queen-size bed, she pulled out three white candles and carried them over to the dresser. She struck a match and carefully lit each one. Candlelight flickered, casting eerie shadows on the walls.

"Close the door," she commanded.

Cain closed the door.

Cleo walked over and made herself comfortable in the wooden chair at the table near the window. It creaked in distress at the heavy weight. Cain hoped it wouldn't collapse.

"What now?" he asked.

"Now we wait." Cleo flicked him a warning glance. "And you both stay quiet while I work."

Cain sat next to Jenny on the bed. He noticed the room had been thoroughly cleaned and the quilt replaced. It still felt as if death lurked in the shadows. Jenny's hand brushed his as she reached for him, and he laced his fingers with hers.

Minutes slipped past. At first, his mind was restless, thinking of things he needed to be doing, thinking of the ranch and Sun King, going over the list of possible enemies he had made, wondering if there were people he should have added.

Time crept past. Midnight turned to one. Jenny sat quietly.

Nothing was happening. His restlessness slowly faded as drowsiness set in, and his eyelids began to droop.

"Who are you?" Cleo asked, and Cain's eyes shot wide open. "Tell me your name."

Jenny's fingers tightened on his. Her breathing quickened, and he could feel an uptick in her pulse. Nerves burned through him, heightening his own heart rate. In the candlelight, he could read the tension that had crept into Cleo's fleshy face.

As the minutes ticked past, the room seemed to narrow to the three points of light coming from the dresser. Cain shifted on the mattress, an odd pressure settling on the back of his neck. He blinked as a headache began to form behind his eyes.

"Stay away from him," Cleo warned. "I know what you're doing. I know what you've done. I can help you. Tell me your name."

An icy breeze sifted through the air, although the window was closed. An instant later, all three candles went out. Cain could hear Cleo's voice, but he could no longer make out what she was saying. His chest felt leaden. His headache increased until it pounded ruthlessly in his ears.

His heart was thudding, his mouth bone dry. He looked at Jenny, at her long, thick brown curls, her smooth skin, and plump lips. Lust swelled inside him, beating at his control. He was hard, he realized, throbbing with every heartbeat. His hands were shaking, his palms sweating.

He wanted to reach for her, bare Jenny's breasts, wanted to squeeze them, pinch her nipples until she cried out. He wanted to shove her down on the bed, rip off her clothes, force her legs apart, and plunge himself inside her.

He looked at her slender throat and wanted to wrap his hands around her neck, to hear her struggling for breath as he pounded his hard length into her again and again.

Horror filled him, and Cain shot up from the bed. He rushed for the light switch next to the door and flipped it on, then opened the door and ran out into the hall. He was shaking, breathing hard, his mind spinning, barely able to catch his breath.

Then Jenny was there, wrapping her arms around him, holding

him close, telling him everything was going to be okay. For a moment, he was afraid to touch her, afraid of the man he had become in room 10. Afraid he would hurt her.

"It's all right," Jenny said. "I know what you were feeling in there. I could sense it. See it in your face. It wasn't you in there, Cain. It was someone else."

Cleo appeared beside them. Cain heard the click of the lock as the door closed behind her.

"We'll talk downstairs," she said. Turning, Cleo marched back down the hall.

CHAPTER TWENTY-FIVE

Cain stood in the hallway outside room 10. Jenny left his side long enough to double-check the door, be sure it was securely locked; then she slid her arm around his waist and pulled him close, keeping him firmly against her side as they followed in Cleo's wake. Still half-dazed, he didn't pull away.

When they reached the bottom of the stairs, they went into Jenny's office. Cleo took up most of the velvet settee. Cain sat down in one of the chairs in front of the desk, and Jenny sat down in the other. She reached over and took hold of his hand.

Cain knew he should say something, try to explain what had happened to him upstairs, but he couldn't find the words.

"You all right?" Cleo asked him.

"I'm not sure."

"I saw what he was doing to you," she said. "But you were too strong for him."

Cain just shook his head.

"You felt him," she said. "Now you know what he's like. He won't bother you again as long as you don't invite him in."

"Is that what I did?"

"No. He took you by surprise. That's what he does."

"You talk as if he's a person."

"He was, but it was a long time ago. He was a miner. Near as I can tell, a real bad hombre. He was shot dead right in the street. In front of a bordello, I think. I could see women standing on the sidewalk in front of the building."

"He told you all that?" Cain asked.

"Not in words. It's sort of a nonverbal thing. I watched it happen. It's like you're looking down on the scene. I saw him arguing with someone in front of a small single-story, wooden building. I saw the bullet slam into his chest, the gush of blood. I watched his soul lift away, but something went wrong. Maybe he fought it—I don't know."

"If he died in the street, why is he here?" Jenny asked.

"Earlier, I saw him sitting at one of the card tables in the saloon. He liked it here. After he died, he came back. The bad news is he's made a place for himself in room ten, and he doesn't want to leave."

Cain said nothing. Whatever had happened in that room, it was something he had never experienced before, something he would never forget. Something terrifying.

"What I'm telling you isn't a hundred percent certain," Cleo said. "It's my best guess from the feelings I got, but there's still a lot I don't know, and my information's not always reliable. You might be able to do some research, see if you can find out something about him, find out if what I'm suggesting is true."

"I can do that," Jenny said.

Cleo turned to Cain. "You gonna be okay?"

He managed to nod. "I'm okay, but . . . I'm not sure Jenny should stay with me tonight. The way I felt in that room . . . what if I hurt her? What if—"

"You aren't going to hurt her," Cleo said firmly. "There are a lot of things spirits can do, and a lot more they can't. You just have to remember who's in control. That person is you."

Jenny squeezed his hand. "You would never hurt me, Cain. You didn't do it in that room. You won't do it when we're somewhere else."

He hoped she was right, because he wasn't leaving her alone to spend the night in her room at the Star.

"It's getting late," he said, rising from the chair. "Can I drive you home, Cleo?"

"I'm only a block away. Harder for me to get in and out of that fancy car of yours than it is to walk."

"I'll go with you," Jenny volunteered.

"We'll both walk you back," Cain said.

They made the brief trip, waited until Cleo was inside her apartment building, then headed back to the Jag.

It was nearly two in the morning by the time they were up in his suite, ready to go to bed.

"I'm staying in the guest room tonight," Cain said.

"What?"

"You heard me."

"But—"

"It's not open for debate." He tipped her chin up and settled a brief kiss on her lips. "Get some sleep. I'll see you in the morning."

He left her in the living room, his mind still heavy with the weight of what had happened in that hotel room. Was there really an entity inhabiting it?

One thing he knew—something had preyed upon the darkest parts of his soul, urging him to do unspeakable things.

Whatever it was, whoever it was—it was evil. The question was what to do about it. He hoped Cleo had an answer.

After a restless night alone in Cain's big bed, Jenny joined him for breakfast in front of the big glass windows in the living room. They didn't talk about the night before. Cain didn't mention what had happened at the Copper Star, and neither did Jenny.

They both needed time to sort things out, plan what to do next. When the meal was over, Cain suggested driving up to the ranch.

"It isn't that far away," he argued, when she insisted she had to work. "We can relax for a few hours, breathe some fresh, high-desert air, spend the night, and drive back in the morning."

Jenny could see the stress in Cain's face, the lines across his forehead, the tension around his mouth. He was still struggling with the scary moments up in room 10. Cain needed a break, and knowing what she would be dealing with when she returned to the Star, Jenny figured a short break might be good for her, too.

"All right. A night away sounds like a good idea. I just need to grab a few things from the Copper Star before we leave."

His eyes darkened.

"You can wait for me in the lobby. I'll only be a few minutes."

Surprisingly, Cain didn't argue. He didn't want to go upstairs, and she didn't blame him. Jenny hurriedly grabbed a few items, including her boots and a warm outdoor jacket. More items that would end up in Cain's suite.

Her clothes were beginning to fill the guest closet, but Cain didn't seem to mind. He took the satchel she brought down and carried it out to the Jag.

"I called ahead," he said. "They'll be expecting us."

In minutes, they were on their way down the mountain, the Jag hugging the curves, Cain relaxing more with every mile farther away from Jerome.

"So how's the grand-opening party coming?" he asked as he made a steep turn. It was a great day to be outside, the sun shining, the sky a clear azure blue except for a few stray white clouds.

"Millie and I have almost everything done." The party was scheduled for the last Saturday in October. With Halloween the following Wednesday, they had decided on a glamorous masked affair, formal, the guests wearing elegant sequined and feathered masks a la Mardi Gras that would be handed out at the door.

It would be memorable, Jenny was sure.

"We'll be ready," Cain said. "The crew is just doing pickup work. Completing the last of the finish work. Should be done in a day or two. Millie's got most of the furniture in place."

"She'll have the rest in by the middle of the week."

"What else is there to do?" Cain asked.

"With your permission, we're going to open the bar and restaurant early, serve anyone who happens to come through the door, invite a few of the locals to try us. The staff has already been working, learning their routines, but serving outsiders would give them a little more confidence before opening night."

"That's a good idea."

"We've already sent out the invitations. We got most of the guests' email addresses from your assistant in Scottsdale. She was a big help with that. Millicent also had a list. We've already gotten RSVPs from some of the digital invitations we sent out, but considering the caliber of people we're hoping to attract, we also sent a printed invitation."

Jack Barlow, a Copper Star customer, had put in extra effort to get the invitations printed in a short time, an elegant, gold-embossed picture of the hotel on expensive white, deckle-edge card stock.

Bridget Hayes, Summer's mom, had volunteered to address the envelopes, as calligraphy was her hobby. Bridget and Summer, along with a select number of local business owners, were on the invitation list.

Guests from out of town would be staying in the hotel, which Jenny figured would be full that night.

"Believe it or not, I'm actually starting to look forward to this," Cain said. "I need to have my assistant pick up my tux and messenger it up to the hotel."

"Which reminds me, I have to buy a dress."

Cain flicked her a glance. "We'll go shopping. I'll drive you down to Scottsdale. We'll make a day of it."

"I can find something here."

"You don't have to worry about the price. It'll be a gift."

She shot him a look. "No, thank you. It wouldn't be right for you to pay for my dress."

Cain laughed. "You're the first woman I've known who wouldn't let me spend money on her."

"That's because I'm nothing like the other women you've known."

He grinned. "I figured that out a while back." The Jag rolled out of the mountains into the high desert.

"How's your enemies list coming along?" Jenny asked, changing the subject.

Cain surprised her by reaching into the pocket of his denim shirt and pulling out a folded piece of paper. "Take a look. Maybe you can think of someone I'm missing."

She took the list and gave it a brief perusal. "Let's run through it. Hearing the names out loud might jog something that will help."

"All right."

Some of the names were grouped together. "Roger Duffy, Alvin Cline, and Maryann Whelan."

"Ex-employees. They were all let go for different reasons. There were others over the years—that's just business. But those three resented it more than anyone else. Roger even threatened to sue me if we didn't give him his job back."

"Severance pay?"

"Yes. More than they deserved."

She read the next name on the list. "Raymond Aldridge."

"Outbid him on a deal to buy a cluster of moly claims. Claims turned out to be very productive, worth way more than we paid for them. Ray wasn't happy."

She looked back down at the list. "Rance Decker, Tank Rosen, and Butch Steel."

"Guys in the gang I ran with after I dropped out of high school. They were pissed when I reformed, went back to school, and left them behind."

"Even more pissed, I imagine, as you became more and more successful."

He just shrugged. "Probably." He flicked her a sideways glance. "Like I told Nick, depending on how you look at it, I've probably got an army of enemies out there."

Jenny studied the list. "I don't see Barton Harwell's name. Your former partner couldn't have been happy after you bought him out and then found molybdenum on the claims he sold."

"I haven't seen Bart in years. Last I heard, he was somewhere down in South America. Besides, the price I paid him at the time was more than fair. Bart was happy to take the money."

"His name should still be on the list."

"Fine, if that's what you think, write it down."

Jenny took a pen out of her purse and made a note on the paper.

"I see Ryder Vance's name." Steel Cobras was typed in parenthesis beside it. "Your run-in with Ryder happened after King was stolen."

"True, but this is a list of my enemies, and I think Ryder would consider himself one of them."

She nodded. "Couldn't hurt to have him checked out." She looked back down at the list. "What about women? Maryann Whelan, your former employee, is the only female on the list."

Cain's gaze sliced to hers. "I try not to make enemies of the women I spend time with."

"I don't think that's possible. There are bound to be a few you've slept with who felt used or betrayed, some who might want to take revenge for being dumped."

Cain sighed. "Let me give it some thought."

Jenny didn't press him. There had to be a string of women who were pissed when he ended their affair, brief as it might have been. It wasn't hard to imagine herself in that role. She wouldn't be angry, she realized. She would be brokenhearted.

Since it was bound to happen sooner or later, Jenny shoved the depressing thought away.

For the rest of the trip, the scenery kept her entertained. Before they reached Prescott, Cain made the turn north toward Kirkland. As the Jag drove through the rolling desert hills, the miles slipped past. Up ahead, she could see the green, irrigated pastures of the ranch. The Jag turned down the narrow lane toward the sprawling Spanish-style house, and Maria came out on the front porch to greet them.

Cain stopped the car, turned off the engine, and both of them climbed out.

Maria smiled as they approached. She wiped her hands on the yellow apron tied over her jeans. "Welcome. You are just in time for lunch, Señor Cain."

"Great. I'm starving. You remember Jenny?"

"*Sí.* Welcome back, Señora."

"Thank you. It's nice to see you again."

"I will set places for you both in the sun-room."

Cain grabbed the small overnight bags they had brought, carried them into the house and down the hall to his room. Jenny wandered the house, ending up in an intimate glass-walled space filled with plants, some of them overgrowing their colorful pots. It was the perfect room for a day like today, sunny, but tinged with a sharp October chill.

The table was set with bright-colored place mats and pottery plates. Maria walked in, carrying a tray laden with bowls emitting the delicious aroma of chilies and brazed meat.

"That smells delicious," Jenny said.

Maria flicked her a glance. "So the two of you are still together." She took the food off the tray and set the bowls in the middle of the table.

"You didn't think we would be?" Jenny replied. "Well, neither did I."

Maria's chin went up. "Cain is a good man."

"Yes, he is. That's the reason we're still together."

Some of the stiffness went out of Maria's shoulders. "Perhaps I have been wrong about you. Perhaps you are good for Señor Cain."

"I'd like to think so."

Maria's smile actually looked sincere. "Enjoy your lunch."

Cain passed the broad-hipped woman as he walked into the sun-room. "What was that about?"

"I think she was surprised to see me here again. Apparently, a relationship that lasts any length of time is a novelty where you're concerned."

Amusement touched his lips. "I suppose that's true. In your case, we're only getting started."

Jenny felt an expected pang. Half of her hoped it was true. The other half was terrified it might be. "We better eat before it gets cold."

The *chili Colorado* was delicious, the tortillas freshly made. After lunch, they put on their boots, grabbed their jackets, and headed for the barn. Billy saddled Rosebud, the palomino mare she had ridden before, while Cain saddled his big red roan, Gladiator.

Once they were mounted and on their way, the wind died down, and the sun on their shoulders kept them warm. It was a lovely way to spend the afternoon, though Jenny noticed Cain was carefully working to keep his distance. There was no making love on a blanket near the stream, as she had fantasized about on the way to the ranch. There were no fun sexual innuendos.

It bothered her until she realized that, after what had happened in the hotel last night, Cain was afraid of what he might do to her when they made love. What he'd experienced had affected him greatly. Brian Santana was dead. Leslie Owens and Mary Dennison had almost been killed.

But Jenny knew in her heart that Cain would never hurt her. He was stronger than whatever had tried to control him. Tonight, she was going to prove it.

They were back in the barn, Billy unsaddling the horses, when Denver walked toward them through the open barn door. His suntanned face looked pale, his features drawn tight.

"What is it?" Cain asked.

Denver pulled off his hat and held it in front of him. "King's back. Sanchez found him in the east pasture. No idea when or how he got there, but . . ."

"Is he all right?" Cain frowned at the look on Denver's face. "Something's wrong. What is it?"

Denver ran his tongue over his lips. "He's not the same horse, Cain. He went after Sanchez, chased him clear out of the pasture. He attacked Quinn, bit him, chased him, and tried to stomp him into the ground. He's gone completely crazy." Denver's fingers tightened on the brim of his hat. "The thing is, whoever took him . . . they gelded him, Cain. King's not a stallion anymore."

CHAPTER TWENTY-SIX

Cain heard Jenny's soft gasp. Tears sprang into her eyes. "Oh, my God, poor King. What a terrible thing to do."

Cain's jaw went tight. "I need to handle this. I've got to call the sheriff. I need to get the vet over here to look at King. Why don't you go inside and get warmed up? I'll be in when we're finished. It may take a while."

"I'm all right. I'd rather stay with you."

Cain just shook his head. Jenny seemed to understand what he was feeling, the helpless rage, how this had gutted him, but Cain didn't want her sympathy. He wanted to vent his fury on whoever had hurt his stallion. He wanted to pound them into the dirt, end their miserable time on earth.

"I need you to go," he said, his voice harder than he intended. "Please."

Jenny's gaze searched his face; then she nodded. Rising on her toes, she brushed a kiss over his cheek. "I'll see you when you finish up."

The hours slipped past. He spent time with Dave Petersen, the local veterinarian. Denver, Sanchez, and Quinn had to physically restrain King so the vet could examine him. Cain hated to do it after the trauma the horse had suffered, but the doc wanted to look at the area where the crude surgery had been performed and give King antibiotics to prevent infection.

At eight years old, the stallion was too mature to be gelded.

The healing process would take far longer and be much more painful, the risks far greater. In addition, gelding the stallion so late wouldn't alter the horse's biological urges. King would still want to breed the mares, though he could no longer reproduce.

Any plans for a foal out of Kitty Cat by Sun King had been sabotaged completely.

Cain's hand fisted. He thought of his enemies list and mentally went over each name. What kind of man would make an animal suffer as revenge for some imagined misdeed? It was cruel and twisted.

He couldn't think of anyone who would stoop that low, but someone was responsible. Cain vowed to find out who it was and make them pay.

It was early evening when deputy Hank Landry arrived. He took cell-phone pictures of King and drove out to the east pasture, where the horse had been returned. Landry took statements from Denver and the rest of the hands, as well as a statement from Cain, but Cain had purposely left Jenny out of it.

This was bad business. He had no idea where it was heading or when it would end.

It was dark by the time he returned to the house. Not in the mood for conversation, he spent a couple of hours in his study. It was almost eleven o'clock when he finally gave in to the rumbling in his stomach and went into the kitchen, where a plate of roast chicken and mashed potatoes waited for him in the oven.

Cain picked at the meal, put the dishes in the dishwasher, then headed down the hall to the guest room. He wanted Jenny with a deep, fierce urgency, but he wasn't ready to chance a repeat of what had happened to him at the Copper Star.

He figured Jenny would be asleep by now, but when he reached the end of the hall, a light burned under the door to his room. Maybe she had fallen asleep and forgotten to turn off the lamp.

Quietly, he opened the door, saw Jenny sitting up in bed reading. She'd been waiting for him. The knowledge tightened something in his chest.

"Cain," she said, tossing back the covers. Her bare feet hit the floor, and she walked toward him. She was wearing a short, white silk nightgown, the sheer lace bodice barely covering her high, full breasts. He could see the dark areolas at the crest, see the womanly shadow at the juncture of her thighs, and his body hardened.

"Are you okay?" she asked. "How is King doing?"

He forced himself not to move toward her. "He's having a rough time of it. Denver is spending the night in the barn, doing his best to reassure King that he's home and safe, but he's been badly mistreated. It's going to be an uphill battle."

She took a few more steps, rested her palms on his chest. "Cain, I'm so sorry."

"Get some sleep," he said, easing away from her. "I'll see you in the morning."

"I don't want you to go. I want you to stay here with me."

He wanted her tonight. Wanted the comfort of her body after such a difficult day, wanted the softness he knew he would find afterward when he held her.

His mind shot back to the sinister thoughts he'd had last night. "It's late," he said gruffly. "You need to get some sleep."

She moved closer, pressing herself against him, went up on her toes, and settled her mouth over his. Her arms went around his neck. Unable to stop himself, Cain kissed her back, his hands circling her waist to pull her even closer. The kiss turned rough and hungry, his mouth moving hotly over hers. God, he needed her tonight. Everything inside him craved her, craved the release she could give him, the gift of her sweetness wrapping around him.

But what if the lust he'd felt last night overcame him? What if he snapped and hurt her? Or worse?

Cain broke the kiss. Gently, he caught her wrists, dragged them away from the back of his neck, and eased her away.

"Not tonight," he said. "We'll talk about it in the morning."

Jenny's chin firmed. "Talking is the last thing we need to do." She slid her hand over the front of his jeans. He was thick and hard beneath the zipper. Cain hissed in a breath.

"I feel bad about what happened to your horse," Jenny said,

"but you're still a stallion, Cain. Don't tell me you don't want me. We both know it wouldn't be true."

"Jenny . . . honey, please. I'll make it up to you another time."

Her green eyes found his darker ones. "I know what's going on here. I know you're afraid of becoming the person you were in that room, but you aren't him, Cain. You're nothing like him, and I'm going to prove it."

Unzipping his jeans, she freed him. His eyes closed as he felt her small hand wrap around him, then the warm wetness of her mouth. It took every ounce of his will to stay in control, but somehow he managed.

He wanted to be inside her, needed to feel the snug, welcoming heat of her body. He couldn't resist any longer. Drawing her to her feet, he swept her up in his arms, carried her over to the bed, and settled her on the mattress.

He was hard as steel, aching with every heartbeat, but so far he hadn't turned into a raving lunatic. Vaguely, it occurred to him that the last thing he wanted to do was hurt her.

In minutes, he had stripped off his clothes and joined her on the bed. When he lifted her astride him, Jenny pulled the nightgown over her head and tossed it away, leaving her naked and making him harder still.

She had the prettiest dark-tipped breasts, full and tilted slightly upward. He cupped them, gently caressed them. When she leaned over to take him inside, her silky brown curls cocooned them. Jenny started to move, and Cain clamped down hard on his control.

He needed to make love to her gently, prove he wasn't the animal who had taken over his mind last night, but the faster she moved, the deeper she took him, the more she tested his will.

"I want you," she said, and Cain groaned.

Finding himself nearing the edge, he gripped her hips to hold her in place and drove himself deep, took her and took her until Jenny's head fell back, sending her curls tumbling around her shoulders, and she moaned.

Cain didn't stop, not even when she cried out in release, not until his own release burned through him. In seconds, he was hard again, aching for more. Rolling her beneath him, he drove her up again, pushing her to a second powerful climax, pushing himself to the very brink, then over.

For long seconds, they drifted, trapped in the sweet pleasure, enjoying the moments of pure contentment.

Time passed, and little by little, reality began to seep in, but the sense of peace remained. Cain lifted himself away and lay beside her, eased her into his arms. Jenny rested her head on his shoulder.

She ran the tip of her finger over his pecs down his abs and tilted her head back to look at him. "Are you okay?"

Cain smiled. "I didn't turn into a demon, so the answer is yes." He stroked a hand over her silky curls. "Thanks for what you did."

"It wasn't just for you. I wanted you. I did it for both of us."

It went unspoken that, in giving herself to him, she had shown him how deeply she trusted him. Cain kissed her temple. He thought of King and what the horse had suffered. He thought of the unknown enemy he had made and Nick Faraday's warning.

What if his enemy came after Jenny?

His chest clamped down. No one, he vowed, was going to hurt her.

No one.

It was early when Jenny returned with Cain to Jerome the next morning. Cain dropped her off at the Copper Star; then the Jag continued up Hill Street to the Grandview.

When Jenny walked into the lobby of the Star, ringing the bell above the door, Heather was checking out two hotel guests. While the husband loaded their luggage into the trunk of their compact SUV, Jenny noticed the wife, a saucy little blonde with short, spiky hair, writing something in the journal. Her husband honked, and she raced out the door toward the car.

"The woman who just left?" Heather said, drawing Jenny's attention. "They stayed in room nine last night. She told me she thought there was a ghost in the room. She said she was sitting at the table by the window when her hairbrush lifted off the dresser, flew across the room, and slammed into the wall. She said it barely missed hitting her in the head. You don't think it could be true, do you?"

Jenny hoped to God it wasn't. "I have no idea. Let's go up and take a look."

Heather grinned and nodded, more intrigued than afraid of spirits.

The bed in room 9 was unmade. Damp white towels sat in a pile on the bathroom floor. There was a soda-can ring on the nightstand, but the tops were covered with a plastic coating, so nothing sank into the wood. It looked the way rooms usually did when people checked out.

"Mrs. Grogen told me the hairbrush hit the wall," Heather said, surveying the interior. "But the room looks okay to me."

The room was done in shades of rose and cream, with pink-rose wallpaper behind the table near the four-poster bed. Jenny took a close look at the walls, but didn't see anything.

"This might be something," Heather said, pointing toward a spot next to the chair beside the table where the woman had been sitting.

Jenny moved closer. It was hard to see the spot in the pink-rose paper, but there was definitely an indentation. She ran her finger over the place where the plaster had been dented. Something had caused it, and from the fresh tear in the paper, it was recent.

Her stomach knotted. "Do we have guests in this room tonight?"

"I checked. Unless we get a call, there's no one coming in until next week."

"Okay, let's get it cleaned and leave it empty, at least for now."

"I'll take care of it."

Jenny nodded, distracted by the possibility there could be more trouble in the new wing of the hotel. Back downstairs, she checked in with the kitchen staff to make sure they didn't need anything before the saloon opened for the day, then walked out the front door.

She was on her way to the library to see if she could find something to validate Cleo's story about the miner who had been shot. Glancing up, she saw Dylan step onto the sidewalk in front of her.

"Hey, sis."

"Dylan!" She smiled as he bent and kissed her cheek.

"Last day off before I'm back on duty," he said. "I thought I'd come up and say hello."

"It's always great to see you."

"You, too. No more ghosts, I hope." He kept his tone light, but she had called him after the murder, so he knew something terrible had happened. He'd wanted to come up then, but she had told him the police were handling the investigation and there was nothing he could do.

"No more than usual," she said evasively.

"So nobody else is dead."

Jenny made no reply.

Dylan glanced up the hill. "How's your job at the Grandview working out?"

Jenny thought of Cain and the way he had made love to her last night at the ranch, with a desperate need and vulnerability that touched her as nothing he had done before.

"It's going great. I like my job. If you want to know whether I'm still seeing Cain, the answer is yes."

His lips thinned. "I can't tell you what to do. Just be careful."

She managed to smile. "The Grandview's almost finished. We're gearing up for the grand-opening party. Your invitation's in the mail."

Dylan just nodded. "I got the email." He was looking over her shoulder at something on the boardwalk and smiling. Jenny turned to see Summer walking out of the Butterfly Boutique, headed in their direction. A light breeze ruffled her long, pale-blond hair and the fringe on the knit shawl around her shoulders.

"We're, umm . . . going to lunch at the Haunted Hamburger," Dylan said.

One of Jenny's eyebrows went up. "How did that happen?"

"Summer called me. She told me she was invited to the grand-opening party at the Grandview. She figured I would be going and asked if I might be interested in the two of us going together."

"And you said yes?"

He shrugged his broad shoulders. "Why not? After she called, we started Face-Timing each other. I thought I'd stay here the night of the party and go back in the morning."

"That's great." Jenny knew how her friend felt about Dylan. "I'll book you a room." Her gaze shifted between Summer and her good-looking brother. "A double."

Summer walked up just then. "Hi, guys."

"Hey, Summer." Dylan bent and kissed her cheek. "You hungry?"

Summer smiled. "Starving."

"Me, too." He cast Jenny a glance. "We'll see you after lunch." Dylan took Summer's hand, and they headed across the street to the stairs leading up the hill to the restaurant on Clark Street. Summer looked back at Jenny and mouthed, *Talk later.*

Jenny waved, glad Summer had taken the initiative, proud of her brother for taking a chance. She hoped it worked out for the two of them.

CHAPTER TWENTY-SEVEN

INSTEAD OF HEADING UP TO THE LIBRARY, JENNY ROUNDED THE CORner and walked downhill, past the Liberty Theatre to Hull Avenue. In the old days, this area was part of the Tenderloin, the toughest section of town.

Both Hull and Queen, the street below, had been lined with saloons, bordellos, and cribs. There was even a set of stairs that led down from Main Street—Husband's Alley, it was called—a not-so-secret passageway for businessmen who wanted to spend the afternoon with a working girl.

Some of the old buildings remained, turned into souvenir shops, art galleries, and boutiques. Jenny wanted to see where the shooting—if it had actually happened—might have occurred. If Cleo were there, perhaps the woman could sense the exact spot the man had fallen.

Coming up empty, Jenny headed back up to Main, then on up the hill to the Jerome Public Library. The search through old newspapers was overwhelming. The *Jerome Chronicle,* 1895; the *Jerome Mining News,* 1897; the *Daily News* and the *Reporter,* 1898, and at least half a dozen others.

There had to be a better way.

Spotting the librarian, Evelyn Dunning, one of the town's most respected historians, Jenny went up to the front desk.

"Mrs. Dunning?" An attractive woman with silver-touched hair worn in a buzz cut, Evelyn wore tiny, round silver spectacles attached to a silver chain around her neck.

She looked up. "Yes?"

"I'm Jenny Spencer. I own the Copper Star. I was hoping you might be able to help me."

The woman smiled. "I'd be happy to. What do you need?"

"I'm trying to dig up information on a shooting that occurred way back in the mining heyday. I understand you're an expert on Jerome history."

"I'm interested in the history of the area. It's part of my job, but I'll admit it's also an obsession."

Jenny smiled. "After everything I've learned, I understand your fascination. I'm looking into the possibility of a shooting that might have occurred on the street in front of a bordello. I'm thinking it could have happened on Main Street, Hull, or Queen. Unfortunately, I don't know the time frame. I've been told the victim died and that he was a miner."

Evelyn laughed. "Well, that certainly narrows it down. There must be dozens of incidents that fit your description. Jerome was a notoriously lawless town."

"I know it isn't much to go on. I don't know the man's name or who shot him. I just thought something might pop into your head, something you've read or heard."

"You've checked old newspaper articles?" Evelyn asked.

"I spent a few hours at it, but there are so many papers, printed over so many years. I didn't even make a dent."

Evelyn nodded in understanding. "I can't think of anything offhand that might help, but give me a little time. There are indices available, ways to access information by subject matter. I might be able to narrow it down, even run across an article about the shooting."

"That would be wonderful. I don't have a business card, but I can write down my—"

Evelyn smiled. "If you own the Copper Star, I know where to find you. Should I run across something of interest, I'll get in touch."

"Thank you so much."

Jenny left the library feeling slightly better. Evelyn Dunning was clearly an expert. She prayed the woman would find what they needed.

Jenny sighed as she walked back down to the saloon. Unfortunately, even if they discovered the name of the miner and the circumstances of his death, she had no idea how to get rid of him. He was, after all, a ghost.

She imagined Cleo had already talked to Nell about it. Maybe if they all put their heads together, they could figure out what to do.

In the meantime, she would take Cleo's advice and stay out of room 10.

Cain spent the rest of the morning in the study in his suite. Problems had come up with the Titan acquisition. He should have stayed in Scottsdale, made certain everything was in order, remained there until the deal was officially closed.

Instead, his mind had been filled with Jenny, a distraction he couldn't afford. He'd driven back to Jerome, had a fit of jealous temper, which had never happened before, then fortunately managed to extricate himself from the mess he had made. He hadn't returned to Scottsdale, though he should have. Now problems had surfaced, and the closing had been postponed.

He checked his watch. He was meeting Nick Faraday in the bar. His detective friend had Cain's enemies list, but they hadn't discussed it. Cain shut down his computer and headed downstairs.

Nick was waiting when he arrived, sitting at the bar, a rocks glass in front of him.

When Hannah walked up behind the bar to take Cain's order, he simply pointed to Nick's drink. Knowing Cain drank Johnny Walker Black, she poured the drink and set it in front of him; then he and Nick carried their drinks over to a table in the corner.

"This place is really looking good," Nick said, surveying the interior, the wood paneling, the low lighting that illuminated the impressionist desert landscapes on the walls. "Looks like you'll be finished in time for the party."

"Unless disaster strikes. Which lately seems to be happening more and more." He took a drink of whiskey and enjoyed the relaxing burn. "You must have gotten your invitation. Will you be coming?"

Nick smiled. "Masks, women in sequined gowns, and guys in tuxedos. Wouldn't miss it." He tipped his head toward the bar. "I got an invitation, but Hannah filled me in. Should make for an interesting evening."

"The girls wanted to make a splash."

Nick raised a black eyebrow. "The girls?"

"Politically incorrect, I suppose. Millicent and Jenny. They figured, with Halloween so close, it should be something that tied in, but had a little more class. It's costing me a fortune. I hope they're right."

Nick grinned. "You can afford it, and the idea's intriguing enough that everyone on the guest list will be there."

"Need a room?"

"I thought I'd stay at the Copper Star, leave your fancy rooms for the people you're trying to impress."

Cain grunted. "Make sure you don't stay in room ten."

"That the murder room?"

"Yeah." He didn't say more. It was embarrassing to realize he believed Jenny's theory about a ghost being responsible for Brian Santana's death. But whatever he'd felt in that room had been murderous, at the very least.

Nick sipped his drink. "About your list . . ."

"What have you got so far?"

Nick pulled out a sheet of paper and began to read. "Roger Duffy, Alvin Cline, and Maryann Whelan, your former employees, all landed on their feet after you let them go. They're employed and making good money. That moves them down the list."

"Down but not off."

Nick shrugged. "We'll see." He glanced back at the information on the paper. "Barton Harwell, your old partner? Last known address is a boarding house in San Cristobal, Bolivia."

"Lithium. That's what they mine there."

"He moved out, but I haven't found out where he landed."

"Good bet he's still there somewhere, trying to strike it rich."

Nick nodded. "Decker, Rosen, and Steel, guys you used to run with when you were a kid?"

"Troublemakers. Thank God, I wised up before it was too late."

"Decker's in prison for attempted murder. Rosen has a rap sheet a mile long, but he's currently not wanted for anything. He's in the wind, which means he's still on the list."

"And Steel?"

Nick smiled. "Michael 'Butch' Steel is married, the father of two kids, a boy, six, and a girl, four. He's gainfully employed, a district manager for Ace Hardware. Sources say it's a happy marriage."

Cain grinned. "Good for Butch. I guess that takes him off our list."

"He's off—unless something changes."

"What's Ryder Vance up to these days?"

"His trial date's been postponed. He's out on bail and in the wind. That moves him up the list. The problem is, Sun King was already missing when you two butted heads."

"Butted heads. That's putting it mildly. At the time, I was trying to kill him. But that's just between you and me."

Nick sat back and took a sip of his drink. "It's a good thing you didn't succeed. You'd need an attorney a lot more than a detective."

"I still might if the bastard comes near Jenny again."

One of Nick's black eyebrows went up, but he made no comment. He looked back down at the paper.

"Ray Aldridge, the guy you beat out of a deal, lives in Phoenix. I went to see him. He's working a couple of new moly claims, still trying to hit the jackpot. Since he's making barely enough to survive, he's up at the top of the list."

Cain just nodded.

"Last but not least, your lady friends, women who might want revenge against you for dumping them."

"That was Jenny's idea. Frankly, I don't see any of them stealing a bunch of horses, then castrating the one that belongs to me."

"According to Shakespeare, hell hath no fury like a woman scorned."

"Actually, it was William Congreve, *The Mourning Bride.* I still don't buy it."

"Maybe not. I ran a background check on all of them, but didn't find anything to convince me any of them were involved. I also made some phone calls."

Cain sipped his drink.

"Rebecca Carter, the former assistant DA you dated for a couple of weeks, called you a few choice names, but the rest of them gave you at least a four-star review."

"Very funny. Rebecca and I had a slightly hostile parting. I didn't know she was separated from but still married to her husband, who occasionally showed up at her apartment—and he didn't sleep on the couch. I don't date married women, and I certainly don't share them with their spouses."

"How'd you find out?"

"Showed up unexpectedly one morning, and there he was. Rebecca was angry I hadn't called first. I wasn't too happy about it myself. We argued. That was the last time I saw her."

Nick just smiled. He glanced down at the paper. "I was surprised to see Anna Hobbs's name on your list. Somerset, I guess it is now. You dated her in high school, didn't you?"

"I wouldn't exactly call it dating. We had sex whenever she wanted a little excitement. That was it. I didn't see her again for years, until a few months back. I slept with her a couple of times in Scottsdale, but ended things after that. I wouldn't have written down her name, but she keeps showing up like a bad penny. That and the fact that her wealthy husband kicked the bucket shortly after their marriage. Makes you wonder how far she'd go to get back at someone."

"I'll give her another look, but on the surface, I didn't see anything."

"As I said, I don't think any of my exes are involved. Most women have a soft spot when it comes to animals. I'm sure that's a generalization, but that's been my experience."

Nick's gaze slid toward the door. "Speaking of women . . ." He rose as Jenny approached.

She smiled. "Hi, Nick."

Cain rose and pulled out one of the upholstered leather captain's chairs around the table. Jenny turned and gave him an intimate smile that instantly filled him with lust. "Cain . . ."

He tamped it down and brushed a kiss over her cheek as she took a seat. "What would you like to drink?"

"I have to work late. Club soda would be great."

He spoke to Hannah as she approached. "Club soda for Jenny."

"No problem." Hannah returned a few minutes later with a tall, iced glass and set it on the table. Jenny took a sip just as Cain's cell phone rang.

It was Martin Cohen, one of his VPs. Martin was frantic.

"I know you're busy, Cain. I really hate to bother you, but this deal is not going to happen without you. We need someone who can put the pressure on, convince these guys they have to stand by the agreement they made or else. We're meeting the top execs for a late supper at Flemings." A fine-dining steakhouse not far from the office. "Is there any chance you could make it?"

He wanted this deal, wanted it badly. Jenny would be working late at the Star, and it was past time he got over this ridiculous need to spend every minute with her. From the start, he had planned to enjoy her, enjoy the relationship, for as long as it lasted. He'd never intended to get in so deep.

"What time's the meeting?"

"Eight-thirty." It was a two-hour drive to Scottsdale. Cain checked his watch. It was six o'clock now. He could make it.

"Save me a seat at the table. I'll be there." Cain ended the call and rose from his chair. "I'm afraid something's come up. I've got a meeting in Scottsdale I can't afford to miss. I need to change, and then I'll be heading out." He looked at Nick. "Let me know if anything new turns up."

"Will do," Nick said, rising.

Jenny also rose.

"Ride up with me." Cain set a hand at her waist as they headed for his private elevator. "I won't be back tonight," he said, as the elevator door slid open and they walked inside. "Will you be staying in my suite?"

As the door slid closed, Jenny cut him a glance. "I'm not staying here without you, Cain. I'll be staying at the Star. I have to close up anyway. Will you be back tomorrow?"

"I'm not sure. I'll call you in the morning."

Jenny must have heard something in his voice. She looked as if she wanted to say something, but the elevator door opened, and he walked out into his entry.

Jenny followed him out, rested a hand on his cheek, leaned up, and kissed him. "Drive safely." Stepping back inside the carriage, she hit the button and closed the door.

Cain took a deep breath, missing her already. Chiding himself, he headed into his bedroom to change out of his jeans into a sport coat and dress pants. His feelings for Jenny were growing. They were interfering with his work. Jenny was becoming an obsession he couldn't afford.

He wasn't coming back tomorrow, he decided, or the rest of the week. It was past time he slowed things down, gave himself a chance to think.

He would come back for the party. By then, maybe he'd have his head on straight.

Maybe.

CHAPTER TWENTY-EIGHT

SATURDAY NIGHT AT THE COPPER STAR WAS A LITTLE MORE RAUCOUS than usual. A group was in town for an outdoor wedding the next day at the Surgeon's House, a popular venue. Many of the guests were staying at the Star, some at the Clinkscale or B&Bs in the area. The groom's bachelor party was being held in the saloon, a rowdy group of young guys doing tequila shooters and having fun. So far, they hadn't done any damage.

Summer dropped by early in the evening, excited to talk about her lunch with Dylan and their upcoming date for the grand-opening party.

"Your brother is amazing." Summer fanned herself and grinned. "He is just soo sexy. Plus he's smart, and he has a great sense of humor. I haven't laughed so much in . . . maybe never."

"He was like that when we were kids. After the breakup with his ex, he changed, became a lot more serious."

"He didn't say anything about her. If you hadn't told me, I never would have known."

"The engagement didn't last long. She wore the ring about three weeks before Dylan found out she was cheating on him while he was on duty."

"Fidelity in a relationship is crucial," Summer said. "I would never cheat on someone. It isn't fair to either party. I think Dylan feels the same."

Jenny thought of Cain. He had called after his dinner meeting to tell her wouldn't be back tomorrow. He'd be busy till the end of the week, but he promised to be back in time for the party.

"You don't think Cain would cheat, do you?" Summer asked, guessing the reason for her sudden quiet.

"His word is important to him. I don't think he would break it by cheating. More likely, he would simply end our relationship—if that's what it actually is."

Cain owned a huge corporation. He worked hard to make it successful. It was a miracle he'd been able to spend as much time in Jerome as he had. But she couldn't help thinking of Anna Hobbs and that Anna lived in Scottsdale. Anna wanted Cain, and the beautiful blonde was definitely a temptation.

"So Cain gave you his word he wouldn't cheat?"

"More like we made a mutual agreement to be monogamous as long as we're together."

"Well, I guess that's something."

"I guess." Only time would tell how long the relationship would last.

"But he's coming back for the party, right? You're his date for the evening?"

"That's the idea."

Summer grinned. "It's a formal affair. We need to go shopping. Tomorrow's Sunday. You're off, right? We'll drive down to Prescott. Lots of stores are open on Sunday in Prescott. We'll go to Dillard's. Oh, and I know this little boutique right next to the Palace Saloon on Whiskey Row. They have amazing clothes in there."

She did need something to wear. She wanted to look good for Cain. This was a special night for him, the opening of the hotel he'd worked on so hard. She wanted him to be proud to have her with him.

"Sunday works for me. It'll be late when we close tonight. Ten o'clock okay?"

"Ten o'clock is perfect." Summer rose from the table. "I'll meet you in the lobby in the morning."

Jenny kept the bar open until midnight, when the last few stragglers wandered out. Barb had worked the day shift and had already gone home. Jenny bartended through the evening; then she and Molly closed up. Molly headed home, and Jenny went upstairs.

She had only stayed in the suite a few times since the night Ryder Vance had attacked her. But Vance had been arrested, and though he was out on bail, she didn't think he would risk coming after her again.

At least she hoped not. And the chain locks were now on the doors.

Jenny opened the windows as she undressed, and the fresh air dissipated her tension. She yawned. She was tired after such a long night. Dragging on a cotton sleep-tee, she crawled into bed. She thought she might have trouble sleeping, but her tired body slipped into dreamland just minutes after her head hit the pillow.

The digital clock read 2:15 when her eyes slowly opened, her sleep disturbed by odd sounds in the room. Her heart jerked as she thought of Ryder Vance, and she bolted upright in bed. Her gaze shot to the door, but it was firmly locked, the chain in place, and there was no one in the bedroom.

Her heart rate slowed, then settled as she lay back down, and little by little, the drowsiness returned. She was just on the edge of sleep when she heard the clank of metal against metal. It took a moment for her to identify the sound as chains being dragged across the floor.

She shot back up and quickly scanned the room, but as before, nothing was there. She strained to hear the sound, which seemed to be coming from several different places. Then, as suddenly as it had begun, the rattle of chains disappeared, and quiet settled in.

Only a few seconds passed before new sounds began. The plinking notes of an old upright piano coming from the bar downstairs. She could hear what sounded like people laughing and talking. Sounds she remembered from before.

Jenny didn't bother to get out of bed. She had closed the bar. If she went downstairs, she would discover exactly what she had the last time—no one would be there.

She lay awake for a while, listening to the ghostly play of music and laughter from a time long past. The sounds soon disappeared, but Jenny kept listening. The clock read half an hour later when she finally gave in to the silence. Determined to get some badly needed rest, Jenny closed her eyes.

But she couldn't fall asleep.

As tired as she was the next morning, her Sunday shopping trip was a success. It was fun to spend the day with Summer, and the outing kept her mind off Cain.

In a weak moment on the way down the mountain, Jenny told Summer about the ghostly sounds in her room the night before.

"The last time I heard noises in the saloon, I went down to see what was going on, but there was no one there. No people, no piano playing, nothing. I've read a number of the old journals the hotel used to keep. In the old days, more than a few guests mentioned hearing the same sounds."

"You shouldn't be surprised. Jerome is full of ghosts. Everyone who lives here knows that."

Jenny sighed. "I guess so. It's just hard to believe until it happens to you."

They didn't talk about the murder, and Jenny didn't mention Cleo or what had happened to Cain in room 10. They were having a girls' day out, and problems had no place in it.

They went to the boutique first. The French Hen had unique, gorgeous clothes, lots of formal wear, long sequined dresses, jackets, pants, and skirts, and the prices were fairly reasonable.

Summer ended up with a long silver gown and matching short jacket. Jenny chose a floor-length, black-velvet dress with a narrow skirt split up one side. The square-cut bodice, trimmed with white satin, was low enough to show some cleavage, something she rarely did. She wondered what Cain would say. She hoped it would make his mouth water.

They had lunch at St. Michael's Bistro, not far from the boutique, a charming restaurant in a redbrick building with tin ceilings, old-fashioned wooden booths, and a beautiful dark-wood bar.

Afterward, they bought shoes and evening bags at Dillard's.

The day was fun but tiring. They got back to Jerome in time for Jenny to take a nap before she took over for Barb, who was subbing for Troy. Technically, Jenny was off on Sundays, but with Cain gone, it didn't really matter.

No sounds bothered her that night. In the morning, she headed up to the Grandview to help with final preparations for the party. Cain didn't call that day or the next.

She'd seen Nell only briefly, long enough to learn she had heard from her grandson, as Jenny hadn't. She told herself it was nothing to worry about. Nell left for a visit with a friend in Sedona, and Jenny hadn't seen her since.

Cain called on Wednesday, but they spoke only briefly. He called again on Friday to tell her he would pick her up at six on Saturday night for the party, a brief conversation, nothing personal, his tone strictly business.

He was busy, she knew. She hadn't realized how much she would miss him.

Or how obvious it would be that Cain did not miss her.

By Friday, after working with Millicent, Jake Fellows, Opal, Lydia Thompson, manager of the housekeeping staff, and others of Cain's employees, Jenny felt confident both hotel and staff were ready for the party.

"We'll be handing out the masks as the guests walk in," Millicent said. "There'll be a lovely selection to choose from. I think everyone will be pleased."

"I hope Cain doesn't see the bill," Jenny said. "The masks are beautiful, but they cost a fortune."

Millie just smiled. "They'll be nice mementos of the evening. We would have had to give people something. The masks work perfectly." Millicent tossed her a glance. "Have you picked yours out yet?"

"Not yet."

"Let's go do it right now."

Millicent led the way. Their unlikely friendship had continued, grown even stronger. Jenny thought it was based on mutual respect. They were both good at their jobs and proud of the work they had done to make the Grandview a success.

An array of masks was spread across a table in the bar. "What color is your dress?" Millie asked.

"It's black velvet, with a touch of white satin."

"Good choice. You can never go wrong with black." Millie sorted through the display. Some were full masks, but most were half masks designed to cover the top of the wearer's face. Millie plucked out a red-satin mask with tiny devil horns and held it up.

Jenny shook her head. "Reminds me of Dante's Inferno. Definitely not for me." Especially after what had happened in room 10.

Millie held up a gold Venetian butterfly mask.

"I don't know . . . it's not too bad," Jenny said.

"Wait! What about this?" Millie held up a black-sequined half mask with gleaming black feathers around the eyes. "Simple and elegant."

Jenny smiled. "I'll take it." Some of the masks had elastic bands to hold them in place; others had a wooden handle. Jenny picked up the handle, held the mask over her face, and looked at herself in a mirror over the bar. "I like it. What about yours?"

"I want to stand out," Millie said. "I deserve it after all the work I've done on this place."

Jenny nodded. "You're right. What color is your dress?"

"Teal-blue taffeta. Very short, low-cut front and back, and accented with sequins."

Jenny laughed. "That ought to stand out." She held up a mask. "How about this one?" Dark blue satin, with gorgeous waving peacock feathers. It was flashy, but it was beautiful.

"Perfect."

They laughed and wound up having a glass of wine at the bar. It was a good day. Work at the Grandview had gone well all week, and she'd had no more problems with ghostly sounds in her room. Still, she hadn't slept very well. She missed Cain, missed his big, powerful body curling her against him.

Part of her dreaded seeing him tomorrow night. She was afraid he was going to tell her it was over.

She would deal with it, of course. She was a strong woman. She'd dealt with other disappointments. But nothing that had happened in the past had broken her heart.

CHAPTER TWENTY-NINE

He'd made a mistake. Cain knew it as he drove too fast through the mountains, back up the hill to Jerome. He'd spent a week determined to get Jenny out of his system, give them both a break and himself time to think. It hadn't worked.

He'd thought of Jenny every day, every hour. And he'd worried about her. What if Ryder showed up? What if something else happened in the new section of the hotel? He'd asked Barb to let him know if any problems came up, but if they did, he was too far away to help.

Ten times a day, he'd almost picked up the phone on his desk to call or punched her number into his cell phone. But he had made a promise to himself, and he was determined to keep it.

He needed to clear his head, think things through. He had done the best he could, but his plans were still unclear. In the week since he'd left Jerome, all he'd discovered was that he was hooked on Jenny and hooked badly. He was seeing her tonight, and he was going to let her know how much she meant to him, how much he cared.

He had no idea where things would go from there, but admitting that much was a start.

As he passed the city-limits sign, he wanted to drive the Jag straight to the Copper Star. But even more, he wanted the night to be special for Jenny. He headed for the Grandview, parked in back, and took the elevator up to his suite.

His tuxedo waited in a plastic bag spread over the bed, messengered up earlier that week. He showered and dressed, checked his appearance in the mirror, then the time on his watch. It was a little too early to pick her up, so he contented himself with a scotch on the rocks at the bar in his living room.

When it was finally time to leave, he opened the door to the refrigerator under the bar and took out the white-orchid corsage he'd had delivered to the hotel.

Cain left the suite and headed back to the Jag. He was eager to see his woman. And he was nervous, he realized. Not like him.

There wasn't a parking place in front of the Copper Star. He circled around until he found one, then walked back to the hotel lobby to wait. He had texted Jenny earlier, told her he would be there at six-thirty to pick her up.

Officially, the party started at seven, though most of the out-of-town guests had arrived early to check into their rooms. Cain wanted to be there to greet them when they appeared at the door of the Grand Vista Salon. And he wanted Jenny beside him.

Waiting at the foot of the stairs in the lobby, he glanced at his watch. 6:30. Jenny was always prompt. At 6:35, he began to fidget, shooting the cuffs of his pleated white shirt, straightening his black bow tie. By 6:40, he was ready to go up and beat on her door, but a sound caught his attention, and he looked up to see her coming down the stairs.

His chest clamped down. She looked so beautiful his mouth dried up. The long black-velvet gown couldn't have been a better showcase for Jenny's sexy curves. He caught a glimpse of shapely legs in a pair of strappy high heels as she descended the stairs and felt a primal shot of lust he barely managed to contain.

She had swept her glorious golden-brown curls up on one side and held them in place with a rhinestone clip that matched the long rhinestone earrings dangling from her ears.

Cain had to remind himself to breathe.

When she reached the last step, he moved toward her, allowed his gaze to drift over the soft mounds above the neckline of her gown.

He bent and kissed her cheek. "Saying you look beautiful isn't nearly enough."

She gave him a tentative smile. "Thank you. You look very handsome yourself." There was something in her eyes. He wasn't sure exactly, uncertainty maybe, and something more.

He took her hand and pressed it against his lips. "I made a mistake," he said. "I was going to wait until later, but I need to say it now."

Her face went pale. Keeping her hand in his, Cain led her over to the velvet settee in the lobby, and Jenny sat down. "This thing between us—"

"Wait! Please, Cain . . ." She pulled her hand from his, and it went to the base of her throat. She looked up at him, and her eyes filled. "If you do this now, I won't be able to make it through the evening. Please, Cain, please wait till later."

His chest tightened. "Honey, what's wrong?"

"I know you wouldn't cheat. You said you would tell me when things were over. When you didn't call, I knew, but just for tonight—"

"My God." He hauled her up and into his arms, his throat tight as he held her. "You don't understand. I wanted to tell you how much I missed you. What a mistake I made in leaving. I'm crazy about you, baby."

Jenny clung to him. He could feel her trembling. "Cain . . ."

He realized he had dropped the corsage box onto the floor at his feet. Flowers weren't enough. He needed jewelry, something beautiful to go with her dress. A ring, he thought and immediately blocked the notion.

He eased her away from him, saw a tear rolling down her cheek. He felt unsteady as he whisked it away with the tip of his finger. "Sweetheart, I'm so sorry. I wanted . . . needed some time to sort things out. Please forgive me for being a fool."

When Jenny said nothing, he bent and brushed her cheek with a kiss. "I missed you. So much."

Jenny's features softened. She managed a wobbly smile. "You did?"

"Yes."

"I'm really glad you're back."

Cain drew her closer. "I thought of you every day."

She smiled up at him. "I thought of you, too." Her fingertips smoothed over the satin lapel of his jacket. "Every woman in the place will be jealous of me tonight."

Cain smiled. "Every guy in the place is going to wish he were the man taking you home with him." He tipped up her chin. "I have to do this. You'll just have to fix your lipstick later." And then he kissed her.

He'd meant it to be gentle, a sweet way to apologize and show her how much he cared. But the minute her lips softened under his, heat exploded inside him.

Cain deepened the kiss, taking what he had missed so badly. When Jenny clutched his shoulders and kissed him back, it took every ounce of his will to pull away.

He inhaled a steadying breath and slowly released it. "As much as I wish I could just skip all this and haul you upstairs to my bed, we have a party to attend."

Jenny's smile reached all the way to her beautiful green eyes. "I believe we do."

Cain picked the corsage box up off the floor and took out the ruffled white orchid. "I know this is old-fashioned, but I wanted to bring you something pretty."

Jenny smiled. "It's beautiful."

Cain pinned the flower on her shoulder. "Ready?"

Jenny smiled and took his arm.

After a brief ride up the hill in Cain's Jag, Jenny walked next to him into the Grandview, down the hall into the Grand Vista Salon. The room was large, but they weren't using all of the available space. The party was intended for a very select crowd. Forty or fifty couples, no more than a hundred people.

Millie had suggested minimal decorations, and Jenny agreed. With its dark wood paneling and art deco chandeliers and wall sconces, the room was lovely on its own, and the idea was to feature the elegant hotel itself.

Jenny picked up the black, feathered mask that had been set aside for her and held it up, covering the top half of her face as she looked at Cain.

"You are a true temptation," Cain said. "I don't know how I'm going to make it through the evening without dragging you into a closet somewhere."

Jenny laughed and ignored a little curl of lust at the thought.

Cain chose a black-and-silver mask in the style of *The Phantom of the Opera.* When he put it on, covering half his handsome face, Jenny's knees felt weak.

She turned to survey the room. In sky-high, teal-blue satin heels that matched her dress, Millicent walked toward them across the room, a handsome man with a touch of gray in his hair at her side.

"Everything seems to be in order," she said. Peacock feathers waved from the mask in her hand. "Cain Barrett and Jenny Spencer, I'd like you to meet Mark Ellison. Mark is CEO of Ellison-Price Manufacturing."

"Mark." Cain pulled off his mask and extended a hand, which the man shook.

Millie smiled. "We have a good deal of Ellison-Price furniture in the hotel."

"I thought I'd seen the name," Cain said.

"Good to meet you," Mark said. He turned. "Ms. Spencer."

"Jenny." Smiling, she shook his hand.

They made small talk. Jenny could see the interest in Millie's face as she looked at her date, a look returned twofold by her handsome escort. Inwardly smiling, Jenny excused herself to check on the setup of the bars at both ends of the salon. It wasn't really her job, yet she felt a strong sense of duty when it came to the success of the Grandview, and especially the party tonight.

The bartenders wore tuxedos, as did all of the servers. Since the party would be more lively if the guests kept moving and talking, there were linen-draped high-tables scattered around, along with a few regular tables for older people.

Long, black, plumed feathers mixed with brilliant purple waved from silver vases in the center of the tables. Elegant and simple, the opulent purple provided color for the affair, adding to the gala mood created by the masks.

Satisfied that everything was running smoothly, Jenny returned to Cain's side as guests continued to arrive.

"You did a great job, Millicent," Cain said, using the name she preferred. "Everything looks perfect."

Millicent smiled, clearly pleased.

"Now, if you'll both excuse us, I believe we're needed at the door." Cain took Jenny's hand, and they headed for the entry.

Having studied the guest list, Cain personally greeted each person as they arrived. Then partygoers chose one of the beautiful handmade masks from the display on the table. Feathers, sequins, velvet, and satin shimmered. Servers circulated the room, silver trays sparkling with stemmed glasses of Veuve Clicquot champagne.

Others carried trays of hors d'oeuvres: cold paté, potato napoleons with caviar, smoked salmon on cucumbers, and various other canapés. A light buffet was being served featuring small plates, easy-to-eat items like antipasti, oysters, shrimp, chicken, and filet mignon kabobs.

Fruit tarts and profiteroles were among a variety of small desserts. The Scottsdale caterer, with Opal's assistance, had done a magnificent job.

Most of the guests had arrived by the time Cain's grandmother showed up at the door. Emma left the wheelchair in the hallway, and Nell, with the use of her cane, walked proudly into the salon. Cleo walked with a swaying motion into the room beside them.

Upon seeing the women, Jenny's pasted-on smile turned sincere. "I'm so glad you all could make it."

Nell wore a navy-blue dinner suit with a long skirt and beaded navy jacket. Emma kept it simple with a knee-length black suit piped with satin, and a string of pearls.

Cain leaned down and brushed a kiss on Nell's cheek, did the same to Emma, then turned to the big, heavyset woman beside them.

"Well, look who's here," he drawled, eyeing Cleo with what appeared to be speculation.

"Cleo's a friend," Jenny defended. As large as she was, in her flashy fuchsia skirt and flowing-silver sequined top, she stood out among the sophisticated crowd. "Of course, she was invited."

Cain just smiled. "Cleopatra," he said and surprised Jenny by leaning down to brush a kiss on the older woman's powdered cheek. "Welcome to the Grand Vista Salon."

Cleo grinned. "You handsome devil. You haven't changed a bit. Still charming the women the way you did when you were a boy. You're just better at it now."

Cain laughed. He waited for each of the women to choose a mask, then ushered them to the table he had reserved for Nell and her friends. He stopped a passing server. "The ladies will have champagne."

The lanky young man took three crystal flutes filled with golden liquid and set them on the table.

"Jason, isn't it?" Cain asked.

"Yes, sir, Mr. Barrett."

"I'll expect you to personally take care of this table, Jason. See that these ladies have everything they need. Food, drinks, whatever it might be."

"Yes, sir."

Cain spoke to Nell. "Jenny and I need to mingle." He smiled at the group of women. "Enjoy yourselves." Taking Jenny's arm, he led her through the crowd, pausing here and there to renew old friendships and make new ones.

An hour slipped past.

Dylan and Summer arrived, Summer looking like a beautiful angel in her silver gown, Dylan in a rented tuxedo that fit his lean, broad-shouldered frame as if it had been perfectly tailored for him.

Her brother leaned down and kissed her cheek. "You look beautiful, sis."

Jenny smiled. "You both look incredible. I hope you have a good time."

They looked at each other as if the answer was a given, and behind her back, Jenny crossed her fingers, hoping it would work out for them.

Nick Faraday showed up with a flashy redhead. He looked great in a tux, and his date was gorgeous.

A few more minutes passed. "I need to visit the ladies' room," Jenny said to Cain. "I'll be right back."

Cain just nodded as Jenny slipped away. By the time she returned, he had drifted a little farther into the salon. Jenny froze when she recognized the woman he was talking to.

Anna Hobbs Somerset. In a full-length, gold-lamé designer gown that made her blond hair seem to glow, she looked gorgeous. It was a slip dress, the thin material held up by two narrow gold straps, the shiny fabric draping so low in front it barely covered her pale breasts.

Jenny had gone over the guest list with both Millie and Cain. Anna wasn't on it.

Should she disappear back into the ladies' room before they spotted her, or join them and stake her claim? Or should she simply wait for Cain's next move?

The question was resolved when a good-looking, silver-haired man appeared at Anna's side. Her date, Jenny presumed, when he set a hand at Anna's waist.

With a rush of relief, Jenny pasted her smile back on, walked up to Cain, and rested her hand possessively on the sleeve of his black tuxedo.

"I don't believe we've met," she said, a little too sweetly, as she studied the couple. She didn't have to worry that Anna might remember her. They had never been introduced, and in high school Jenny had been too far down the pecking order for Anna to notice.

Cain introduced them. "Jenny, this is Lucien Rossi, president of Overland Industries, and this is his companion, Anna Somerset."

"A pleasure." The silver-haired man made a polite inclination of his head. He was tall and lean, with Italian features and a suntan. Maybe he played a lot of golf.

Anna's gaze swept over Jenny as if she should have been one of the servers instead of Cain's date. "Jenny."

Jenny kept the smile glued to her face. "Anna."

"Overland produces different types of bulk-handling equipment used in mining," Cain explained.

Lucien smiled. "That's right. Word is Barrett Enterprises may be expanding. Perhaps I should have my people get in touch with yours."

Cain nodded. "We'll make it happen." Jenny felt Cain's hand on her bare back as he guided her away from Anna, and she breathed a sigh of relief.

"I swear I had no idea Lucien would be bringing her," Cain said, leading her to a spot away from the crowd.

"I remember seeing his name on the guest list. There's no way you could have known Anna would be his date."

"She's a conniving little witch. I don't trust her not to cause trouble."

"Tonight?"

"She's already caused trouble tonight just by showing up. I hope this is the end of it."

"But you aren't sure."

"No."

Determined to enjoy herself, Jenny was grateful Cain steered clear of Anna and her date for the rest of the evening.

They stopped by Nell's table a couple of times. The women didn't stay late, but from the sound of their laughter, they were having a good time.

"We need to talk," Cleo said to Jenny as she and the others prepared to leave. "Call me as soon as you can."

"I'll call you tomorrow." She watched Cleo make her way to the door and wished she'd had more success tracking down information on the spirit that haunted room 10. Maybe Evelyn Dunning would find something.

She felt Cain's dark eyes on her and glanced up into his handsome face.

"I think we've accomplished what we set out to do here." He smiled, and the gold in his eyes glittered. "I've got something else to accomplish tonight, and I'm more than ready to get started."

Desire slipped through her. Cain's urgency was contagious as he guided her out of the salon to his private elevator. The minute the door slid open in his entry, she was in his arms. His hungry kiss left no doubt of what he planned to accomplish before morning.

Jenny was all in.

CHAPTER THIRTY

After the long evening and several satisfying rounds of sex, they slept late the next day. Cain awakened to the feel of silky curls and soft kisses trailing over his chest. With a groan, he gave in to the heat building between them.

They made love, dozed again, then finally roused themselves enough to realize both of them were starving. With the hotel fully booked, room service was going to take a while, so Cain made coffee in the pot he kept behind the bar, and they relaxed in front of the windows overlooking the valley while they waited for their food to arrive.

"You're off today," Cain said. "I thought we'd ride up to the ranch, spend the night, and come back in the morning."

Jenny took a sip of the rich, dark French roast. "I probably shouldn't."

Cain smiled. "I'll take that as a yes."

One of Jenny's eyebrows went up. "Do we get to go riding?"

Cain laughed. "I don't see why not."

"Okay, then."

By afternoon, they were unpacked and settled in his bedroom at the ranch. With the hands off on Sundays, it was Denver's weekend on duty.

"How's Sun King doing?" Cain asked him.

"We're making progress," Denver said. "But it's slow. Sanchez and I are both working with him, trying to regain his trust, but we've had to start completely over. Rotten sonsabitches ought to be castrated themselves."

Cain's jaw hardened. Every time he thought of what had happened to his stallion, he felt a nearly uncontrollable rage. He wasn't sure what he'd do if he ever got his hands on the men responsible.

It didn't take long to saddle the horses. He hadn't told Jenny, but he'd been carrying a little .380 semiautomatic since the day Sun King had been returned, and he had accepted the fact that someone had a personal vendetta against him.

Cain went inside the house and took a .30-30 Winchester lever-action out of the gun safe, then went back to the barn. They'd be out in the open today. It never hurt to be careful.

Cain shoved the rifle into the saddle scabbard and swung up onto Gladiator, while Jenny mounted Rosebud. Leaving the barn behind, they rode up the trail, into the rolling desert hills, disappearing over the rise behind the ranch house and out of sight.

At the bottom of the hill, Cain pulled the big red roan to a halt beneath a cottonwood tree next to a shallow stream that crossed the property.

"We'll ride a little more after we eat." Reaching up, he lifted Jenny down. It was Maria's day off, so Jenny had poked around in the kitchen and found cheese and crackers, apples, salami, and a bottle of good Chablis. He handed her the bundle that he'd packed in his saddlebag, then walked over and hobbled the roan near the stream.

He was grabbing a second pair of hobbles out of the saddlebag for Jenny's palomino just as the crack of a rifle echoed across the desert landscape. Rosebud shrieked and bolted, and Cain felt the impact of a bullet slamming into his chest.

"Get down!" He stayed on his feet long enough to pull Jenny behind the cottonwood, where both of them crouched on the ground.

He could feel the blood dripping down his arm, soaking into the sleeve of the shirt beneath his jacket, running over the tattoo on his arm, down the back of his hand.

"Oh, my God, you're shot!" Horrified, Jenny reached for him. "Where . . . where are you hit?"

"Bullet's in my upper-left shoulder."

Another shot rang out, the lead ball slamming into the trunk of the tree a foot above their heads. Jenny dragged off the wool scarf she had tied around her neck for warmth while Cain dug out his cell phone. "No service."

"Press this against the wound," Jenny said, handing him the scarf. "Maybe we can slow the bleeding."

Cain stuffed the scarf into the bullet hole, then zipped up his jacket to help hold it in place.

He pulled the little handgun out of the pocket of his jeans. "Can you shoot?"

"My dad taught me, but—"

He shoved the gun into Jenny's hand. "This won't reach far enough to do much good, but we can use it as a diversion. I need to get to the rifle."

"Yes, but—"

"I'll count to three, and you start firing."

Jenny shoved the pistol back into his hand. "You fire. I'll get the gun. The less you move, the less you bleed."

He didn't like it. Not one bit. But he was already feeling lightheaded. Jenny was right. If he passed out, their attacker could kill them both.

Cain nodded. "Don't run in a straight line." Damn, he hated putting her in even more danger. But they had no other choice. "You ready?"

"I'm ready."

"On three. One, two, three." He started firing in the direction the shots had come from, while Jenny raced in quick-turning movements toward the roan. Wild-eyed, the big horse reared and nickered, but didn't try to run. More gunfire erupted as Jenny slid the rifle out of the scabbard and ran a zigzag pattern back to where they crouched behind the trunk of the tree.

Blood still pumped from the wound. Cain could feel the wetness oozing down his chest and arm. He was lightheaded and dizzy, losing too much blood. He took the rifle and gave Jenny the handgun. He moved a little, lay flat on his belly, and propped the rifle on a chunk of rock next to the tree.

"Fire off a couple of rounds," he said.

Jenny aimed the pistol and fired. Once, twice. A rifle shot cracked in return. Cain adjusted the barrel of the rifle, sighted, and fired toward the sound.

Return fire told him he was close. He shifted and fired, got more return fire, shifted again, caught a flash of movement and fired.

Silence followed. He was pretty sure he had hit the bastard. He had no idea if the guy was wounded or dead, but he couldn't take the chance the man was still out there, waiting for them to move. He kept the rifle aimed toward the spot where he had last seen the attacker, blinking to keep his eyes open and focused.

"Someone's coming," Jenny said.

"Where?"

"Down the trail." Her eyes brightened. "It's Denver!" She rose a little and waved.

Cowboy hat pulled low, Denver rode full tilt in their direction, rifle in hand, sliding Jenny's palomino to a halt in front of the tree, dismounting and hurrying to join them.

"Rosebud came back with an empty saddle," Denver explained. "I figured you might be in trouble. Didn't have time to saddle another horse, just took off as fast as I could. I heard gunshots as I neared the rise. When I started down the hill, I spotted a guy on a dirt bike hauling ass across the desert toward the road."

"You think he's gone?" Cain asked.

"I didn't see anyone else." Denver looked down at Cain and saw his shirt and sleeve soaked in blood, more running over his hand. "Jesus, you've been hit."

"We need an ambulance," Jenny said in a shaky voice. "But there's no cell service out here."

"I'll ride back up the hill and call 911. Tell them to send a medevac chopper." He looked at Cain. "You gonna be okay till it gets here?"

"I'm too stubborn to let that bastard kill me." But his vision was beginning to darken around the edges. He took a last look at Jenny, then his eyes drifted closed, and he slipped into blackness.

"Put pressure on the wound," Denver said. "I'll be right back." Denver grabbed the saddle horn and swung up on Rosebud, then urged the palomino into a run.

Jenny rolled Cain onto his back. Forcing down her panic and fear, she unzipped his jacket and swallowed against the sight of the blood on his chest. Leaning over him, she pressed her hands hard on the scarf covering the bullet hole. Silently, she began to pray, asking God to help Cain. She looked up to see Denver riding hell-for-leather back toward them.

He pulled the palomino to a halt. "Medics are on the way. Hospital's only thirty miles from here. Shouldn't take a chopper long to get here." He looked down to where Jenny was keeping pressure on Cain's bloody wound. "How's he doing?"

Jenny fought back tears. "He's lost a lot of blood. I hope they get here soon."

"I'll ride back up on the ridge and watch for them, make sure they know where we are. Ground's flat all along the bottom of the hill. They shouldn't have a problem landing."

"Be careful, Denver. We don't know for sure whoever it was isn't still out there."

Denver nodded. He spun and gigged the horse, took off at a gallop for the ridge.

"You're going to be okay," Jenny said. Tears returned to her eyes and began to roll down her cheeks. "Just hold on." She wished she could rest his head in her lap, let him know she was there, but she didn't want to move him, and she had to keep the pressure on.

It seemed like hours until she heard the *whop whop whop* of a helicopter overhead. The chopper began to descend, blowing up dust and debris; then the skids settled on the ground, and the engine went silent. As the doors slid open, two EMTs in black uniforms, one young and brawny, the other older, tall, and slender, jumped out carrying a stretcher.

Ducking the blades, they hurried over to where Cain lay next to the tree.

"Thank God, you're here," Jenny said. "It looks really bad, and he's lost a lot of blood."

"He's in good hands now," the older man said.

While she and Denver looked on, the men worked over Cain's body, checking his vitals, cleaning and packing the wound, administering an antibiotic, preparing him for the short ride back to the hospital.

All the while, Jenny watched, feeling useless and sick inside.

"You want to come along?" the younger of the techs asked as they made final adjustments, securing Cain to the stretcher.

"Yes. Absolutely. Thank you."

"I'll call the hands and Maria," Denver said. "Let them know what's going on."

"I'll let Cain know what's happening as soon as he wakes up." She refused to consider the possibility that he wouldn't.

Following the two men, she waited while they loaded Cain into the chopper, then climbed aboard and settled herself beside him. Then the pilot was lifting the chopper away, swooping into the air, veering off toward the hospital in Prescott.

Jenny bent over Cain and pressed a soft kiss on his lips. She didn't want to believe she was in love with him. But the tears in her eyes, the way her heart was aching, the way her insides trembled with fear for him, she couldn't fool herself any longer.

She prayed that he would be all right and clung to his hand as the chopper flew toward town.

CHAPTER THIRTY-ONE

Cain awoke slowly, dragging himself from the depths of a heavy, drugging sleep. His eyes felt gritty, his mouth dry. He wasn't sure what time it was, but the curtains were drawn, and it was dark in the room. The sound of beeping drew his groggy attention to the monitor hooked up to a stand beside the bed. There was an IV in his arm, a bag of fluid dripping clear liquid into his veins.

Little by little, memories returned—riding Gladiator over the ridge, getting ready for a picnic by the stream, the echo of gunshots. The pain and the blood.

The bastard who had shot him.

He turned his head a little, saw Jenny curled up asleep in a chair next to the bed, her head propped against her shoulder. She looked uncomfortable and exhausted, and the knowledge she was there tightened something in his chest.

Eased by her presence, he closed his eyes and drifted back to sleep.

Night turned into morning; the hours slipped past and it was noon. Jenny sat with Nell and Emma in a waiting room down the hall from Cain's hospital room. There was a row of vinyl-cushioned chairs along the wall, more placed back-to-back in the middle of the room. Sunlight streamed in through the window.

After the shooting, Cain had been flown to the Yavapai Regional Medical Center in Prescott and taken directly into surgery. Doctors had dealt with his loss of blood, torn ligaments, and tendons, removed the bullet, and stitched up the wound.

Emma had driven Nell down yesterday as soon as Jenny had called to tell her about the shooting. After the doctors had assured her that Cain was going to be all right, she had gone home for the night, but came back early this morning. According to Emma, nothing could dissuade her.

Jenny thought of the mother she had barely known. It was good Cain understood how lucky he was.

At the Copper Star, Jenny had relied on Troy, Barb, Heather, and the rest of her employees to take care of things while she was gone. The Cross Bar ranch hands had all shown up at the hospital, including Maria. The men stayed in shifts, one of them outside Cain's door at all times.

Someone had tried to kill their boss, who was also a friend. The men were there to protect him until he could protect himself.

Jenny checked the time on her phone. Currently, hospital staff were finishing the paperwork needed to release Cain.

"They'd better hurry this along," Nell grumbled. "Cain'll be chomping at the bit to get out of here."

"I doubt he likes hospitals any better than the rest of us," Jenny said.

"He spent some time in 'em off and on. Got beat up pretty good when he was a kid. He was runnin' with a bad bunch. Found trouble one night with another bad bunch. Took four of them to take him down. Cain spent three days in the hospital that time. Turned out to be a good lesson."

"I knew he had problems when he was a teen." Jenny glanced toward the door, hoping the nurse walking down the hall was coming to tell them Cain was ready to leave, but the nurse kept walking, heading farther down the corridor.

"What about the scars on his hands?" Jenny asked. "Those are burn scars, aren't they? How did it happen?"

"He never talks about it," Nell said. "Happened in a mine he was workin'. There was an explosion, then a fire. One of the miners got pinned beneath some heavy timber. The other men took off and left him, but Cain stayed behind. Boy's strong as a bull. He managed to free the man before the fire swept over them, but his hands got badly burned. My boy was a hero."

Jenny's throat tightened. The more she learned about Cain, the more she was drawn to him. It worried her. Getting more deeply involved was the last thing she wanted.

"After the way he protected me, I'm not surprised. I'm glad you told me. What about the tattoo on his arm?"

One of Nell's silver eyebrows went up. "The skull wearing a hard hat? He was just young and dumb."

Jenny laughed.

Another hour passed before the nurse finally came in to tell them Cain was ready to leave. Jenny headed down the hall, while Emma pushed Nell in her wheelchair.

When Jenny shoved open the door, Cain was getting dressed. Apparently, the nurse had helped him into the gray sweatpants that Denver had brought, but he was naked from the waist up.

Her pulse thrummed. He had the most incredible body, his arms and chest heavily muscled, his waist narrow and flat. She had never liked muscle jocks, but there was something about a man who had earned all those sexy muscles by doing actual hard work.

She grabbed the matching gray sweatshirt off the bed and handed it over. "Looks like you're ready to go. How does your shoulder feel?"

"Like a cannon ball tore through it, but I'll live." His left shoulder was covered with a thick white bandage, his arm in a sling. The doctor had said Cain had been lucky in a way. The path the bullet had torn had missed most of the major muscles and tendons.

"Sanchez is in the hall," Jenny said. "Your men have been staying outside the door in shifts. They're probably armed, even if they aren't supposed to be."

He nodded. "They're good men."

"And good friends. They were worried about you."

Nell made a disgruntled sound in her throat. "Who'd you piss off bad enough to try killing you?" she asked.

Cain clenched his jaw. "I wish I knew." He bent and brushed a kiss over Nell's cheek. "You can bet I'm going to find out. In the meantime, I don't want you to worry, I'll be fine." He smiled. "Why don't we get out of this place and go home?"

"Good idea," Nell said. "You goin' to the ranch or back to Jerome?"

He glanced at Jenny.

"I have to get back to work," she said. "Tomorrow night's Halloween, one of the busiest nights of the year." She wished she could stay with Cain at the ranch, make sure he was okay, but she was determined to make the Star a success, and she had a responsibility to the people who worked there.

Cain's dark eyes locked with hers. "I'll be going back to Jerome."

A look passed between them. He was going back for her. He was worried about her. Jenny felt a pinch in her heart.

"Emma, can you give us a lift?" Cain asked.

"Of course. I'll go get the car and pick you up out front."

The door to the room opened, and Cain's nurse, a short, buxom woman dressed in green scrubs, walked in, pushing a wheelchair. "Take a seat," she said.

"It's my shoulder, not my legs," he grumbled. "I can walk just fine."

"Standard procedure." The nurse cast him a warning glance. "Get in or you don't leave."

Jenny bit back a smile as Cain muttered something no one could hear and settled himself in the chair. The nurse pushed him out into the hall, where he stopped to thank Sanchez, who was sitting on a bench near the door.

"I want you to know how much I appreciate the way you and the other guys looked out for me. Tell them that, and tell them I plan to find the a-hole who shot me and make him pay."

Sanchez just nodded. "We are *amígos*. Friends take care of each other."

Cain squeezed the older man's shoulder. "Tell the boys to be careful out there. This bastard is dangerous, and we don't have a clue who he is."

They left the hospital and headed through town, back up the curvy road to Jerome. Jenny got out of the car at the Copper Star.

"I'll be right back," Cain told Emma as he followed Jenny out of the vehicle.

Jenny stopped and turned. "You need to relax, let yourself heal," she reminded him.

Cain ignored her. "I'm putting someone on you until this is over."

"What? A bodyguard? I don't need a bodyguard. They're after you, not me."

"And a good way to get to me is through you."

"I don't need—"

He leaned down and kissed her, lingered, went a little deeper. "I'm overruling you on this. I need to make some calls, then I'll be back. I'll stay with you until he gets here."

She could still feel his mouth on hers, the possessive way he'd kissed her. Jenny just nodded. "Okay . . . if you think it's necessary."

"I hope it isn't, but I'm not taking any chances."

He kissed her one last time, then climbed back into the car, and Emma drove off toward the Grandview.

Jenny thought of Cain and how close he had come to being killed. As she crossed the saloon to where Troy stood behind the bar, she said a silent prayer for Cain's safety.

The first call Cain made went to Nick Faraday. He told Faraday about the attack at the ranch and that the shooter had escaped on a mountain bike.

"You sure there was only one of them?" Nick asked.

"That's the only one Denver spotted. Doesn't mean they didn't split up and scatter, but the shots all seemed to come from the same direction. One rifle, I'd say. I think I hit the bastard, but he still managed to get away."

"I'll check the hospitals in the area, see if there were any reported gunshot wounds. You talk to the sheriff?"

Cain leaned back in the chair behind the desk in his study. "Denver called him, gave him a report. I haven't talked to him yet. Just got out of the hospital." And his shoulder hurt like a bitch. "I figure he'll show up in Jerome sooner or later. But I don't have much faith in the guy."

"Maybe he'll surprise you."

"Maybe," Cain said. "I need to hire a bodyguard."

"Good idea."

"Not for me—for Jenny. I'm not completely up to speed, and I don't want to leave her unprotected. You know anyone local?"

"I work with a guy named Will Price. He's a vet, stays in shape. He's done this kind of work before. Will lives in Scottsdale. I'll call him, see if he's available."

"If he is, send him up. He can stay at the hotel when I don't need him."

"I'll text to let you know."

"Making any progress on Sun King?" Cain asked.

"I've narrowed down your list. Your old buddy Tank Rosen was busted two weeks ago in California for armed robbery. He's cooling his jets in the San José County jail."

"So he can't be our shooter."

"No. Turns out he's been living in California for the past five years. Has a girlfriend, a life of sorts. I talked to the girl. Said they needed money, so he robbed a Fast Trip convenience store. Cutting the balls off your horse wouldn't have solved the problem."

"Which means he's likely not our horse thief, either."

"Doesn't sound like it. But after the shooting, Ryder Vance has moved up the list. Could have been Vance who shot you. Might not have had anything to do with stealing your horse and everything to do with your woman."

Cain thought of Ryder's attack on Jenny. The guy was exactly the sort who would want revenge. "I wouldn't put it past him, but a dirt bike isn't a Harley."

"A bike's a bike. He moves up the list."

Cain scrubbed a hand over his face, felt the roughness on his unshaven face. "So, aside from Rosen, we're right back where we started."

"I'm going to try to locate Harwell and dig deeper into Ray Aldridge. In the meantime, keep your head down and an eye on Jenny."

"Believe me, I intend to." He ended the call, went into the bathroom, and popped a couple of Advils. The doctor had given him some meds, but he didn't like the groggy feeling they gave him, and if he ran into more trouble, he needed to be alert.

He rode his private elevator down to the main floor. He wanted to check on things at the hotel, but he needed to get back to Jenny. His shoulder was aching, throbbing like a thousand drumbeats, but the Advil would soon kick in.

The elevator door slid open, and he walked out into the hallway off the lobby. The Grandview was now open to the public. Tomorrow night was Halloween. The whole town would be masked up, people's identities hidden. The perfect night to cause trouble.

Cain planned to spend the evening at the Copper Star.

CHAPTER THIRTY-TWO

JENNY WAS WORKING BEHIND THE BAR WHEN SUMMER WALKED IN. SHE was wearing a black turtleneck and black slacks, which set off the pale color of her hair. She hurried toward Jenny and climbed up on a barstool on the opposite side.

"I heard about the shooting," Summer said. "Everyone in town is talking about it. Is Cain all right? What happened?"

"Word travels fast," Jenny said as she dried a shot glass.

"One of the paramedics has a sister who lives up here," Summer explained. "He told a friend, who told a friend, and well . . . you know how it goes. He's okay, then?"

"He was shot while we were horseback riding on his ranch. It was terrifying. I thought the guy was going to kill us both."

"Oh, my God, I didn't realize you were also in danger."

"Cain lost a lot of blood. They did surgery to repair the muscles and tendons and close up the wound. But he's back at the Grandview now. I hope he's resting, but with Cain, it's not a good bet." She smiled, hoping to hide her worry. "You want a Diet Coke or something?"

"Sounds good."

Jenny filled a glass with ice, poured in the cola, and set it on the bar.

Summer took a sip. "I'm glad Cain's all right. Have they caught the man who shot him?"

"Not yet. No idea who did it." Jenny prayed it wasn't Ryder

Vance. The idea of her being responsible for nearly getting Cain killed made her physically ill.

Jenny sighed. "Cain's coming so close to death made me realize how much I care about him."

Summer's head came up. "You aren't falling in love with him?"

"I'm trying to convince myself I'm not."

Summer smiled. "How's that working out?"

"Not too well so far." She moved down the bar to wait on a couple of guys who had just climbed up on a stool. She drew them each a beer, then returned to Summer.

"So how about you? How did your date go with Dylan?"

Color crept into Summer's cheeks. "He's just . . . It was a wonderful two days."

"Two days? I thought he was only staying in town the night of the party."

"We . . . umm . . . spent that night in a room upstairs, then drove up to Sedona the next day. We had such a good time, Dylan decided to stay another night."

"And the extra night included you."

Summer nodded. "It felt so right being with him." She took a sip of her Coke. "But, in a way, I wish I hadn't slept with him. I've always had a crush on your brother. Now I know he's exactly the guy I thought he was. I'm half in love with him already, and I have no idea what he feels for me."

Jenny reached across the bar and squeezed Summer's hand. "He stayed with you an extra night. That's a good sign."

"I guess." Summer's blue eyes filled. "I'm going to be miserable if he doesn't call me again."

Jenny's stomach tightened. "I know what you mean." She thought of the way she'd felt last week when Cain hadn't called. Everything inside her had ached. Maybe Cain had been right in leaving for Scottsdale, trying to slow things down. That week had given her a glimpse of how she was going to feel if things didn't work out between them.

Only it was going to be much, much worse.

She should pull back, give herself some room, try to protect her heart.

But the sad truth was, it was too late.

Summer left to return to the Butterfly Boutique. Molly filled in while Jenny took a break. She hadn't had time to check with Heather, make sure everything in the hotel was running smoothly.

Heather was at work behind the front desk. She looked up, tucking a strand of pink-streaked dark hair behind her ear as Jenny approached.

"I didn't see any messages on my phone while I was gone, so I guess everything's okay," Jenny said.

"We had a busy night," Heather said. "I heard about Cain. They said someone shot him. Is he going to be okay?"

"He's out of the hospital and mending." She wondered how many more times she would have to tell the story. "He's strong as a bull, so he should be all right. How's everything here?"

"The only interesting thing that happened was the couple in room eight—the Johnsons? When they checked out this morning, they claimed they saw the transparent figure of a man walking down the hallway last night. He was dressed in old-fashioned clothes, a vest and a bowler hat. Scared them half to death. They said they wouldn't be back."

Jenny's heart sank. Dear God, things in the new section weren't bad enough with a murder in room 10? Now there were spirits in the hallway.

"I thought people came to Jerome specifically to see ghosts," she said.

"Not everyone. Most people come here to get out of the city, to shop, and visit the restaurants."

She knew that. People said they wanted to see spirits, but she knew from personal experience, it wasn't always fun.

"The Johnsons stayed in room eight," Heather said. "That's in the new section. Seems like everything bad that's happened has been in that part of the hotel."

Jenny thought of Uncle Charlie's words. *Odd things happen in the rooms in that section. Dangerous things.* She should close those rooms off, just as her uncle had done, but if she did, the hotel wouldn't make enough money to repay the loan she'd taken out for the remodel.

"I'm afraid to ask if there was anything else," Jenny said.

"No, that's it. We're completely booked for Halloween—except for room ten, which you said to leave empty. Every place in town is sold out."

"I ordered extra supplies for the kitchen and restocked the bar. The saloon will be packed. Everybody's working that night. We do this every year, so we should be able to handle it."

"I'll stay until all the guests are settled in their rooms, then come in early the next morning for checkout."

"Thanks, Heather. I know I can always count on you."

Heather smiled appreciatively. As an employer, Jenny did her best to take care of her staff. She had no trouble hiring people. It was paying them that was a problem. For now, she would keep the new section open.

When she returned to the bar, she saw Cain sitting at a table in the corner, going over a stack of files. He had removed his sling, much to her chagrin. Damn, the man was stubborn.

She continued setting things up for the big crowd on Halloween. Troy and Barb would both be bartending. Tim and both part-time servers would also be there, while Myrna worked in the kitchen. Jenny's job was to keep things running smoothly and fill in wherever she was needed.

She prayed there would be no new calamities tomorrow night.

Cain took some work he wanted to review and sat at a table in the saloon until Jenny was able to leave that night. After closing, she stayed with him at the Grandview, but left the following morning. She had a lot to do to prepare for the biggest night of the year.

Ignoring her protests, Cain accompanied her again that morning. A meeting with Will Price, the bodyguard he had hired, was scheduled for eleven a.m. at the saloon. Price shoved through the batwing doors at exactly one minute before.

Cain rose, and Price walked toward him, forty years old, a touch of silver in his hair. He had a lean, hard-muscled body, and the bulge beneath the leather jacket he wore with a pair of dark blue jeans said he was armed.

"Pleasure to meet you, Mr. Barrett," Will said, extending a hand.

"It's just Cain." He accepted the handshake, and they talked for a while. The conversation was easy, no pressure. Cain was impressed by the man's no-nonsense attitude and the homework Will had done on Ryder Vance.

"You're sure you'll be able to spot him?" Cain asked.

"I've read his file, studied his mug shots—more than one. I've got his picture on my cell phone. He comes in, I'll spot him."

"The problem is everybody is going to be in costume. No way you can tell one person from another."

"I'm aware. I intend to keep a close eye on your lady. Anyone who gives her any trouble is going down."

"Good. That makes two of us. I'll be sticking to her like gum on the bottom of my shoe. Unfortunately, if Ryder shows up with his friends, you'll be up against more than just one man."

"That where you come in?"

Cain nodded. "Or the other way around. The two of us should be able to handle whatever comes up." He wished his damned arm was a little more functional, but life happened.

"I'll introduce you to Jenny."

Jenny was in the kitchen, working with the cook. All the employees were in costume today, the bar already full. But the crowd was a drop in the bucket compared to the horde that would be descending on the town that night.

He stood up and waved, and Jenny walked over. She was wearing her boots, black jeans, and a black T-shirt that said MEOW on the front. She had drawn whiskers and a small black nose on her face. The black band across her head had two fuzzy little cat ears sticking up.

Cain grinned. She looked so damned cute, he fought an urge to haul her upstairs and finish what they hadn't had time to start that morning.

At the grin on his face, Jenny flashed him a look and set a hand on her hip. "It's Halloween, remember? I wear this every year. It's easy to work in, but it's still a costume."

"I love it. I just hope you'll wear it for me when we're alone."

She laughed.

"Jenny, meet Will Price. He's going to keep an eye on things this afternoon and tonight."

"Hello, Will. Nice to meet you." They shook hands.

"I realize you're going to be busy," Will said. "I'll do my best to stay out of your way, but I won't go far, and I'll be watching you. If I miss something and you need me, just raise your hand."

"With the two of us here," Cain said, "you should be safe enough."

"I'm sure I will be."

But Cain was far less certain.

CHAPTER THIRTY-THREE

JENNY WORKED ALL AFTERNOON AS THE PLACE FILLED TO OVERFLOWING, people in ghoulish costumes, including a man with a black ski mask that revealed red, murderous eyes. That one made her nervous, but it wasn't Ryder Vance, just some guy having fun with his friends.

There was a vampire, a man in a long, black robe carrying a plastic sickle with a fake bloody blade on the end. There was a lady pirate, a sexy, blond female devil, more black cats. Lots of fake blood and gore.

So far nothing threatening, everyone just having fun.

She was in the kitchen, checking on a food order that was delayed when she heard a loud crash in the basement. Myrna, dressed as a plus-size version of a 1920's flapper, was busy filling plates, and Tim, the busboy, in a sailor suit, was clearing tables.

Jenny headed for the basement. Just as she was about to disappear out of sight, Cain appeared in the kitchen doorway.

"You need to stay where one of us can see you," he said darkly. He and Will were both wearing cowboy boots and hats as their costumes, except the clothes looked perfectly fitted and slightly worn, clearly not just "pretend" for the night.

Jenny glanced at Cain, whose gaze was hard with warning, and irritation trickled through her. "There was a noise in the basement. I need to go down and see what's going on."

If it hadn't been for the shooting, she could have justified being annoyed. The man could be ridiculously protective. As it was, she simply ignored him and continued on down the stairs. Before she reached the bottom, she heard Cain's heavy footfalls behind her.

She kept walking. There wasn't a lot of light down there, but it didn't take long to figure out what had happened. Her mother's precious china, one of the only things she had left that had belonged to her mom, had fallen off the shelf. The box had split open and the dishes were in bits and pieces all over the floor.

Her heart sank. As she knelt beside the pretty flowered porcelain cups and saucers, tears burned her eyes.

Cain's hard gaze followed hers. "What the hell . . . ?"

Jenny rose to her feet, knuckling a tear from her cheek as she looked up at Cain. "My mother's good china. I thought we'd stored it in a place where it would be safe."

Cain's jaw hardened. "We did. It was in the last load we brought from your house. I double-checked it myself. There is no way that box accidentally fell off the shelf."

"You think someone did this on purpose?"

"Who has access to the basement?"

"Everyone who works here. There's all kinds of stuff down here: paper goods, flatware, plates and glassware, food supplies, anything we need." Fighting an urge to cry, she looked back down at the pile of broken dishes.

She took a shaky breath. "I can't stop right now. Maybe I can salvage something later."

Cain softly cursed. He crouched and put the broken pieces back in the box, then shoved it out of the way for the night. Rising, he eased Jenny into his arms. "We'll come down first thing in the morning, see what we can find."

Jenny just nodded. She felt hollow inside. And worried. Who would have done something like that? Maybe it was just the hotel shifting, jarring the box off the shelf. There were eighty-eight miles of tunnels under Jerome. In the old days, whole sections of the town had collapsed.

But surely she would have felt a jolt strong enough to move the heavy box.

She didn't believe it was a ghost. Not for a second. The box was important to her. This felt personal.

Cain took her hand, and they headed back upstairs, into the saloon. The place was packed. Cain squeezed Jenny's hand as she started back to the bar to help with the swelling crowd demanding drinks.

She spotted Will Price at one end of the bar, his gaze scanning the room. She could see Cain's head above the crowd in another section of the saloon.

Troy and Barb filled drink orders behind the bar while Jenny helped the servers take orders and deliver the drinks. She was setting a tray of tequila shooters on a table when she heard a familiar voice next to her ear.

"Well, if it isn't my sweet little cousin, Jenny!" he shouted above the din of the crowd.

She turned. Uncle Charlie's son, the black sheep of the family. "Eddie . . ." He was wearing a white sheet with a hole cut for his head and a bloody, gruesome mask he had pulled off and left hanging around his neck.

His smile looked vicious. "Looks like you're pulling in some major bucks tonight, just like my old man."

"We're busy, Eddie. I have to get back to work."

"I just dropped by to say hello. I'll be back tomorrow so we can talk."

"I've got nothing to say to you!" she shouted. "It's over, Eddie. Finished!"

Will Price moved closer, leaned down, and spoke to Eddie. "You heard the lady. Time for you to leave."

Jenny left Eddie with Will and went back to work. She knew what her cousin wanted. Money. He believed his father should have left the Copper Star to him. The last time he'd shown up, Jenny had given him two thousand dollars, half of what he had demanded. He had taken the money and left, and Jenny had hoped that would be the end of it. Unfortunately, here he was again.

Uncle Charlie had willed the Star to her, not the son he didn't trust to continue his legacy. Jenny wasn't giving her no-good cousin another dime.

As she delivered trays heavy with food and drinks, she couldn't help wondering if Eddie had been the one who'd destroyed her mother's dishes. She had no idea how he could have known they were down there, but maybe someone had told him.

In the back of her mind, she thought about the shooting. Eddie was an alcoholic and a drug user, but she didn't think he was a killer.

They closed the bar at two a.m. Both Cain and Will looked tired. She could read the pain Cain was dealing with in the tight lines of his face.

Jenny knew how the men felt. Her feet were aching, her head pounding. She said good night to Troy, Barb, and the rest of the crew and thanked them for a job well done. Cain spoke to Will, who left for his room at the Grandview, and she and Cain headed upstairs.

She had asked him to stay with her tonight. The hotel was packed, lots of drunk and disorderlies on the street. She needed to be close at hand in case something happened.

She prayed nothing would go wrong.

Cain waited for her to walk past him into her small suite, which looked even tinier with him in the room. She was still wearing her black-cat clothes, eager to get them off.

"You look so damned cute in that outfit, I could just about eat you up." Cain's gaze ran over her, and his mouth edged up.

Jenny sighed, tired to the bone. "Have a little mercy," she said.

Cain laughed. "I'm not in much better shape than you are. No easy job running a bar on Halloween night."

"No."

"We'll save it for morning. Let's just get some sleep."

They didn't even bother to shower. Jenny checked the bandages on his shoulder; then they finished undressing and fell into bed. The queen-size was too small for Cain's big frame, but when he curled her against him, there was plenty of room, and it felt perfect having him hold her that way. Both of them were asleep in seconds.

It was four o'clock in the morning when a noise in the room had her eyes cracking open.

"What the hell is that?" Cain asked groggily.

Jenny recognized the sounds from before. "It's like a bunch of chains clanking together."

"Chains," Cain repeated, sitting up and swinging his long legs to the side of the bed.

The sound came again. "Like heavy iron being dragged over a wooden floor," she whispered. It was followed by the creak of a metal gate swinging open, then heavy footsteps.

Both of them listened hard. "Like a criminal being dragged into an old iron jail cell," Cain said when the noise came again.

"Yes . . ."

The grating noise of a rusty key turning in the lock cut through the silence. A man's deep voice groaned.

Jenny's heart was racing, her mouth bone-dry. It was getting worse. She had to do something. Close this part of the hotel—at the very least.

Cain shot to his feet. "This is bullshit. I don't believe this crap for a minute." He strode into the tiny living room, pulled open the door, and glanced into the corridor. He closed the door and returned to bed.

"Not a damned thing out there." He raked his fingers through his thick dark hair. "Snakes and broken dishes. Demons and murder. Now this. God knows what's next."

"While we were gone, room eight reported seeing a transparent man in the hallway."

Cain swore beneath his breath. When the room fell silent, he climbed back into bed and pulled her against him, planted a soft kiss on the side of her neck. "Don't think about it tonight. We both need sleep. We'll figure this out in the morning."

Jenny closed her eyes. She could feel his hard body slowly relax around her, and then he was sleeping. It took a while, but eventually, she fell asleep, too. It was late the next morning when she awakened.

Cain was already gone.

* * *

Cain had phoned Will Price before he left the Copper Star. Jenny would find him in the hallway outside her door when she left her room for work.

After the broken dishes and the noises in her room last night, protection for Jenny was more important than ever. Someone was purposely causing her trouble, and it wasn't a bunch of ghosts.

He refused to think about what had happened to him in room 10. There had to be an explanation, and Cain intended to find it.

To start with, Jenny was going to sit down and write an enemies list—just as he had done. She had told him about her cousin Eddie's appearance last night and the man's belief she owed him money.

Eddie Spencer held the number-one spot on her list, along with Ryder Vance. Cain picked up the phone and called Nick Faraday. It was Wednesday, but Nick wasn't picking up.

He left a message asking Nick to call. Maybe by the time Nick phoned back, Cain would have a few more enemies to add to Jenny's list.

Sitting at a table in the bar, Jenny went over the receipts from last night. It looked as if the evening had been extremely profitable, not unusual for Halloween night in a ghost town. She smiled.

Barb and some of the staff had arrived early to clean the place up, though they'd done most of it last night.

Will accompanied her down to the basement, then stood by while she sifted through her mother's pretty dishes and tried not to cry. She managed to salvage a gold-rimmed, flowered porcelain tea pot and four matching cups and saucers. Most of the plates and serving dishes were cracked or broken. She saved as much as she could, wrapped it all in newspaper and boxed it up, then carried the box to a different part of the basement and hid it behind some cartons on the floor.

Thinking of her mother and swallowing past the lump in her throat, she returned upstairs with Will.

The bar and kitchen opened, but very few customers showed up. After the late-night partying, most people were still recovering.

Cain had called earlier to tell her he had some things he needed to take care of and asked about Will. Jenny assured him Will Price had been looking out for her since she had walked out of her room that morning.

She spotted him seated at a table just a few feet away, watchful, leaning back in a captain's chair, sipping a cup of coffee.

Jenny sighed. Between Will and Cain, she never had a moment to herself. She hated living like a prisoner, but for now, she had no choice.

She was continuing to work on the receipts when she glanced up to see a woman pushing through the batwing doors. Silver-gray hair worn in a buzz cut, tiny round spectacles. Evelyn Dunning. Jenny rose and walked toward her, hope rising that the librarian had found something useful.

Jenny smiled. "Evelyn. It's good to see you."

"It's nice to see you, too. I brought some information I thought might interest you."

"Great. Why don't we sit down?" Jenny led Evelyn over to the table where she had been working, and both of them sat down.

"So what have you found?" Jenny asked anxiously.

Evelyn took out a copy of an old newspaper article and set it on the table.

"The Jerome *Daily News,* dated June 1904." She slid the copy over to Jenny's side of the table. Jenny skimmed the page and began reading the article out loud.

During an arrest attempt by Sheriff John Mackey, a miner named Boris Koblinsky was shot and killed in front of the Cuban Queen Bordello on Queen Street. He was wanted in connection to the murders of three known prostitutes who died between the years 1898 and 1904.

"Wow." She glanced up. "A miner who was shot in the street in front of a brothel. Maybe this is him."

There was more to the article, including the names of the women: Sadie Murphy in 1898, Blanch Milford in 1900, and Lily Dubois in 1904. Each of them had been strangled to death. The article went on to say that there may have been others, but there wasn't enough evidence to include them in the charges.

Strangled. She thought of the journal and Mary Dennison. She thought of what Leslie had said.

Jenny finished the article, both appalled and excited. "This could be what I've been looking for. Thank you so much for working on this."

"Now that you know the date and the names of the people involved, you can probably find out more."

She nodded. "Yes. I'll definitely look into it." But she wanted to talk to Cleo first. "Can I buy you some lunch? It's the least I can do."

Evelyn rose. "Thanks, but I have to get back to work."

Jenny walked her to the door, then gave her a grateful hug. "Thanks again, Evelyn." She smiled. "Whenever you're ready, I still owe you lunch."

Evelyn laughed. "Not necessary. Research is what I do."

As soon as the librarian walked out the door, Jenny grabbed her cell phone.

"Hi, Cleo, it's Jenny. I think I may have found what we were looking for. Or actually, Evelyn Dunning over at the library found it."

"Good. The more we know, the better our chances of getting rid of the bastard."

"I've got names and dates. Cain's busy, so as soon as I can take a break, I'll go back to the library and take another look."

"You do that, and then we'll get together."

"Great. Thanks, Cleo."

Cleo just grunted and hung up the phone.

CHAPTER THIRTY-FOUR

Cain was on his way down the hill to the Copper Star when his cell phone rang. Nick Faraday. One of the few people who had his private number.

Cain paused on the sidewalk and pressed the phone against his ear. "Nick, what's going on?"

"New location on Bart Harwell. Apparently, he was making job inquires in Bagdad. That's a mining town—"

"Not far from the ranch."

"That's right. It was three months ago. Harwell didn't get the job, and that's the last anyone has seen of him."

"So he was back in the area before the horses went missing."

"Well, he might have been. He was there three months ago, but I'm not sure where he went after, or where he is now. I'll stay on it. The thing is, your old buddy, Ray Aldridge, just filed for bankruptcy. Word is, he's blaming all his troubles on you. Says you cheated him out of the claims he was buying."

"That's a crock of bull."

"I'm sure it is. Doesn't mean he doesn't have it in for you. Either of those guys could have stolen those horses. Doesn't take much to hire the kind of thugs who would do it. Think either of them could be trying to kill you?"

"If you'd asked me that a few months back, I would have said no. Now I guess anything is possible."

"I'll keep you posted," Nick said.

"And while you're digging, check out Jenny's cousin, Eddie Spencer. He was in the bar last night. Jenny says he wants money. Thinks he deserves it because her uncle, Charles Spencer, left the Star to her and not him."

"Charles and Eddie's names both came up when I was looking into Jenny's background. I'll check him out and get back to you."

The call ended, and Cain tucked the phone into his jeans. He had set up a meeting at the Copper Star. He figured Jenny wasn't going to be happy about it, but he wasn't giving her a choice.

By the time he pushed through the batwing doors, the group was already inside, waiting for him. One woman and two men. They were sound and video experts. A guy named Max Bradley was in charge. Mike Stockton and Carrie Garner worked for him.

Cain motioned them over to one of the tables, and they all sat down just as Jenny walked up. He could see Will Price standing not far away.

Jenny gave Cain a warm smile, which he figured wouldn't last long. "You should have told me you had a business meeting this morning. I could have had everything set up for you."

"This meeting involves you, I'm afraid. You and the hotel."

"What?"

Cain introduced the group. Max was bulky, with dark hair and a speculative gleam in his eyes. Mike was red-haired, easy to remember. Carrie was petite and pretty, a brunette who exuded confidence and ability.

"Nice to meet you, Jenny," Max said for all of them.

"They do technical production in Scottsdale," Cain explained. "Make commercials, short video clips, documentaries, that kind of thing. Mostly for TV."

"So they're here to help with marketing?"

"They're here to find out what the hell is going on in your hotel."

"Wait a minute!"

Cain ignored her. "You have the equipment you need?" he asked Max.

"It's in the van. We're parked right out front."

"Get it." Cain turned back to Jenny. "I assume most of the guests have checked out by now."

"Yes, but you can't just come in here and take over like this!"

"They're going to look around upstairs. If there's something going on we don't know about, there's a good chance they can find out what it is. You want to know the truth, don't you?"

"Well, I . . ." She turned as the swinging doors opened and the small group walked back in carrying equipment.

"You want the truth, right?" Cain repeated.

"Yes. What is that stuff?"

"I have no idea. Whatever it is, they'll be looking for audio feeds, video cameras, things like that. They need access. If they do any damage, I'll pay to have it repaired. Deal?"

Jenny set a hand on her hip and glared at him. "There is no way that murder in room ten was caused by a couple who got in a fight. Not after what I read in the journal and what Leslie said. Think about what happened to you in that room, Cain. You don't believe that was real?"

"I don't know. Let's find out. Room ten hasn't been rented since the murder, right?"

"No, it hasn't been rented."

"Fine, we'll start there." He walked over and dismissed Will for the day, then motioned for Max and the others to follow him and led them through the saloon into the hotel lobby next door. Jenny walked behind them, clearly pissed off.

Cain turned back to her when they reached the front desk. "We'll need keys to the empty rooms in both sections."

Jenny's sigh held resignation. "All right, fine." Heather stood by as Jenny sorted through the room keys, checking to be sure which rooms were unoccupied, and handed them over.

"The cleaners are working up there," she said to Cain. "I'll go up with you and explain what's going on."

Cain just nodded, and the two of them headed upstairs, trailed by Max and his crew. Cain knew Max Bradley from Scottsdale. They'd been introduced by a friend who was trying to convince him to make some commercials. It would improve Barrett Enterprises' image, his friend had said.

Cain hadn't been interested, but he'd liked Max Bradley, respected his professionalism. With all the trouble happening at the Star, Cain had phoned, explained to Max what he wanted, and Max had promised to bring in some of his best people.

The group stopped outside room 10, and Cain opened the door. It smelled musty and closed-up inside. The carpet had been stripped, the bedding replaced. Still there was something eerie about the space that bothered him.

"See if you can find anything unusual in here," Cain said, hoping like hell they would.

"We'll take a good look," Max promised, and his crew set to work. Jenny watched for a moment, then went down the hall to explain to the women cleaning the rooms that guests had checked out of that morning.

"I'll leave you to it," Cain said to Max. "The room keys have numbers. Dig around, poke some holes in the walls, do whatever you need to. I'll take care of the repairs."

"All right."

"I'm particularly interested in this room. Let me know what you find. Jenny and I will be downstairs."

An hour later, Cain glanced up to see Max walking toward him. Cain rose when the man reached the table.

"Nothing so far," Max said. "And believe me, if there was any kind of equipment in the room, we would have found it. We took a look at the electrical, tested for something in the walls, knocked a hole in the ceiling, and looked up in the attic. Nothing."

Jenny walked up just then. "I heard what you said. Are you sure, Max?"

"As sure as I can be without tearing the whole damn room apart."

She flicked Cain a sugary smile, but spoke to Max. "Thank you, Max. I don't think that'll be necessary."

"Nothing in there, but we're just getting started on the rest of the hotel." Max left to go back upstairs, and Jenny went back to work, staying mostly where Cain could see her. That was something, he supposed.

Irritated with the results of Max's search, he sat back down in his chair. He'd been sure they'd find something in that room.

He amended that. After the things that had been going on, including the disturbing sounds he had heard in Jenny's room last night, he wasn't sure of any damned thing.

But there was something about room 10 . . . It took a lot to scare Cain. He'd been afraid that night—afraid of himself. Half of him was sorry it wasn't all fake. The other half was relieved to discover that whatever had happened, he hadn't been played for a fool.

He took a couple more Advil and was glad when they finally kicked in.

An hour later, Cain was going through his email and text messages on his phone when he looked up to see a grinning Max walking toward him.

"You need to come see this." Max glanced over at Jenny, at work behind the bar. "You both need to come."

Cain signaled for Jenny to join them.

"Max has something to show us," Cain said. Jenny flicked Max a glance, and then the three of them walked to the stairs. As they reached the top, Max turned right and headed into the new section.

"We didn't find anything in the older part of the hotel, but in the new section . . ." He joined Mike Stockton, who stood in the middle of the hallway next to an aluminum ladder. Mike pointed up at the ceiling, where a hole had been cut.

"What'd you find up there?" Cain asked.

"Better if you just go up and see for yourself," Max said.

"I'll go," Jenny said, but Cain rested a hand on her arm, letting Mike go up first.

Mike waited next to the opening to help Jenny into the attic. Cain went up behind her, and Max followed. The attic was coated in a layer of dust, the air choking with it.

Cain frowned at the cluster of odd-looking instruments in the dim space. "What is that stuff?"

Max spoke to Jenny. "You told Cain some of the guests reported seeing a transparent man in a bowler hat walking down the hallway."

"That's right." Jenny cast Cain a glance.

"What they were seeing was a hologram." Max ducked to avoid the low ceiling and made his way over to a laptop computer sitting on a card table.

"The actual video was made somewhere else," Max said. "It was brought here and projected by a laser. They used holographic film plates, optical lenses, mirrors, and an anti-vibration setup to make it all happen. The hologram was controlled by the computer. There's a tiny opening where the image was projected into the hallway."

"I can't believe it," Jenny said, her eyes big as she stared at Max. "So all of it was fake?"

"This is all we've found so far. Cain told us about the sounds you heard in your bedroom. That's where Carrie is now."

"Bring the laptop," Cain said. "Leave everything else the way it is. This is a problem for the police."

When they returned downstairs, Carrie was waiting for them in the hallway. "I found something in Jenny's bedroom. Bring the ladder."

They all marched in that direction, Mike carrying the lightweight aluminum ladder.

Carrie pointed to something wedged out of sight in the molding around the ceiling over the bed. "One up there. Another one over near the corner." She pointed to a spot mostly hidden by the drapes. "Small wireless speakers. Whatever you heard was a recording, probably controlled by the laptop."

"I can't believe it." Jenny sank down on the bed. She looked up at Cain with such despair it made his chest clamp down. "Why would someone do this to me?"

His jaw tightened. "That's what we're going to find out."

Mike climbed the ladder and pried the small speakers out of their hiding places. "I'll take another look around, make sure there aren't any more."

"We'll need to check the rest of the rooms," Max said.

Jenny just nodded.

Cain set a hand at her waist. "Come on, honey. Let's let them do their job. We'll be downstairs," he said to Max.

Back in the saloon, Cain seated Jenny at one of the tables. Noting the pale color of her face, he went over to the bar and had Barb pour her a shot of whiskey, then set it on the table in front of her.

"Drink that," he commanded. "You look like you need it."

For once, she didn't argue, just took a long swallow of the dark liquid and relaxed back in her chair "So none of the ghost reports are real? What about room ten?"

"Let's wait till Max is finished."

Jenny nodded dully. "I still can't believe it." She looked up at him. "What about the ghost I saw at the Grandview? You don't think . . . ?"

"What . . . ? That the Grandview has also been bugged? I doubt it, but I'll have Max and his crew check it out. Whatever is going on, it's happening here. It's directed at you personally."

"Like my broken china?"

"Yes, and the snakes."

She shivered. "I still can't believe it. Not after so many reports of ghosts over the years."

"We'll find out. Drink your whiskey. I'm going back to the bar to get myself a beer."

CHAPTER THIRTY-FIVE

MAX AND HIS CREW FOUND SPEAKERS IN TWO MORE ROOMS IN THE new section. On the laptop computer, Carrie found recordings of chains rattling, of a music box playing, of children laughing, of a man's voice and an iron door opening and closing. There was a recording of footsteps and heavy breathing.

There was no explanation for other incidents—guest entries in the journal for several decades that reported faucets turning on by themselves, small handprints appearing on the windows, the ghost cat, closet doors swinging open and closed.

There was nothing to explain the old-fashioned piano music she had heard downstairs in the middle of the night, or the sounds of people talking and clinking glasses in the saloon.

They found nothing in the old section, though stories about those rooms had been abundant too over the years. Cain believed it could all be fake, but Jenny wasn't convinced.

As soon as the team had wrapped up their work, Cain called ahead and made arrangements for Max and his people to take a look at the Grandview. As it was such a quiet day, Jenny left Barb in charge, and she and Cain went up to the Grandview to see what Max had found.

Knowing what to look for now, Max made a search of rooms on each floor, but by the end of the day, he had found nothing. The hours were slipping past, and a big storm was predicted for that night. Jenny and Cain were waiting in the bar before going in to supper when Max approached.

"Have a seat," Cain said, indicating a chair across from him.

"I can't stay long. The others are loading the equipment into the van, and then we're driving back to Scottsdale."

"What's the final word?" Cain took a drink of whiskey.

"We gave it our best shot," Max said. "But it looks like the place is clean."

"We tore the entire hotel apart for the remodel and completely rebuilt it," Cain said. "Jake Fellows, my contractor, kept a close eye on everything being done. I didn't expect you to find anything."

"Glad we could help solve at least part of the mystery at the Copper Star."

Cain rose and extended a hand. "I really appreciate the work you did today."

Smiling, Max shook his hand. "You paid me plenty to do it."

Cain smiled. "Worth every penny."

Max left to join the rest of his team for the drive back down the mountain. Cain escorted Jenny into the dining room for supper.

The server, a young man named Robert, in black slacks and a crisp white shirt, arrived. Jenny ordered chicken cordon bleu, Cain ordered a steak, and they compromised on the wine, asking Robert to bring out a bottle of Duckhorn merlot to accompany the meal.

Cain tasted, and Robert poured the wine into the crystal glasses Millie had chosen. Lovely, but thanks to Jenny, sturdy enough to stand the wear.

"I've been thinking about what Max found in the Copper Star," Jenny said, taking a sip of wine. "There was nothing in the old wing. All the equipment was hidden in the new section. You think it was set up during the remodel?"

Cain nodded. "No other way they could have done it without being noticed."

"But why?"

"I think someone is trying to put you out of business. The kind of stuff that happened wasn't just the usual, occasional ghost sighting. Those are good for business, right?"

"In the past, they certainly have been."

"People report all kinds of things at the Grandview, ghosts on the balcony, the sound of a gurney rolling down the hall—this previously being a hospital. But none of it is dangerous."

He took a drink of wine and set the glass back down on the linen-draped table. "The stuff happening in the new section of your hotel isn't good for business. It's downright scary."

"A man was murdered. That's more than just scary."

Cain's gaze found hers. "We still don't know what's going on with that."

"Evelyn Dunning came to see me—the librarian?"

"What about her?"

"I think she may have found something that could help us figure things out. I'm going to do a little more research in the morning, then talk to Cleo. She wants to try again."

"No way," Cain said, setting his wineglass down a little too firmly.

Jenny gave him a tight smile. "I appreciate everything you've done for me, Cain, but the Copper Star belongs to me. I don't interfere in the way you run the Grandview. I'm going to handle the problem in room ten the way I see fit."

Cain swore softly.

"You don't have to go with us. In fact, I'd rather you didn't. I think we might do better if there isn't a man in the room."

"You mean the kind of man the presence in the room can dominate—that's what you're thinking, right?"

Jenny shook her head. "I don't think he would be able to dominate you this time. You're one of the strongest people I've ever met."

He relaxed, his lips edging into the faintest of smiles. "I guess that's a compliment. If I ever run into another demon, I'll keep your words in mind."

"That's what you think it is, a demon?"

"How the hell would I know? I don't even believe in ghosts, let alone demons."

Jenny laughed. "Well, we really don't know what's happening in that room. I'm going to do some more research on Boris Koblinsky. Maybe that will help us figure it out."

"Boris Koblinsky? Who's he?"

"I'm not sure yet. I think he might be the spirit in room ten."

Cain opened his mouth to say something, but Robert arrived with their meals just then. After he left, they started eating, and the conversation turned to other subjects.

"Speaking of problems . . ." Cain said between bites.

"Do we have to?"

Cain didn't smile. "We were talking about people who might want to do you harm. You helped me make a list of possible enemies. Now I need a list from you. Who would be willing to go to such extremes to put you out of business?"

"I have no idea."

"Is there anyone who wants to buy you out? Devaluing the property might give them a good opportunity."

"I can't think of anyone who seems interested."

"All right, how about personal enemies? Your ex-husband, maybe? What about good ol' cousin Eddie?"

"My ex wouldn't be interested. He's married to a very wealthy woman, but Eddie . . ."

"Eddie thinks he deserves to own the Star, correct?"

"That's right."

"Okay, he goes to the top of the list."

"There isn't any list. He's the only person I can think of who might do something to make me fail."

"Then for now we focus on Eddie. I've got Faraday looking into him. Maybe he'll find something that puts all of this together."

Her head came up. "You don't think Eddie could be the guy who shot you?"

"No idea. I'm not overlooking any possibility."

They finished their meal, then went into the bar for a brandy before heading up to Cain's room. By the time they got there, both of them were running a fever, the kind that made her want to tear off his clothes. Cain had been gone for a week. They'd made passionate love after the masked ball, then gone to the ranch, where Cain had been shot.

He'd been in the hospital, finally gotten out, but they had both been exhausted on Halloween night, and there was the problem of ghosts. Or as it turned out, fake ghosts.

Jenny needed him tonight, and from the hot glitter in his dark eyes, he needed her, too. They went up to his suite, barely made it into the entry before he was kissing her. In seconds, the kiss turned hot, wet, and hungry, and Cain began pulling off her clothes.

Jenny tugged Cain's white shirt out of his black pants, saw the ragged scar from the stitches in his shoulder, and gentled her touch. Frustrated, Cain began to help her, tugging so hard, one of the buttons went flying across the room.

Jenny ran her hand over his bare chest. The man had the sexiest body. Jenny couldn't get enough of him.

"Damn, I want you," Cain said. They kissed as he finished stripping her out of her clothes. The next thing she knew he was lifting her up, wrapping her legs around his waist, carrying her over to the new live-edge table next to the window. He kicked one of the chairs out of the way and set her on top.

Long, deep kisses followed. Jenny's arms went around his neck as he moved between her legs. Sliding his zipper down, he freed himself and slid inside.

Jenny moaned. Cain moved out and drove in, taking her with long, determined strokes. Sweet pleasure rolled through her, making her tremble, and her body tightened around him.

Cain didn't stop until she climaxed, kept going till she tipped over the edge again, dragging him along with her to a powerful release. They were spent and clinging to each other by the time he was finished.

He tipped his forehead against hers. "I don't know what I'm going to do about you. I can't seem to get enough."

Jenny softly kissed him. "You're just making up for the time you were gone."

He smiled and kissed her again. "Yeah, one of my worst ideas."

"Let's go to bed," Jenny said. "Your shoulder still isn't completely well."

He smiled. "For some reason, I've forgotten all about it."

True to his word, Cain carried her into the bedroom, and they started all over again, slower this time. Jenny still worried about his injury, though it seemed to be healing well. Cain was the only man who had ever satisfied her, but it was more than just his physical size and strength.

It was the way he looked at her, the way he touched her. As if she were the most important person in the world. Deep down, she knew it was a feeling she would never find with another man.

Jenny refused to think about it. She had no idea what the future held for either of them. There were too many problems, too much happening.

Some of it deadly.

Cain met his grandmother downstairs for breakfast the following morning. There was a bit more color in Nell's pale face, her carriage a little straighter than when she had first arrived in town. His grandmother was happy in Jerome. The thought that he had been able to give Nell her dream made him smile.

Cain rose and pulled out a chair, bent and kissed Nell's cheek as he seated her. She took the linen napkin next to her plate and spread it over her lap. They both ordered, then sipped coffee as they waited for the food to arrive.

"I heard a wild rumor that you had a bunch of ghost hunters workin' over at Jenny's place yesterday."

"Not true. In fact, Max and his crew are the exact opposite of ghost hunters. I hired them to debunk what's been happening at the hotel."

"And did they?"

"Somewhat."

"What does that mean? They found ghosts or they didn't?"

His grandmother had always been far too perceptive. She could recognize a half-truth a mile away. "They figured out that someone installed small wireless speakers and video equipment to scare the ballocks off the guests in some of the rooms."

Nell laughed. "Is that so?"

"Yes, that's so."

"Does that mean that what happened to you in room ten was all a prank?"

"How did you know about—"

"Cleo's my best friend."

"Of course," he drawled sarcastically. "How could I forget?" He took a drink of his coffee, set the cup back down on the table. "All right, so they didn't find anything fake in room ten. They found all sorts of stuff in the new section—especially in Jenny's room—nothing in the old section."

"And nothing that explains what happened to you in room ten."

"No."

"Cleo says Jenny is investigating, tryin' to figure out who the spirit is."

"She's been at the library all morning. Will's with her, of course. I'm more worried about the guy who shot me going after Jenny than I am about the demon in room ten."

Nell's silver eyebrows shot up. "Demon, is it?"

"Who the hell knows. Pardon the pun."

Nell smiled. "You know, you just keep gettin' smarter and smarter. Or at least more open-minded."

Cain took a sip of coffee. "Two things I've learned—anything is possible, and never underestimate Nell Barrett."

His grandmother laughed.

The food arrived, and they ate for a while, enjoying the bacon, eggs, fresh-squeezed orange juice, more coffee, and each other's company.

"So how's it goin' with you and Jenny?" Nell finally asked.

"I wondered how long it would take you to get around to that subject."

"Well . . . ?"

"Well, I like her." Nell's snowy eyebrows climbed. "I like her a lot, okay?"

Nell said nothing. Just kept staring, waiting for a truthful answer.

"Fine. If you must know, I'm crazy about her. I'm just not quite sure what to do about it."

"Maybe you should marry her," Nell said.

Cain choked on the mouthful of orange juice he had taken. He dabbed his mouth with a napkin. "As I said, we like each other a lot. Marriage is a big step. It takes time to sort through all the angles."

"There's only one angle that matters. Do you love her, and does she love you? That's it. The rest will work itself out."

"I have no idea how Jenny feels about me." Which was a fact he didn't like to think about. "She's never really said."

"One of you is going to have to take the first step. If you don't, things could go south in a hurry."

"We've talked about this before. It's none of your concern."

"You're right, of course," Nell said, returning to her breakfast. "What was I thinking?"

Cain scowled, but her words had struck a chord. What was Jenny thinking about their relationship? She was an extremely independent woman. Being tied down by marriage might be the last thing she wanted.

Cain wasn't sure if that was good news or bad.

CHAPTER THIRTY-SIX

WHILE JENNY SEARCHED FOR INFORMATION IN THE LIBRARY, WILL sat at a table a few feet away from where she had piled her purse and notepad, his sharp gaze surveying their surroundings. The man was dependable, that was for sure.

Jenny used search indices to find information on the three women whose names appeared in the article Evelyn had brought: Sadie Murphy, Blanch Milford, and Lily Dubois.

There were no obituaries, nothing but the single article. She did find, however, in the Jerome *Daily News,* a record of Sheriff John Mackey's death in a huge fire in Jerome in 1917. The blaze engulfed an entire city block, destroying homes and boardinghouses and displacing ninety people.

He'd been forty-five years old at the time of his death, which made him thirty-two in 1904, when he had shot Boris Koblinsky. She felt oddly bereft at the sheriff's passing, the hero who had found justice for the women Koblinsky had murdered.

Too bad Sheriff Mackey wasn't still around to get justice for Brian Santana, whose death was likely the result of Koblinsky's possession of his body. Though it might sound ridiculous, Leslie would have believed it, and so would Mary Dennison.

After what had happened to Cain in that room, Jenny had a feeling that, deep down, Cain believed it, too.

She made a copy of the article about the sheriff, then walked over to let Will know she was ready to leave.

Jenny called Cleo on the way back to the Star and offered to buy her a late lunch. Cleo eagerly accepted. Living so close, the heavyset woman was seated at a table waiting when Jenny arrived. Nell Barrett sat across from her.

Jenny made a quick check with Barb, who was bartending today, to be sure everything was running smoothly, then went over to join them.

"Cleo. Thanks for coming." She smiled at Nell. "Well, this is a nice surprise." She glanced around. "Where's Emma?"

"Had some shopping to do. She'll pick me up when we're finished."

"I'm glad you're here," Jenny said. "Have you ordered?"

"Thought we'd wait for you," Cleo said.

"I had something earlier. What would you like for lunch? My treat."

Both women ordered the Copper Star's famous Miner's Burger with fries. Jenny put the order in, adding a Diet Coke for herself, then returned.

"Time's a'wastin'," Cleo said. "What'd you find out?"

Jenny flicked a glance at Nell, hoping she wouldn't think this whole thing was crazy. "I'm pretty sure the spirit in room ten is a miner named Boris Koblinsky. Cleo, you said he was a miner. Looks like you were right."

"What else?" Cleo asked.

"Koblinsky murdered three women—that they know of—between 1898 and 1904. Prostitutes. He strangled the women to death."

"*Strangled.*" Nell repeated. "That fits what Leslie Owens told you."

Jenny nodded. "What Leslie said and what Mary Dennison wrote in the journal. According to Mary, her husband tried to strangle her. But it wasn't really her husband; it was someone—or something—else."

"Yeah, something named Boris Koblinsky," Cleo said.

"Yes, and today I found out what happened to him. He was shot by a sheriff named John Mackey in June of 1904 when the sheriff tried to arrest him for the murders. The shoot-out occurred in the street in front of the Cuban Queen bordello."

Cleo shifted her huge bulk on the chair, making it creak beneath her weight. "I'd say that's our man."

"I think so, too," Jenny said. "Unfortunately, Sheriff Mackey died in a fire in 1917. He was only forty-five at the time."

"Way too young," Nell said.

"Yes," Jenny said. "It makes me sad to know he died in such an awful way." The hamburgers arrived, and the two women dug in. Jenny sipped the Diet Coke she had ordered.

"So, what are we going to do to get rid of the spirit in room ten?" Jenny asked.

"At least we know who he is," Cleo said between bites.

"And what the bastard did," Nell added.

"Maybe we can use it against him," Jenny suggested.

Cleo nodded. "We'll figure somethin' out." Jenny left the women and went behind the bar to relieve Barb for a break. Will sat at one end, sipping the same beer he'd ordered when they'd arrived.

They still needed a plan. She hoped Cleo would come up with something soon.

Cain's cell phone rang. He was talking to Martin Cohen, one of his VPs. They were finally closing the Titan Transport deal, thank God. He was just hanging up when another call came in.

Cain picked up the call.

"Barrett, this is Deputy Sheriff Hank Landry. I got some news I think you'll want to hear."

"I hope it's good news for a change," Cain said.

"It's not good news for Ryder Vance and his boys. We just arrested Vance on drug-trafficking charges. Technically, possession with intent to deliver a controlled substance. Cocaine and fentanyl in substantial quantities. Some of his boys were taken into custody on lesser charges. Since it's Vance's second time around, he'll be going away for a good long while."

"You talk to him about my stallion? Or the bullet someone put in my shoulder?"

"As a matter of fact, I did. He had no idea what I was talking about. I believe him. If he'd done it, he could have used the information to cut a deal. I don't think he's your guy."

Cain thought of the man on the other end of the phone. So maybe the deputy wasn't the dumbass Cain had thought.

"I appreciate your call, Deputy, and the work you've done on the case."

"We're still looking for the shooter who went after you at the ranch. It just doesn't appear to be Ryder Vance."

"Thanks again, Hank," he said, using the man's first name for the first time. "Nice work."

"Just doing my job." But there was a note of pride in his voice.

Cain's next call went to Nick. He relayed the information on Ryder and got an update on Eddie Spencer.

"Spencer's a scumbag," Nick said. "No doubt about it. But I don't think he's interested in anything that won't make him money. Killing you isn't going to do that."

"Neither is castrating my stud."

"No."

"So Spencer's off the list?"

"He's off your list. He's still on Jenny's. He could definitely be the guy who's trying to drive her out of business."

"Except if it's the business he's after, destroying it isn't a great idea."

"Can't argue with that. How's Will working out?"

"He's a good man. He's doing a great job looking out for Jenny."

"She's not out of danger yet."

"I know."

"Which means, with Vance in jail, Ray Aldridge and Bart Harwell are our last two suspects."

"Unless it's someone else entirely."

"Yeah. Hold steady. And don't do anything that will put you in the crosshairs."

"I'll do my best to stay alive. Thanks, Nick." Cain ended the call.

Aldridge or Harwell? He and Bart had ended their partnership on a satisfactory note—at least at the time. But Cain had made a lot of money after he'd found moly on the claims they'd once owned together.

Aldridge flat-out hated his guts and made no bones about it.

Which one wanted him dead? Or was it someone else?

Unease slipped through him. No more walking down to the Star. Too much exposure that could make him an easy target. Too many spots for a shooter to hide.

He didn't want to die of stupidity.

Cain thought of Jenny, and his unease deepened. He made his way to his private elevator and rode down to the lower floor. At least his shoulder was feeling better.

He checked the area around the parking lot before he walked outside. He needed to see Jenny. Will was a good man, but if it came down to life or death, he didn't trust anyone but himself.

Crossing the lot, he climbed into the Jag that Denver had delivered after Cain had been released from the hospital. Sliding behind the wheel, he fired the powerful engine.

His instincts were nagging him.

He needed to be sure Jenny was safe.

CHAPTER THIRTY-SEVEN

JENNY SAT BEHIND THE COMPUTER IN HER OFFICE. AFTER NELL AND Cleo left, she'd decided to do a little more digging, see if she could find anything more on the history of the Copper Star.

She had been Googling for a while, skimming through several well-known ghost stories, when she spotted an article that involved the hotel.

A prominent local woman, notorious for her violent temper and certain her husband had been having an affair with the town's pretty schoolteacher, had left her room, gone downstairs to the café, and thrown carbolic acid into the teacher's face.

"Wow," Jenny thought, unable to imagine doing something so brutal.

The teacher had survived her injuries, and the woman, whose name was omitted, had been arrested. She'd been stunningly beautiful, the tale continued, the kind of woman men couldn't resist. She'd been released after only two years, then arrested again after another attack on someone else.

After her death in an asylum in Los Angeles in 1951, her ghost had reportedly been seen upstairs in the Copper Star Hotel.

Jenny kept reading, discovered another story tied to the first. The woman's daughter had secretly been seeing a young Mexican boy. After impregnating the girl, the young man was arrested and thrown into the local jail.

Town vigilantes were determined to hang the boy, but couldn't get past the sheriff. They ended up setting the jail on fire, and the sheriff had to shoot the young man in order to keep him from burning to death.

Jenny shivered and closed down her computer. One more reminder why Jerome had been called the Wickedest Town in the West.

Walking out of the office, she found Will waiting exactly where she had left him.

"I need some air," she said. "One more trip up to the library should do it. Are you game?"

"There's a lot of open space between here and the library. I'm not sure it's a good idea."

He'd been reticent the first time, but Jenny looked forward to any excuse to get outside, into the crisp, early-November air. It was overcast this afternoon, with heavy rain predicted sometime in the next few days. It might be her last chance.

She smiled up at Will. "This is my final trip, I promise."

Will nodded, and Jenny headed for the door in the hotel lobby. When she opened it, Will stepped in front of her to check the street, then shoved open the door.

"Looks okay," he said, walking out onto the sidewalk to survey the area. "Not many folks around today."

Jenny joined him. They'd started across Main Street toward the stairs up to Clark when a shot rang out from somewhere above them. Blood erupted on Will's back as he grunted and went down, and Jenny screamed.

She turned to run back into the saloon, but a man blocked her way. He was tall, lean-muscled, and wiry, Jenny noticed, as he jerked her against him and clamped a white rag over her nose and mouth. Lashing out, she tried to fight him, tried to scream, but she only sucked in more of the brain-numbing drug. She continued to struggle, but his hold was too tight, and the rag left no room to breathe.

Her legs and arms were going weak, her head spinning. She swayed, gripped the man's shirt to stay on her feet. She was beginning to lose consciousness when the man holding her knelt next to Will and stuffed a note in his pocket.

That was the last thing she remembered as the darkness at the edge of her vision closed in, and the world slowly faded.

Will stirred enough to see a group of people clustered around where he lay on the sidewalk. He could feel blood leaking out of a wound in his back.

"An ambulance is on the way," a heavyset man with a short beard said. "The EMTs will be here any minute. Just take it easy."

Will stirred, tried to sit up. "Jenny . . ."

"Just take it easy, sir," a young woman said.

"Get . . . Barrett."

"Barrett?" someone said. "Cain Barrett?"

"He owns the Grandview Hotel," a woman added.

"What the hell's going on here?" Someone was shouldering his way through the crowd, tall, barrel-chested. It was Cain. Will felt a wave of relief, followed by a sweep of nausea, and fought the lure of darkness.

"Jenny . . ." Will said as the big man knelt beside him.

"The EMTs are on their way," Cain said. "I can see them from here. Just hang on."

"Sniper . . . shot me. Second man . . . took Jenny."

Cain felt a rush of fury that had his hands balling into shaking fists. "We'll find her. You just stay alive."

"Sir, you'll have to step away." EMTs had just arrived, this one young, fresh-faced, and anxious to help.

Cain started to rise, but Will gripped his hand. "Note in my . . . pocket."

"Sir, this man is bleeding very badly," the young tech said. "Please step away."

Cain shoved the young guy off him long enough to search Will's shirt pocket and pull out a white piece of paper. He rose and moved out of the way.

"Take good care of him," Cain said.

The young tech relaxed. "We will."

Cain wanted to stay, make sure Will was going to be all right, but for now, finding Jenny had to come first. His rage swelled as he read the note.

I have Jenny. You want her back, you'll have to figure out where I am.

It was signed, *Your old friend, Bart.*

Fucking Bart Harwell, once his partner, never much of a friend. He hadn't believed Bart would want payback this badly. Cain wanted to crumple the note and grind it into the dirt with the heel of his boot, but instead he stuffed it into the pocket of his jeans.

The police were arriving on the scene. He recognized the two deputies, Jerry Simmons and Neal Gibbons. The Verde Valley ambulance was less than fifteen minutes away. He left the EMTs working over Will and phoned Nick Faraday as he walked back to the Jag.

"Bart Harwell's got Jenny," Cain said. "He's working with a partner. One of them shot Will Price in the back, while the other took Jenny. Will's alive, but he's badly injured. The EMTs are with him. The ambulance should be here any minute. I'll be at the Grandview till I can figure out where Harwell's taken Jenny."

"I'm on my way," Nick said.

Cain got into the Jag, pulled out of the parking space, and drove back up the hill. Bart and another man. Bart was a damned good shot. He remembered the two of them practicing out in the desert around their mining claims. Most likely, he was the sniper. Probably been the guy who had shot him on the ranch.

Absently, he rubbed his shoulder. His wound was healing. He had full range of motion, but his shoulder still ached off and on.

His jaw hardened. Bart had wanted him dead. Now he had Jenny, the leverage he needed to get a second crack at him.

He thought of his Jenny at the mercy of a man like Barton Harwell. Bart had been rough-and-tumble back in their mining days, loved nothing better than a drunken night and a good barroom brawl. Only thing better was a few hours with a woman. Any woman. Didn't matter much to Bart.

Cain's stomach knotted. What would he do to Jenny? Bart wanted payback. What better way than to hurt the woman Cain loved.

The notion hit him hard. He loved Jenny Spencer, and Bart Harwell meant to hurt her.

The answer was simple. Cain was going to find Jenny and bring her home. He was going to find Bart Harwell, and when he did, Cain was going to kill him.

Jenny had no idea how much time had passed. For several seconds, she didn't move, just lay there, trying to figure out where she was, fighting to remember what had happened. The ground was rough dirt beneath her, and she realized her wrists were bound behind her back. When she opened her eyes, there was nothing to see but all-consuming darkness.

Her heart jerked and started pounding. She told herself to stay calm, try to figure things out, give her eyes time to adjust. Hearing no footsteps or the sound of voices around her, she slowly sat up. More seconds passed before her head stopped spinning and her pupils dilated enough that she could see a patch of gray light about twenty feet away.

She was in a tunnel, she realized with a jolt of fear. There were eighty-eight miles of tunnels beneath Jerome, and she was in one of them. Or a tunnel somewhere else.

Oh, dear God! How would anyone find her?

The faint patch of gray had to be the last hint of daylight shining through the entrance. She had to get out of there before full night set in and she couldn't see at all.

Think! You've seen a hundred movies where the heroine is kidnapped. Cain isn't here this time. You have to help yourself!

His handsome, beloved face appeared in her mind, but Jenny forced down the image. Cain had no idea where she was. She had to get away before whoever had taken her returned.

Rising to her feet, she managed to link her fingers together behind her back, then she stretched her rope binding enough to bend down and step through the circle she had made.

The stiff rope cut into her wrists and made her shoulders burn, but it worked!

She let out a sigh of relief and ignored the pain she had caused in her shoulders. At least her hands were now bound in front of her. She moved, searching the area around her, felt the rough wall of the tunnel off to one side and one of the timbers shoring up the tunnel. Using the wall to guide her, she headed toward the fading gray light.

She had almost reached the entrance when she heard men's voices near the tunnel opening. Two people, she figured, as she hurriedly made her way back to the place they had left her. Lying back down, she curled up on her side against the wall so they wouldn't notice her hands, and pretended to still be asleep. It was so dark she might have a chance to fool them, even with the lantern each man carried.

She prayed they would ignore her a little longer, prayed that Cain would come for her.

Knowing without a doubt that he would.

Jenny prayed that when he got there, it wouldn't already be too late.

Cain was studying the US topographical map of the Clarksdale, Arizona, quadrant when Nick rapped at the door to the suite. Cain strode across the living room to let him in.

"How's Will?" Cain asked as he led Nick back to the study, where the map was spread open on a table near the corner.

"Critical condition is all the hospital would tell me on the phone. He's still alive. That's something."

"Dammit!" He slammed a hand down on the table. "I was trying to get to Jenny when it happened. I was just a few minutes too late."

"If you'd been with her, you'd likely be the one in critical—or you would be dead."

"Or maybe Bart would have missed his shot, and I would have killed the sonofabitch before he could hurt her."

One of Nick's black eyebrows went up, but he made no comment. Cain went back to reading the map, and Nick's gaze followed.

"You think he's taken her into one of the tunnels?"

"His note said if I wanted to find her, I'd have to figure out where he took her. He wants me to find him. He wants to settle this personally, so it has to be someplace I know."

"Where would he take her?" Nick asked.

"When we were prospecting, we worked a lot of old mining claims. Some of them are in this area. I don't think he's gone too far. He's cast the lure—now he's trying to reel me in."

Cain studied the map. "We worked a claim right next to the Josephine Tunnel. That's right here, not far from Jerome."

He set his finger near a spot on the map. "There's an old dirt road heading north off 89A before you get to Clarksdale," Cain said, tracing the faint line on the map. "We were looking for gold at the time. We found a trace, not enough to keep us working up there. The old mine tunnel we worked goes into the side of the mountain, but it's not that deep."

"Just deep enough to hide a kidnap victim."

"Yeah." Cain looked up. "And it's not far away. Bart was never a patient man. He wants this confrontation. He's got to be tired of waiting."

"You're making a good argument."

Cain scrubbed a hand over the rough shadow of his afternoon beard. "Bart and I worked a lot of claims before I bought him out. It could be any one of them. I could be wrong about this. If I am, Jenny's the one who's going to suffer."

"I can't tell you what to do, Cain. All I can say is I do my best work when I follow my instincts."

Cain's gaze held Nick's for a long, silent moment. "So do I," he said. "Let's go."

CHAPTER THIRTY-EIGHT

JENNY TENSED AS THE MEN'S HEAVY FOOTFALLS CAME TOWARD HER, echoing down the tunnel. Lying on the cold dirt floor, she pressed herself against the rough rock wall and closed her eyes.

The lantern light ran over her. "She's still drugged up," one of them said, the voice of the tall, mud-faced man who had abducted her. She had only caught a glimpse, but she remembered his thick, black eyebrows and the scar that ran from the base of his nose to his upper lip. It made him even homelier than he was already.

"Get out of the way, Clyde. Let me have a look at her." The second man nudged her body with the toe of his heavy leather boot. His voice was deep, with the hint of a drawl. Jenny kept her eyes firmly closed. Clyde moved close enough to examine her.

"She's faking it, Bart," he said. "I tied her hands behind her, not in front."

Bart Harwell. Cain's old partner. The man who had shot Will and probably Cain when he was out at the ranch.

Her eyes flew open as he gripped her arm and jerked her roughly to her feet. "Well, ain't you the clever one."

In the lantern light, he had thinning, dark brown hair and dark eyes a little too close together. He was shorter than Clyde, but well over six feet, bulkier, heavily muscled through the chest and shoulders. Like Cain, he had worked the mines. Her stomach knotted to think how strong he must be.

"He'll come for you," Bart said. "You know that, right? And when he does, I'll be waiting."

"Cain's no fool. You tried to kill him once already. He won't just walk into your trap."

She could see the hard grin spread over his face. "Maybe he'll take his time, give me a chance to enjoy his woman. How would you like that, darlin'? Have a little fun before he gets here?"

A shudder ran through her. "You touch me and Cain will kill you."

"He shot me out at the ranch, but his bullet only grazed me. I plan to see he's dead before he gets another chance."

Too bad Cain's bullet hadn't done more damage. "You hate him that much?"

"He cheated me! He's rich as Croesus, and I got nothing!"

"He bought out your half of the partnership at a more than fair price and kept working the claims until one of them paid off. You didn't stick, and he did."

"I was drinking too much at the time, doing a little dope. Cain took advantage."

"If you had kept working as hard as he did, you would be rich, too. Instead you were a worthless drunk who wasn't willing to do your share!"

Bart slapped her so hard her ears rang, and she crashed back down onto the tunnel floor, out of the circle of lantern light. She landed hard on a rough-edged flat rock and bit back a groan. Grabbing the rock, thinking it might serve as a weapon, she shoved it into the waistband of her jeans and pulled out her flannel shirttail to cover it before she staggered back to her feet.

"Stay away from me, Bart." The corner of her mouth was bleeding, blood trickling down to her chin.

"How about me, sugar?" Clyde grinned, making his features look distorted in the lantern light. "I could make you feel real good."

"Shut up, Clyde. She's mine. I might give you a taste when I'm done."

Clyde chuckled softly. "I'm a patient man."

"Go take a look outside. Check real good, make sure nobody's out there."

"You think Barrett could figure out where we are that quick?"

"Like Jenny here said, Cain's no fool. He'll figure it out sooner or later." He cupped the front of his jeans and squeezed. "Right now, I'm hoping it's later."

As Clyde moved off toward the tunnel entrance, taking his lantern with him, the interior grew darker.

"I'll be right back," Clyde called down the tunnel.

"Take your time," Bart answered.

"You stole Cain's stallion," she said, just to keep him talking.

"So I got a little pleasure out of seeing him squirm. He deserved it." He shoved her, tripped her as she stumbled backward, knocking her feet out from under her. Jenny landed hard in the shadows, the breath rushing out of her lungs.

She steadied herself and pulled the rock out of her jeans. In the darkness, her hands shook as she raised her makeshift weapon over her head and waited. *Please . . . just give me one good shot.*

"You can make this easy on both of us," Bart said. "You're Cain's bitch, so I mean to have you." He set the lamp on the floor and moved closer. "Why don't you take off them jeans and this'll go a whole lot smoother."

"Why don't you fuck the hell off."

Bart laughed. "I think Cain hit real gold when he found you, sweet thing."

He knelt on the floor beside her and leaned over her. Jenny tensed. Gripping the rock in both hands in the darkness, she waited until he moved a little closer. When Bart reached for the zipper on her jeans, she crashed the heavy weight down on his skull with all her strength. Bone cracked. She heard Bart's grunt of pain; then he collapsed on top of her.

Oh my God oh my God oh my God. Blood was soaking into her clothes, blood on the rock she quickly tossed away. She didn't have time to find out if she had killed him. Clyde could be back any second.

Shoving Bart's heavy body off her, she surged to her feet, grabbed his lantern from the tunnel floor, and raced for the entrance. She had almost reached the opening when Clyde stepped into the tunnel, blocking her way.

"Where you going, sugar?" He stared past the light cast by her lantern into the darkness behind her, must have caught a glimpse of Bart sprawled on the floor.

"Well, ain't that sweet? You got rid of ol' Bart and left your pretty little self all to me."

She ducked, tried to dart around him. Clyde just laughed. He was twice her size, and the gleam in his eyes said he was determined.

She needed to distract him. "So . . . are you going to take up where Bart left off? Are you going to kill Cain?"

Clyde shook his head. "Nope. I don't need to kill him. I got somethin' belongs to him, somethin' he wants real bad, and I figure he'll be willing to pay big money to get her back."

"You're right. Cain will pay you. Just let me call him, explain what's going on."

Clyde laughed, the grating echo booming into the darkness. The moon was rising, and she could see the scar on his face.

"We'll get around to it," he said. "In the meantime, if I give you back to him a little the worse for wear, it ain't gonna matter."

Fury engulfed her. Jenny put her head down and charged like a wild thing, knocking Clyde backward out through the tunnel entrance. He stumbled and landed on his back a few feet below the opening.

Jenny burst past him, running as fast as she could. Clyde was up and running right behind her. He caught her ankle as she leaped over a rock and jerked her down, then landed hard on top of her.

"You are one helluva lot of trouble, sugar."

"Get off me!" With her arms pinned between them, Jenny could barely move.

"Randy as I'm feelin', this shouldn't take long." She heard the swish of the knife Clyde pulled out of his boot.

He pressed the blade against the side of her neck. "I don't want to hurt you, sugar, but I will. Now why don't you just relax. I'll take what I need, then we'll call Barrett, see how much he's willing to pay for used goods."

A whimper escaped.

She felt one of Clyde's hands slide between them as he tried to unzip her jeans. Jenny started struggling and Clyde pressed the knife a little deeper.

"Take it easy. I won't waste no time."

She wanted to fight him, but she didn't want to die.

Tears blurred her vision the instant before a slight movement in the darkness caught her eye. The blue metal barrel of a gun appeared as Cain stepped out of the scrub brush near the entrance to the tunnel, the semiautomatic gripped in his hand.

"If it's money you want, let her go, and we'll do business."

Clyde rolled off her, at the same time jerking her to her feet. The knife pressed even more solidly against her throat. "So I guess the Lone Ranger got here just in time."

"Where's Bart?" Cain asked, the gun never wavering.

"Your little gal here took care of him. Bashed him in the skull with a rock. Got to admire her grit."

"I admire a lot of things about Jenny. The one thing I won't allow is anyone hurting her."

In the darkness, Jenny caught the quick flash of Clyde's smile. A trickle of blood slid down from the thin slice in her neck.

"How much is she worth to you, Barrett? You bring me a bag full of money, and I'll let her go."

"I'm not leaving her with you. Not for an hour. Not for a minute. Not for another second."

Jenny shoved Clyde, knocking him off balance, and Cain fired, the bullet slamming into the other man's shoulder, the knife flying into the air, landing with a clatter against a rock somewhere in the shadows.

Swearing foully, Clyde staggered backward, and Nick Faraday moved out of the shadows. Cain grabbed Clyde by the front of his shirt and punched him hard enough to send him sprawling, dragged him up and punched him again. Punched him in the stomach, doubling him over, then punched him in the face again. Clyde grunted as he hit the ground and didn't get up.

Jenny raced across the clearing toward Cain, whose long strides carried him toward her. He pulled her into his arms and pressed her tight against him.

"I'm here now. No one's going to hurt you again."

She was trembling, burrowing into him, trying to absorb his warmth and strength.

"I'm all right . . . now that you're here." She buried her face against his shoulder, and his hand stroked over her thick brown curls.

"I'm sorry you got dragged into this. None of it had anything to do with you, and yet you were the one who paid."

She looked up at him, her eyes wet and glistening. "I don't care about any of that. I needed you, and you came. I knew you would. I just had to hold out long enough for you to get here."

She felt the shudder that moved though his tall, hard body. "I love you, baby. This whole thing showed me just how much."

Cain loved her. It took a moment to absorb the words. Her arms slid up around his neck. "Cain . . ." She blinked, and a tear rolled down her cheek. "I love you, too."

Cain lowered his head and kissed her, brief and hard. A finger gently wiped away the tear. "I wasn't sure. I hoped you felt the same way." He kissed her lightly one last time. "We need to talk, but this isn't the place. Where's Bart?"

Jenny swallowed. "I think I . . . I think I killed him."

"Where is he?"

"In the tunnel."

Cain grabbed Clyde's lantern. "Stay with Nick. I'll be right back." He strode toward the tunnel entrance and disappeared inside.

Nick walked toward her. Clyde still lay on the ground, unconscious. She could see Nick had zip-tied the man's hands behind his back.

"You're bleeding," Nick said, turning her face with his hand to survey the injury. He frowned. "It doesn't look too bad, but Cain's not going to like it."

"I think I might have killed Bart."

Nick's jaw hardened. "Self-defense, sweetheart. There won't be any charges."

She swallowed. "I suppose I should feel something, but I don't. I'm just glad it's over. I really appreciate your helping Cain find me."

Nick smiled. "He didn't need me. If he'd had to, he would have turned over every rock in Yavapai County to find you."

Her eyes burned. "Bart knew Cain would figure it out. He planned to kill him."

"Thanks to you, that isn't going to happen."

She heard Cain's voice then as he walked back out of the tunnel. "The bastard's still breathing. He was just getting to his feet when I found him." His knuckles were scraped and spotted with blood. "They'll need a stretcher to get the sonofabitch out of there now."

"He still got his balls?" Nick asked.

"I was tempted to even the score for Sun King. But I wasn't sure Jenny would approve. Odds are he'll live, but he's not going to feel very good when he wakes up."

"I'll call the sheriff," Nick said. "And an ambulance. With any luck, Bart will die on the way to the hospital."

"Or in a prison cell," Cain said darkly. He turned to Jenny and opened his arms. Jenny went into them and just hung on.

He frowned at the blood on the corner of her mouth, took out his handkerchief and gently wiped the trickle away.

"I should have finished the job you started," he said.

"Let's let the sheriff handle it," Nick said. "You don't need more trouble."

Cain looked down at her, saw the abrasions on her hands and the side of her face. "I wish I'd killed him."

Jenny said nothing.

Cain ran a hand over his jaw. "We should probably wait for the ambulance. Get you checked out when it arrives."

"It's mostly just scrapes and bruises. I want to go home, Cain."

He kissed the top of her head, hesitated. "Are you sure?"

"I'm sure."

"All right, we'll go home. Your place or mine? As long as you're with me, it doesn't matter."

Jenny slid her arm around his waist and looked up at him. "Your place. I don't want to face any more problems tonight."

"You're right. Tomorrow's another day. Tonight we just take care of each other."

Jenny leaned up and kissed his mouth. Cain loved her. He wasn't a man who spoke rash words. If he said it, he meant it. And God knew, she loved him. She had never met anyone like him. She was sure she never would again.

Tomorrow they would talk things over, try to straighten out the rest of the problems they were facing.

Try to end the danger lurking at the Copper Star.

CHAPTER THIRTY-NINE

Cain hadn't intended to make love to Jenny that night. She was battered and bruised and exhausted. But when they'd climbed into bed, she had turned to him, wrapped her arms around him, and kissed him, not a sweet, goodnight kiss, but a deep, fiery kiss that made him hard.

After all that had happened, she needed him, he realized. As much as he always needed her.

He had taken her gently, let her set the pace. He was in love with her. It might have taken him a while to figure that out, but he knew it now, deep in his bones.

And Jenny loved him. He had never met a woman he trusted more, never met a woman he respected more, and he intended to keep her.

They slept late that morning, made love again before they dressed and walked down to the Copper Star. Ryder Vance was in jail, his bail denied. Bart Harwell was in the hospital, chained to the bed, on his way to prison as soon as he was well enough to travel.

Cain was grateful to have his own problems wrapped up, but there was still something going on at the Copper Star. Will Price was going to be all right, but he was in no shape to act as Jenny's protector. That left Cain, and he intended to be sure this time she was safe.

He was seated at one of the barroom tables when he looked up to see Jenny getting ready to leave.

"Where are you going?" he asked, his voice a little harsher than he'd intended. "I thought we agreed you'd stay close until we figured out what's going on here."

"I was only going to the library. I just wanted to check one more thing before Cleo and I made a plan."

"If I recall correctly, the last time you headed off to the library, Will was shot in the back and you were abducted."

Jenny's cheeks flushed. "That was different. Those men were after you, not me."

"A fine line of distinction. You want to go to the library? Fine, let's go." Since he was no longer a target, he didn't mind the walk. The day was overcast, a chilly wind racing up from the flat desert lands below the mountain.

The librarian, Evelyn Dunning, was at the front desk when they walked inside.

"Maybe Evelyn can help speed this up," Jenny said.

"I'll wait right here." He took a seat at one of the tables while Jenny spoke to the librarian at the counter. He had yet to have the conversation with Jenny he'd been wanting to have.

He wished he had time to make a trip to Scottsdale, pick out an engagement ring. Then again, he had no idea what Jenny would say when he broached the subject of marriage. Loving someone and becoming that person's wife were two very different things. Jenny Spencer was extremely independent, and Cain was demanding and used to people doing whatever he told them. Not an easy man to love.

Cain shoved the thought away and pulled out his cell phone to check his email, but seconds later, he was back to thinking about Jenny.

He'd take her somewhere nice for dinner. Or maybe they would drive up to Sedona, spend the night. There were five-star hotels and gourmet restaurants in Sedona, and the town was only forty-five minutes away. It occurred to him there were first-class jewelry stores in Sedona. Surely, he could find a nice diamond for Jenny.

If she said yes.

Cain straightened in his chair. If he wanted something, he could be damned determined, he reminded himself, and Cain wanted Jenny. He wasn't about to let her say no.

He was smiling, his mind going over his plan, when Jenny walked up beside him.

"You find what you were looking for?" he asked, forcing himself to focus on the current situation.

"I did. It was even more interesting than I thought. Evelyn made me copies of the articles. Let's go back to the hotel, and I'll tell you all about it."

And maybe they would get the chance to talk about that trip to Sedona.

Jenny walked through the swinging doors to find her brother pacing impatiently in the saloon, waiting for her. Behind him, a few feet away, Summer sat on a barstool, sipping a Diet Coke.

She slipped off the stool and hurried over, gave Jenny a fierce, sisterly hug. "Everyone knows about the kidnapping. I'm so glad you're okay."

"I'm okay." She hugged Summer again. "I'm just glad Cain and Nick found me before it was too late."

At one time or another since she'd arrived at the Copper Star, half the town had come in to see her. They all wanted to express their concern over her abduction and tell her how thankful they were that she was all right.

Her brother didn't bother to hug her, just strode up to Cain and got right in his face.

"I'm not having any more of this, Barrett. Everything that's happened to Jenny has been your fault. You're just using her, and everyone knows it. I want you out of her life once and for all."

"Dylan! What on earth is wrong with you?"

Cain didn't budge. "You realize you're insulting your sister. Obviously, my opinion of Jenny is much higher than yours. Your sister is no fool. If I was using her, she would have ended our relationship a long time ago. You're her brother, but I won't tolerate your attitude. Jenny doesn't deserve it."

Dylan just stared.

Jenny tried to get between them. "Dylan, for heaven's sake, this is none of your business."

Her brother's look turned hard. "You were kidnapped! You could have been killed! You know Barrett's reputation. You're smart enough to know what he wants from you!"

Cain eased Jenny out of the way and moved even closer to Dylan, forcing him back a step. Cain's jaw looked as hard as steel.

"For your information, Dylan, I'm in love with your sister, and I'm going to ask her to marry me. I have no idea what her answer will be. Whatever it is, Jenny's right—it's none of your business."

Dylan flashed a surprised look at Jenny, then glanced back at Cain. His dark frown relaxed. Little by little, a wide grin spread over his face.

"Sorry. I guess I can be a little overprotective when it comes to my little sister."

The tension in Cain's powerful shoulders eased. He smiled. "That's a good thing, I guess. As long as you remember we both love her."

Dylan's smile broadened. He stuck out his hand. "I hope she says yes."

Cain gripped his hand. "So do I."

Jenny felt a stinging behind her eyes.

"I'm hoping those are happy tears, or I'm in big trouble," Cain said.

Jenny turned and went into his arms. "I love you so much."

Cain kissed her. "I refuse to ask you in here. We're going somewhere romantic. I was thinking Sedona. Maybe we could leave tomorrow, spend the night, maybe two."

Jenny just nodded. She wanted to say yes right then and there, but she could see Cain wanted to do it right, do it his way.

Inwardly, she grinned. Nothing new there.

"Sedona sounds perfect," she said.

It was an hour before Dylan and Summer slipped away. They would be spending the night in a room upstairs in the old wing.

Dylan always stayed at the hotel whenever he was in town. Lately, he'd been showing up more and more often.

Jenny thought of Summer and smiled.

With the cold weather moving in, there were plenty of rooms. Jenny was still not certain what was happening in the new section, so she'd kept those rooms unrented.

She needed to talk to Cleo—and soon.

The afternoon was sliding into dusk by the time there was a lull in business and Jenny sank into a chair next to Cain, where he sat behind his laptop at one of the tables.

"You were going to tell me what you found out at the library," Cain said, closing the computer down.

"It's about this article I read." She went on to tell him about the woman who had been staying upstairs at the hotel. "It happened in March of 1921, right here in the saloon, which was then a café."

She told Cain how the woman had been so jealous of her husband that she had come down to the café during breakfast and, believing her husband was having an affair with the town's pretty schoolteacher, threw carbolic acid into the teacher's face.

"She was insanely jealous," Jenny said. "Apparently, she had a history of violence even before the acid incident. Her husband was a wealthy, powerful man in Jerome, so she kept getting away with the things she did."

Jenny looked at Cain. "Today's the first time I've had a chance to read the whole story."

"I'm listening."

"According to the internet article, the woman was beautiful and desirable, able to wrap men around her finger. Even the governor was charmed by her. In May, she was arrested for the assault and put in jail. In June, on her birthday, the governor sent flowers and a birthday cake to her in prison. At the end of August, she got out on parole."

"Must have been some woman."

"More like a devious, jealous, half-crazy woman. After she died in an asylum in L.A., her ghost was supposedly seen walking the halls upstairs in the hotel."

Cain just smiled.

Jenny smiled back. "Who knows, right? But the thing I found most interesting was her name."

"Which was?"

"Anna Hopkins."

One of Cain's dark eyebrows went up. "I doubt Anna Hopkins and Anna Hobbs are related."

"Probably not. Have you seen Anna lately?"

Cain frowned. "She stopped by the Grandview Wednesday morning on her way back to Scottsdale. She said she'd spent the night with her girlfriend and was just heading home."

"You didn't mention it."

"No. Anna's not one of your favorite people, and I didn't want to upset you. For the record, she's not one of my favorites, either. I told her I was busy, then headed down to meet Max and his crew at your place."

"I trust you, Cain—that isn't it. The thing is, Anna Hobbs is obsessed with you. The same way Anna Hopkins was obsessed with her husband back in the twenties. It made me wonder if there was a chance Anna could have something to do with what's been happening at the Star."

"Wait . . . what?"

"Maybe Anna thinks that if she could get me out of the picture—"

"I haven't encouraged Anna. I've told her we were through a dozen times."

"I'm not sure Anna believes it. I'm just wondering how far she would go to get what she wants."

His eyes darkened. "Which you think is me."

"Maybe."

Long seconds passed as Cain considered her words. "She'd have to have help. Someone on the inside."

"I know."

"And she'd need a professional to install the right equipment to create the illusions upstairs."

Jenny made no reply. She could see Cain's mind sorting through possibilities.

"Who's bartending tonight?" he asked.

"Troy should be here any minute to take over for Barb. He's working the night shift and closing up."

Cain shoved to his feet. "Which leaves us free to head back to the Grandview. I've got some calls I need to make."

Jenny rose beside him. "Including Nick Faraday?"

"He's my first call, but he won't be my last. Let's go."

CHAPTER FORTY

It was just after midnight. They'd had a late supper in his suite, then gone to bed, both of them feeling restless and uneasy in some inexplicable way.

Cain kept thinking of what Jenny had said about Anna Hobbs, and his mind swirled with possibilities, discarding some, reviewing others. He remembered the first time he had seen Anna in Jerome. It wasn't long after he had slept with her in Scottsdale. He'd been surprised to see her in town. He'd thought he'd made it clear he had no interest in continuing the relationship, such as it was.

The Grandview remodel was well underway at the time, and he had begun coming up to supervise the final stages. Anna had stopped by the hotel a couple of times, but he had always been busy, and she had left after just a few minutes.

He remembered another occasion, remembered seeing Anna at the Copper Star. He had begun stopping by for a beer with Jake Fellows or one of the guys in Jake's crew. He'd liked the atmosphere and been intrigued by the pretty little bartender. He'd talked to Jenny a few times, eventually remembered her from high school.

He'd been attracted to her almost from the start.

At the time, they'd been remodeling part of the Copper Star, getting ready to open a new batch of rooms. He'd been laughing at something Jenny said when Anna sat down on the barstool beside him.

Cain had chatted with her politely, then excused himself and gone back to the Grandview. After that, she'd shown up several more times, even gone out to the ranch. Now he wondered . . .

He'd know more after he heard from Nick. Until they figured things out, he would just continue to keep a close watch over Jenny. Not an unpleasant task, he thought.

That was when he heard someone banging on the door to his suite. At this time of night, whatever was happening couldn't be good.

Jenny stirred as he climbed out of bed, grabbed his white terry robe, and shrugged it on.

"What's that noise?" Jenny sat up in the bed.

"I don't know. Someone's banging on the door. I'll go find out."

But Jenny was already up and pulling on her robe, following him into the living room. They were both bar owners, a business that stayed open late at night. Problems were a barkeep's constant nightmare.

The pounding came again, harder this time. Cain jerked open the door. "What the hell—"

"There's a fire at the Copper Star! The whole town is pouring into the streets!"

The color leached from Jenny's face. "Oh, God! Summer and Dylan are in there!" Turning, she raced back to the bedroom.

"We're on our way," Cain said to the guy in the hall, closing the door and hurrying to catch up with her.

In minutes, they were dressed and rushing down Hill Street toward the Star. With fire and police vehicles blocking the streets, parking would be impossible. Faster just to run, so they did.

Even from a distance, they could see the flames spreading rapidly through the upper story of the building, the glass panes in the rooms upstairs starting to explode from the heat.

He could hear Jenny praying as they ran. Cain thought of the people in the hotel, thought of Summer and Dylan. *Dylan's a firefighter,* he told himself. *He'll know what to do.* But as the flames leaped and grew, Cain started praying himself.

* * *

Summer could see flames eating through the ceiling of the room. "Oh, God, Dylan, we're trapped up here! What . . . what are we going to do?" She was shaking all over, more terrified than she'd ever been in her life.

Dylan was in the bathroom, wetting down a couple of towels. He draped the soggy fabric around her shoulders.

He caught her arms. "Listen to me. I'm getting you out of the hotel. Then I'm coming back for anyone who hasn't gotten out already."

Smoke was seeping into the room from every direction, and the roar of the fire in the hall was so loud she was terrified of what would happen when Dylan opened the door.

He draped the other towel around his own shoulders, pulled Summer's towel up over her head, and handed her a wet washcloth. "Put that over your face. You ready?"

Summer clutched the towel together in front of her. "No, Dylan. We get everyone out who is still on the second floor. You might not have time to come back for them if we don't."

She could see by the look in his eyes it was true. He gripped her shoulders and kissed her quick and hard. "Hang on to my belt. No matter what happens, don't let go."

She nodded and grabbed hold of the leather band around his waist, pressed the wet rag over her nose and mouth. Dylan did the same. He checked the door for heat, then opened it into a blazing inferno. It took every ounce of courage Summer possessed to keep from fainting and remain on her feet.

Her fingers tightened around the back of Dylan's belt as they ran through the flames around the doorframe, Dylan in front as they moved down the hall. Both sides were on fire, flames climbing the walls and licking down from the ceiling overhead. Dylan kept moving, pounding on doors as he made his way along the hallway, dodging spouts of fire that erupted here and there.

It seemed impossible they would make it to the staircase.

A door swung open. A young woman and a little girl, their eyes huge in their faces, stared out into the smoke-filled hallway. The little girl was crying, tears streaking down her face.

Dylan grabbed the child and swung her up in his arms, while Summer grabbed the woman with her free hand. Their fingers linked, and the small group hurried on down the hall.

Another door opened, closer to the lobby stairs. A young Hispanic couple raced out.

"Stay low and head for the stairs!" Dylan shouted.

Bent over and coughing, the couple hurried to join the fleeing guests.

Dylan continued pounding on doors, and another door swung open.

"Get out now!" Dylan shouted. "Stay low and head for the staircase!"

A heavyset man and his wife stumbled into the hall in their nightclothes and followed them, but Summer could see it was too late—the staircase was engulfed in flames. The bottom half fell away as the terrified group approached.

"What . . . what about the emergency exit in the new wing?" Summer shouted, her voice shaking so badly she hoped Dylan could hear her. She was covered with soot, her skin hot to the touch.

Dylan looked toward the far end of the hall, but it was blocked by a wall of flame. "Can't get through!"

Even as he said the words, Summer turned to see the thick wall of flames that now blocked the way.

"We're all gonna die!" the heavyset man screamed into the roar of the fire.

"We're all getting out!" Dylan promised, determination in every word. "We'll use the old wooden stairs!" Dylan rounded up the desperate little band, turning them back the way they had come, moving toward a door Summer had never really noticed.

When he opened it, Summer could see an old wooden staircase she hadn't known was there, probably the original exit out of the hotel. It was just beginning to burn, but the wood was dry and rotted and would quickly flash into flames.

With the little girl over his shoulder in a fireman's carry, Dylan urged the older man and his wife down the rickety stairs. The young Hispanic couple followed. Summer felt Dylan's hand cover hers on his belt and squeeze as he herded the little girl's mother ahead of him; then Dylan and the little girl led Summer down the rickety wooden stairs.

The entire hotel was in flames. A group of firefighters working on the back side of the hotel spotted them and started spraying water on the old staircase.

One of the firemen helped the other couples, while another took the little girl from Dylan's arms.

Just when Summer thought they had made it, just as Dylan reached back for her, the bottom dropped out beneath her feet. Summer screamed. She heard Dylan's roar, then everything went black.

Jenny gripped Cain's hand as they reached the street in front of the hotel.

"Get back!" one of the firemen warned. "This whole place is coming down!"

Windows shattered overhead, spraying shards of glass down on top of them. "All of you get back before you get hurt!" In unison, the crowd moved backward. Cain forced Jenny back out of danger.

She looked up at him. "My brother's in there—and Summer! We have to do something!"

When she would have moved forward, Cain stepped in front of her. "I know you'll probably hate me for this, but, honey, there is nothing we can do. We have to hope Dylan knows enough about fire to keep the two of them safe."

She glanced around wildly, desperate to find them. It seemed the entire town of Jerome was on the street in front of the burning hotel, but there was no sign of Dylan or Summer.

"How many people in the hotel tonight?" Cain asked.

"I'm not . . . not sure. Fewer than usual, thank God. And the new section is empty."

The fire chief walked up just then, tall, silver-haired. Jenny searched her mind for his name but couldn't remember. She hurried toward him, Cain at her side.

"I'm Jenny Spencer. I own the Copper Star. Did . . . did everyone get out?"

"The bar had just closed. We're sure all the customers got out of the saloon. We're pretty sure the staff had all left for the night."

"What about the guests in the hotel?"

The chief shook his head. "Looks like the fire started upstairs. By the time we got here, the place was already engulfed. We're hoping they got out, but we aren't really sure."

A little sound came from Jenny's throat.

"Her brother and his girlfriend were in there," Cain said.

"His name is Dylan Spencer. He's a firefighter." Jenny glanced around, desperately hoping to see them.

"I know Dylan," the chief said. "I haven't seen him. I'm sorry. At the moment, we aren't sure of anything." The chief hurried to join his men, who were shooting huge streams of water up at the burning structure.

Jenny looked at Cain and couldn't stop the tears from rolling down her cheeks. "Oh, God, Cain. What if they . . . didn't get out?"

Cain gripped her shoulders. "Dylan's smart, and he's good at his job, right?"

"He's . . . he's the best."

"And he knows his way around the hotel, right?"

"That's right. We both spent a lot of our childhood up here."

"So if he can't come down the front stairs, how does he get out?"

Jenny looked up at him, trying to collect her thoughts. "Through the new section. We installed a new emergency exit when we remodeled. The stairs come out behind the Liberty Theatre."

"Let's go!"

Clutching each other's hands, they raced around the corner, skirting the flames, then ran down Jerome Avenue, past the theatre, heading toward the back to the building complex that covered most of a city block. Firefighters from Jerome, Clarksdale, and Cottonwood surrounded the blaze, fighting the flames, working frantically to keep the fire at the Star from spreading to the businesses around it.

When they rounded the rear of the building toward the emergency exit behind the hotel, there was a sea of firefighters, but no sign of Dylan or Summer.

Cain pulled Jenny into his arms, but she couldn't control the trembling. "They aren't here."

Cain gave her a little shake to gain her attention. "Okay, he couldn't get out through the main entrance or the emergency exit in the new section. What's he do next?"

She tried to think, but she was petrified, her brain scrambled and foggy.

"If there's a way, Dylan knows it," Cain said. "What's he do, Jenny?"

Smoke burned her eyes. The tears kept coming. So did a vague memory from her youth. "The original fire escape. An old wooden staircase in the old section. It was rotten, a hazard that needed tearing down. I meant to do it. I-I just hadn't gotten around to it."

His grip tightened on her shoulders. "So it's still there, and Dylan knows about it?"

"Yes." Cain took her hand, and they started moving again, heading farther around behind the main brick structure. The staircase was close to the far end of the old section. But when they reached it, the stairs were no longer there. Instead a crumpled pile of smoldering ashes lay on the dirt where the stairs should have ended.

Jenny's legs went weak, and Cain scooped her up in his arms. He started striding farther along the block, and she realized he was heading for a cluster of people gathered around an ambulance.

Jenny's heart seemed able to beat again. "I see them!"

Cain set her on her feet, and she raced toward her brother, threw herself into his arms. He was covered with soot and sweat, but he was alive.

"I'm okay," Dylan said. "We're both okay. When the outside stairs collapsed, Summer dropped the last few feet and broke her leg, but she's going to be all right."

"Oh, thank God." She swayed a little, felt Cain's arm go around her waist to steady her.

"Your brother saved us," a woman said, coming forward. "Me and my daughter and the others. We'll never forget how brave he was."

Jenny smiled at Dylan, then turned back to the woman. "He's a fireman. That's what firemen do."

Dylan grinned, his teeth flashing white in a face black with soot. The firemen were still working hard to contain the blaze, but the hotel continued to burn.

Jenny spotted Summer sitting on a stretcher at the back of the ambulance and hurried over.

"Oh, Summer, I'm so sorry. Dylan told me some of what happened. I know you broke your leg, but I'm just so glad you're both alive."

"Your brother was amazing," Summer said. "None of us would have made it out of there if it hadn't been for him."

Dylan walked up just then, reached down and took hold of Summer's hand. He brought her fingers to his lips and kissed them.

"Summer was brave, and she was smart. She did everything I told her." He flashed her a grin. "Well, almost everything."

"I feel like this is my fault," Jenny said. "I should have closed the hotel when the trouble started."

"We don't know what happened yet," Cain said, but Jenny caught her brother's glance, which locked with Cain's.

"You both think it was arson," Jenny said.

"There's no way to know until the arson team goes in," Dylan said.

"But if you had to guess?" Jenny asked.

Dylan rubbed a soot-covered hand over his face, leaving a black streak along his jaw. "I could smell gasoline. I'd say the fire was set."

Jenny turned away, her chest clamping down. Between the smoke, the worry, and now this, she could barely breathe.

"You gonna be okay?" Dylan asked.

"I wanted the truth, but in my heart I already knew the answer."

"What we don't know," Cain said, "is who's responsible. But I promise you—we're going to find out."

CHAPTER FORTY-ONE

THE FIRE WAS STILL BURNING WHEN CAIN LED JENNY BACK TO THE front of the building. Flames licked out of upper- and lower-story windows, their sills blackened with soot. Several firemen told them there seemed to be no casualties, but Cain wanted to talk to the chief to be sure.

The chief was busy, so they waited. They were watching the flames, Jenny's face pale with worry, when Cain spotted Cleopatra Swift, swaying from side to side as she walked toward them.

She stopped in front of where they stood on the far side of the street, away from the blaze and the heat. Cleo flicked Cain a glance, but spoke to Jenny.

"I'm sorry about your place, hun. Seems like you got nothing but bad news lately."

Jenny glanced over at the business that had meant so much to her. "Dylan thinks it was arson."

Cleo grunted. "Considering what's been going on, I'm not surprised."

"We'll find out who did it," Cain said darkly. "You may be certain of that."

"I don't doubt it," Cleo said. "You've always been a man of your word."

She turned back to Jenny. "Something happened up there tonight."

"Besides half the block burning down," Cain drawled.

Cleo ignored him. "I don't live far. I was one of the first people out here on the street. You remember Boris Koblinsky, the guy in room ten?"

"I'm not likely to forget," Jenny said.

"Well, he ain't there no more."

"What do you mean?"

"When I got here, the fire was really blazin'. I started thinking about room ten, wondering about Boris. I began to feel something. I realized I could feel the bastard in that room."

Cain scoffed. "What the hell, Cleo? You aren't saying the fire killed whatever thing was in that room?"

"Not exactly." She turned back to Jenny. "You know that young sheriff who shot him?"

"John Mackey. What about him?"

"You recall he died in a fire."

Jenny's shoulders straightened as her gaze sharpened on Cleo's. "Yes."

"Well, he was here tonight. I could feel him. He dealt with Boris Koblinsky, once and for all."

"That's absurd," Cain said.

Cleo continued to ignore him. "I'm not sure how it works, but the sheriff was here—handsome, he was—and a few seconds later, that rotten bastard went up in flames. Boris is exactly where he oughta be—burnin' in the fires of hell."

"That's total and complete—"

Jenny gently set her fingers against Cain's lips. "I guess we'll never know for sure, but I'm willing to believe what Cleo says. The hotel is gone, but if Boris is gone, too, maybe it's worth it. Boris was responsible for the death of Brian Santana and at least three women. Maybe he finally had to face the wrath of God."

Cleo started nodding, moving her triple chins. "Could be," she said.

Cain considered Cleo's wild story. Since he didn't want to think about what had happened to him in that room, he changed the subject.

"We're rebuilding," Cain said, snagging Jenny's attention. "How many times has the Star burned down?"

Jenny looked up at him as if he'd lost his mind. "Four."

"So what's one more? We rebuild the Copper Star—but not until we find the sonofabitch who burned it down."

Cleo cackled a laugh. "Sounds like a good plan to me. Since my building is still standin', I'm going home. I'll call Nell tomorrow, see if she'll meet me for lunch." Cleo smiled. "I'll give her all the gory details." She looked at Jenny. "I suggest you both go home, too."

"We have to talk to the chief," Jenny said wearily.

Cleo's glance swung to Cain. "Take her home and give her some lovin'. You're good at just about everything. I imagine you're good at that, too."

Cain just smiled.

Cleo set off for home in her side-to-side sailor's gait, and Cain nudged Jenny forward.

"Let's get this over with," he said.

Jenny nodded. Cain could tell the shock of what had happened was returning.

"Tomorrow we'll figure it out," he promised, keeping a firm hand at her waist.

Jenny looked up at him. "You really think so?"

"I know so." Because Cain had already figured it out.

It was late the next morning when he finally awoke. Jenny lay next to him, still deeply asleep. Cain rolled onto his side and just watched her, enjoying the way her pretty golden-brown curls spread over his pillow. He had never really considered marriage and family. He was extremely self-sufficient. He'd never needed anyone but himself.

Then he'd met Jenny. She'd brought light and love into his life, and Cain finally found something he needed more than his freedom, something he had been searching for without even knowing. Cain needed Jenny. He wanted to marry her. Have children with her.

He wanted them to make a life together.

Cain left her sleeping and went into his study. First, he needed to solve the problems at the Star.

He had phoned Nick late last night and left a message, but hadn't heard back from him. Nick was digging deeper into Anna Hobbs. Cain was sure he'd come up with something that would prove what Cain already believed.

That Anna Hobbs was behind the trouble at the Copper Star.

Cain made a few more calls before Nick's return call came in.

"I can't believe the Copper Star burned down last night," Nick said, responding to the message Cain had left on his cell. "I hope everyone got out all right."

Cain spotted Jenny standing in the doorway, dressed in jeans and a dark green sweater, her pretty hair pulled back in a curly ponytail. They would have to go back down to the Star today. It was an ugly reality, but they had no choice.

"We're waiting for final word. So far it looks that way." Cain motioned Jenny over. "Jenny's here. I'm putting you on speaker."

"Hi, Jenny," Nick said. "Sorry about the fire."

"It was really bad, Nick."

"If there's anything you need me to do . . ."

"Jenny's brother was staying in the hotel with his girlfriend last night," Cain explained. "He's a firefighter in Prescott. His actions last night saved lives."

"I've met Dylan. He's a good man. Looks like he's a hero now."

"Looks that way."

"I probably shouldn't be making any wild leaps here, but after your call last night . . . are you thinking Anna Hobbs set the fire?"

Cain grunted. "I don't think Anna would want to get her hands dirty. I think she paid someone to do it. I'm expecting Jenny to get a call this morning from the arson squad."

"So I guess I'm still working the case."

"Until we know the fire was accidental."

"If it was."

"Yeah." Which Cain doubted. "Tell me you found something on Anna."

"That's easy. Anna's about to go down for the murder of her husband, Arthur Somerset. Turns out the grieving widow bought a box of thallium over the internet a week before poor old Arthur succumbed."

"Rat poison."

"That's right," Nick said. "No odor. No taste. Just a sprinkle here and there in a cup of coffee or Arthur's five o'clock martini."

"Conveniently, he died just a month or so after their marriage," Cain said.

"Correct," Nick said. "Right after he'd changed his will."

Cain flicked a glance at Jenny, who perched on the edge of a chair on the other side of the desk. "I didn't think you could buy that stuff on the internet anymore," Cain said.

"It's hard to get hold of, but Anna managed. Too bad she wasn't able to erase the record of her purchase."

"Have they arrested her yet?"

"Not yet, but according to Detective Elliot, they exhumed the body. They're waiting for the autopsy report, but they're pretty sure what the ME is going to find."

"Let's see if we can find a link between her and the fire at the Star."

"Any idea who might be the inside man?"

"My guess would be Troy Layton, the bartender." He looked at Jenny. "I know you trust him, honey, but—"

"Troy loves money," she said. "He also loves beautiful women. If Anna was willing to go far enough, Troy would be putty in her hands."

Cain agreed. "After what we just learned about her husband's murder, I think we can safely assume Anna would have no trouble doing whatever was necessary to get what she wanted."

"I haven't trusted Troy for a while," Jenny said. "I think he might have been skimming the till. I've been watching him, but I didn't want to accuse him without any proof."

"I think it's time we talk to Police Chief Nolan," Cain said. "As well as the head of the arson squad."

"Let me know how it goes," Nick said. "Call me if you come up with anything new."

"Will do." As soon as Cain hung up, a call came in on the landline from the front desk.

"Mr. Barrett? Sorry to bother you, but Police Chief Nolan is here to see you."

"Thanks, Debbie. I've been expecting to hear from him. Send him up."

"I'll make a fresh pot of coffee," Jenny said.

"Good idea. Maybe we should put a shot of whiskey in our cups before he gets here."

Jenny laughed. It was the first time Cain had heard the sound since the fire.

CHAPTER FORTY-TWO

JENNY CROSSED THE LIVING ROOM NEXT TO CAIN, AND HE OPENED THE door in the entry. In his police uniform, Chief Nolan walked into the suite, but he wasn't alone. The man with him, in a slightly different uniform, was shorter, lean, with weathered olive skin and sun wrinkles at the corners of his dark eyes.

"Come on in." Cain stuck out a hand, which both men shook.

"Good morning," the chief said. He turned to Jenny. "I was hoping I'd find you here. I'm glad Cain is with you."

"We've been expecting to hear from you," Jenny said, her worry beginning to build.

The chief nodded. "This is Captain Dean Kendall. He's with the Yavapai County Fire Investigation Task Force."

"Hello," Jenny said. At the serious looks on their faces, she didn't mention the coffee.

"I'm afraid we've brought bad news," Captain Kendall said. "We were hoping there were no casualties involved in the fire last night, but unfortunately, not everyone got out of the building."

Jenny's heart jerked. She felt Cain's big hand settle at her waist.

"Why don't we sit down?" Cain suggested. The men moved over to the sofa, and everyone took seats around the coffee table. Jenny sat down next to Cain.

"Please go on," she urged.

"As soon as the debris was cool enough for the team to go in this morning," the captain said, "we made an inspection of the premises. One of the team members found human remains up on the second floor."

Nausea rolled in her stomach, and Jenny fought not to tremble.

"Has the body been identified?" Cain asked.

"The remnants of a wallet were found on the victim's person. Most of it was destroyed, but a portion of a driver's license remained. We believe the deceased is Troy Alexander Layton, the bartender."

Jenny swayed against Cain, and he reached for her hand, laced her fingers with his.

"The police checked Layton's apartment," the captain continued. "But there was no indication he returned home after work last night, which supports our assumption."

"It'll take an autopsy to officially confirm," Nolan said. "But the wallet and a few other items found on the body lead to the same conclusion."

Jenny said nothing. Her throat was too tight to speak.

"I'm afraid there's more," Kendall said. "I'm not sure if this will make the news easier or more difficult to handle."

"What is it?" Cain pressed.

"From the trail left by the accelerant—a number of empty cans of gasoline were found on the second floor—the fire was clearly arson. The trail led straight to the body of the deceased, which leads us to believe Layton is the person who set the fire. Since he had no previous record of arson-related charges, we think he may have accidentally spilled gasoline on himself as he splashed the fuel around the upstairs hallway."

Jenny swallowed, fighting to keep the image out of her head.

Chief Nolan spoke up. "I don't think Troy realized when he lit the fire that he was going to be its first victim."

Jenny's eyes filled, but she still didn't speak.

Cain said, "There's a chance a woman named Anna Somerset hired Troy to cause problems in the Copper Star. She may have paid him to set the fire. The Phoenix police are investigating her in connection with the murder of her husband, Arthur Somerset. Word is an arrest is imminent."

Nolan's eyes widened. His stone-gray eyebrows pulled down in a frown. "So the Somerset woman had a beef with Jenny?"

She forced her voice to work. "Anna was obsessed with Cain. She just wanted me out of the way."

"We think she was paying Troy—in more ways than one—to cause Jenny trouble. Last night was the culmination of other events."

"Looks like I need to be talking to the Phoenix Police," Chief Nolan said.

"It's all speculation at this point," Cain reminded them.

"If you're right," said the chief, "this could all be wrapped up in a very neat bundle. The arsonist is dead, and the woman who paid him is going to prison for murder."

A long pause ensued.

"I'll need a statement from both of you." Chief Nolan stood, along with Captain Kendall.

Cain rose to join them. "We gave you our official statement before we left last night. As I said, what we told you today is purely speculation."

"Fair enough," Nolan agreed. "Once we get things pinned down, I'll come back and we can talk."

"I'm sure we'll have follow-up questions," Captain Kendall said. "I hope you'll both stay close for a while."

Cain glanced down at Jenny, his eyes locked with hers. "We won't be more than an hour away."

The pressure in Jenny's chest eased. *Sedona,* she thought. She wanted to smile, but it was too soon.

Cain accompanied their visitors to the door and closed it behind them. He turned and walked back to her, pulled her into his arms.

"It's over, baby. That portion of our lives ended this morning. There are loose ends we'll have to tie up, problems we'll have to deal with, but we'll handle them. Today we're starting a new life together." He bent his head and very thoroughly kissed her. She was clutching his shoulders, her insides melting, by the time he was done.

"This morning, I called the Enchantment Resort in Sedona

and made a reservation. Starting tomorrow, we'll hole up in one of their bungalows for a couple of days, enjoy the spectacular red-rock scenery, and do nothing but relax. We'll eat fabulous food and do some shopping. When we come back, we'll be ready to tackle whatever comes next."

He brushed a kiss over her lips. "Okay?" he asked.

There were a hundred reasons she should say no. She should be thinking of the Star, trying to put things in order, make sure her people were all right.

She opened her mouth and said, "Okay."

The breath she hadn't realized Cain had been holding whispered out.

"Okay, then. There are things we have to take care of today, but we can handle that. Your stuff is all gone, but you have a few clothes here you can wear. We'll get you some new things in Sedona."

She thought about the fire, the death and destruction, and it all seemed so daunting.

Cain caught her chin with his fingers. "You won't be doing this alone. We'll take things one at a time. Today, we'll talk to your people, take care of them. Tomorrow, we go to Sedona and take care of ourselves. When we get back, we'll handle whatever comes next."

She thought of how he was always there for her, and her eyes filled.

"Dammit, don't cry. I feel bad enough about all this as it is. Everything that's happened to you has in one way or another been my fault."

"No . . ."

"Yes. But being a prospector, I learned one thing. A man's bad luck can't last forever. Change my luck, Jenny. Will you marry me?"

The tears in her eyes trembled onto her cheeks. "Oh, Cain. Of course, I'll marry you. I love you so much." She gave him a smile that widened into a grin. "But you have to ask me again in Sedona."

Cain laughed out loud. He pulled her close and kissed her. "Deal," he said.

EPILOGUE

THE CROSS BAR PASTURES WERE LUSH WITH GREEN GRASS, THE horses' coats gleaming as they raced across the fields. Black Angus cattle grazed contentedly, enjoying the sunshine now that winter was gone.

As Cain had arranged, he and Jennie had gotten engaged in Sedona—after a romantic proposal that ended with Cain slipping the perfect diamond ring on her finger.

Nell had been thrilled at the news, saying she believed her grandson had finally found the right woman, perhaps a soulmate he had recognized on some level back in high school when Jenny had stood up to a group of school bullies. Nell was happy, enjoying time with Cleo, Emma, and the rest of her friends.

A week after the fire, Anna Hobbs was charged with the murder of her husband, Arthur Somerset. Bank deposits from Anna to Troy proved she had paid him to set the fire in which he had died, which resulted in an additional charge of second-degree murder.

Payments from Troy's checking account had incriminated Troy's friend, Junior Belmont, who worked in special effects for the Hollywood studios.

Junior admitted he'd placed recordings in various Copper Star hotel rooms, as well as set up hologram images in the hallway. He denied hiding anything in room 10 or using any sort of recording that sounded like old piano music and laughter in the saloon downstairs.

Jenny wasn't surprised. There were things that went bump in the night. Things, she had learned, that could never be explained.

Bart Harwell and Clyde Foley were serving time in prison for kidnapping, attempted murder, and numerous miscellaneous charges. Ryder Vance was still fighting drug charges, but prison time loomed.

The Grandview was running smoothly while reconstruction progressed on the Copper Star. Jenny and Cain were doing their best to make the old hotel and saloon look the way it had for more than a hundred years, even using the same bricks on the exterior for authenticity.

During the fire, firefighters had dropped heavy fireproof cloths over portions of the saloon and hotel lobby. Though the second story collapsed onto the first, beneath the cloth, the old bar and ornate back bar, as well as the original lobby desk, which held the journals, had been saved.

The saloon had always been an important part of the town. That would continue.

Two months ago, Dylan and Summer had gotten engaged. Until their fall wedding, they were living in Dylan's Prescott apartment, though Summer often returned to Jerome for the days he was on duty. Both of them seemed ridiculously happy.

"You ready to go?" Cain asked, leading Gladiator and Rosebud out of the barn and walking toward her.

Jenny smiled, taking the reins of the beautiful palomino. "More than ready." She swung easily into the saddle on Rosebud's back, accustomed once more to riding, which they both loved.

Cain mounted the big roan and settled himself in the saddle. Looking at him in his scuffed boots and battered cowboy hat made her mouth water. The heat in his dark eyes said his thoughts ran much the same.

"Did you bring that blanket?" he drawled.

Jenny grinned. "Absolutely. Maria packed it in your saddlebag along with our lunch."

Cain flashed a devilish smile. "The sooner we get there—"

"My thoughts exactly." Both of them laughed and nudged their horses forward, passing Denver, Billy, and Sanchez as they rode toward the trail into the hills. In the distance, Sun King grazed peacefully in one of the pastures.

The future looked bright. But the past would always be with them, making its presence known.

Jenny had learned that from the ghosts of Jerome.

AUTHOR'S NOTE

I hope you enjoyed Cain and Jenny's story. Though the novel is fiction, the town of Jerome, Arizona, is real. Once known as the Wickedest Town in the West, today Jerome is one of the state's most haunted places.

Almost all of the incidents I've described about the history of the town are true. Copper mining made Jerome incredibly rich, but the mining accidents were brutal, driving up astonishing death tolls. Many men were gruesomely injured or killed in fires and explosions. Gunfights and shoot-outs killed dozens of others.

More than nine thousand people died in the hospital, now the Jerome Grand Hotel, and the sidewalks were indeed made from a mixture of concrete and the ashes of the dead.

Most of the ghost stories are alleged to be true, reported by visitors who have relayed the same experiences over and over through the years. A number of such tales are written in the pages of the journal in the lobby of the Conner Hotel, originally built in 1898 and still in business on Main Street today.

Sadie Murphy's death represents the astonishing number of prostitutes murdered in the town's heyday. Belgian Jennie Bauters and the infamous Mrs. Sammie Dean were among those strangled to death. There were unknown numbers of others killed in various unpleasant ways.

From personal experience, I can say that Jerome is one of the most fascinating places I've ever visited. Though I was there regularly doing research, I am smiling as I tell you I decided not to spend the night.

Until next time. All best wishes and happy reading,
Kat